ACKNOWLEDGMENTS

I would like to thank the following individuals who served as readers for this project:

Estonian immigrant Paul Vesterstein—whose real life journey inspired this fictional tale, Scott Vesterstein, Dr. Alexis Pogorelskin, Dr. Pasi Tuunainen, Irina Haller, Gerry Henkel, Richard Pemberton, Cynthia Anthony, Hanna Erpestad, Jim Kurtti, Parnell Thill, Harry Munger, Renata Skube, Mark Rubin, Ron McVean, Sheila Packa, Harry Teder, Marlene Wisuri, René Munger, and Rev. Dave Hill.

Without these dedicated family, friends, and professional scholars devoting their time and effort to reading the manuscript, the content and flow of this novel might be vastly different, and—more than likely—vastly inferior.

Funding for this book was generously provided by Finlandia Foundation and Paul Vesterstein. Without their support, this novel would still be in a drawer.

Lastly, a word of thanks to my wife, René, and my son, Jack. Many days and nights have been lost to family while I type away at the keyboard, struggle with revisions, or sleep in my chair because I've been up at five in the morning working on this book. Their patience through the duration of this project is much appreciated.

Mark Munger
2014
Duluth, Minnesota

Dedicated to the innocents.

How very good and pleasant it is when kindred live together in unity!
Psalm 133

Sukulaiset:

The Kindred
(A Story of Estonia and Finland)

THE FAMILIES

Finland and America

Karl Gustafson: Swedish-speaking Finnish immigrant to the United States. Married to Laina. Father of Elin Gustafson and Alexis Gustafson. A lawyer and conservative.

Laina Gustafson: Finnish-speaking Finnish immigrant to the United States. Mother of Elin Gustafson. A suffragette and Progressive activist.

Sofia Wirtanen Gustafson: Mistress (and second wife) of Karl Gustafson. Mother of Alexis Gustafson. A maid in the Gustafson household before her marriage to Karl.

Elin Gustafson Ellison Goldfarb Peltomaa: Daughter of Karl and Laina born in Duluth, Minnesota. Wife of Horace Ellison (divorced). Widow of Hiram Goldfarb. Wife of Matti Peltomaa. A teacher and journalist. Raised her half-sister Alexis as her own daughter.

Alexis Gustafson: Daughter of Karl and Sofia born in Duluth, Minnesota. Treated by Elin as her daughter. College educated. Medical doctor in New York City. Married Elmore Tate, MD. Two children: Josiah and Janine Tate.

Elmore Tate, MD: Married Alexis Gustafson. Two children: Josiah and Janine. Director of women's health clinic in New York City.

Hiram Goldfarb: Elin's second husband. A Jew, communist, and journalist from New York City.

Josiah Tate: Son of Alexis and Elmore. Has children.

Janine Tate: Daughter of Alexis and Elmore. Has children.

Matti Peltomaa: Elin's third husband. Emigrated from Finland to the U.S. and then immigrated to Karelia, U.S.S.R. Logger and machine operator. Served in the Finnish Army during the Winter War, Continuation War, and Lapland War. Wounded three times.

Estonia and America

Andres Kristian: Husband of Hele and father of Nigul and Karl. Deep familial roots in Estonia. A farmer and *kannel* (lap harp) maker.

Hele Kristian: Wife of Andres and mother of Nigul and Karl. Her maternal and paternal families immigrated to Estonia from Finland. A singer and homemaker.

Nigul Kristian (aka *Nigel Christian*): Eldest son of Andres and Hele and brother of Karl. An electrician. Served in the Forest Brothers and the Finnish Army during World War II. Winner of the Mannerheim

Cross. Immigrated to North America. Married Grace Sippola. Two daughters. Lives in Biwabik, Minnesota.

Grace Sippola Christian: Married to Nigel Christian. Iron Ranger related to Congressman John Blatnik. Mother of Emily and Emma Christian.

Emily Christian: Eldest daughter of Nigel and Grace. Physical therapist. Lives in Biwabik. Divorced. One son.

Emma Christian: Youngest daughter of Nigel and Grace. Registered nurse. Lives in St. Paul. Married. Three sons.

Karl Kristian: Youngest son of Andres and Hele. Brother of Nigul. College educated teacher and poet. Served in the Forest Brothers and the Finnish Army during World War II and in the Forest Brothers during the Soviet occupation.

Lovlise "Marju" Sabbe Kristian: Also known as "Marju". Wife of Karl. Mother of Emily and Emma. Daughter of Kolt and Lahja Sabbe.

Tiia Kristian: Eldest daughter of Karl and Marju. Settled in Tallinn. Married. No children. A hospital aide.

Jannika Kristian: Youngest daughter of Karl and Marju. Settled in Tallinn. Married. No children. A waitress going to school to become a bookkeeper. Also the administrator of a charity named in her father's honor and established by her uncle Nigul.

Kolt Sabbe: Father of Lovlise. Father-in-law of Karl Kristian. Grandfather of Tiia and Jannika Kristian. Husband of Lahja Sabbe.

Lahja Sabbe: Mother of Marju. Wife of Kolt. Killed during the German retreat from Estonia.

PREFACE

"Damn," the old man muttered. "Never saw that coming."

Nigel Christian sat in an over-stuffed easy chair, the fabric worn from use, sipping coffee, early morning light falling gently over his aging, blade-like body. The sunlight also touched sprigs of blond hair surrounding a sea of baldness crowning Christian's head.

A color television set—a vacuum tube dinosaur enclosed in an oak cabinet—sat against the far wall of the living room: a small, cramped space, one of three rooms the old man occupied above Tanner's Bar, a speakeasy crammed into a corner lot of downtown Biwabik, Minnesota. Smoking wasn't allowed in the apartments above the bar. Despite this prohibition, a glowing Camel straight balanced on the rim of a crystal ashtray on an end table next to the old man. Smoke curled against advancing dawn and migrated towards the slender crack of an open window. Christian smoked because he could. He owned the building. In fact, he owned the entire block of the little town the tavern and apartments occupied. The rest of the buildings under Christian's control had, like Tanner's Bar and Rooming House, been reconditioned with government money—federal dollars pumped into Minnesota's Mesabi Iron Range by its longstanding champion and native son, Congressman Jim Oberstar. It was Oberstar's electoral demise that had caused the old man's outcry.

"Oberstar and Blatnik were good men," Christian said softly, his weary gray eyes following the tabulation of votes from the election across the twitching screen of the Sylvania. Long serving Eighth District Congressman Jim Oberstar and his predecessor John Blatnik were Democrats, the party the old man usually preferred. "Maybe stayed too long, I'll grant you that. But he's a good man."

Oberstar's challenger, a young Tea Party upstart named Craavack, had outworked the veteran lawmaker and, in the process, had captured at least two years in Congress, returning the seat to conservative control for the first time since 1948—the year Nigel Christian immigrated to the United States.

"Shit."

Christian stood up, mashed his cigarette into the bottom of the ashtray, picked up his coffee mug, the tri-color flag of his native country displayed on white porcelain, and despite being eighty-seven years old, moved with agility towards the kitchenette to refill his cup with coffee.

The apartment was painted white. The room's maple trim was varnished and revealed the burl of the wood. Christian's stocking feet padded softly against maple flooring: the thin strips of wood protected by identical varnish—the flooring original to the building, which had once housed a dry goods shop on the cavernous main floor but had always featured a hotel or boarding house above street level.

The old man's eyes adjusted to light entering the kitchenette through a window over the sink.

Not much of a view, Christian thought as he lifted a dented aluminum coffee pot off a glowing burner of a tiny range.

Across the street, the town's only undertaker polished chrome on the town's only hearse.

Sonofabitch Abernathy won't get me today. Hell of a way to make a living; taking money from grieving widows, widowers, children, and the like. Sonofabitch probably thinks I'm good for one of his ten thousand dollar vaults. Ha! More like a puff of smoke, a few nice words from the priest, and I'm gone. That's the way to do it. No need to waste money on ceremony.

Christian watched the middle-aged funeral director—Abernathy's fat belly jiggling with each swipe of the rag held in his smallish hand—shine rims of silver around the Lincoln's headlamps. The undertaker was dressed for business; a black suit, a white dress shirt with button down collar, and a prim blue necktie announced he was, despite the fact the clothing was at least a size too small, ready to receive the grieving. A smile crept over the old man's face as he watched a passing beer truck nearly take Abernathy out.

Who makes ready the funeral for the town's only mortician?

"Slow down, asshole!" Abernathy shouted as he executed an ungainly pirouette in the slipstream of the departing Leinenkugel's truck.

Christian diverted his attention to a plate littered with toast crumbs and a glass harboring residual orange juice pulp on its rim. He turned on the hot water spigot of the sink and rinsed the plate and glass thoroughly before placing them upside down on a dishtowel on the Formica counter. The old man picked up his coffee cup, wandered back to the living room, reclaimed his favorite chair, sat down with a grace usually lost to age, and studied the headlines scrolling across the bottom of the television screen. He was a news junkie. He rarely watched suspense or comedy shows. He was a man of the world: curious and always interested in understanding the status of things in far distant places.

"*In Darfur, efforts by the African Union forces to calm recent unrest seem destined to fail...*"

War.

He remembered when his homeland seethed and teetered on the brink of destruction. There had been inordinate periods of time after his beloved country was invaded, not once, not twice, but three times in a five year period, when, like Darfur, all hope seemed lost. He had been a young man when he donned a uniform and took up arms in defense of his country.

It was complicated.

Indeed. Christian's homeland was distinguished by a nearly indecipherable history, a past where horrific events and incalculable loss had cannibalized Nigel Christian's youth and very nearly his soul.

Tires rolled over pavement. A car pulled to a stop in front of the tavern. A buzzer sounded. Someone was demanding admittance. Christian cleared razor sharp memories from his mind, placed his cup on its saucer, rose from the sagging chair, and approached the apartment's front door.

"Can I help you?" the old man asked through an intercom speaker.

There was a slight pause before a scratchy voice replied. "Mr. Christian, Chief Eddelstrom here. Mind if I come up? There's a matter we need to discuss."

Why in the devil's name would the chief of police need to see me? The delinquents who broke into the tavern last month to steal cigarettes and booze were caught. Maybe that's it. Maybe he wants my take on what their punishment should be.

The old man pushed another button to unlock the security door. A mechanical click was followed by footsteps. Eddelstrom wasn't alone.

What the hell is going on?

A knock. The old man opened the door. Dusty light illumed four men. The chief of police and three strangers wearing black trench coats, black wingtips, smartly knotted neckties, and business suits, stood outside Apartment 2A.

Bud Eddelstrom, fifteen years the chief of the three-officer Biwabik Police Department, thirty years with the force, five years past retirement, stood patiently in the hallway without speaking. The delay allowed the old man to get his bearings.

Eddelstrom was a compact man of average height dressed in a blue uniform. His sidearm was holstered and his utility belt was crammed with police gear. Age hadn't yet infiltrated the chief's alert brown eyes, though it had touched his cropped blond hair, leaving wisps of light gray around the temples and ears. The cop's face was ruddy from effort.

"Nigel," Eddelstrom said softly, "we're here to talk to you about something that's come up. These two fellows, Stano and Hobbs," the chief continued, gesturing to the two men furthest behind him, their tall, athletic bodies nearly equal to Nigel Christian's physique in his prime, "are with the FBI. And Agent Jones, here," Eddelstrom concluded, "is with Homeland Security in the immigration division."

"What's this about?"

"Mind if we come in?" Jones asked.

The old man moved aside and the officers entered the apartment.

"Have a seat."

"No thanks," Eddelstrom replied. "This shouldn't take too long. Just a few questions and we'll be out of here."

Nigel Christian shifted nervously on the balls of his stocking covered feet.

"How can I help you?"

"Does the name 'Aleksander Laak' mean anything to you?" Jones asked.

Chief Eddelstrom watched the old man reach for his coffee, grasp the cup's handle with a steady hand, and sip gingerly.

"Mr. Christian?"

Agent Hobbs spoke as he moved towards a large window in the living room, his attention drawn to the antics of the undertaker still polishing the hearse.

Nigel Christian nodded, put his cup back on its saucer, and looked directly at the FBI agent. "I know the name."

BOOK ONE: KARELIA

CHAPTER ONE
October 1936

Waves lapped the stony shoreline of Lake Onega. Alexis Gustafson trudged from water's edge to an empty birch bark basket resting on the ground a few meters from the lake's cold reach, her arms strained by a clutch of newly washed clothing.

Paradise, the girl thought derisively in Finnish. *Some workers' paradise this turned out to be.*

Cold wind, something the girl had come to expect even in autumn, gusts blowing in as they did from across the forests, lakes, bogs and undulating terrain of Soviet Karelia from neighboring Finland, stung Alexis's face as she labored. She was dressed in a patchwork skirt, threadbare white peasant blouse, ratty silk leggings, and a blue sweater of pilled wool—all hand-me-downs from her journalist mother.

Mother.

The girl paused and looked back across the rolling waves of the second largest lake in Europe.

I wish I'd never listened to her nonsense.

Two years earlier, Elin Gustafson Goldfarb, her husband, New York newspaperman, Hiram Goldfarb, and Elin's daughter, Alexis Gustafson, had left New York City on a grand adventure. At least, that was how the journey had been pitched to the girl.

Hiram, Elin, and Alexis—who was actually Elin's half-sister, though Elin always treated Alexis as her child and not her sibling—crossed the Atlantic aboard the *RMS Georgic*. After a brief stay in London, the trio booked passage on the *Smolny,* a Russian passenger and freight ship several notches below the palatial *Georgic* in decorum, which brought them to Leningrad, where they boarded a train for Karelia. From Petroskoi, the family took a lake steamer across Lake Onega to Kontupohja, where Hiram was to serve as the editor of the local Finnish language newspaper in addition to his duties as Karelian correspondent for his father's paper, the *New Worker.*

Many North American Finns who immigrated to the Soviet Union during Karelian Fever did so because they were disillusioned by the economic stagnation of the Great Depression. But the Goldfarbs and Alexis made their journey not as economic refugees but as witnesses to history. In this respect, Hiram, the son of a Jewish father and a Finnish Canadian mother, and Elin, a woman of Finnish heritage on both sides of her lineage, had much in common with Oscar Corgan, one of the

North American promoters of Karelian Fever. All three left behind comfortable lives in the United States to experience the Karelian experiment in socialism first-hand.

Difficulty loomed for the newcomers. The language spoken by native Karelian Finns did not correspond exactly with Finglish, the dialect of Finnish used by North American Finns. Words and phrases often required translation. For the first two years of Alexis's life in Kontupohja, much of what she tried to say was misunderstood. Two years of study at the Finnish language school in Kontupohja instilled in Alexis an understanding of the nuances between Karelian Finnish, Finnish, and Finglish.

Language had not posed a problem when the Goldfarb-Gustafson family first settled in a logging camp upon arriving in Karelia. Surrounded by other Finglish speakers, the family's first linguistic experience as immigrants was grounded in familiarity. The same cannot be said of the living conditions the new arrivals encountered in the rustic camp.

Mud. Mosquitoes. Black flies. Filthy latrines. Foul water. Leaky dormitories. Cold nights and sultry days. Unceasing toil.

These were the memories that Alexis Gustafson carried with her as she considered the four miserable months her family spent in the logging camp. It had taken that length of time for Hiram to firm up his editorial position with the local newspaper. Elin accepted a copy editor position with the same paper three months after the family moved into a two bedroom flat located in the tavern and wharf section of Kontupohja: a rough and tumble district distinctly different from the neighborhood in lower Manhattan the family had left behind.

The tenement in Kontupohja had no running water. A communal well fifty feet from the building served the entire block. The flat had no indoor toilet. Two privies were located in close proximity to Lake Onega for use by the tenants. A copper bottomed communal bathtub shared by six apartments was available for personal hygiene but most often tenants bathed in the sturdy log sauna North American immigrants had built on the shores of the balmy lake three blocks away. Though much progress had been made in the two years since the first pioneers from America and Canada arrived, rolled up their sleeves, and went to work, indoor plumbing, consistent electricity, central heating, and other such improvements remained elusive.

For two years, Hiram and Elin worked hard at their positions and applied their respective talents to the pages of *Työläinen* (Laborer). Though Elin was hired as copy editor, she quickly assumed additional duties as a reporter, a role she had held with *Työmies* in Superior,

Wisconsin before the tragic deaths of her mother, father, and stepmother. Though her writing style endeared her to her new audience, she did not pen dispatches from Karelia to the States for the *New Worker*. She left such efforts to her husband. Had she written the "Letters from Karelia" column that appeared back home—Hiram's words telegraphed to Leningrad and from there via underwater cable to London before reaching New York via transatlantic cable—Elin Gustafson Goldfarb would have done something remarkable, something her husband was loath to do. She would have told the truth.

Things were not going well. Politics, even utopian socialist politics, are subject to change. The winds of fortune and misfortune gather and blow across the political landscape of any era. And in 1936, the clouds gathering above the Finnish immigrant communities in Soviet Karelia were darkening by the moment.

Alexis was no fool. She knew that danger was lurking in her life and the lives of her parents. They had come to Lake Onega under the protection of Edvard Gylling. Gylling, a native born Finn, was, like Corgan, an early and fervent recruiter of North American Finns for immigration to Soviet Karelia. But, over time, Gylling's prominence waned. His political clout in Moscow, where he once held sway, diminished. Alexis paid attention when her parents talked in low tones about such matters. She heard them fret about the fact that they had turned their American passports over to the NKVD (Stalin's secret police). She understood that it was questionable whether they were free, of their own volition, to leave the country.

The remembered voices of her parents, the tenseness of their discourse, weighed heavily on Alexis Gustafson as she hoisted the basket of wet clothing, turned her face to the escalating wind, and retreated to her family's apartment.

CHAPTER 2

"How goes the studying?" Hiram Goldfarb asked.

Alexis Gustafson sat on a wooden chair constructed by a friend of her parents from the Karelian logging camp, Russian language text books in front of her on the smoothly polished surface of a long, narrow kitchen table, and worked equations on oily paper. With Edvard Gylling's influence waning and with Stalin's paranoia rising, schooling for the immigrant children had changed significantly. Where once Alexis's lessons had been in Finnish, now all her instruction was in Russian. Having been forced to abandon her second language, Finglish, to learn more proper Finnish, and having been required to, in turn, abandon her newly acquired skills in *that* tongue, Alexis struggled to master Russian.

The young woman looked up from her homework. Flickering yellow candlelight, the tallowy flame sending black smoke into the depressingly close air of the apartment, illumed Alexis as she scribbled.

"I think I've figured it out, she said. "No thanks to Mr. Boykin. His accent is so thick, I can't understand a word that man says!"

"Ah," her stepfather said lightly, his small black eyes focused on the girl as he loaded another pine log into the wood stove that served as both furnace and range for the apartment. "Perhaps you need to spend more time studying Russian and less time studying Juha Rintala."

The remark was said in jest. Juha was Alexis's beau, a strapping, thickheaded dockworker and fellow immigrant who'd left his sickly wife and two small children behind in Port Arthur, Ontario for the promise of a new beginning. There was no confirmation that Rintala had actually divorced his wife. Some swore that to be the case. Others claimed he'd simply abandoned her. The rumors didn't dissuade Alexis. The young woman's lack of concern over Juha's unsettled history bothered her parents but appeared to have little effect on Alexis's infatuation with the handsome dockworker whose parents had immigrated to Canada from Joensuu, a city located in the Finnish province of Northern Karelia. There were also unflattering whispers that Juha Rintala, who spent considerable time visiting relations in Joensuu, had also fathered a child there and had shirked his duties in that regard as well. Alexis didn't know whether the rumors were true and, in fact, her ardor for the man seemed to increase upon hearing about Juha's alleged indiscretions.

"Time spent with Mr. Rintala has not interfered with my ability to learn Russian. In fact, he's helping me with my tense and verbs.

Working with so many Russian speakers, he's as fluent in the language as if he were born here."

The diminutive Jewish newspaperman removed a pair of wire-rimmed spectacles from the bridge of his nose. The round lenses were clouded from pine smoke. Hiram pulled a white handkerchief from the front pocket of his brown wool trousers and fastidiously cleaned the lenses. He held the glasses up in flickering light to check his work before replacing them on his bony nose. Goldfarb's misshapen septum was the result of the newspaperman having been disciplined by a local NKVD operative for a story he'd supposedly written. The immigrant had suffered the beating without outcry despite the officer's plain error: the Jew had not written the offending article—his wife had.

Elin Gustafson, forty-seven years old, her shoulder length auburn hair tending to gray, her steely eyes dimmed by hardship, opened the door to the apartment and stepped into the room.

"Hello, dear," Hiram said softly, turning to greet his wife. "How was your day?"

The woman dropped a canvas sack onto the wooden floor and hung her wool overcoat on a peg on the wall. "Tiresome," she replied. "The back of my head is pounding like someone hit me with a hammer."

Elin was prone to frequent headaches. The pain, which began at the base of her skull and spread to the top of her head, was but one symptom of her body's internal struggle. She picked up the sack, its weight heavy in her right hand.

Diverting her thoughts from her throbbing head, seeking to avoid descending into self-pity, Elin spoke about the work she had done that day. "I went to another meeting of the education committee. Nothing much happened other than complaining—the same old whining," Elin observed, pausing briefly to catch her breath. "And the interview with the man from agriculture? An utter disaster!"

She placed the bag on the counter next to the kitchen washbasin and began removing items. Rutabagas, meat wrapped in brown paper, carrots, onions, and smallish red potatoes were placed in turn on the roughly planed pine countertop.

"But I see the market is abundant. A sure sign that things are improving!" Hiram noted.

"Things always improve right before Stalin gives a speech. It is magical indeed how food appears just as the Great Leader reveals new policy."

Elin's reference was to speeches Stalin was giving that outlined upcoming changes to the Soviet Constitution. *Pravda* described the document—written by a special commission which, for the first time, allowed universal, direct, secret voting in all elections—as evidence that

Stalin was a "genius of the new world, the wisest man of the epoch, a great leader."

Elin Goldfarb doubted that Stalin's promise of universal suffrage and economic rights would amount to much. But until that moment, she had never voiced such views: views that were, in a word, dangerous even if uttered in private.

Hiram frowned. There was great risk lurking behind his wife's apostasy. Though he remained supportive of the Soviet regime, he was a practical man. He knew that the political landscape in the U.S.S.R. had changed and that there was no longer room for even the gentlest of criticism of the government or the Party. Hiram Goldfarb thought better of engaging in a political debate with his wife. He simply shook his head in disagreement.

Elin moved slowly, the weight of depression heavy across her shoulders, her head still pounding, as she scrubbed vegetables free of dirt and manure under cold water poured from a white porcelain pitcher.

"But there is meat. We've not had meat for what, two weeks?" Hiram said.

"Three. And don't get too excited, my love," Elin replied, a note of tenderness softening the conversation. "It's lamb. I'm not sure how fresh. I'll likely need to doctor it significantly with spices and onion to make it palatable."

"I *hate* lamb." Alexis muttered the words as she considered another equation, her blue left eye reminiscent of her natural father's Swedish roots: her brown right eye evidence of the heterochromia that had appeared shortly after her birth.

"That's enough, 'Lexis. It's the best your mother could do. We'll enjoy the bounty of the harvest and not complain."

"I *hate* lamb."

There was petulance in the girl's mantra. She had lost any sense of awe or marvel in their collective journey. There was little other than Juha Rintala to interest Alexis in her station in Karelia.

The young student looked up again from her work. She was far ahead of the other students in the Russian language academy she was attending through her parent's affiliation with the Communist Party. Both her parents had been members of the American Communist Party, a fact that had not made their entry into the Karelian Communist Party easier. There had been questions of loyalty to be answered. There had been long periods of silence from Moscow. And then, by written fiat of some official in some smoky room in some far away bureaucratic office, both Hiram and Elin Goldfarb were admitted as full-fledged members of the Party. But with membership came the confiscation of their American passports, a circumstance that Alexis, always the skeptic, eyed with suspicion.

The girl studied her mother. There was no doubt in Alexis's mind that Elin Gustafson Goldfarb retained beauty. The hard life in the logging camp had caused some of the extraneous weight Elin had gained eating starchy foods during their voyage to vanish. To Alexis's eye, her mother was as striking a figure as she'd been when the family lived in Manhattan.

Manhattan.

The word drove Alexis to consider the Gustafson family history, at least the portions of the story she was privy to, certain details having been deleted from the sanitized version handed down to Alexis by her mother.

• • •

Elin Goldfarb's parents Karl and Laina Gustafson had lived at the pinnacle of American society in the fresh water port of Duluth, Minnesota where Karl was a respected lawyer. Their marriage—that of a Swede-Finn and a Finnish commoner—had crossed lines that, in Finland, were rarely crossed.

Beginning with the rise of the Fennomen (Swedish speaking Finnish intellectuals), there was serious prejudice amongst those who embraced Finnish culture and language, including Lönrot's translation of traditional Finnish-Karelian fables into *The Kalevala*, against anything Swedish. The fact that Laina, a Finnish speaker from Turku, was able to overcome such ingrained prejudice and fall in love with and marry Karl, whose family roots ran deep in the Swedish speaking Åland Islands, evinced Laina's pragmatic nature. Working through their differences, the couple rose to become an American success story: Karl, as a well-respected attorney and Laina as a socialite and activist in causes at odds with the conservative politics of her husband. Their life was exquisitely complete until, as Elin related to Alexis when the girl was old enough to appreciate the tragedy, Elin's father became entangled with a servant girl. Laina, though liberal in her politics, was not liberal in her idea of marriage. She put the young, single, and very beautiful Sofia Wirtanen out on the street upon discovering the sin of her husband. But cancer took Laina, and Karl—whether he had continued the affair outside the home or merely re-kindled the fires of passion upon his wife's death—went back to Sofia with determination. Alexis was born from the subsequent marriage of Karl and Sofia and was actually a half-sister to Elin, a young woman in 1918, the year of Alexis's birth, already working as a journalist in Duluth.

At the time of Alexis's birth, Elin was trapped in a loveless marriage. Upon the deaths of Sofia (to influenza) and her father (to a fatal heart attack), Elin shed her husband, gathered up her things and the infant Alexis, and moved to New York where her mother's friend Alice Munger Silvey, a survivor of the *Titanic*, had connections. Alice, heiress to her lumber baron father's fortune, enjoyed a comfortable life in Duluth upon returning from the sinking that claimed her first husband, William Silvey. Elin left Duluth for New York with a substantial divorce settlement in hand: enough money to allow her to live comfortably, if not elegantly. But the crash of '29 ruined Elin Ellison as it did so many others and ended her dreams of completing a graduate degree in literature at Columbia University. Her fortune gone, Elin found work as an editor of textbooks. She rented a walk-up studio apartment in the Finnish cooperative association building located in Sunset Park. The neighborhood was, before the onset of the Great Depression, a bustling center of blue-collar employment, home to thousands of longshoremen working the piers of New York Harbor and thousands of men and women working the mills, lathes, and other industrial machinery of the waterfront.

Originally settled by immigrant Norwegians and Finns, Sunset Park accepted waves of newcomers. Poles and Czechs and Italians sought the freedom of America and the bounty of her shores and came to live in the neighborhood. Despite the watering down of their influence in Sunset Park, the Finns persevered in their efforts to indoctrinate new arrivals concerning the unfairness of American capitalism and Elin Gustafson (the divorcée had reclaimed her maiden name) was one of many writers documenting worker demands for economic justice.

Elin braved the rain, sleet, cold, snow, dirt, heat, and grime of the metropolis in search of political stories. Aided by a public transportation system that made sojourns from Sunset Park to Queens, Manhattan, the Bronx, and the other boroughs and neighborhoods of the city routine, Elin arrived one October evening, with five-year-old Alexis in tow, at the Finnish Progressive Society Hall in Harlem. Erected on 126th Street between 5th and Lenox, the hall was an impressive edifice to communist clout during the period following the Finnish Civil War.

On the heels of the October Revolution, Finland had declared its independence from Russia. Communists (the "Reds") battled the conservatives (the "Whites") for control of Finland. The Reds occupied major Finnish cities between January and March of 1918. Lenin's attempt to mobilize Soviet troops stationed in Finland on the side of the Reds proved problematic. The Russian soldiers, (who had been at war for nearly five years) ignored their new leader's pleas and deserted. The

Whites, led by General Carl Mannerheim (a Swedish speaking Finn who had served as an officer in the Russian Army during the Great War), sought to wrest Finland from communist control. Mannerheim drove the Reds from Tampere and German troops allied with the Whites liberated Helsinki. These victories spelled the end of Lenin's attempt to establish a "People's Republic" in Finland.

From 1918-1922, the so-called "Kinship Wars"—involving Finland, the newly formed Republic of Estonia, and the Karelian Autonomous Soviet Socialist Republic—dominated the region. Estonia emerged from the Kinship Wars as an independent, non-communist state. But Finland's tepid support of Karelian intrigue failed to foster the emergence of a Greater Finland, a dream of Finnish conservatives who longed for an expansion of Finnish influence into places such as Karelia and Estonia, places whose language and culture were compatible with those of the new Finnish Republic.

It was after these events, events far removed from America, that radical Finns in New York City built their hall on 126th Street. The Finnish Progressive Society Hall, which was located in Harlem to influence political thinking among the blacks, boasted conference rooms and offices, an elegant auditorium, saunas, a swimming pool, and restaurants. Like other Finn halls throughout North America, the Harlem edifice hosted plays, concerts, political debates, pageants, and athletic contests.

A debate between former Socialist candidate for president Eugene Debs and C.E. Ruthenberg, Executive Secretary of the American Communist Party, drew Elin Gustafson to Society Hall in October of 1923 as a free-lance reporter.

"Excuse me sir," Elin had said, while standing on the top step of the granite staircase leading to the main entrance of the hall, her words addressed to a stranger smoking a pipe. "Is there a place I can store my coat during the debate?"

Elin stood before the man, with Alexis draped in her arms. The child's face was buried against Elin's wool coat. The weight of the sleeping girl was heavy against Elin's right hip.

"Surely. Let me tap this pipe out and I'll lead you to the cloakroom," the stranger said.

Elin had waited as the man knocked the cherry wood bowl of his pipe against a stone archway. The sun's orange and magenta demise was reflected in the glass of the hall's entry doors as bits of charred tobacco fluttered to the ground. The stranger slid his pipe into a pocket of his black suit coat, the fabric cheap and frayed, opened the nearest door, and urged Elin to enter. Elin had smiled wearily, the weight of the child, the reality of spending a full day at Broadstone's, the textbook company where she worked, clear in her exhaustion.

"I didn't even ask you your name," Elin said quietly, joining the milling crowd in the building's foyer.

Many of the debate attendees were black. The ebony faces of the crowd caused the woman to consider her own history. Before she could offer an observation about the differing immigrant paths of Finns and African slaves, her companion had replied.

"Artie Sillanpaa."

"Elin Gustafson."

"Ah. The reporter."

She raised her eyes tenuously. "You know my work?"

"My folks live in Houghton. They send me *Työmies* when they're done reading it. I haven't seen anything by you for quite some time. You're an excellent writer. I miss your insights."

Elin had smiled. Before she could respond further, Alexis stirred and slid free of her mother's grip.

"Where are we, Ma?"

"'*Mother.*' 'Where are we, *Mother*?'"

The child had been ready to stomp her booted foot on the stone floor in protest, but saw that her mother wasn't in the mood for shenanigans. The girl paused, a hint of maturity at odds with her age, before speaking.

"Where are we, *Mother*?"

The child's inflection had been sugary and false.

"Worker's Hall. In Harlem."

"Where all the colored people live?"

"Yes."

The child pivoted on her heels and took in the crowd. "There sure are a lot of colored people here."

Elin had smiled.

"Yes there are. Hush, now, 'Lexis. And don't stare. And don't call them 'colored'. That's disrespectful. Call them 'negroes'. That's the proper term. They're folks just like you, me, and Mr. Sillanpaa, here."

"Who's Mr. Sillanpaa?"

"This nice man who's helping me."

The girl studied the athletically built man in the cheap suit. "He doesn't look like much."

Sillanpaa had smiled and tousled the girl's blond hair. "You're a smart little slip of a thing, aren't you?" he said in English, the language Alexis was speaking.

"More like a little demon devoid of manners," Elin observed, opening the girl's coat and straightening her jumper.

Elin removed her black leather gloves, slid them into a pocket of her blue overcoat, and lifted the hood away from Alexis' face, revealing the glowing skin of a beautiful child. Alexis's hair was cut short in the style of the day.

"He's quite the stunner," Sillanpaa had remarked as they moved through the crowd towards an enclave marked "Woman's Coat Check" in both Finnish and English.

"*She*."

"How's that?"

"*Her* name is Alexis. After the poet, Aleksis Kivi."

"Oh. Sorry," the man said as they stood in front of the coat check counter.

Sillanpaa helped Elin shed her coat. Elin slipped her daughter's coat off the girl's slender shoulders. The reporter handed the garments to a dowager woman on the other side of the counter. The cashier ambled away on short legs. Inordinate time passed before the woman returned.

"That'll be ten cents," the attendant had advised between gasps, the brief walk having taxed her endurance.

"Here," Elin replied, as she simultaneously tried to hold Alexis's hand, open her black leather satchel, and dig for coins in a coin purse.

"Don't be silly," Sillanpaa said, pulling out two Liberty nickels from his wrinkled dress slacks. "It's the least I can do for a famous writer."

The attendant accepted the coins and gave the man a numbered receipt, which he'd presented with undue formality to Elin.

He's a working man, the writer had noted, taking in the calloused fingers and palm of Sillanpaa's hand. *I shouldn't accept money from him. He likely needs every nickel he earns.*

"Thank you," Elin replied, ignoring her own silent admonition.

Sillanpaa had nodded. They joined a line of attendees snaking its way into the auditorium. The men and women seeking entry had been polite. There was no jostling or pushing or shoving. Elin stood behind the square shouldered Finn who had come to her assistance, Alexis by her side, the child's attention riveted on the excitement building in the crowd.

"Would you care to sit with me?"

Artie Sillanpaa turned towards Elin as he spoke. His sea foam eyes shone bright in the electric lights of the hall's foyer. The details of his features, the lines of exhaustion under his eyes, the weariness clear in the paleness of his skin, spoke volumes. Elin had met and known thousands of workers and farmers and miners like Artie Sillanpaa. They were all good men: men destined to live existences of agonizing sameness, meager earnings, and expectant tragedy.

"Certainly. I may ask you to watch the child from time to time if she gets fidgety. I'll want to take a few notes. Generally, 'Lexis is well behaved. But one never knows about a five-year-old. They have wills of their own."

"It would be my pleasure. Come—my friends Tania and Lena, from the steel fabricating shop I work at—have saved a seat for me towards the front of the hall. I'm sure we can squeeze in two more."

The debate had been a boring exercise in discourse. Neither Debs nor Ruthenberg landed any major blows. In the end, Elin's notes revealed extreme disappointment regarding the evening's events:

All in all, the purported "war of words" between the two giants of the Left never materialized. What I heard, what the crowd observed, was two men of great intellect unable to translate their thoughts into the rhetoric of the common men and women who sat on bated breath awaiting revelation. Instead, the audience received a sampling of tired theories and exhortations.

But Elin Gustafson took away something far more important, far more life changing from that evening than the words of two politicians. She met Hiram Goldfarb—the man who would become her second husband—at the debate.

Artie Sillanpaa's fellow workers had drifted off after the debate ended and goodbyes were said. Alexis had fallen asleep once the speechifying commenced. As Elin waited for Sillanpaa to retrieve the coats, the child continued to slumber in her mother's arms despite the din of the departing crowd. When the factory worker returned and attempted to assist Elin as she held the sleeping child, Elin's coat became a hopeless tangle.

"Here, let me lend a hand."

A man dressed to the nines in a finely pressed, expensive suit, black bowler, and shiny black boots, offered to hold Alexis.

Elin had handed the slumbering child to the stranger. In quick fashion, Sillanpaa resituated Elin's coat and the stranger handed the child back to the woman. Elin slid the child's inert arms into the sleeves of her wool coat and buttoned the garment.

"Thanks, mister," Sillanpaa had said. "I don't think I've had the pleasure..."

"Hiram Goldfarb."

"Artie Sillanpaa," the factory man had replied. "This is Elin Gustafson and her daughter, Alexis."

"Please to meet you, Mr. Sillanpaa. And you," the smaller man continued, extending his hand with vigor to the woman, "must be the writer. *Työmies*. Am I right?"

Elin Gustafson had nodded but did not shake the man's hand.

"I haven't seen any of your columns for a while," the Jew said, his hand persistently extended, his dark eyes locking on the woman. "I take it you no longer write for the paper?"

Elin shifted Alexis and shook Goldfarb's hand without uttering a word.

Idiot. Why am I unable to respond? He's not striking, not handsome at all. But there's something about meeting Hiram Goldfarb, editor of the New Worker that *has got me tongue-tied. What is wrong with me?*

Elin had blushed.

Sillanpaa, noting that something was stirring between the two, conceded that he was not going to escort the woman and her daughter to the train station.

"I best catch up with my crowd," the mill worker announced, the volume of his expression displacing disappointment. "It was nice to meet you."

Sillanpaa's exit prodded the woman to recover her native calm.

"Thank you for all your kindness, Mr. Sillanpaa. I appreciate all you've done for us tonight."

Sillanpaa waved a hand in the air but did not turn around. His stride carried him into the departing crowd where he became just another worker in the throng.

Hiram Goldfarb stood in the cool October air, his eyes watching the competition yield to his intellect and bearing, his heart pounding with anticipation.

"Do you still write Mrs. Ellison?"

Elin had shifted Alexis in her arms. "'*Miss Gustafson*'. I am divorced. Have been for quite some time, though I only recently reclaimed my maiden name. Since coming to New York, I have only written the occasional piece for local tabloids. My job, such as it is, is as an editor. For Broadstone's. I am trying to get back into writing. That is what brought me here tonight."

"Broadstone's? They publish textbooks, don't they? My, *that* must be exciting," Goldfarb had teased.

Their relationship had started slowly. Elin had little history with Jews. Though she had always been curious about the Hebrew faith and Jewish ethnicity, her Finnish lineage and Lutheran upbringing created a homogeneity that, outside of chance interactions with Leftist Jews during political events, left her ignorant of specifics.

Despite Hiram Goldfarb's views on the rights of the fairer sex, including views on women in the work force, politics, and contraception that mirrored Elin's, theirs had been a decidedly old fashioned courtship.

Hiram introduced his new friend to his culture, his family, and his favorite places in New York. She, in turn, brought the small, darkly complected man with the stunning black eyes and unceasing mind around to meet Finnish émigrés living throughout the city. And Alexis adored Hiram. The Jew made the child laugh. He bought her trinkets and books and clothes for her dolls. In the end, a justice of the peace married them. Elin quit her job at Broadstone's and accepted a position at the *New Worker*, where, over time, Hiram convinced her of the rightness of communist doctrine, the correctness of joining the Party, and their need to leave America to experience revolution first hand.

• • •

Slices of lamb sizzled in a cast iron skillet on the front burner of the woodstove. Fried rutabagas, onions, potatoes, and carrots waited in a covered ceramic bowl. Elin wiped sweat off her brow with the corner of the grease-stained white apron tied around her waist. After injecting her medicine, the headache had abated. She was working shoeless and without stockings, standing with her toes spread for balance, on the cold pine floor of the kitchen.

"Smells good," Hiram said.

Approaching Elin from behind, the Jew wrapped his arms around the woman's waist.

Hiram kissed Elin in the cleft where her neck joined her shoulders. She shuddered, a reaction of surprise, not delight.

"Don't. I'm tired."

The Jew backed off but remained connected to his wife in a loose embrace.

"I'm sorry you had a bad day," Hiram said, his native patience obvious in the steadfast way he approached her.

"Rotten. Absolutely rotten. The interview with the Assistant Commissar of Agriculture was a waste of time. He said nothing. No matter how many times I changed directions, he never once gave me anything solid on the rumored famine."

"Too bad. The people need to know, to prepare themselves, to stockpile whatever may be short. Maybe try again in a day or so."

Elin turned in Hiram's arms and looked sternly at her husband.

"It won't be just a few isolated shortages. I'm hearing that even bread and flour will be lacking," she said softly, dampening her tone. "Maybe it's time we thought about going home."

Upset flared in Hiram's eyes at the suggestion, a suggestion that Elin brought up regularly as the connection between the Finnish-speaking immigrants and the Soviet hierarchy strained. But the emotion passed quickly. Before the man could voice a thoughtful objection, their daughter interrupted.

"I finished my homework. May I go out before supper?" Alexis asked as she stuffed papers into the green canvas daypack she lugged to school.

Hiram loosened his embrace, moved to a shelf above the sink, and began removing plates and cups.

"After we eat, young lady," Hiram Goldfarb said. "I presume you're ready for your entrance examinations?"

"*Yes.*"

There was resignation in the word. Juha Rintala would have to wait beneath the eaves of the abandoned warehouse across from the Goldfarb apartment, new rain pummeling the unpaved streets of the wharf district, while Alexis bided her time, while she ate tough lamb, undercooked carrots, small potatoes, and bitter rutabagas. Salt was at a premium. Pepper was nonexistent. Only the fried onion would give the food flavor.

But Juha's kiss will make up for a dull, unappetizing meal.

"Done," Elin announced.

The family ate quietly. The wind howled. Rain battered the pine siding of the frame building and Elin's concern about remaining in Karelia, where even rutabagas were becoming scarce, was displaced by hunger.

CHAPTER 3

They had carried little with them from America: four place settings of china, four glass tumblers, four sets of silverware, a ladle, a spatula, a wooden stirring spoon, two carving knives, a sharpening stone, assorted pots and pans, their kitchen table, a Victrola, five symphonies by the London Philharmonic (all featuring Russian composers) on 78 rpm records, two crates of books—mostly Hiram's texts dedicated to Marxist theory, though Elin insisted on taking Whitman's *Leaves of Grass* and Alexis managed to cram two Jane Austen novels into her suitcase—their clothing, and two very heavy and very well-used Underwood portable typewriters with extra ribbons.

The journey from Leningrad to the lumber camp had been hell. Day after day—riding uncomfortably on hard wooden benches in a series of chattering, rollicking rail cars—the family had eaten sour black bread and sipped meatless turnip broth. When they arrived at *Hyvämetsä* (Good Forest) camp, their stomachs famished, their energies low, the presence of freshly baked Finnish rye bread and moose stew were a godsend.

They were assigned bunks in a communal dormitory. Their quarters were divided by a tarp strung across the log rafters, one side for Alexis, the other for her parents. They had failed to listen to the admonitions of those who'd made the journey before them and did not bring caustic powder to deal with the infestation of biting, digging, gnawing bedbugs that swarmed the camp's bunks. Placing dishes of water under the feet of their beds discouraged the bugs from climbing the bedposts but did nothing for vermin already embedded in the straw mattresses. Alexis suffered mightily. Her backside and legs became a mass of sores that didn't heal during the family's stay in the logging camp.

Hiram—whose love of good tobacco was his only vice—was sorely pressed to find anyone to sell him factory-made cigarettes or loose tobacco and papers. At best, he was able to scrounge *mahorka*—homemade cigarettes of poor quality Soviet grown tobacco and newsprint. At worst, he smoked native grasses wrapped in old news. Unaccustomed to physical labor, Hiram Goldfarb learned to sweat. Blisters caused by the bucksaw Hiram tended with another immigrant in the conifer forest turned to callus. Biceps developed. The Jew was, in the course of one summer, transformed into sinew. But the flies and the mosquitoes: there was no escaping their appetites. It made working the woods, even at night—when the flies disappeared but the mosquitoes came to life—a scene reminiscent of Dante's *Inferno*. Only the smoke from Hiram Goldfarb's cigarette, a dangerous habit to engage in amidst the slash and debris accumulated on the forest floor, offered respite from flying pests.

The working conditions were crude. Whereas, by the 1930s, North American logging operations had advanced from horse and sledge to steam powered tractors and narrow gauge locomotives, in Karelia, logging remained dependent upon horses. But the influx of hard working and innovative Finns from the United States and Canada modernized Karelian logging. Finnish-speaking immigrants brought tractors and other machinery with them. Technology increased the economic output of Karelia beyond projections. The Finns' success gave Stalin pause. In the dictator's view, there was a danger that Soviet Karelia would, on the heels of its economic stardom, seek independence or strive for union with Finland.

Winter approached. As Alexis bundled up in her coat and hat, the wool damp from her walk home from school in the perpetual autumnal mist and fog of the inland port, she lamented following her parents' utopian vision to the shores of Lake Onega. Despite being born in a similar climate in a similar freshwater town thousands of miles to the west, Alexis Gustafson did not relish the geographic resemblance between Kontupohja and Duluth, Minnesota. She was a New York City girl, if not by birth, then certainly by acclimation, and the smallness, the dullness, the intellectual sameness of her existence in Karelia weighed on a young woman used to a plethora of choices: cinema, opera, orchestral performances, and coffee shops full of intellectuals discussing poetry, prose, and politics of every stripe—not just the mundane mumbo-jumbo language of class warfare. Though she enjoyed the occasional visits by the Karelian Symphony Orchestra to Kontupohja, Alexis found little beyond the walls of the family's apartment to engage her mind and hold her interest, the exception being the time she spent with Juha Rintala.

Alexis first met Rintala, a man seven years her senior, on a trip into town from *Hyvämetsä* a month after the family arrived in Karelia. Juha Rintala had already lost his first job in Karelia after pummeling his boss to the ground in an argument over Rintala's intentions towards the man's fifteen-year-old daughter. There had been whispers of an abortion after Juha scrambled away from the logging camp to escape other fathers intent upon justice for their own daughters, daughters who also pined after the thick blond hair, the clarion blue eyes, the plate-sized hands, and the square jaw of the towering Finn. The rumor of Alana, the foreman's daughter, being spirited off to Petroskoi to "correct" her error in judgment with Juha Rintala persisted. But these unkind whispers did not deter Alexis's ardor.

Though Elin worried about the liaison between her daughter and the more experienced and presumably still married man, Elin recognized the anticipation in her daughter's eyes, the lighting up of 'Lexis's face, whenever the handsome logger-turned-stevedore happened by.

Far be it for me to interfere. She's a young woman. She needs to make her own choices.

Elin's own past, her own sexual awakening, and the scandal she had caused when she ran off with a miner to the wilds of Upper Peninsula Michigan colored her thinking. Her illicit affair with Andrew Maki, torrid and deeply rooted, had been the stuff of Victorian romance novels and like most such tales, had come to a bad end, with Elin marrying someone else: a cad, a man whose power and wealth approached that of her father's but whose integrity paled in comparison to that of the miner she left behind. Her first husband, Horace Ellison, had finally given up, finally yielded to Elin's spirit, and let her go. Their divorce allowed Elin and Alexis to flee Minnesota for New York City.

Memories of the simpler, purer love Elin once felt for Andrew Maki faded but never entirely evaporated from her consciousness. Despite her fondness for the past, Elin did not leave her daughter defenseless. The lessons Elin learned from young adulthood: bowing to her overbearing father's insistence, failing to follow her heart and marry the man she loved, using contraceptives to prevent pregnancy (until Horace's infidelity with a whore infected her and cost her the ability to bear children), were imparted to Alexis once the girl began to show signs of interest in boys. At eighteen, Alexis knew about condoms and other measures to prevent conception. She knew more about such subjects than many married women. Alexis carried this knowledge with her as she briskly said "goodbye," closed the thick pine door to her apartment, and clambered down the crude wooden stairway to meet her beau.

It was raining. Dusk had fallen. The dockworker stood beneath the eaves of a frame building across the street from the Goldfarb flat, in a blue-gray great coat, a castoff he'd found in a local surplus store, a reminder of the Russian Army's sad retreat from the Eastern Front during the Great War, the rabbit fur of the collar pulled snug, a store-bought cigarette smoldering between his lips. Water dripped from a ruined gutter, plastering Rintala's blond to his scalp as he watched Alexis cover her head with her hands for the mad dash across the muddy street. Safely across, the girl threw her arms around her lover, pulled his cleanly shaven face towards her, and kissed him on the lips.

"What took you so long?" the big Finn asked, as they separated.

"Homework. And supper. And discussing politics."

"Best keep those conversations behind closed doors," the dockworker said furtively, his eyes darting, knowledge that the political landscape of Karelia had changed, that immigrant Finns were out of favor with Moscow, clear in his caution.

"We're not stupid," Alexis said, creating more distance. "My parents write what they think is the truth, but truth colored with nuance to satisfy the censors. What we talk about in the privacy of our kitchen isn't repeated in public."

Rintala nodded, removed a tin flask from the front pocket of his coat, and pulled the cork. "Care for a nip?"

"No thanks. I've a bit of a headache."

Rintala smirked, took a pull of vodka, corked the flask and shoved it back into his pocket. "I hope that's not an excuse."

Alexis frowned. "What's that supposed to mean?" she said in perfect Russian, her effort at grammar and tense paying off in fluency.

"The headache..."

"I'll not use it as an excuse."

They began walking towards Rintala's room. A wooden sidewalk led them away from the waterfront and towards downtown. There was scant traffic. Night cloaked the city. The rain continued.

"Did you get them?" Alexis asked.

"Yes. Damn Aho charged me twice the normal price. Said it was 'mark up,' the cost of doing business. Sheepskins are damn hard to find in Karelia."

The woman smiled.

"No sheepskins, no Alexis. You know the agreement. I'm not interested in carrying a child. I'll not be tied down to you or any other man until after I pass my entrance examinations, complete college in Leningrad, and finish medical school in Moscow. Then, maybe, if the stars are in alignment and the man I am with at the time suits my fancy, I *might* consent to carry his offspring. But until then..."

Rintala glanced at her as they walked. "I have two brats already. I don't need a third."

Juha's *partial* disclosure (he omitted any reference to the child allegedly fathered in Joensuu) was something Alexis Gustafson had mulled over for a considerable period of time before becoming involved with the man. Even though Alexis was not, at that point in her life, religious, she was, after her own fashion, moral. Sleeping with a married man had not been a casual decision.

Their first union had been painful. His sex was as manifest as his hands. Alexis had no experience in her role, despite the sermons her mother had preached on the topics of love, sex, and reproduction. Then there was the circumstance of location. Her apartment. Her bed. Her parents away. The weather outside dreadfully cold and stormy. The perpetually grey Karelian sky had added its own brand of melancholy to the day. No work at the docks. No lake steamers for Juha to unload. A hot cup of real coffee—not the weak *tee* or rye-based substitute that was their usual fare—shared at a local cooperative deli. Eyes meeting. Hands touching. Kisses fluttering. A dash back to the Goldfarb tenement. Juha slowly disrobing her in the dark. Shame at her underthings—her shame, not his. Alexis unable to assist. Her eyes had been riveted on the buttons of his trousers as he slowly, inexorably, undid them one by one. She had never, until that moment, despite all the airs of superiority, of confidence, of maturity she cast about when surrounded by boys her own age, seen a grown man in the altogether. And there it was. Magnificent. Frightening. Its uncircumcised countenance rising from folded skin like a tulip seeking moisture. Her bare back met cold sheets, the scratchy wool blanket tossed aside, her small breasts sagging, her nipples rising from cold. Or was it due to excitement? She couldn't recall exactly. And then, he was pressed against her, his hairless chest forcing her into the bed, his fingers touching her private hair—blond, the color of straw, the color of *his* hair. A finger. Parting. Wetness.

Her breath had quickened and then, inexplicably, Juha's face had locked on hers.

"Your eyes…"

She struggled to comprehend the interruption of the inevitable.

"Yes?"

"One blue. One brown."

She had grinned. His sex, sheathed in sheepskin, had been rigid and rested on her bare thigh.

"And you are just noticing this now?"

A slight laugh. "What does it mean?"

She had frowned. "That it is three o'clock in the afternoon and you best get about your business or my parents will see things that will haunt them for the rest of their lives!"

He had nodded. There had been pain. She had grimaced. And then, the thrusting had commenced.

Since that day, she had learned much. There were ways, when no protection was available, that they could pleasure each other without risk, though with Juha, one always had to guard against impulse. His desire to find release in her warmth was so strong it was all she could do to restrain him. She understood. She appreciated the biological urge that compelled him to try. She was capable of redirecting him, of rising to the challenge. She was not about to follow some fifteen-year-old Canadian farm girl to the abortionist.

They rested, his naked body next to hers, the warmth of blankets surrounding them like a cocoon as she stared hard at the imprecisely joined tin ceiling. Rintala's apartment was located in a single-story frame building crammed between storefronts on a side street near the center of Kontupohja. Lulled to contemplation by the calm of resolution, she daydreamed.

Someday, I will take a boat from Lake Onega to Moscow. A summer trip. Up the Mariinsk canal system. Through the river valleys and woodlands. Birds darting. Fish leaping. The smell of flowers, clover, and leaves. Like a scene from a Jane Austen book. I would be the heroine. But who would play Mr. Darcy? Certainly not Juha. He's a solid man for purposes unrelated to the future. Marriage to Juha? I could not trust him, not for a minute. When I am thirty-five, my belly scarred from bearing children, my breasts sagging from gravity, Juha Rintala's eyes would wander. He would not intend to hurt me. But he would. That is for certain. No, he is not the man of my dreams. He is not my knight in shining armor.

"What are you thinking?" Juha studied 'Lexis's face. The question drew her back to their circumstance. His fingers touched her thigh. There was tenderness, not urgency, in the gesture. She lowered her gaze to search his eyes, to determine his intent.

He is satisfied. So satisfied, that when he climaxed, I thought he had died. Would that I could feel the same certainty. A stirring and a release of tension—that is what I am able to achieve. Mother said it is possible to achieve more, much more, with a man. So far, with Juha, the miracle has not happened. Still…

"That I am comfortable here, in this bed, with you," she replied.

He smiled. "But do you love me? Do I complete you like those men you fawn after in those books you read?"

There were times, when they were alone, that she read passages from *Pride and Prejudice*, her favorite Austen work, to Juha. The words seemed to affect the handsome Finn. His efforts at seduction became more refined, more subdued after such readings. But the result of their union, even with Jane Austen providing the mood, was less than earth shattering. Alexis achieved release but not at the level of an earthquake or thunderstorm, a failing that troubled her to a degree. Despite this truth, Alexis knew that she was inexperienced as a lover and that, in time, she would likely find what she was looking for in the warmth of Juha Rintala's bed.

She considered his question. There was a need for great delicacy in her answer. "Love is something that emerges over time," Alexis whispered. "Affection is the beginning of love and I certainly have affection for you."

Juha understood that little good would be gained by pressing the issue.

"Well," the dockworker said, glancing at a pocket watch on the nightstand next to his bed. "It's time to get you back to your parents. Any later and they might suspect that we're up to more than just a cup of coffee and conversation."

A fragile laugh. "Oh, Mr. Rintala, I think Mother, if not Father, has figured out there's more to our night time strolls than just coffee."

CHAPTER 4
October 1938

***I** have lost weight.*

Elin Goldfarb scurried through Petroskoi, clutching a canvas satchel full of pencils and paper, an abused Finnish-Russian dictionary, and a sandwich. Her once fashionable black leather boots had worn thin and were barely able to keep out the snowmelt. She dodged scruffy peasants, recently arrived immigrants to Karelia—another wave of Russification—Stalin's forced transplantation of former *kulaks* to work the forests. Elin stared straight ahead as she navigated the sea of men and women crowding the sidewalk.

Am I starting to look like these poor creatures? she wondered. *Workers' paradise? That's a laugh. Gylling, Rovio, and Corgan all gone, swallowed up by the very Russian culture they praised. Where can the music of Choi and Rubenstein and Tchaikovsky be heard? Who are the pretenders, the charlatans that Stalin promotes over the masters? And the men of letters: Dostoyevsky. Turgenev. Tolstoy. Where are their words? Banned. No longer acceptable. Declared illegal by edict of the Central Committee of the Karelian Communist Party.*

As she hurried to a meeting at the labor hall, snow falling gently around her, an overcast sky shrouding the unremarkable architecture of the unremarkable provincial capital, intent upon reporting on the latest restrictions imposed by the Soviet regime, she silently reviewed the risks attendant to her journey.

The promoters of Karelian Fever had been removed from power. Gylling, Rovio, and Corgan, along with dozens of other Finnish-speaking immigrants, were presumably bound for inglorious "re-education" in Siberia, or worse—the firing squad. As Elin Goldfarb waded through the crowd, late as she was for her appointment with a minor Party official, she considered what the years between 1934 and 1938 had wrought.

On the positive side of the ledger, Alexis had passed her entrance examinations, been accepted by St. Petersburg State University, and was doing well, at least according to her occasional letters and infrequent visits home. There had been a moment, when Alexis seemed infatuated with Juha Rintala, where the girl's future appeared at risk. But the relationship soured when Juha's eyes and hands wandered. The man's intractable need to possess any decent looking woman who glanced in his direction proved too great a temptation. The fling between Alexis and the dockworker ended when, arriving unannounced at Rintala's rented room one evening, Alexis found Juha's rugged face buried between the thighs of a Russian barmaid. There had been a scene, at the conclusion of which the dockworker and the Russian girl ended up wearing the contents of Rintala's chamber pot. After the police escorted Alexis home, the incident was never again referenced by anyone in the Goldfarb-Gustafson family. And Juha Rintala did not attempt to win Alexis back. He sent no messages or letters or lines of sweet poetry to woo her heart, the embers of their steamy affair having been extinguished by a bucket of stale piss.

Alexis moved to St. Petersburg after being accepted by the university. She lived in a women's dormitory, far removed from the dockworker's influence, and achieved the highest grades possible in anatomy, chemistry, and advanced biology. She studied dutifully, in hopes of winning a scholarship to the I.M. Sechenov First Institute of Medicine in Moscow so she could pursue her dream of becoming a physician.

If there is a God, Elin considered as she walked through steady snow, *He intervened that cold night in Kontupohja.*

The hesitancy of her belief fit the journalist's religious background. Elin had been born into Lutheranism, had made her confirmation answering the bishop's questions, questions that had been posed to her and the other children for months before the service at Bethany Lutheran church in Duluth's West End took place. Elin had attended services, church weddings, and funerals as an adult. Then, one day, after marrying Hiram Goldfarb, Elin Gustafson Goldfarb began to question her faith.

It was the war. How could God allow men—for it was men and men alone who sent their sons and grandsons to perish in the trenches—to engage in such slaughter? And to what purpose? There was nothing noble or sacred or honorable or even great at stake in the "Great" War. Ancient familial ties and insignificant insults led to conflagration. It is unlikely that God oversees this experiment on Earth. There is only randomness and chaos beyond the limits of the sky and after that, only the dark cold void of the grave.

Despite this critique of her beliefs, somewhere in Elin Goldfarb's innermost thoughts, or perhaps lodged even deeper, there existed a kernel of residual faith. She wanted there to be a God, desired for there to be something more than what she had witnessed during her life of love and loss.

That I still have some slender hope in a Hereafter, in a life after the last scene of this bitter play has been acted and the curtain has been drawn, she considered, sidestepping a sleeping drunk on the sidewalk, *is another positive, I guess.*

On the negative side of the ledger, she and Hiram had come under renewed scrutiny. A year earlier, the newspaper had been forced by Party edict to switch from printing in Finnish to Russian. In addition, Elin, Hiram, and the paper's other writers could no longer express their frustrations, concerns, and opinions regarding the path Karelia was on. No more could their writing question the wisdom of the regime's retrenchment from Gylling's vision. That dream, the dream of an autonomous Finnish-speaking republic within the structure of the U.S.S.R., was dead. "Report the news and report it with an eye towards the correct Marxist ideology or you will join Gylling and the others!" was the message delivered by the Party apparatus in the simplest of terms. As a journalist, the new censorship grated on Elin: it galled her like encountering vinegar in what had once been sweet wine. But she found that, as she aged, her penchant for challenging authority waned.

She arrived at the labor hall in response to an invitation to meet with the immigration officer for the People's Commissariat for Internal Affairs (the NKVD). The invitation had been addressed to her husband but when the envelope arrived at *Työläinen* earlier that morning, Hiram was away, spending the day with city officials regarding new sanitation works being planned to treat the city's sewage and was unavailable to make the afternoon meeting.

This looks interesting, Elin had thought, reading the elegantly scripted invitation. *I'd best see what the boys in Petroskoi are planning.*

She had jotted a note to her husband, gathered up her satchel, coat, and purse and left the newspaper office to catch a ferry bound for the capital city.

There was a large crowd milling outside the entrance doors to the concrete block structure. The building was a testament to uninspired architecture springing up as a result of Stalin's First Five Year Plan. The hall had been hastily erected without consideration for aesthetics. Five stories of ordinary gray block rose above the street, the thick, fortress-like walls of the structure interrupted only by narrow windows. No color. No adornments. No embellishments of any sort interfered with the message of the building: *This is a serious place; where serious issues are discussed. Enter only if you are a serious man or woman.*

Elin clutched her black leather purse and canvas satchel and walked through a door held open for her by a stranger. Her eyes darted as she scrutinized the crowd.

Why are all these Finns here? I was to have a private interview with Mr. Toivinen. What is this all about?

She recognized the faces of other émigrés: men and women of Finnish ancestry who had climbed aboard tramp streamers and ocean liners to journey thousands of miles to Karelia. There was, to her reporter's intuition, something odd, something untoward about the folks assembled in the labor hall because all the faces she recognized belonged to members of the elite: journalists like herself or lawyers, doctors, engineers, architects, teachers, logging camp bosses, or factory managers.

Why are there no ordinary working people here?

The question gnawed at her, increased her anxiety, as she advanced. She nodded and offered occasional greetings to folks she knew. But Elin's attempt at pleasantry was tenuous. There was a current of unease circulating through the crowd. An element of risk, given the recent disappearance of immigrants Elin had come to know as friends—an elementary school teacher and his wife vanishing in the night, the head of the local forest products committee disappearing, leaving his wife and two small children without a husband and father, a poet she once interviewed mysteriously summoned to Moscow to never return—permeated the smoky air.

She approached a man wearing a black fedora and black storm coat, his face serious, his manner threatening, standing near the entrance doors to the auditorium.

"Excuse me, sir. Can you tell me what is happening?"

"Get moving. No questions," the man grunted.

He's with the NKVD.

Elin suppressed her uneasiness.

"I am a reporter. From Kondopoga. *Työläinen* newspaper. I'm here for a meeting with Mr. Toivinen."

"Inside. He's inside with the rest. Now get moving, before I escort you in myself!" Loathing colored the man's words as he pointed through an open door into a cavernous room filling with attendees.

Head bent in pious reflection, eyes focused on the wet concrete floor in learned compliance, Elin Goldfarb followed the crowd into the auditorium, found a seat, placed her satchel on the floor, removed her damp coat and draped it over the back of a theater style chair, and sat down. Elin straightened the hem of her skirt, removed paper and pencil from her canvas bag, and sat upright in expectation. Her stomach growled.

I am glad the insulin treatments are effective, she thought, referencing the diagnosis of diabetes she had received from her physician. *Without the injections, I would be dead by now.*

Diabetes had once been treated with raw quinces, gruel, ground coral, and other dietary supplements. Some of these remedies had a palliative impact on the Type II (non-insulin dependent) form of the disease but had no impact upon the more serious, Type I (insulin dependent) form. Elin Goldfarb experienced adult onset Type I diabetes after arriving in Karelia. The free medical care available to her—one of Stalin's more positive programs—included regular injections of insulin, a regimen adopted by physicians worldwide after a Canadian scientist discovered that, by injecting canine pancreatic extract into a child, a patient's blood sugar could be controlled. This miracle of science came just in time to save Elin Goldfarb. Prior to the discovery of insulin, Type I diabetics universally slipped into semi-consciousness and suffocated. In the U.S.S.R., state laboratories were busily manufacturing insulin and supplying the hormone to the government-run health care system, though a shortage of glass syringes plagued the delivery of the drug to patients. Dr. Petrov, Elin's physician—whose brother Borya was the head of procurement for the Karelian Health Service—had no difficulty in keeping a steady supply of insulin, syringes, and needles on hand for patients.

The reusable needles Dr. Petrov supplied were insanely large, crude by modern standards, and the injections, originally done in the doctor's office once a week, but more recently, accomplished by Elin on her own, were unpleasant. But Elin dutifully attended appointments with Dr. Petrov to replenish her supply of insulin vials, glass syringes, and needles and checked her blood sugar level by using a complex system of test tubes and chemicals and felt stored along the wooden backsplash of the kitchen sink in her apartment. She also ate wisely, avoiding extraneous sugar and maintaining a safe distance from tempting sweets. The reporter favored small meals to keep her stomach full—a schedule she had failed to adhere to while traveling to Petroskoi.

How could I be so forgetful? Elin thought as her stomach rumbled. *Oy veh!* she thought, repeating a phrase Hiram often uttered when exasperated. She touched her left index finger to her temple. *What's this? I forgot to eat and remove my scarf!*

She untied the scarf, turned in her seat, and hung the garment over her coat. As Elin took in the crowd, she felt renewed hunger: a sure sign that she needed something to tide her over until dinner.

Best make sure I eat lunch before too long, Elin thought as she studied the man seated to her left. *Wait—I know this man…*

"Excuse me, sir," Elin said in Russian, loud enough to be heard over the buzz of the crowd, "but haven't we met?"

The man looked at Elin with deep brown eyes. His black hair was slicked to his scalp. His salt and pepper beard was well trimmed. He was dressed in a modest brown tweed coat, black slacks that had seen better days, and work boots that, despite the application of boot black, showed signs of a hard life.

"Sorry. I don't speak Russian very well. And this noise isn't helping."

She smiled.

"Matti? Matti Peltomaa?"

The man, who was older than Elin Goldfarb, stared intently. A glimmer of familiarity slid across his brow. "Elin?"

"*Todellakin*," she replied in Finnish.

"It's been, what, twenty years?"

"It has."

The man sat back in his seat and took in the woman. "I can't believe it! I travel three thousand miles to run into an old friend from Duluth!"

Elin recalled her connection to the man: Matti Peltomaa had been a friend of her first love, Andrew Maki.

"How is Duluth?"

"Cold. Rainy. Foggy. Jobs are tough to come by. The good timber is gone. Most of the big logging camps have shut down. And the docks are as still as a tomb. There's no work for men like me, none at all."

The woman nodded. It was a story she had heard from other immigrants. Most North Americans who made the arduous journey to Karelia had assets and didn't make the trip empty-handed. There was little money available through the cooperatives and Finn halls sponsoring Karelian Fever. Universally, the men and women who came to Karelia came because the Great Depression had stifled their opportunities for advancement and not because they were impoverished. North American Finns who had relied upon strong backs to make a living and who had bank accounts or other assets sufficient to finance the journey came to Karelia by the thousands, hoping to escape lives of physical labor.

Matti Peltomaa is one of them.

Peltomaa's mouth opened to speak. His teeth were stained from chew, a habit that he had carried with him to Karelia despite the shortage of good snoose in the Soviet Union.

"How is Mr. Maki?" Elin posed the question with delicacy.

"Andrew's good. No longer logs. He and his wife, Heidi, still live on the farm on Papoose Lake. Their son Joey—actually her son, his stepson—lives in Minneapolis. Went to the university on an athletic scholarship. Played football and ran track. All Conference in both. Now he's studying to be a dentist. Wants to move back to Aurora and set up shop."

The man paused to breathe.

"And Mr. and Mrs. Maki? Did they ever have children of their own?" Elin asked, trying to restrain her wishful hope that the answer was a resounding "no".

Peltomaa studied Elin's face.

She's not the young girl who stood up to her asshole husband and regained her freedom. She has matured, aged gracefully. Not an easy task in this godforsaken place. She wears a wedding band but still she asks about Andrew. She hasn't forgotten, hasn't put the past behind her.

"Two. They have two children. A boy, Timothy, named after Tim Laitila. I don't know if you remember him. Laitila died in an accident while working for Andrew. And there's a daughter: Lila. Tim is fifteen and is finishing up his studies at Aurora High School. Lila is ten, in elementary school. Beautiful children, bright as new pennies."

The woman frowned as she listened to Peltomaa's description of Maki's life, a life Elin Goldfarb could have shared with the logger had she stood up to her father.

Choices, she thought. *We all make them. Good. Bad. I love Hiram. I have made that choice.*

Elin feigned a smile, but her attention was elsewhere.

She was engaged by a vision, a daydream of washing her hair in water heated on a wood cook stove in a remote cabin on the bulrush-clogged shores of a northern Minnesota lake. She'd never been to the Maki farm, never seen the cabin that Andrew Maki crafted out of tamarack logs cut and hewn from the land adjacent to Papoose Lake. Still, the vision was clear. Elin was washing her hair over a porcelain basin, the water draining directly under the cabin, no indoor plumbing to make the task easy. A sturdy man dressed in the clothes of the north woods approached her from behind, put his arms around her waist, and drew her into his body. *Andrew.* His smell hadn't changed. Though there was age to his face, she knew him. She would always know him.

"Why are you here?" Elin asked after completing her silent contemplation.

Peltomaa pulled a crumpled slip of paper from the inside pocket of his suit coat and handed it to the woman.

"Supposed to be a meeting of plant managers. I'm the production manager at the ski factory here in Petroskoi." Matti Peltomaa stopped speaking and searched the crowd. "But I don't think this is a meeting to discuss productivity, do you?"

"No. I am sure that's not the case," Elin replied, in a voice colored by uneasiness.

Before Elin Goldfarb could say anything further, a man dressed in a carefully pressed brown tweed business suit climbed stairs leading to the auditorium stage. The doors to the great hall closed with simultaneous "thuds".

Elin glanced around the room. Every entrance was guarded by NKVD men.

"It was nice to see you again," Elin whispered in Finnish. "Even under these circumstances."

Peltomaa nodded but made no reply.

The Russian on the stage moved behind a wooden podium, adjusted a microphone, cleared his throat, and began to address the audience.

CHAPTER 5
A Year Before

Oscar Corgan vanished in the middle of the night. During the winter of 1937, Corgan and dozens of other foreign-born Finns were roused from sleep, allowed a few moments to dress, and escorted from their homes. Most of "The Taken" were never seen again. A handful of men and women who disappeared in this fashion returned to their communities after being interrogated. These lucky few said nothing about what they had endured because they were the exceptions rather than the rule. Oscar Corgan, former editor of *Työmies* and one of the primary promoters of Karelian Fever, was not so fortunate.

Most often, *troikas*—a trio of men who arrived unannounced during the night—snatched up the unfortunates. In Corgan's case, only two men came. One, Mr. Kiuru, an immigrant from Finland and a Party operative, was a trusted family friend. The other man, a faceless, nameless Russian, large backed and hulking in the standard black trench coat and fedora of Stalin's secret police, was unidentified—a man of mystery who remained in the background as Kiuru explained that Oscar Corgan was being summoned for an "interview" with the NKVD.

"But, you know me, Kiuru. You know that I am a loyal communist."

Kiuru had shaken his long narrow head. "Nationalism is a crime against the State. Party affiliation cannot hide the damage your tendencies have caused."

Corgan knew that further argument with the man, in the face of the accusation being made, was useless.

"Oscar, what is happening?" Corgan's pretty wife Katri asked, rubbing her eyes in the dull light of a kerosene lantern as Oscar searched for clothing in the couple's bedroom. "Who is here?" she added, from the safety of their bed.

"Go back to sleep," Corgan answered. "I'm needed by the Party. I'll be back as soon as I can."

Kiuru stood watchfully in the doorway as the doomed man pulled a pair of pants over his woolen Union suit and a flannel shirt over his torso, donned a coat, gloves, and hat, and bent at the waist to kiss his wife. Paul, the eldest child still at home, stood in the shadow cast by Kiuru outside the master bedroom.

"No need for that," Kiuru said as Corgan picked up a pocket watch and fob. "Leave the watch—it might be useful for your family in the days ahead."

Paul Corgan would later recall that Kiuru's voice, rather than being authoritative, seemed conciliatory.

"Let me borrow your wristwatch, will you?" Oscar asked his son, as the men moved into the living room. Corgan snatched Paul's cheap timepiece from a shelf near the boy's bedroll on the cold floor, rolled up the left sleeve of his jacket and shirt, and secured the watch. "I'll give it back when I return."

Despite his youth, Paul suspected that it was unlikely he'd see his watch or his father again. The boy maintained silence as the Russian gathered up Oscar Corgan's typewriter, the family's camera, radio, birth certificates, other documents of importance—including Oscar's journals and a photograph album. The big intruder tossed the items into a rucksack before following the prisoner and Kiuru outside. The cottage's thin wooden door closed with a bang. A black sedan clattered away under a cloudless sky. There had been no moon visible that night as the car roared south on brutal roads towards an interrogation room in Petroskoi.

The Corgan family waited to hear of Oscar's fate. Rumors circulated: *Oscar Corgan has been shot. Oscar Corgan is in a Siberian labor camp. Oscar Corgan is in Moscow being interrogated by the NKVD.*

It was not as if the family mutely accepted the disappearance of its patriarch. Inquiries were made but the answer was always the same.

"The State does not arrest innocent people," Mayme Corgan, the eldest Corgan child, home from her schooling during the summer of 1938, was told. "If your father was taken, he is guilty of something."

Still, the family held out hope that Oscar would one day reappear, perhaps thinner, a little grayer at the temples, but alive. The Corgans clung to a desperate belief that communism would right itself, that peace and order would return to Karelia and that, with the end of the purges, their father and husband would come home. It would be years, long after Stalin's death, before the truth would be revealed.

He was a broken man. A dimly lighted cellar in an unnamed warehouse in the darkest, foulest recesses of Petroskoi's underbelly became his home. Day after day, men assigned to interrogate Oscar Corgan beat him with thick canvas straps cut from a conveyor belt. Day after day, they immersed his head in cold water from Lake Onega, forcing Corgan's mouth and nose underwater until he was near drowning. These tactics achieved nothing. There were no great secrets locked in the recesses of Oscar Corgan's mind. He was not, as his tormentors continually screamed in Russian, "a nationalist." He had no grandiose dream of uniting Karelia, Finland, and Estonia into a "Greater Finland." He had only the prideful notion, as did Gylling and many other Finnish immigrants, that Soviet Karelia could be an example of worker brotherhood to the rest of the world. This revelation did not satisfy his captors. This revelation did not mollify the powers that be.

On January 9, 1938, Oscar Corgan and a dozen other detainees were loaded onto an army truck—a truck identical to other army trucks winding their way through the Karelian countryside. There was a harsh wind that day, a wind that cut through the thin jackets and coats of the captives as they were driven through the logged-out forests surrounding Petroskoi, the landscape barren, wasted, and littered with rotting stumps as thick as a man's waist. The truck came to rest in the last vestige of uncut timber. The prisoners were ordered out.

The despondent men and women were slow to disembark because the length of the journey and the cold had crept into their joints. They were beaten for their hesitancy. The little band was marched by six Soviet soldiers carrying submachine guns along a frozen dirt road winding through a deserted logging camp.

We're likely going to be put to work for our perceived crimes, Oscar Corgan thought, as the column moved past empty barracks. *Once they find out this is a mistake, I'll be freed. Katri and the children will be waiting for me in Utuha. I will find a way to get them out of this place. I have done what I could. It is time to recognize that this is not my home—that Karelia is not what I envisioned.*

"Line up!" one of the NKVD men supervising the operation screamed. "Face the woods!"

Apprehension caused Oscar Corgan to stumble but not fall. He realized, as he took his place on the edge of a crude ditch, that there would be no labor camp and no reunion with his family.

A young woman began to wail. "I have those boys," she cried out. "I have those boys!"

The man in command walked briskly to the woman, raised his revolver, placed the cold steel of the gun against the back of the young mother's head and, without a word, pulled the trigger. The report of the gun echoed. The woman made no sound as she crumpled to the frozen earth. Oscar Corgan closed his eyes as the soldiers raised their machine guns and leveled their sights.

"They took Oscar Corgan," Hiram Goldfarb had whispered to his wife in the sanctuary of their bed in the couple's drafty flat in Kontupohja when the news began to circulate throughout the Finnish community.

"When?" Elin had replied through chattering teeth.

"A month ago. There has been no word. No one knows where he is."

That night, the night Hiram disclosed that the purge had claimed Oscar Corgan, Elin had thought back to her connection to the communist organizer. She had preceded Corgan at *Työmies*: not as the editor, which had been Corgan's title, but as a reporter. The two had never worked together, though, sometime later, at the Finnish Hall in Harlem, they did meet.

Elin and Hiram had been swimming in the hall's pool. As Elin worked on her backstroke, she noticed Oscar Corgan, whom she recognized from newspaper photographs, speaking to Hiram. She had kept her distance and allowed the men their privacy. It was only a matter of weeks before Hiram's desire to travel to the U.S.S.R. as a reporter for the *New Worker* became a topic of discussion in the Goldfarb home. It took Hiram a year of lobbying to convince his wife to leave New York City for Karelia. Elin was reluctant to drag Alexis across the ocean on a whim. But in the end, Elin succumbed to the same dream of socialistic brotherhood that drove Oscar Corgan and nearly ten thousand Finns to leave their homes and migrate half a world away.

Elin suspected her decision to accompany Hiram to Karelia was a poor choice long before Oscar Corgan went missing. There had been tremors and vibrations of ugliness in the Soviet system that alarmed her after the assassination of Stalin's adjutant, Sergie Kirov, in 1934. Following Kirov's death—a murder rumored to have been orchestrated by Stalin himself—the autonomy allowed Finnish immigrants began to contract. Friends and neighbors started to vanish. By the time Hiram Goldfarb embraced his wife in their bed and whispered that Oscar Corgan had been taken, Elin Goldfarb was convinced that her family had made a terrible mistake.

CHAPTER 6

Months after Oscar Corgan disappeared, a truck arrived and whisked the rest of the Corgan family away. The Corgans began a bitter odyssey all too familiar to Finnish immigrant families living in Karelia. Some Finns, whose faith in socialism collapsed at the first sign of trouble, or whose ability to endure hardship vanished in the face of the poverty, hard work, and poor food, left before the purges became commonplace. Over half of all Finnish émigrés from the United States and Canada left Karelia within two years of arrival. As Elin Goldfarb sat in the labor hall in Petroskoi, she knew about these defections. But Elin did not—until the moment the Russian at the podium began to speak—realize the folks who'd returned to North America were infinitely smarter than she was.

"My name is Victor Mendakoff," the tall, stoop shouldered man began. "I am the Assistant General Secretary of the Communist Party of Karelia."

Elin reached for her notepad and pencil and began scribbling in Russian. The man's face had seemed familiar to her. And now, with his introduction, she placed the name to the face. She had once interviewed Mendakoff for an article she had written for the *New Worker*. The piece was written against Elin's better judgment as a journalist in that it was propaganda. The interview with Mendakoff was intended by the Party to be a recruiting tool, a revelation of the great spirit of brotherhood prevailing in Karelia.

A sense of uneasiness crept over Elin Goldfarb as she listened to the man speak.

I doubt we were called to this hall to receive praises from the Party.

"You have been summoned here because our leaders in Moscow are troubled."

Fretful whispers buzzed amongst the crowd.

"Please, friends, please hear me out."

The hubbub died down.

"As I was saying, this gathering has the approval of the most senior of our leaders. They have considered the situation in Karelia with great care, in the most thoughtful of detail. They have discussed these matters with the men and women who brought you here. Edvard Gylling, Oscar Corgan, and the rest. It has become apparent that there are elements amongst you who are nationalists, who are enemies of the People."

"That's a lie!" a bearded Finnish Canadian logging boss shouted in Russian as he gained his full height and shook a fist at the stage. "That's a damned dirty lie!" he repeated in Finnish.

Other men and women stood in unity with the camp boss and added catcalls.

Mendakoff did not remonstrate. He did not anger. He simply bided his time until the undercurrent of emotion settled to a dull murmur.

"I am sorry, friends, but it is indeed a proven fact that there are those among you who support the idea of the Karelian Autonomous Republic becoming a province of the Finnish anti-proletariat state. Indeed, there are so many of you in this gathering in support of such treason, that…" Here, Mendakoff paused for what seemed to Elin Goldfarb to be at least five full seconds before continuing. "…the Republic and the Party have no choice but to order your internment for re-education and possible expulsion."

"Damned bastards!" another bearded man, a New Englander by accent, yelled in English upon rising to his feet. "I came to this country a free man. I'll leave it the same way!" he shouted, leaving his seat and moving towards the main aisle.

Crack.

An NKVD man drew a nasty looking automatic from inside his coat and fired a round into the hall's high ceiling. Plaster fragments showered the crowd.

"Sit down!" Mendakoff said harshly. "This hall is surrounded by soldiers. They are here to prevent bloodshed. But if you insist on causing a disturbance, they will have little choice but to enter the building and deal with those of you who cannot follow instructions."

A woman in front of Elin began to weep. "I have babies at home," the young woman said between sobs. "Who will care for them? How will they come to me? How will they know where I am?"

Elin paused her note-taking to consider the woman's outburst. Alexis was away at school and would not return until summer. But Hiram would be puzzled by her disappearance, for Elin knew, upon reflection, that what was about to happen to her and the hundreds of other Finns sitting in the hall was just that: a mass vanishing, a Soviet magic act where everyday folks disappeared. She knew such things happened. But she always, until that moment, believed the words uttered by those who discovered the haunting emptiness of the Corgan apartment in Utuha: *The Soviet system does not make mistakes. The Corgans must have done something wrong.*

Now she knew. Now she appreciated the randomness, the arbitrariness of the world she and her family had entered. It was too late for lament. It was too late for remonstrating.

I'd best keep my mouth shut.

"You will be taken to camps, well-appointed and furnished, where the sorting out of your respective *situations* will commence," the Russian continued. "Mr. Turgov, would you please ask the commander of the guard to assemble his men?"

A pinch-faced NKVD operative nodded stiffly, opened the door, and exited the auditorium. He returned with a Soviet military officer and soldiers armed with submachine guns. A hum of concern emanated from the crowd and filled the hall.

"Beginning with the front row, you will accompany your escorts peacefully. No one, I repeat, no one shall talk. No one, I repeat, no one, shall deviate from the commands given by their escort. Do I make myself clear?"

Crying jags erupted from some of the women. A few heads shook in defiance. But the vast majority of the crowd knew they were damned, knew that protest would yield nothing. And so, the Finns waited apprehensively for further instructions.

Hiram will have no idea what has happened, Elin Goldfarb fretted. *He will have no idea where to find me.*

A Russian soldier arrived at the end of her row. Elin stood up, slipped on her coat and scarf, and began to slide between the rows of seats. Concern overcame the reporter as she followed Matti Peltomaa towards the hall's main aisle.

I only have two vials of insulin, one syringe, and one needle. Without access to medical supplies, I am a dead woman.

Outside the hall, satchels, purses, briefcases, and other items carried by the detainees were tossed into a pile. Elin considered keeping her purse and satchel as she approached the growing heap.

My notes, the reporter thought. *It is important to keep my notes: to preserve them so the truth can be told. And I must keep my insulin, the stone, the syringe, and the needle.*

She slipped a gloved hand into her purse, removed the medical supplies and shoved them into a coat pocket. Elin considered doing the same with her notes. But faced with the reality of a PPD 40 submachine gun, the reporter threw her purse and satchel onto the pile.

The young soldier scrutinizing Elin grunted, lowered his weapon, and broke into a faint grin as he barked at her. "Move along."

But there's been a mistake.

Even if she wasn't punished for speaking, she knew what the response from the soldier would be.

"The Party doesn't make mistakes."

But the message was addressed to my husband and not to me. I came in his stead. He is the one you want to interrogate, to re-educate, not me.

"If you live with him, if you write articles with him, you are as guilty as he is," would be the likely response.

In point of fact, the most politically dangerous article written for *Työläinen* had been her work. As the paper's editor, Hiram had accepted responsibility for the piece and Elin had never stepped forward as the author. She knew that she was as guilty, if not guiltier, than her husband of the disloyalty being alleged.

Protest will yield nothing.

Though she held her tongue, Elin wanted to ask the soldier why he was doing this to innocent people, people who had journeyed thousands of miles and endured countless hardships to become fellow citizens. But the admonition of Comrade Mendakoff resounded in her head and those of her companions: *Keep your mouth shut.*

When Elin arrived at the line of transport trucks, she lifted the hem of her skirt with her left hand, grasped the rung of a ladder with her right, and climbed into the truck. Matti Peltomaa was already waiting in the truck's cargo area. He offered Elin his hand. Elin accepted her friend's assistance, felt the strength of the man as he pulled her up, offered a weak nod in appreciation, and took a seat on the roughly planed wooden bench next to him. Peltomaa rested the back of his head against canvas and closed his eyes. Elin Goldfarb did likewise; fully cognizant that another long journey was about to begin.

CHAPTER 7

The border between Russian Karelia and Finland was crawling with NKVD men, border guards, and Soviet soldiers. Even if Hiram Goldfarb wanted to turn tail and run, he was trapped.

The Jew had discovered the neatly scripted *faux* invitation and Elin's hasty note that she had gone to the Karelian capital in his stead. He recognized that the invitation was a ruse. He threw on his overcoat to seek out a minor Party official who might know why he was being summoned, who might know where his wife, who did not return home from her journey, had been taken. The official knew only that those who assembled at the labor hall in Petroskoi were no longer visible to their *sukulaiset,* their kin. They had evaporated into the interrogation system of the NKVD and there was no news, no information, about Elin Goldfarb—or any of the other unfortunates—to be had.

Hiram was beside himself. He wrote a quick letter to their daughter and posted it. He urged Alexis to come home to assist him in searching for her mother. NKVD agents watching Hiram Goldfarb intercepted the envelope. The letter was read and held as evidence in the treason case against the unfortunate newspaperman.

"Mrs. Goldfarb, you are a reporter, no?"

Elin Goldfarb sat in a hard backed wooden chair in a small windowless basement room of an isolated warehouse, the same building that had once housed Oscar Corgan. She sat across a grey metal desk from a wide-hipped, large-paunched investigator whose face bore acne scars of such depth and frequency it appeared as if the man had been shot in the face with a shotgun. The man's eyes revealed evidence of alcoholism. Elin's interrogator, Comrade Litvin, was indeed a drinker: a liter-of-vodka-a-day man.

The woman stared directly into the jaundiced eyes of the Russian as she replied. "I am."

Litvin narrowed his gaze so that his dispirited eyes bore into the woman. He shifted his heft in his chair behind the desk. "And these?"

The agent pointed to the syringe, needle, vials, and pumice stone that guards had confiscated from Elin.

I've been here three days. Without adequate food. Without cold water to drink. The water here, wherever it comes from, is lukewarm and foul. My condition, she thought, *is precarious.*

Elin was overdue for an injection. She had used the bucket in her cell that functioned as a toilet repeatedly since arriving at NKVD headquarters. She craved water beyond ordinary thirst. Intense hunger, inordinate fatigue, and a feeling of her skin beginning to shrink and itch all signaled that her body craved insulin.

How much do I reveal? How much information am I willing to share with this man who holds the key to whether I walk out of this place a free woman or end up working at hard labor in some distant camp?

She had little choice but to be candid. "I am diabetic."

"Diabetes? I have heard of the condition but have never been acquainted with someone who has been diagnosed."

Litvin's right index finger stroked the glass vial.

"Fascinating. So, as I understand it, you will die from too much sugar accumulating in your body if you aren't able to inject yourself with…" The man picked up the vial and read the Russian label on the bottle. "…insulin. No?"

Elin nodded. She felt dizzy. Fainting due to her condition became a real possibility.

"Fascinating," Litvin repeated, carefully placing the vial back on the desk.

A mechanical clock on the cement block wall behind the agent ticked loudly in the musty, cool space of the basement room. Two single light bulbs hung from frayed wiring and provided yellow light; light nearly identical in color to the pale eyes of Elin's captor.

"What can you tell me about your husband?"

A lump formed in Elin's throat. "What do you mean?"

Litvin smiled, revealing broken incisors. "Hiram Goldfarb. You are married to him, no?"

She nodded.

"So. Tell me why he has chosen to become an enemy of the People. I mean, his writings, madam; surely you understand that what he has been writing and publishing in that little paper of his is unacceptable."

My article. He's talking about my article criticizing the Karelian Communist Party for backtracking. He thinks, as the policeman who came to beat Hiram did, that Hiram was the author of that piece.

"I don't understand," she lied.

Litvin diverted his eyes and studied a wooden joist supporting the building. "Sure you do. You know what I am talking about. This article," he said slowly, opening a red cardboard folder and removing a copy of the piece from *Työläinen,* the edges of the newspaper clipping revealing the carefulness of the man in the sharply clean edges of the fragment, "has all the hallmarks of being the product of a nationalist. It is your husband's work, no?" The agent slid the article across the desk.

Elin blinked. Her head pounded. Her eyes stared at the words, words she, not her husband, had typed on the Cyrillic typewriter that had replaced her beloved Underwood at the newspaper. Unconsciously, her gaze fixed on the vials of insulin.

"Answer my question and I will allow you your medicine. You look terrible, Mrs. Goldfarb. Your face is haggard, your expression, limp. Are you feeling ill? Maybe you need an injection of your precious insulin, no? Am I correct? The piece is your husband's work, yes?"

The words became gibberish. Elin's head pounded. Pain spread from the back of her skull to her forehead. Thirst welled up in her throat. An itch clawed at her skin. Her stomach churned. She felt the room spin. Her breath took on a sweet odor. She began to pant and hyperventilate, which increased her dizziness and confusion.

"You were not asked to come to the meeting at the labor hall," Litvin said quietly, studying the distressed woman with predatory eyes, eyes at odds with the conciliatory tone of his voice. "The invitation was meant not for you, but for your husband. There has been…" Here the agent paused to collect his thoughts, to select the right word. "…a mistake. That is not a word I use lightly, Mrs. Goldfarb. It is unusual for someone in my position to admit that the system has made an error, that our net has caught the wrong fish. But that is what appears to have happened."

Elin blinked. She was battling an urge to reveal the true authorship of the article. But in the back of her mind, her responsibility to Alexis loomed like a gigantic shadow.

If I tell him the truth, I am going to disappear like Oscar Corgan. What good will come of that? On the other hand, if I reiterate his belief, it will fall upon Hiram. What has he done to deserve such a fate? Nothing. Where is his crime? Where is his wrong that he should be fated for a labor camp or worse? God, I wish I could think clearly. The sugar is rising inside me. My mind is cloudy. I haven't much time. What should I do?

"You have something to say about this article, about your husband's connection to this, this…" Litvin pointed to the clipping with a fat index finger, "…piece of trash?"

Elin's eyes fixed on the glass vials, the muted light of the electric bulbs repeated in their cylindrical shapes. A power surge caused a momentary flicker in the lights and disrupted her concentration.

"He is the editor of the newspaper," she finally whispered.

"Meaning?"

"Whatever appears in *Työläinen* must meet his approval."

It was not a lie. It was the truth. Hiram *was* the editor of the newspaper and controlled its content. Still, she was concealing the authorship of the article from Litvin to protect her own skin.

A half-truth.

The NKVD man slid the syringe, pumice, needle, and medicine across the table. "The People thank you for your cooperation. I'll leave you so you can deal with your condition privately," Litvin said, as he pushed himself away from the table, stood up, and exited the room.

CHAPTER 8

The Goldfarb apartment was in disarray when Elin returned home from her interrogation. Every item that could be linked to the family's "nationalistic" tendencies: paper, pencils, pencil sharpener, pen tips, quills, ink, files, records, photographs, camera, personal records, newspaper clippings, and the Victrola and the symphony records was gone. Nearly every stick of furniture had been reduced to kindling. Mattresses were torn in half and stuffing was strewn throughout the apartment. Sheets and blankets were ripped to shreds. Clothing had been removed from dressers and tossed randomly throughout the flat. Elin saw her expensive silk slip dangling from a door handle: the garment had providently snagged the metal handle on its descent. The small larder of food Elin had stockpiled was gone. The flour bin was empty. An overturned sugar bowl spilled its contents across the wooden floor. There were no potatoes left in the rack Hiram had bought in Leningrad. Onions had vanished: only the smashed remnants of the wooden nail box Elin used as their receptacle remained. Candles were broken. Glassware was shattered. Dish fragments littered the floor. But despite the violation of her home, it was the disappearance of Hiram, the complete and utter absence of his presence that weighed heaviest upon Elin Goldfarb.
What have I done?

Elin, until the moment when, in diabetic confusion, she gave Comrade Litvin what he desired, had always considered herself as possessing moral, if not physical, courage. Her constitution had been strong enough to put her first husband out of the familial home when she discovered his unfaithfulness. She had dutifully, and at some personal danger, investigated the murder of Olli Kinkkonen, an itinerant Finn who was lynched in Duluth. She stood up to her father—and to the conservative side of Finnish American society in her hometown—with nary a blink of an eye. But when affected by disease and on the brink of collapse in that ugly room in the basement of NKVD headquarters, the moral moat around her integrity had been breached and she had given Litvin her husband.

I am no better than Judas, she thought as she righted the only unbroken chair remaining in the lightless apartment and sat down on the chair's hard pine seat.

I broke every promise I ever made to Hiram. Sweet Hiram. Trusting Hiram. He's done nothing wrong, nothing but try to make the world a better place for those who were not born to money or power.

She scratched the back of her head, where her long hair was tied in a dirty bun and held off her neck by a barrette. There had been lice—there had been dirty, filthy lice in the mattress in her cell where the NKVD had kept her. There had been no light and no sound in the bowels of the dungeon, save the occasional report of a pistol being discharged somewhere down the hall. She later learned what the gunshots meant. She pieced together that some suspected of treason, of nationalism, never made it out of that basement. She did not know, and never personally saw, the killing room just down the hall from her cell: a long, narrow, windowless room lined with rock walls and containing a shallow trough, like those found in cattle barns, cut into the cement floor. Had she seen the room, had she been privy to its secrets, she would have known the purpose of the channel. But she did not see the room. She only heard the muffled report of Litvin's revolver punctuating the night as she shuddered beneath the licey blanket, waiting for Litvin to call for her.

He hadn't. Litvin hadn't called for her again, not after she had given the man what he asked for. Elin Goldfarb thought that there was a chance that she could barter her favors to save her husband from what came next. Elin Goldfarb still retained a beautiful face, a striking figure, a bust that was poised and not defeated by gravity, and luxuriant graying hair.

I should have tried to seduce the Russian. I doubt he would have been interested. But, who knows? Men are what they are and Comrade Litvin is likely no different than any other man I've ever met. Maybe I could have saved Hiram, had I acted on my impulse.

Tears flowed down Elin's downy cheek. She bent at the waist, retrieved a dishcloth from the debris surrounding her chair, and dabbed her eyes.

Where is Hiram?

The thought had occupied every second of her existence since she had injected herself with insulin after bowing to the NKVD man's insistence. She closed her eyes and sought to recall the scent of Hiram's aftershave, sought to feel the texture of Hiram's skin as he pressed himself against her in the privacy of their marital bed.

She had been lucky enough to find another man after Andrew Maki who completed her. The unions she experienced with the Finnish miner in her youth had been the stuff of legends. That their thrashing about in bed had produced no child was indeed a miracle. Or, perhaps, a tragedy.

If there had been a child, Elin considered, tears abating as she reviewed her life, *things may have been vastly different. Of course, I would have been forced to cease teaching. No respectable school retains a woman who becomes impregnated outside of marriage. But nothing would have stopped me from working as a reporter. That path would still have been open to me, even with a child. It was open for me when I took Alexis to New York. It would have been available had I stayed with Andrew and made a life with him in Minnesota.*

Elin Goldfarb stood up from the chair to gather her clothing. As she retrieved her things, she stuffed them in a small rucksack, selecting the most practical, the most ordinary of her clothing, leaving the expensive and the dressy on the floor. She retrieved her reserve supply of insulin, needles, and syringes, all curiously undisturbed in the kitchen, and added them to the remaining vial, pumice stone, needle, and syringe taken from her coat pocket. She wrapped the medical supplies in her underthings and placed them at the bottom of the canvas pack.

I need to find Hiram. The illusion of what could have been with Andrew isn't reality. Hiram is my husband. I love him. He was the only man after Andrew who made my heart stop in mid-beat. The only one. He made a mistake, bringing us to this forsaken place. But I forgave him that error in judgment long ago. I could have said "no" but I wanted to see for myself what all the fuss about Karelia entailed. I am just as much to blame for what has happened as he is. No, that's not true. I am more to blame. It was my pride that caused the NKVD to seek Hiram out. It was my words, written in the newspaper, that may well have killed him.

The door to the apartment opened. A shaft of winter light entered the room from a bank of windows lining the drafty hallway. Two Finns whom Elin Goldfarb did not recognize, one tall, one short, and a Russian, strode confidently into her home.

"Mrs. Goldfarb?"

The tall Finn stopped next to her as he spoke in Russian with a Finnish brogue.

"Yes?"

"Come with us."

Elin's eyes narrowed. Fear invaded her mind.

"There must be some mistake. I was just interviewed by Comrade Litvin. In Petroskoi."

The Russian moved towards her. "Litvin? I know no one by that name. But whoever this 'Litvin' is, we have our orders. From the Central Committee. You are on the list," he said gruffly.

"Surely you can check with him. He's with the NKVD, an investigator. In Petroskoi."

"Yes, yes," the Russian said with disdain. "I heard you the first time. Petroskoi. This is Kondopoga (he used the Russian name for the city) not Petroskoi. We are charged with rounding up folks suspected of nationalism. You're one of them. You're on the list despite whatever your Comrade Litvin may or may not have told you."

Elin's gaze lowered.

"Put together whatever it is you need for your journey," the Russian said, the harsh edge of his speech making it clear to the woman that there was little time to waste. "You'll miss the boat if we don't hurry."

Elin stuffed cosmetics, jewelry, hose, and an extra pair of comfortable shoes into the rucksack. When she reached towards the floor to retrieve her copy of *Leaves of Grass*, the NKVD man grasped her wrist tightly.

"No capitalist trash. You've wasted enough time."

The Russian led her by her wrist from the apartment into the common hallway. The air outside the flat was cool but sunlight streaming into the corridor warmed Elin's face as she followed the Russian towards the stairway. The silent Finns brought up the rear.

Snow fell as they stepped outside. The flakes were sharp and icy and stung Elin's cheeks. She buttoned her overcoat. The canvas pack clung to her, its leather straps biting into her bosom as the group hurried towards the harbor.

"Where are we going?" Elin asked, mindful that the Russian had used the term "boat".

"Not *we*. *You*. *You* are going to a re-education camp."

"Where?"

The Russian said nothing. The little group marched through the squall. The snowfall obscured everything beyond a few meters in front of them. They continued at a fast clip until, without warning, Elin and her captors found themselves at water's edge.

"One more for you, captain!" the tall Finn called out, as they stood at the bottom of a gangway leading to the deck of a lake steamer.

The boat—a freighter named the *Minsk*—was old. Its wooden deck and hull were blackened with rot. All along the steamboat's rail, faces manifested between gusts of swirling snow. There were children. And women. And old folks. And hardy workingmen: all standing apprehensively at the rusty iron rail and staring blankly at Elin Goldfarb and her escort.

"Get aboard!" a lanky Karelian, an officer by deportment, shouted from the top of the gangway. "We were due to leave for Kalajoki Island five minutes ago. Waited for you to arrive, as an accommodation to Comrade Belikov," the man said, acknowledging the NKVD agent. "But now it's time to leave."

"Get on board!" Belikov said gruffly, emphasizing his command with a shove.

Elin moved towards the ship but felt resistance as she tried to climb the gangway. The shorter of the two Finns escorting her had a hand on her rucksack. The Finn disguised his actions from Belikov and slid the Whitman into Elin's backpack.

"The flap was loose," the man lied, stepping away. "Best get on the boat or the captain will likely blow his cork."

A whistle shrieked. A dirty contrail belched from the boat's smokestack. Elin turned towards the *Minsk* and began climbing.

CHAPTER 9

"Your wife is beautiful, no?"

Mikhail Litvin sat behind his desk, his eyes fixed on the man seated across from him, the NKVD investigator's sausage-like fingers entwined, his thick hands resting on the leather desktop.

"You have seen my wife?"

Litvin nodded.

"Where?"

The NKVD man sighed. "Here."

Hiram Goldfarb, one corner of his mouth crusted with blood, the result of a blow he'd received during the short boat ride from Kontupohja to Petroskoi, his right eye beginning to blacken from additional blows delivered by the NKVD interrogation unit, sucked greedily on a factory made cigarette as he studied the wide, pockmarked face of his opponent.

"When?"

"Four days ago."

The Jew inhaled deeply and blew a perfect smoke ring into the musty air. "Where is she now?"

Litvin smiled quixotically. "I am the one who is supposed to ask questions." The Russian's smile vanished.

I have work to do. This man is a great danger to the stability of our country. The powers that be have indicted him, found him lacking in patriotism. Though I am also a Jew and have some sympathy for his present station, I must not let my personal feelings interfere with my work.

Mikhail Litvin had immigrated to Karelia from Kiev, the capital city of the Ukrainian Republic, during the *Holodomor*: the famine that killed millions of Ukrainians in 1932 and 1933. He was a member of the Communist Party and used his Party affiliation to out-distance the anguish that claimed many, many Jews and non-Jews living in and around Kiev. Litvin discounted the rumors that Stalin had ordered the mass starvation of Ukrainians in an attempt to "purify" the U.S.S.R. of non-Russians. Litvin believed that he was lucky and that those who starved were unlucky. It was as simple as that. In the agent's view, the tragic deaths did not occur because Stalin hated Ukrainians as Hitler hated Jews: millions died because there was not enough food to feed them. Litvin was unaware that grain, eggs, and meat had actually been *exported* from the Ukraine at the height of the famine. But, given his strong political beliefs, it is unlikely that the NKVD man would have altered his views even if he possessed such information.

Litvin would, however, have quickly corrected both Elin and Hiram Goldfarb's supposition that he was Russian. Despite his love for the Soviet Union, Mikhail Litvin remained, at his core, a Ukrainian Jew.

"Tell me where my wife is," Goldfarb said quietly, "and I will answer any question put to me. I only want to know that she is alive…"

Goldfarb nearly added, *…and will one day be reunited with our daughter…*but thought better of giving the NKVD any more information. *Perhaps they don't know about Alexis, or, if they did know, they have forgotten.*

Litvin took a drag from his cigarette before resting the butt on the edge of a tin ashtray. The NKVD man scrutinized his prisoner before clasping his hands, cracking his fat knuckles, and speaking.

"She is alive. On Kalajoki Island. Being re-educated. No harm has come to her."

Hiram drew heavily on his cigarette and held the smoke. The gray cloud he eventually released through his parched lips momentarily obscured his interrogator. "On Lenin's grave?"

Litvin nodded. "On Lenin's grave."

"She was here, you say?"

Litvin nodded again.

"No harm came to her while she was under your watch?"

Goldfarb knew his wife's beauty, knew every sweet inch of her body like a jeweler knows a diamond. He had heard rumors, unsubstantiated but repeated often enough to be believed, about the treatment women endured at the hands of the NKVD. She would be a target for untoward advances, touches, or worse, if Litvin, or those who had brought her in, had any sort of eyesight at all.

"She was not touched."

Goldfarb finished his cigarette and stubbed it out in the bottom of the ashtray. "In any way?"

Litvin grew impatient. "You ask too many questions. It is my turn to ask you something."

Goldfarb nodded.

"Is this your work?"

Litvin removed the newspaper article he had shown Elin from its folder and slid it towards Hiram. The prisoner picked up the document, read it quickly, and nodded as he held the clipping in his small hands.

"It is from my paper."

"But did you write it?"

Hiram studied the clipping.

What did Elin tell him? Did she tell him she wrote it? Or did she remain silent and simply allow the Russian to form his own conclusions?

"Comrade Goldfarb, I asked you a question."

The Jewish newspaperman cleared his throat. "I don't remember," Hiram lied.

"You don't remember?" the fat man asked incredulously. "You are the editor of the paper and you don't remember whether or not you wrote this, this…" Litvin thought a bit more before continuing, "…piece of disloyal trash?"

Hiram looked pleadingly at the NKVD man but found that any semblance of compassion that had been present in the man's demeanor was gone.

"Mr. Goldfarb, do you honestly expect me to believe you don't know who wrote this article?"

The words came out slowly, dangerously, as a warning.

Hiram swallowed hard and placed the document on the desktop. "I take full responsibility for the opinions expressed in this piece," Goldfarb said quietly. "I am the editor. Nothing is printed without my approval."

Litvin considered the admission, noting that it mirrored the information he had obtained from Elin.

"Someone else told me the same thing," the NKVD man said as he rose from his chair.

Litvin replaced the article in its folder, secured the folder in a black leather briefcase on the floor beside the desk, retrieved an official looking document from the same briefcase, pulled an ink bottle and fountain pen from a drawer, and slid the items across the desk.

Goldfarb read the paperwork. Without hesitancy, he picked up the pen, removed the cork stopper from the inkbottle, dabbed the pen tip in India ink, and signed his name to the prepared confession.

Electric light illuminated the narrow room. The chamber had no windows. Though the winter sun stood high above the city outside the building, no daylight entered the space. Hiram Goldfarb stood facing a concrete block wall, his hands tied behind his back. Litvin and two nameless, faceless NKVD agents stood behind the prisoner. Only Litvin spoke.

"Having admitted to treason, it is by decree of the lawful authorities that I carry out the appointed sentence, said sentence having been adjudged to be the correct and appropriate punishment for your crimes against the state. Before the sentence is carried out, is there anything you would like to say?'

I was wrong. I was misguided. Forgive me, Elin. Forgive me, Alexis. I did not bring you to workers' paradise but to hell.

Hiram held back the words, just as he restrained the tears that he wanted so desperately to unleash in the musty cellar. The prisoner shook his head and fixed his eyes on a gutter cut into the cement floor. Hiram Goldfarb discerned blood on the concrete. Though someone had labored to remove evidence of the room's purpose, there was still blood. The Jew heard steel slide against leather. A draft blew into the room and touched Hiram Goldfarb's face as he waited to join the others.

CHAPTER 10

Alexis Gustafson's skis glided over rain-affected snow. Frigid air stung her lungs as she labored to keep up with her class. She was not a physical young woman—her interests involved things decidedly more sedate: reading fiction, knitting, studying in hopes of maintaining her number one ranking in her class, and making love with her new beau, Yuri Godenov. Physical exertion was not something Alexis had an affinity for. Her thigh muscles burned inside the wool trousers she wore over her union suit. Her hands were cold. The wool liners of her leather choppers were wet from a fall that stung her pride but caused no injury. Her face was scarlet from effort.

I need to complete this ten-kilometer ski to pass this course, Alexis thought. *Legs, do not fail me now!*

As she made her way through municipal forest, Alexis became attuned to the rhythm of the trail.

This isn't so bad, the woman thought, vapor expelling from her mouth like smoke from a factory chimney. *Maybe Yuri could take me on some of the trails in the Leningrad parks. He's an excellent skier and I could use the exercise.*

The Austen volumes Alexis had carried with her from New York, *Pride and Prejudice* and *Emma*, were ragged. She kept the books despite the fact she had read them each a half-dozen times. She exchanged them with other female students for books she hadn't read. In the past year, while waiting for word from her mother, Alexis had devoured Russian translations of Melville's *Moby Dick* (too clinical), *Great Expectations* (a fine piece of writing but Dickens was no Austen), and *Lady Chatterley's Lover* (titillating) by battery powered torch beneath the covers of her dormitory bed, as her roommate, Maria Finley, a boney faced, nervous English girl from Surrey, slept soundly in the lower bunk.

Alexis received no word regarding her stepfather. She learned, from gossip that flowed from Karelia to Leningrad on the lips of Finns who came and went from the Russian seaport, that her stepfather was among the taken, but she knew nothing certain of Hiram Goldfarb's fate.

She hoped—no, she prayed—that the gentle man, the well-meaning man who had led his family to the Soviet Union, was alive. But though Alexis's heart prayed for Hiram's good fortune, her head, without knowing the specifics, knew otherwise.

The students wore identical gray fatigue trousers and matching gray parkas against the weather as they climbed a hill. The women ahead of

Alexis sidestepped the incline, inching their way to the top of the bluff. The birch and pines lining the trail were encased in ice left by recent winter rain. A turgid sky stood over the city.

"See, I told you it would be worth the effort!" Mr. Malinkov exclaimed, as Alexis, the last of the skiers, joined the group in a clearing overlooking Leningrad. "There is the Church of Our Savior on Blood," the instructor continued, pointing towards the spires of the all-too-familiar church. "And there is Saint Isaac's," the Russian added, pointing out another famous cathedral to the female students.

Alexis spat phlegm. Her calf muscles twitched. Her mismatched eyes took in the beauty of the city: an old city, a city not yet subdued by Soviet ugliness as she imagined Moscow to be. Her attitude towards her adopted country, never glowingly affectionate, had, since her mother's ensnarement and her stepfather's disappearance, soured. Only her drive to become a medical doctor and her infatuation with Yuri made her station in life tolerable. Never a member of the Young Pioneers as a child, Alexis had not joined the Komsomol—the communist organization for adolescents—and she expressed no interest in joining the Party as a young adult. Alexis was astute enough to keep her beliefs, both religious and political, to herself, despite her generally outspoken ways.

"We need to move along," Malinkov said after a few moments of reflection. "Dinner is in half an hour. I hear the cook has beef and cabbage soup on the menu."

The girls followed their instructor to the hill's cleft. Below, the trail widened to facilitate a glide onto the floodplain of a small stream. Malinkov watched each skier shuffle up to the edge, look down the steep grade, and allow gravity to take over. One by one, the girls sped down the decline, their silence defeated by enjoyment, their voices tittering as they plummeted. A few girls lost their balance and tumbled but quickly regained their skis to finish the run. Alexis was the last girl down the hill. She looked at the cluster of young women standing in the trees on the flats, their voices a din of happiness, the pleasure of a successful run clear in their chattering. She pushed off with the wrought iron and leather baskets of her ski poles. Air rushed past her face as she crouched to lower her center of gravity and gather speed.

This is something Yuri and I can share.

Alexis coasted to a stop on the valley floor.

Her teacher moved next to her. "Nicely done," Malinkov said. "You have some ability. Have you skied before?"

"Never," Alexis said through a broad smile.

The Russian looked at her skeptically. "Never?"

"Where I come from, snow doesn't last. I never skied as a child."

Malinkov considered the disclosure. "That's a pity," the instructor said, his handlebar mustache twitching as he spoke. "You could be very good."

The girls formed a single file column behind Malinkov and began winding their way back to the university.

Maria Finley poked Alexis's rump with the tip of her ski pole as they shuffled forward. "I didn't figure you for the teacher's pet in a physical education class," the English woman teased. "Did you hear him gushing over your 'ability'? Me thinks," Maria continued in Russian, lowering her ski pole and pushing off to keep up, "it's your ass, more than your skiing ability, that intrigues Mr. Malinkov."

Alexis didn't respond. Her mind was engaged in a search, a search for her mother, for her stepfather, and the reasons behind their silence.

CHAPTER 11
March 1938

Blessed *are the poor in spirit,*
for theirs is the kingdom of heaven.
Blessed are they who mourn,
for they shall be comforted.
Blessed are the meek,
for they shall possess the earth.
Blessed are they who hunger and thirst for justice,
for they shall be satisfied.
Blessed are the merciful,
for they shall obtain mercy.
Blessed are the pure of heart,
for they shall see God.
Blessed are the peacemakers,
for they shall be called sons of God.
Blessed are they who suffer persecution for justice's sake,
for theirs is the kingdom of heaven...

Alexis shook her damp, shortly cropped blond hair. Yuri Godenov sat next to her, his naked body red from the steam, his hairless legs draped over the edge of a wooden bench, his dimpled chin tilted towards the planked ceiling of the sauna. Sweat slid down Alexis's pale skin and followed the curves of her post-adolescent body until it pooled beneath her feet. The young woman's eyelids were shut against heat. Another couple sat at the far end of the communal bench, their bodies barely visible through mist. No one spoke. No sound, save that of hissing rocks, the aftermath of Yuri dipping a small birch ladle into the pine bucket and sprinkling water over percolating stones, invaded the couples' privacy.

Since coming to Leningrad, Alexis had lost modesty. She had been raised in the culture of the Finn Hall in Harlem, where prudish American mores frowned upon mixed gender nudity in the baths. But by the winter of 1938, Alexis had become integrated into the local culture of the sauna bath. She had not accepted this seemingly Bohemian tradition while living with her parents in Kontupohja. Even with Juha Rintala, on the occasions when they ventured to the public sauna together, she insisted on wearing a towel when bathing. Her attitude changed when she was dared by her girlfriends at the university to accompany them to a mixed gender sauna in Finnish Leningrad. It had taken Alexis a few visits to become comfortable with the practice and to avoid silently critiquing the physiques of the men and women who seemed unabashed by their lack of towels or bathing suits in public.

Yuri's learning curve had been quicker. He adapted to the custom seamlessly. He saw no shame, no moral failing in adults of both sexes bathing together.

"I am told it is the way families in Finland have taken sauna baths for generations," he had said, when they had made their first joint excursion to a mixed gender bath.

Yuri had accepted the prescribed nudity of the Finnish public sauna without judgment, though he *was* quick to point out that nude bathing in mixed company was the Finnish way and not a custom followed in Russian *banyas.*

Though it was difficult to see due to steam, Alexis detected movement in the sauna. The sound of needles striking flesh, of the other couple excoriating each other, called Alexis back to her own thoughts. She recited the Beatitudes from Matthew over and over in her mind to the cadence of the flogging. Giggles spilled from the lovers. Despite the distraction, the taking of Alexis's mother and stepfather overwhelmed Alexis to the point of obsession. She wanted to know. Whatever the outcome, she wanted to know.

When Alexis had asked Yuri what course she should take, he had embraced her, pulled her close, and whispered an admonition: "Do not go looking for that which cannot be found."

"You don't know that," Alexis had replied. "You don't know that my mother and stepfather can't be found." Her anger rose. Her cheeks flushed. "How can you possibly know that? You don't. You're just being selfish. You want me to stay here, with you, in Leningrad. How can you tell me to ignore what has happened? To forget what is unforgettable?"

The Russian had shaken his head. His black eyes locked on her mismatched irises. He created distance but maintained the embrace. "There is much danger in what you seek. The NKVD is obviously behind your parents' disappearance. Where such men are involved, there can be no questions asked, no searches made. People are taken. They vanish. That is all."

On that first occasion, when she had pronounced her need to contact the NKVD regarding her parents, she succumbed to Yuri's logic. It was during this prior conversation that Jesus' Beatitudes had come to mind.

She had discovered the Gospel of Matthew in a friend's Finnish Bible. She did not experience any revelation or epiphany as she read the verses. But when she stared into the eyes of her Russian lover and talked about finding her parents, the Beatitudes had emerged, word by word, as if being channeled into her mind by the Apostle himself.

I must at least try, she had silently vowed. *I owe them both at least that much.*

Though she had been unhappy to leave New York City to follow Hiram's whimsy, and though she thought that her parents were undertaking a fool's errand, she bore no bitterness towards her mother and stepfather. She had realized, as the words of Saint Matthew insisted themselves upon her, as she clung desperately to the physical presence of another human being, what she must do. She said nothing more to Yuri about her resolve. They had parted on that earlier occasion without further discourse regarding her missing parents.

The other couple climbed down from the bench and stood on the slatted pine floor. The woman was about Elin Goldfarb's age but more thickly built. A fold of belly skin draped over the hairy triangle of her pubis. Her breasts hung like pumpkins in the hot air as the woman pulled a towel from a wooden peg and wrapped it around her body. Her escort, a man not much older than Yuri but years younger than his female companion, his legs, forearms, back, and chest covered in coarse black hair—hair that had somehow absented itself from his shiny, bald head—smiled as he watched the woman leave the room. It was a private gesture, one not meant for anyone to witness. The man retrieved his towel and followed his lover or his wife—the couple's status was unknown—out the door.

Alexis rested her head against cedar. A thermometer testified that it was 71 degrees Celsius in the bathhouse. Alexis's bangs clung to her forehead as she sat in contemplation.

Blessed are they who suffer persecution for justice's sake,
for theirs is the kingdom of heaven…

The final Beatitude repeated itself over and over in her mind like a Hindu mantra.

If I don't seek to uncover the mystery, to find justice for them, then who will?

Alexis shuddered as she considered the possible fates that had befallen her parents. The list was endless: the end result, predictable.

"You can't keep doing this," Yuri said softly, as he placed his left hand on her right wrist.

Alexis opened her eyes. "But I must."

"No good can come of this. I've been in the offices of the NKVD—when my brother was brought in for interrogation," Yuri whispered, never certain that other ears weren't listening. "He survived but he has never been the same. I was lucky. The officer I talked to remembered me from skiing. He'd been a finalist in the club championships. He'd beaten me by a few meters and remembered me. That connection saved me. But you will not be so lucky. If you wander into the NKVD office in Petrozavodsk—the office most likely responsible for your parents' troubles—you will not come back. You, too, will end up 'disappeared'." He paused for a moment, kissed Alexis on the cheek, and continued. "And that is not something I wish to have happen."

The woman studied her lover's face. She nodded, a perfunctory gesture meant to alleviate his concern.

Yuri Godenov knew that the woman was placating him and that her demons, demons afflicting millions of people throughout the U.S.S.R., were not so easily bested.

Blessed are they who suffer persecution for justice's sake,
for theirs is the kingdom of heaven…

"It's time for me to get back to my dormitory," Alexis said, after considerable repose.

"I am late as well," Yuri agreed, rising from the bench, the air clear of mist but the heat still significant. "I am supposed to meet Professor Nulinka to discuss an internship."

"The head of the anatomy department? That's wonderful news," Alexis said with tenderness, as she pinched Yuri's cheek.

They slid off the bench, gathered their towels, and exited the sauna.

Alexis's teeth chattered as she stood under a plume of invigorating water in the women's shower. The cascade washed sweat from her skin and chilled her body as she nestled her chin against her breastbone and began reciting the Beatitudes from memory.

CHAPTER 12

Elin Goldfarb struggled as she loaded firewood into a horse-drawn sledge. A boney, roan-colored gelding of indeterminate breed waited in harness in crisp April air beneath an ashen sky.

"I would be grateful to whoever is in charge," Elin said, though there was no one to hear her as she tossed another piece of split pine onto the sledge, "if the sun would come out and warm my bones."

Diabetes was exerting its power. The camp diet of thin gruel, bad bread, and weak tea was taking a toll on Elin. Her face was gaunt and her cheekbones had been made more prominent by distress. Her eyes were sunken. Her hands trembled and her head ached as her body sought to regulate the fuel in her bloodstream.

It could be worse, Elin thought as she tossed slabs of dry wood onto the sledge. *If I wasn't working as a secretary in the camp office, I wouldn't have access to insulin at all. I'd be a dead woman.*

• • •

Matti Peltomaa had traveled to Kalajoki Island with Elin Goldfarb. They stood at the railing of the *Minsk* as it plowed through the meager ice of Lake Onega. Their trip to the island was the last voyage of the season for the steamboat. Elin searched the shoreline of the low-lying island for signs of habitation, as the bow of the boat cracked ice and pushed water. Here and there, she discerned smoke, wisps of ebony curling in the sun-warmed air against the high blue of the Karelian winter sky. And then, as the boat's whistle sounded their arrival, she saw them. Hundreds of Finnish Karelians appeared along the island's shoreline, as apparitions manifesting behind the vapor rising off the cold lake. But there were no shouts of encouragement, no cries of delight from the children, no voices of greeting from the adults. The islanders, their clothing in tatters, their faces smudged, their bodies protected from November weather by a smattering of threadbare coats, cloaks, and jackets, had stood mutely, their forlorn expressions universally sad, as kapos armed with black batons patrolled the perimeter of the crowd. The quietude of the islanders alarmed Elin Goldfarb as she stood next to Matti Peltomaa in anticipation of the boat's docking.

The voyage from Kontupohja to Kalajoki Island had given Elin Goldfarb time—when not shivering on the exposed deck of the boat—to consider the devolution of her existence. Long before she had immigrated to Karelia in 1934, the dream of Edvard Gylling and the other leaders of Karelian Fever had begun to fade. The Karelian Autonomous Soviet Socialist Republic that flourished under Lenin's tolerant policies began to unravel shortly after the leader's death.

At first, the privileges granted the immigrants, including allowing Finnish as an official language of the Republic, restrictions against Russian immigration to the region, dedicating one-quarter of the proceeds from the forest harvest for the Republic's internal use, and allowing North American immigrants to shop at stores devoted to foreigners (*Insnab* stores: where better food, clothing, and other goods were stocked) remained unaltered. But with the ascendency of Joseph Stalin, the benefits lavished on the immigrants by the central government began to recede. The last of the niceties to disappear was the *Insnab* stores, which were outlawed across Karelia shortly after the Goldfarbs and their daughter arrived. By 1934—the year Elin and her family emigrated from America—Gylling and the other leaders of the Karelian Fever movement were no longer in charge and internal passports had been imposed upon the immigrants. Finnish speakers who voiced dissatisfaction with these changes were encouraged to apply for passports from their countries of origin and leave. But as Elin Goldfarb later learned, this suggestion was a ruse. Making application for a passport from one's homeland was evidence of disloyalty. This snare caught many a wishful Finn unawares: those who didn't wind up dead found themselves crowded into "re-education" camps.

These changes culminated in a decree requiring that all Karelian schools instruct only in Russian. Many Finnish Karelian schools had already adopted Russian as the primary language of instruction but those institutions that had not made the change either made amends or closed their doors.

Despite these dramatic changes in how the Finnish speaking immigrants were treated, astute political observers of Karelian Fever, like Elin and Hiram Goldfarb, were caught off guard when they too finally were trapped by Stalin's abrupt "about face."

Matti Peltomaa sought Elin out on the *Minsk*. There was a selfish motive behind the man's obsession: Peltomaa was in love with Elin Goldfarb. He'd been in love with her since he first saw her at a dance at the Work People's College in Duluth. Though Peltomaa couldn't recall the exact date of their first encounter, he never forgot the occasion. She had been, at twenty-three years old, the most beautiful girl in the room. Peltomaa had encouraged his friend Andrew Maki to approach Elin for a dance. Andrew and Elin fell in love and Matti Peltomaa long lamented the night he encouraged Maki's interest in Elin Gustafson.

If I had been able to muster up the courage, Matti thought shortly after he learned of Elin's marriage to Horace Ellison, *to ask Elin to dance instead of urging Andrew to open his mouth, perhaps I could have spared her the tragedy of marrying that rich, bandy-legged asshole.*

After chancing upon Elin at the labor hall in Petroskoi, these old feelings rushed over Matti Peltomaa like a tidal wave. It was all the deliberative Finn could do to keep from blurting out his repressed admiration for the woman. She was, after all, remarried, remarried to a Jew, no less—a Jew who had vanished without a trace.

There's no doubt of Hiram Goldfarb's fate, Peltomaa had considered, as the *Minsk* steamed across Lake Onega. *Whatever Elin may believe, the man is dead.*

Peltomaa, despite standing next to Elin for much of the *Minsk*'s relentless surge across the vast lake, had not voiced his conclusion regarding the fate of the newspaperman. Nor had he proclaimed his feelings. True to his introspective nature, Matti Peltomaa kept his own counsel. Clandestinely coveting the woman, Peltomaa had chewed tobacco and spit brown phlegm into the distant water while making small talk with Elin Goldfarb at the rail of the old boat.

Upon arrival at Kalajoki Island, the newcomers had been processed, assigned barracks, and given a short period of respite to unpack their belongings and become situated in the drafty bunkhouses that were now their homes. Each barrack contained crude wooden bunk beds. Entire families were housed in the same space as single men and women. The only bow to privacy were soiled bed sheets or dirty tarps suspended across the room on ropes. Beyond these temporary barriers there was no separation by gender: men and women slept in the same room with no thought of the ramifications.

There were no fences, no guard towers to contain the prisoners. Baton wielding kapos, whose barks, Elin learned, were worse than their bites, enforced the rules. The kapos, Red Finns who had immigrated to Karelia after the communists were defeated in the Finnish Civil War, ran the camp with oversight from the Soviet Army.

The forest on Kalajoki Island consisted of virgin pine. The island was an untouched reserve of trees the size and extent of the white and red pines that loggers like Matti Peltomaa had harvested in northern Minnesota and northwestern Ontario during the early 20th century.

Upon their arrival, Peltomaa had been assigned to work one end of a bucksaw and Elin Goldfarb had been assigned to work in the camp kitchen as a dishwasher. But those designations changed as Elin's untreated diabetes asserted itself and Peltomaa's talents became manifest to Urho Metsä, the camp boss.

The sawmill operating on Kalajoki Island (equipment that Metsä brought with him from Eastern Finland at the end of the Finnish Civil War) had first worked the forests on Kizhi Island. When Stalin's purges began, the authorities transferred Metsä and his fellow Red Finns—some thirty in number, including ten lumberjacks but no mechanic (the camp's mechanic having been assigned to an electric power plant being built elsewhere in Karelia)—to Kalajoki Island. The sawmill, which had operated flawlessly under the watchful eye of the mechanic, began to break down, requiring Metsä to seek out repairmen from other camps. Each day the sawmill was inoperable cost production. When the island's declining output began to suggest sabotage to Captain Karashvili—the Soviet Army officer supervising the camp from the comfort of a *dacha* on the west shore of Lake Onega—and Karashvili began to voice his concerns to Urho Metsä, noting that further decline might require "drastic action," including Metsä's "re-education" and "relocation," Metsä had scrambled to find someone who could keep the sawmill humming. Matti Peltomaa's experience at the ski factory in Petroskoi caught Metsä's attention and relieved Peltomaa from manual labor in the forest. The promotion not only saved Peltomaa from blistered palms and an aching sixty-year-old back: it saved Elin Goldfarb's life.

"The office needs some assistance, no?"

Matti Peltomaa had been standing in front of Urho Metsä's desk discussing the camp's need for an inventory of replacement parts to keep the sawmill running. His comment came about as a result of the Finn's furtive inspection of the receipts, invoices, orders, letters, and other documents heaped around the drafty little office Metsä occupied in the camp headquarters building next to Captain Karashvili's far more spacious, though rarely used, office.

Cold had infiltrated the uninsulated walls of the frame building and rustled the disorganized paperwork. Metsä looked at the mechanic as he considered the offhand remark. "What's that got to do with keeping parts in stock for the mill?"

Peltomaa had shaken his overly large head, his black hair and beard still thick but turning gray as he entered his seventh decade of life.

"Nothing at all, boss. Nothing at all. But looking around this place, it seems to me you could use a secretary to put things in order."

Metsä had eyed the room.

It's true. Things would run more smoothly if I were more organized. When Esther Mattila took sick, I lost the one person who was able to keep things tidy in my office. It's been too long. Peltomaa's right: I need help.

"Know anyone with an office background?"

Peltomaa had nodded. "I do."

A moment of silence had occurred as Metsä, a thick shouldered, big block of a man sat staring at the mechanic. "Well, out with it. I haven't all day," he finally said.

"There's a woman. Smart as a whip. Not bad to look at either," Peltomaa suggested.

"I'm not in the market for a mistress," Metsä said tersely. "Aamu is woman enough for me," he asserted, referring to his wife. "Been married thirty-five years. She stood by me when we had to leave Finland, and raised our three girls here, in Karelia, under circumstances that might cause a lesser woman to complain. No, I'm not looking for trouble. Or beauty. But brains, you say? Now that's a valuable commodity in an assistant. What's her name?"

"Elin. Elin Goldfarb."

"The writer?"

"Yes."

Urho Metsä had paused. His brow creased. He knew the woman's reputation. He also knew that her Jewish husband had disappeared. There was danger, both for the camp boss, and for the woman, to be had in increasing her visibility on Kalajoki Island.

Still, the idea intrigued him. "Can she maintain discretion? She is, after all, a bit of a celebrity."

Peltomaa had crossed his arms. "Right now, she's working in the kitchen, doing dishes. She's not well. Diabetes. She's not getting her medicine. I can talk to her. I'm sure she can make herself as small as a mouse in a corner. In return, you'll get one hell of a secretary."

Metsä closed his eyes.

Famous and sick. Shit. What am I getting myself into?

"Look," Metsä had finally said, "you've kept the mill running. I owe you something, that's for sure. I might be in a cattle car bound for Vladivostok if I hadn't stumbled onto you," the camp boss said quietly. "I'll give her a try. For a week. And I'll get her the medicine she needs through Karashvili. Shouldn't be a problem. But she's got a week to prove herself. Understand? If I suspect trouble, she's back in the kitchen. Tell her that. Understood?"

Peltomaa had nodded and left the office to bring the news to Elin.

She commenced her new position the next day and gave Urho Metsä no cause to regret his decision.

• • •

The weather broke as Elin Goldfarb loaded the last of the firewood into the sledge. The sun burned through the overcast sky and warmed the woman's face as she massaged a kink in her left shoulder.

"Much more of this fresh air and exercise," the woman muttered, pulling her aching body onto the sledge, "and they can toss me in a hole with the others who've passed away from starvation, typhus, diphtheria, and God-knows-what other diseases this place is filled with."

Elin clicked her tongue against the roof of her mouth and snapped leather. The gelding, its better years behind it, began to plod down a muddy path towards the headquarters building of the Kalajoki Lumber Camp. Mucky water sprinkled Elin with each footfall of the lumbering horse. The woman did not curse. She did not raise her voice in protest. She simply accepted what was happening and drove the horse and sledge down the tightly forested lane.

BOOK TWO: ESTONIA
(Nigul's Story)

CHAPTER 1

My name is Nigul Kristian. I am Estonian. I was born on April 5, 1923 on a family farm in Tartumaa County, near the village of Puhja. The significance of my date of birth should not be lost upon the reader. I was born on the anniversary of one of the most historic events in Estonian history: the defeat of the Livonian branch of the Teutonic Knights at the hands of soldiers of the Novgorodian Republic.

Though but a skirmish when considered against the great battles of history, the Battle of the Ice, fought as it was by crusaders from Denmark, Germany, and Estonia against soldiers of Novgorod on the frozen surface of Lake Peipus, was decisive in that it ended the West's attempt to convert Orthodox Russians to Catholicism. Prince Alexander Nevsky drew the invaders into the midst of his army, where his archers slaughtered the enemy. Desperate Catholic knights broke ranks and made for the far side of the lake, where thinner ice gave way beneath the Teutonic cavalry: Horses and armored riders sank like stones, ending the battle and thereby ensuring Lake Peipus as the permanent border between West and East.

My father, Andres Kristian, a *kannel* maker and a farmer, always considered my date of birth to be an inauspicious sign. Because of my birthday and our nearly identical personalities, and because of my brother Karl's brilliance at school, my father and I never saw eye-to-eye about much except one thing: our mistrust of Russians. On this, Andres Kristian and I were of one mind. We also shared a physical likeness. We were both tall and lanky, even to old age, though Father boasted a full head of thick, coarse, black hair and beard up until the day he died and I, unfortunately, became bald with age and never grew a beard.

My mother, Hele, a compact, blue eyed, blond woman of strong patrician shoulders, full hips, large bust, and Finnish blood, favored me. Why this was so, all the way up until her death at age 88 in 1986, is unclear. Perhaps she saw in me, in my *sisu* (as she would call it in Finnish; *meelekindlus* in Estonian; fortitude in English), something of my father, the man she loved.

My brother Karl was the pleaser, the perfect child, the boy who earned grades the envy of other children. I was a troubled, difficult child, the little boy who refused to comply, the student who daydreamed and procrastinated, the young man who enjoyed vodka a bit too much and girls even more. Still, Mother loved me: faults, flaws, and all. I guess, in retrospect, having become a father to two daughters who, like Karl and I, are night and day in terms of their personalities, I can understand her preference for the wayward, the prodigal. This is not to say that Mother didn't love Karl. She did. She tried to be fair, tried to give Karl equal measure despite his perfection, though, in the end, her love was ever so slightly tilted towards me.

My brother and I grew up, as I have said, on a farm located on a tiny creek flowing from a marsh north of Puhja into the Emajögi River.

Karl was born on November 24, 1924: exactly nine months to the day from Estonian Independence Day. It was only once we matured that Karl and I came to understand *how* our parents celebrated the anniversary of our nation's independence in 1924!

We were children during a wonderful time in Estonian history. From February 20, 1918, when the Treaty of Tartu was signed ending the Estonian War of Liberation, until the Soviet Union occupied our homeland in 1940, the Republic of Estonia existed as a free nation. Karl and I were blessed with a taste of individual rights and liberties unknown to our ancestors. Prior to Estonia's independence from Russia at the end of the Great War, the story of my people had been a legacy of a small nationality being dominated by world powers.

My country's namesake, "Eesti," first appeared as "Aesti" in the writings of Roman historian Tacitus. Cassidorus repeated this designation and placed the Aesti people on the shores of the Baltic Sea. There was little interaction between the Aesti and the rest of Europe until the Baltic Crusades were mounted in an attempt to force Catholicism upon the pagans and the Eastern Orthodox Christians of northern Europe. The Battle of the Lake was one of many bloody conflicts fought in this regard. Thereafter, parts of what would become Estonia were carved out as niches of Danish, German, and Swedish territory. By 1561, after a succession of conflicts swept over the Baltics, the region became part of the Swedish Empire and King Gustavus Adolphus brought the printing press and modern learning to Estonia. Russia then bested Sweden in another series of wars, culminating in the Treaty of Nystad in 1721, and Estonia became part of the Russian Empire. In 1809, Sweden also ceded Finland to Russia, thereby uniting the two major Finno-Ugric peoples (the Finns and the Estonians) with their kindred (the Karelians and the Ingrians), whose territory had already been absorbed by Russia. The integration of Estonia and Finland into the Russian Empire led to the migration of my mother's paternal and maternal sides from Finland to Estonia in the late 1800s.

My father farmed sixty hectares of rich land adjacent to Kalevipoeg Creek (so named for the national epic of Estonia, *The Kalevipoeg*)—land that Father had inherited as the eldest son. Before Soviet collectivization took our farm, Father grew potatoes, carrots, tomatoes, and cabbage in fields adjacent to the creek. Father also tended a dozen or so rare Ruhnu sheep—sheep named for the Baltic island of their origin—that he had imported to the mainland. Mother shorn the small sheep and spun their wool into yarn. The Ruhnu grazed a pasture near our barn, an ancient but sturdy structure that was a source of endless adventure for Karl and me when we were boys. A few pigs, suppliers of the ever-present pork loins, chops, hams, and sausages that are essential to the Estonian diet, one horse to pull plow and wagon, and a dozen or so laying hens and a proud rooster also shared the land with my family.

As crops were harvested and wool was collected, Father and Mother would hitch Jaak the gelding—a broad shouldered, golden flanked Estonian pony—to the hay wagon, load the wagon with produce, eggs, and Mother's homespun wool, make space for Karl and me, and travel into Puhja, where my parents would sell or trade the farm's bounty for flour, sugar, coffee, and tobacco. On the way home, Karl and I would suck hard candy and Mother would fill Father in on the latest gossip from town, while fragrantly sweet smoke from Father's hand-carved maple pipe would curl above us and hang in the breezeless air of late summer.

Father was content to eke out a living from the land and to supplement our existence by crafting the most beautiful *kannels* out of birch trees that grew along the banks of the creek. In truth, had Father spent as much time behind Jaak and our single bladed iron plow as he did trying to build the perfect lap harp, he would have been envied by other farmers. But it must be noted here that, despite his musical craftsmanship, Father did not play the instruments he created except to tune them or to accompany Mother, who loved to sing old Estonian love songs, laments, and ballads. It was said in Puhja that the beautiful and shapely Hele Kristian could charm the pants off any man with her singing. This, of course, was a talent no one, other than our father, was privileged to experience!

Mother's strong soprano earned her awards in many, many music contests during her youth and early adulthood, culminating with her being asked to sing a solo at the national music festival in Tallinn in 1920, a year after Estonian independence. My parents had not yet married when twenty-one year old Hele Mattila stood alone in front of thousands of patriotic Estonians to sing. She continued to participate in the festival until 1985. During her last performance, Mother bravely belted out Estonia's national song, even though public performances of the anthem were forbidden by the damnable Russians who were then in charge of Estonia.

My native land, my joy, delight,
How fair thou art and bright!
And nowhere in the world all round
Can ever such a place be found
So well beloved as I love thee,
My native country dear!

My little cradle stood on thy soil,
Whose blessings case my toil.
With my last breath my thanks to thee,
For true to death I'll ever be,
O worthy, most beloved and fine,
Thou, dearest country mine!

May God in Heaven thee defend,
My best, my dearest land!
May He be guard, may He be shield,
Forever may He bless and wield
O graciously all deeds of thine,
Thou dearest country mine!

As described by Father over the course of many evening talks, his distrust of the Russians heightened after the Revolution of 1905. That revolt, a short-lived protest against Czar Nicholas II that achieved slightly greater autonomy for Finland and Estonia, failed to meet the bellicose promises of nationalist politicians. Father, who was fifteen years old in 1905, would recount for us the anticipation he experienced after hearing bold pronouncements of Estonian liberation. And then, with bitterness, he would relate the crushing disappointment he felt when Estonia remained subservient to Russia.

Father would candidly tell us that he again felt joy when, on November 14, 1918 (he was 28 years old and had just met Mother), Germany retreated from its occupation of Estonia, turning over administration of the country to a provisional government headed, not by Russian bureaucrats, but by Estonians.

The Russians sought to reclaim the country and fighting broke out. German troops (who had remained in Estonia after Germany's capitulation) and members of the Estonian Defense League met the communist advance. A plea for recruits went out. Father answered the call, became a rifleman in the Tartuman Partisan Battalion, and participated in the liberation of Tartu, a watershed moment for our fledgling nation. But, as many men who have gone to war and seen friends and comrades die close at hand, Father provided scant details regarding his combat experience.

One bit of history from the Great War that Father *was* willing to share was his admiration for the Finns. Two separate units of Finnish fighting men, *Pohjan Pojat* and *I Suomalainen Vapaajoukko,* arrived during the so-called Kinship Wars to assist Estonia. Other aid came in the form of White Russian brigades, a small unit of Danes, a single volunteer company of Swedes, and British naval assistance. Warships from Great Britain patrolled the Gulf of Finland and kept the Russian fleet at bay, thereby protecting the vulnerable Estonian left flank. The Estonians welcomed all of these outside forces. But it was the generosity of the Finns that received special emphasis from my father. This connection, this indebtedness to our neighbors to the north, was something I never forgot.

My life as a child was bucolic. I recall many sun-drenched midsummer days when Karl and I would wade in Kalevipoeg Creek to cool off after chores. I was the one who harnessed Jaak to the plow to turn the soil. Karl and Mother would plant. Father would supervise and offer commentary but rarely—once I was old enough to manage the horse and rig—did he assist us.

During breaks from his woodworking, I would see Father leaning against the weathered boards of our barn, the red paint faded to near pink, an ever-present cloud of tobacco smoke curling above him, his hat tilted against the sun. I could feel his scrutiny, a father's watchful critique of his eldest son, over the distance. He never verbalized what he was thinking. He was a man of few words, but I knew he was gauging my abilities, assessing my worth as the son who would inherit the farm. I must have done my work credibly because he rarely took me to task for my efforts, though Mother was not shy about sharing *her* criticisms of Karl and my work ethic.

"You boys are as lazy as rams," she would often say, catching the two of us during our numerous breaks from the hot summer sun, sitting in the shade of apple trees when we were supposed to be weeding potatoes or carrots. "All you want to do is sit on your behinds or eat."

Karl and I knew at a young age that there was *one* other thing rams liked to do. But, until we were well into puberty *that* was not something we were tempted to try!

"Yes, Mother," we would chime in unison, as we rose from the ground, rich Estonian soil staining the rumps of our trousers. "We will get back to work."

"I hate this," Karl would say, his voice high pitched and whiney, the kind of voice that made you long to strike him on the nose, as we pulled weeds. "It's such a waste of time."

I'd look at my brother from beneath the rumpled brim of one of Father's castoff fedoras and nod. "Ya. I'm sure you'd much rather be cooped up in the house reading a book."

Though he was a year younger than I was, Karl was always reading.

"Books are a way to leave this place for a while, to see things that can't be seen here," Karl would say, sounding much older than his years.

I would scratch my forehead with a dirty finger, the flies and gnats tormenting me in the sweltering heat, and consider my brother's wisdom. "I'm too damned tired to read. Mother has us digging and weeding and carrying and fetching all day long. How in the hell do you keep your eyes open to read?"

Karl would smile, the gesture revealing his likeness to Mother. "It's something, if you love it, you make time for. You stay awake. It's as simple as that."

We had a soccer ball that Karl, I, and other children living nearby would use in three or four kid-per-side games. We let girls play out of necessity: there was a shortage of eligible boys. The local girls weren't half bad. In fact, one of them, a dark-haired, lantern-jawed, well-built girl my age, was probably the best player of the lot. On the other hand, Karl wasn't much of an athlete. He usually played goalie, guarding the two empty milk cans we set up as one goal or the two bales of hay that were the other. I was a good player, maybe good enough, had I pursued it, to play on the town team. But soccer wasn't my sport. Given the personality traits I shared with my father, I was better suited for individual pursuits. I began to run long distances when I turned twelve. By the time the Second World War broke out, I had made a name for myself as the fastest distance runner in our county. And, in the winter, when there was too much snow to safely run on the shoulder of our rural road, I would strap on my skis and lose myself on trails near our farm. I would kick and glide and climb through the forest on old logging roads, usually the first to have skied the new snow, for hours on end. Occasionally, I asked Karl, who possessed, as I did, birch skis made in the workshop by our father, to join me. But Karl was a complainer. And though I loved my brother dearly, skiing with him was no joy. It was drudgery, plain and simple: a circumstance to avoid if at all possible.

When I grew old enough to carry a rifle, I'd strap my father's .22 across my back and shove off across the white blanket of the Estonian countryside in search of hares and black grouse. I learned how to search out prey, how to balance the rifle in my shivering hands, how to take aim, how to hit my target. When I would ski back into the silent farmyard, the moon rising over the eastern hills, dusk cloaking the quiet, Father would appear from his workshop, the bowl of his pipe glowing orange against the gloaming, and offer his version of a conversation.

"Hunting?"

"Yes sir."

"How'd you do?"

"A pair of grouse, one hare."

"Heard you shoot five times. What happened on the other two shots?"

The veiled criticism didn't bother me.

"Too excited I guess. I missed two more partridge."

Father would nod. "Four birds would make for a better meal," he would observe before heading back to his workshop

CHAPTER 2

Books. Karl would bury his head in them. His greatest treasure was a used copy of Tammsaare's epic, *Tõde ja õigus* (*Truth and Justice*), a mammoth five volume fictional study of Estonian history that Mother had bought from a second hand store in Tartu. Karl would read the volumes cover-to-cover, over and over and over again by candlelight, long after the lanterns in our farmhouse were extinguished. Only ten or eleven years old when Mother gave him the Tammsaare, Karl was already reading at a university level, his mind more interested in the written word than reality.

When Estonia broke free from Russia at the end of the Great War, compulsory schooling for all children through age sixteen was instituted. This was modified in 1934 to allow the sons of farmers to leave school at age fourteen to work the land. With little interest in formal learning or farming, I left school at that age to begin an apprenticeship with an electrician named Bruno Talvik. When I left home in 1937, I was certain that I would never open a book again. I was equally certain that Karl would never live a day of his life when he wasn't deeply engrossed in the study of something.

There was little call for electrical work in the Estonian countryside so my training took place in the city. By my sixteenth birthday, as Mr. Talvik's thin-withered black horse Maati pulled the electrician's four wheeled wagon through the cobblestone streets of Tartu, I was a competent apprentice and on my way to becoming a journeyman. I was Talvik's only helper and he was a thoroughly impatient old man. But despite my general laziness of mind, I discovered that I loved the detail, the precision of wiring homes, businesses, and factories so that electricity could flow from the power poles through the buildings, lighting them up, making machinery hum.

Unlike woodworking, which I found painstakingly boring, I was enthralled with the details of electrical construction. I also knew, despite my status as the first-born son, that I was no farmer. With finicky Mr. Talvik as my teacher, I enjoyed learning a trade and by age sixteen, I knew I had found my life's work.

The money I made as an apprentice was modest. There were the expenses of food and lodging. And there was vodka. It was in Tartu when I first encountered the hazy deception that vodka made me a smarter lad. On those occasions, when I found I'd spent too much and couldn't make my rent or buy a meal, Mr. Talvik would begrudgingly advance the necessary sum. And most weeks, though I had a penchant for the bottle, I religiously mailed a portion of my wage to my parents. This was during the Great Depression, a worldwide economic downturn that, given Estonia's agrarian economy, had less of an impact upon my homeland than it did on the more industrialized nations of the world. But even in agricultural Estonia times were hard and Mother appreciated any money I was able to send home.

It was in Tartu where I also met my first lover. Her name was Ellisabet Raun. Old man Talvik was hired by a widower—Ernest Raun—to electrify his storefront law office and the family living quarters above the office. Mr. Raun had been limited to studying legal books by lantern because the section of Tartu the lawyer's building occupied did not have gas service. Flickering lantern light had taken a terrible toll on the lawyer. When I met Ernest Raun, standing behind Mr. Talvik, listening to the men bicker over the price of the work we were about to do, Raun's eyes caught my attention. The lawyer's eyes mimicked shards of tired coal set deep in his skull above a full beard and a crooked nose. Aside from his eyes, Raun was an unimpressive specimen of humanity, boasting spindly limbs and nasty breath. But his daughter? Ah, that was another matter.

Ellisabet Raun had lost her mother—and the lawyer had lost his wife—delivering a second child, a stillborn son. Mr. Raun was left to raise his daughter alone. Try as he might, Ernest Raun was unable to convince another woman to marry him. Even with a successful law practice as incentive, marriageable women ran away at Raun's approach. I suspect their reluctance had something to do with Mr. Raun's ghoulish appearance.

When Mr. Talvik and I returned to Raun's office to begin our work, I encountered Ellisabet studying at her father's desk and I was bedazzled. She was the most stunning girl I had ever seen. There was no question from whence Ellisabet's handsome profile descended. Her mother's portrait hung on the cracked plaster wall above Ernest's desk. Maarja Raun had been beyond striking. She had been, as depicted in the black and white photograph, exquisite. Her eyes sparkled. Ringlets of shimmering hair cascaded down her shoulders. Her nose was aquiline and poised. But what made Maarja Raun's face extraordinary were her cheekbones: her facial structure suggested patrician bearing without seeming haughty or false.

Beneath the portrait sat a younger version of the same woman. After glancing at Ellisabet, I determined that her mother's eyes had been emerald green and that her hair had been raven black.

Young love is impatient love. The angst and gnawing tension of sensuality, of burgeoning hormones, fairly eats away at the expectant participants. But young love is also tender and innocent in a way that couplings between jaded-by-life adults cannot replicate, no matter how well intended. The connection between Ellisabet and me (she was fourteen and I was sixteen when we met) started soon after I began working at her father's office. Our initial encounters did not mimic prizefighters circling each other. Such imagery would be better suited to older folks who have already experienced disappointment. Instead, our first steps towards affection were like the playful advances of two young pups from different litters meeting each other for the first time.

As I worked inside Mr. Raun's building—installing porcelain insulators, running wire, and connecting terminals—there were occasions when I chanced upon Ellisabet while she was alone. In those awkward moments, as we passed each other in the hallways or when I would catch Ellisabet watching me as I worked, the sweat of summer pouring from my face and my underarms and soaking the long sleeved shirt that Mr. Talvik insisted I wear every day of my apprenticeship, our eyes would meet. In the emerald pools defining Ellisabet's lovely, lovely face, I would see honesty. I would see anticipation. I would see inquisitiveness. I would see love. I cannot relate what she saw when she in turn studied me. I have no idea if she thought of love or simple physicality. But whatever she saw in me that summer in Tartu, Ellisabet Raun apparently appreciated.

Given our disparate social positions and the fact that I had quit school at age fourteen and Ellisabet was destined for university, there was little likelihood that Ernest Raun would have approved of what transpired. I know this to be a fact because, whenever the lawyer happened upon his daughter and me talking quietly in his office or on the back stoop, sipping cold water and sharing stories as we began to do sometime during my second or third week working at the Raun place, the lawyer's eyes would flash and he would grunt his disapproval in a way that made it clear he knew what we were up to even if the two of us did not. But teenage love, or more properly, teenage lust, cannot be deflected by parental disapproval. And though Mr. Raun's sudden appearances disrupted our innocent interaction and compelled the girl to withdraw, the lawyer's breach of our connection was only temporary.

As my work at the law office came to a close, attraction and deceit proved too strong for the lawyer's wariness. It was a night—a weekday night—when Ellisabet and I met in the old livery stable at the end of the darkened lane running past Mr. Raun's law office. Old Man Talvik and the lawyer were at a local pub, deep in their cups, likely discussing politics.

Ernest Raun was a Nazi, an admirer of Adolf Hitler. His desk was littered with newspaper articles proclaiming the German leader's triumphs. A black and white photograph of Hitler in uniform addressing a crowd occupied one corner of Raun's desk. There were also copies of pamphlets, typeset in German, a language I was vaguely familiar with from my schooling, stacked next to the photograph. Though I never heard Raun espouse hatred for Jews in casual conversation, the literature amassed on his desk identified Raun's support of Hitler's antipathy towards that race.

At the time, I knew only one Jew myself: Aaron Friedman, a jeweler who lived in Puhja. No, that isn't true. I also knew his son Emil, who was two years behind me in school, and his wife Greta, a short, homely woman who said maybe three words to me in all the years I knew her. So, I knew three Jews. They were nice folks.

Mr. Friedman was a friend of my father's. The two of them had served together during the Estonian War of Independence. I had no problems with the Friedmans being different from us. I discounted the whispers I heard from classmates who claimed there was something sinister, something untoward about Jews. I saw no evidence that the Friedmans intended to roast and eat Christian children (as some of my elementary school classmates claimed) or wished to convert wayward Lutheran boys like myself to the dark mysteries of their faith.

I glanced at the pamphlets Raun had assembled. Though I didn't read them in depth, I took away a sense of looming dread, of something untoward being proposed by the little Austrian with the Charlie Chaplin mustache. I can't say I appreciated Hitler's intentions. The "Final Solution" was years away from its ultimate realization. But I do remember, glancing at the lawyer's collection of propaganda, feeling apprehensive in some vague and ill-defined way. It was a premonition I kept wholly to myself. I did not express my sense of unease to Mr. Talvik. And I certainly did not discuss it with the lawyer's comely daughter.

I was supposed to be tending to Maati, readying the horse and Mr. Talvik's wagon for our departure the next morning. When Mr. Talvik and Mr. Raun wandered off to the pub, they left me to my pedestrian tasks. Unwittingly, Mr. Raun also left Ellisabet to deal, as best as she could, with her loneliness and her curiosity.

The girl found me in the stable. Fresh oat straw became our bed. Fragments of grain stalks clung to our clothing as we reclined. I could not see Ellisabet's eyes but I sensed apprehension from the rapidity of her breathing, from the tension in her fingers as I clasped her delicate hands in mine.

Not that I was calm. I was as nervous, perhaps more so, than she was. My heart raced. Our lips met.

"I've never done this before," she whispered, through a kiss.

"I know," I said, afraid to reveal my own virginity.

Her body tensed.

Fear of pregnancy? Of pain?

I had heard that the first time for a girl was different than for a boy. That often the resistance of flesh made the act uncomfortable. That there might be tearing. And pain. And blood. I stopped to consider this folklore as I held Ellisabet. A horse in the next stall snorted. Another horse, a more distant horse, neighed softly in reply.

"We can stop."

Sparse light from the half-mooned sky infiltrated the barn through an open hayloft door. Ellisabet bit her lower lip. Ignoring my admonition, the girl guided my right hand beneath the cotton of her blouse and the smooth silk of her camisole. My fingers explored. She urged my other hand beneath the straight edge of her skirt.

"This is something I want to do. That I *must* do," she finally answered.

"Are you certain? We barely know each other."

She nodded. Her hair tickled my nose. "I know you well enough."

I said nothing more.

Her lips found mine again. I slipped my hand inside her underpants. My breathing grew erratic. My thoughts raced.

What if we make a baby?

She smiled, as if reading my thoughts. "Don't worry, Nigul. It's nearly my time of the month. I won't become an unwed mother tonight."

I needed little encouragement. I unbuttoned my trousers and slipped off my pants and my underwear. The air chilled my most private skin. I searched for a way inside. I found moistness. I found warmth. My body pressed down on Ellisabet's small frame and I began to move.

When I was finished, there *was* blood. Ellisabet wiped the evidence of our sin away with a white handkerchief she had brought with for that purpose. After rearranging our clothing, we spooned on the warm straw of the old barn. We did not speak of love or plans or the future. I knew that, on the morrow, when Ellisabet's father and Mr. Talvik awoke to pounding headaches and roiling stomachs, I would be in the driver's seat of the electrician's wagon. Bruno Talvik would climb gingerly onto the carriage seat and cast a stupored look at me. I would snap leather, put Maati through his paces, and we would depart.

The next time I saw Ellisabet Raun, things had changed; the world was in flames, Hitler's army occupied Estonia, the Friedmans had vanished, and the lawyer's daughter had embraced her father's politics.

CHAPTER 3
Tallinn, 1939

She was a large woman with the painted face of a whore, hairy armpits, hairier legs, and folds of skin that descended her body like fleshy steps. Liisu Koidula's steady breathing kept time with my heartbeat as I stared at the ceiling of her apartment on Sauna Street in Tallinn. Liisu wasn't attractive—at least to a sober man. But during my seventeenth year, a year spent in Tallinn working as an electrician for the Kinnunen Shipbuilding Company, that wasn't a problem for me.

I was tall and physically mature for my age. No one at the Water's Edge Bar questioned my right to drink or denied me my vodka, including Liisu, the owner of the tavern and the only woman who frequented the place save for whores who wandered in looking for desperate shipyard workers and drunken sailors.

God, how I loved my vodka in those days! The bitter fire. The dulled senses. The feeling of invincibility. I knew as I staggered upstairs to Liisu's bedroom for yet another wild romp that Mother would die if she discovered what her eldest son was up to. Liisu was thirty-three. Unable to have children, there was no fear of procreation between us, a circumstance that only increased our frenzy. And there was no danger of my falling in love with Liisu Koidula. There was only teaching and learning between us. How to caress a woman's breast. How to kiss. How to use one's mouth and tongue. These were the things that I learned from Liisu Koidula. These were the lessons she taught me in the dark, late at night, through the gauzy lens of vodka. Unlike the professional whores prowling her bar, Liisu was monogamous and did not charge for her expertise. But there was, as I slowly came to realize, a cost to her lessons; a deep and abiding moral cost was attached to what I was learning in the arms of Liisu Koidula.

Father and Mother had instilled in Karl and me basic values bestowed upon *them* by *their* Lutheran upbringing. But I don't want you to get the wrong idea. Our parents weren't church people. Beyond occasional Sunday visits to appease the sequence of itinerant pastors who guided our little parish, and obligatory attendance on Easter and Christmas Eve, our parents spent little time in church. Beyond singing a solo or two when asked by the pastor, Mother did not participate in the circle of pious women who made church a priority. Father never sat on the church council or spent more than an occasional Saturday morning pitching in to help maintain the little white frame building that sits—to this day—on a tidy lot on the edge of Puhja. But despite their lack of enthusiasm for organized religion, our parents were moral people. They were in love with each other. They loved God in their own private way. And they loved their children. There was no hint of scandal associated with Andres and Hele Kristian. Thank God my antics with Liisu Koidula never became more than distant rumors in Puhja—bits and pieces of unverified gossip that seemed at odds with the maturity I displayed during my visits home.

"Do you love me?" Liisu once asked.

What woman has not raised this question as she rested in nude repose? I knew at that moment, even as inexperienced as I was in such things, that Liisu did not expect candor. I understood this truth at an early age. But how to answer? How to tell the woman whose bed I occupied night after night such a thing without inflicting pain? For even though I did not love my lover, I had no interest in causing her injury.

"No, Liisu," I had finally replied, "I do not love you. But I love what we do."

Though the lights were off in her bedroom, I studied the woman's thick face as she considered my answer. Like I've said, Liisu clearly knew the parameters of *us*. There was no permanency, no love, no possibility of "until death do us part" in the equation we shared. She was taking advantage of my youth and I was taking advantage of her experience. It was as simple as that. Still, as I learned that night when she broached the question, unless it is a professional transaction between a whore and her customer, sex always, and I mean *always*, descends into the same moral quagmire.

I thought I detected slight tearing in the fat woman's brown eyes as she mulled over a response to my honesty. I didn't have the *sisu* (as my mother would say) to say more, to delve deeper into what she was thinking. I suspected my bluntness would end what we had and, despite the loathing that would pester me every morning I awoke in Liisu's bed, losing whatever it was we had was something I did not want to face.

The woman had nodded, turned away from me, and, within a matter of minutes, was snoring.

As I fell deeper into decadence, the pace of the world at large accelerated in ominous ways. By August of 1939, Hitler had perfected the process of provocation and destruction. German troops invaded and occupied the Rhineland in 1936. Two years later, Austria was incorporated into "Greater Germany" and the German army occupied the Sudetenland of Czechoslovakia. In November of 1938, the Night of Broken Glass (*Kristallnacht*)—the event that revealed Hitler's enmity towards the Jews—occurred. The following year, Hitler swallowed up what remained of

Czechoslovakia, signed his "Pact of Steel" with Mussolini, sponsored Franco's Fascist victory in Spain, and entered into a secret agreement with Joseph Stalin known as the Molotov-Ribbentrop Pact, which prospectively carved up and distributed Latvia, Lithuania, and Estonia between Germany and the U.S.S.R.

CHAPTER 4
Winter 1939

On September 24, 1939, the Soviet Navy appeared in Estonian waters and Joseph Stalin "requested" that Estonia allow 25,000 Red Army troops be quartered in Estonia to "protect" it from "foreign aggression." At the very moment Stalin forwarded his "request" to the leaders of my country, 160,000 Soviet troops were poised on Estonia's eastern border, a force ten times the number of soldiers in Estonia's standing army. My nation capitulated. A mutual assistance pact was signed. Tensions mounted. Soviet troops built and occupied new military bases within Estonia just as the invasion of Poland by Germany and the U.S.S.R. began. By early October, Poland no longer existed, carved up like a Christmas pork roast between two hungry diners. The Molotov-Ribbentrop agreement also granted the U.S.S.R. the right to invade Finland, a small detail that was not acknowledged by Stalin as he expanded his military presence in Estonia.

Indeed, there was much I did not know about the larger world at the time. I had no grasp of international intrigue. I did, however, pay close attention to what was transpiring in nations surrounding Estonia. I knew, for example, without having much formal education, that the quick strikes by the Soviet Union and Nazi Germany against Poland, a country more populous and possessing a far larger military than Estonia, did not bode well for Lithuania, the Baltic nation immediately adjacent to Poland. And given my mother's roots in the Republic of Finland, I paid special attention to news regarding Estonia's northern neighbor just a short ferry ride across the sea.

Diverse groups inhabited Soviet Karelia, an area of vast pine forests, lakes, and marshes. Karelians and Ingrians and Votes and ethnic Finns and Russians and Finnish speaking immigrants from North America occupied the forested region surrounding Europe's largest lakes. Stalin looked at Karelia's border with Finland as vulnerable. These things, of course, were unknown to me as a young man working in a shipyard and reading Estonian newspapers of the time. But from my casual reading, I came to understand that negotiations between the Finns and the Russians began shortly after the ink on the Molotov-Ribbentrop agreement was dry. I also learned that Finland was ill prepared for war—that Finnish leaders were working furiously to maintain peace. Thus, I was shocked to read a headline in early December of 1939 proclaiming the beginning of what came to be called "The Winter War."

"Take a look at this," I said, handing my father the front page of *Eesti Päevaleht* while home on brief holiday.

Soviet Union at War with Finland: Fierce Battles Rage on Eastern Border.

"Goddamned Russians," my father muttered, holding the newsprint in his strong hands. "Goddamned Stalin. Hele, come see this," Father commanded. "The bastards have invaded Finland."

Father and I were in the living room of the farmhouse, sitting in front of a roaring birch fire. Mother was kneading bread dough in the kitchen, making ready the family's Sunday dinner. Karl was not at home. He was in town, staying with a friend's family. Mother entered the warm room, flour covering her arms from the tips of her fingers to her elbows, and stood over Father's shoulder to read.

"Oh my God," she whispered. "Oh my God."

My father chortled. "Hele, my dearest one, God has very little to do with it. This is the work of politicians. I've seen their work up close, too close. The result of their work is, in the end, slaughter. And for what? To gain a few more hectares of swamp? Trees? Fields?"

This exchange was as near as my father had ever come to talking about the details of his wartime service. Oh, he would talk in generalities about how the Great War—the precursor to the Estonian War of Independence—started; how foolish it was for the world's great powers to embark upon a conflict that began when a crazy man shot a prince in a backwater country. The way Father explained things, the Great War started over something as inane as a child being affronted by another child's insult, a conflict that, by its end, engulfed most of Europe in a cesspool of senseless warfare. Treaties between despots had been engaged. Pride was at stake. And so, common men like Andres Kristian were called upon to sacrifice. There was no reason for it, according to Father. It was all a colossal quagmire of hurt feelings and petty grievances that led to the deaths of sixteen million human beings. My father's part in it all, such as Karl and I learned as children, was minor: a few engagements against the communists during the War for Independence. He was not a victim of the horrific trench warfare that ground young men to dust along the main fronts of the Great War. And still, when he would remember, you could see a lurking appreciation for death in Father's eyes.

"They claimed that the last war, the one that gave us our freedom, the one that you so bravely fought in, was the 'war to end all wars'," Mother said quietly.

Father reached out and patted Mother's flour covered right wrist. "It surprises you that the men in charge of the world are liars?"

My mother shook her head and retreated to the kitchen without reply.

"This isn't right," I said, after Father returned the newspaper to me.

The old man picked up the *kannel* he was stringing, the varnished birch a natural extension of his arthritic fingers, and returned to his work. The mantle clock ticked as I read details about the Russian invasion of Finland.

"Päts," I continued, referring to Konstanin Päts, the president of Estonia, "has said little about the attack on Finland."

Father did not look up from his work. "There was a time," he said quietly, "when I trusted that man. Back during the Great War, when he was just getting started, he said some things that made sense. He was one of the few men in Estonia who realized that our size, our lack of geographic distance and natural obstacles along our border with Russia, coupled with our small population, magnified our weakness. He tried hard to address those deficits."

The fire diminished. I stood up, walked to the wood bin, selected a piece of dry birch, the bark curled and eager to burn, pulled back the fireplace screen, and arranged the wood on glowing coals. Sparks flew from the new log as I returned to my chair and my newspaper.

"How's that?" I asked.

"Greater Finland."

I wasn't familiar with the term. Before I could ask another question, my father explained.

"Greater Finland: the joining of Finland, Estonia, and Karelia into one nation, one people. It's an old dream. For a while, Päts tried to pursue it. There were some attempts—the Kinship Wars, they were called—to make it happen. White Finns crossed into Karelia and tried to bring about a revolt against the new Soviet regime. Didn't get very far. My belief? Men had little stomach for killing after the armistice ended the Great War. Folks wanted things left alone."

"Says here," I said, tapping the article in the newspaper, "that several brigades of Estonians are mobilizing to fight alongside the Finns."

"The Finns have as much chance of winning a war against Russia as I have of becoming King of Denmark," Father said quietly. "You'll accomplish nothing by thinking such nonsense. No good can come of you dreaming about fighting in Finland."

"I didn't—"

"Enough, Nigul. Enough. I can see it in your eyes. I can hear it in your voice. War isn't some parade of pretty toy soldiers marching to glory. It's filthy business. It eats away at a man's heart, his soul, to kill another human being. I know. I've been there."

Father placed the *kannel* across his knees and began to strum the instrument. Mother returned to the living room, softly humming the melody Father was playing.

I rested my head against the fabric of the chair, closed my eyes, and dreamed of acts of heroism and glory in defense of my country.

CHAPTER 5
June 1940

Pork loin, potatoes, and heavy gravy steamed on my plate as I sat on a wooden chair at a small table in front of dirty windows at the *Rohke Söökla* (Plenty Diner) located at the intersection of Sauna and Viru Street. Steam drifted from boiled carrots in a small bowl next to the main course. Between bites of food, I studied the front page of *Tõde* (*Truth*), a newspaper published by the trade unions of Tallinn. My union, the electricians' union, was a member of the consortium. A machine-rolled cigarette smoldered in a glass ashtray on the table. Customers—people from the neighborhood I recognized but did not know—came and went through the front door to the café. Their pace was harried. It was the news. Bad news was prompting Estonians to rush about like panicked rabbits.

The talk at the shipyards had been excited and, in some sense of the word, *pöörane* (crazy). Big Peeter Saul, who, because of his nickname, received daily barbs cast in his direction by the bravest of our crew, declared that it was time for Estonia to stand up to Stalin, no matter the cost. After reflection, I had changed my view on that point. In my estimation, this determination to fight was silly talk. What in God's name were we, a country of one million men, women, children, and old people, going to accomplish against one of the best-armed nations in the world?

Soviet Troops Secure Estonian Borders

"Damned communists," Big Peeter had roared, as more Soviet troops were "welcomed" into Estonia. "If the idiots in charge of this country had only paid attention, they would have learned from Chamberlin. *Appeasement.* Ha! It didn't work with Hitler and it won't work with Stalin. You cannot appease a fat man's appetite for cake by giving him a slice, or satisfy a glutton like Stalin by letting him sneak one cookie from the Estonian cookie jar. Not fighting the damned Russians a year ago, when Russian ships appeared in Tallinn Harbor, was a huge mistake: A mistake I am afraid all of us are about to pay for."

As I recreated the impassioned speech Big Peeter had made earlier that day in my mind, I drew a fork laden with hot pork into my mouth and savored the meat and the rich gravy. Smoke curled from my cigarette and framed my little corner of the world in gray. I reached across the wooden table top, the pine scarred from countless prior customers, hefted a thick mug and sipped strong coffee as I considered how dumbstruck the men on my crew had been by the news that Stalin had finally done it; he'd finally taken Estonia away from the Estonians.

Being that I was the youngest on my crew and had little experience in the ways of politics, I kept my mouth shut as Big Peeter ranted and others, including our foreman Miik Salu, tried to minimize the impact of Stalin's move.

"He's no tyrant," Miik had argued. But then, Miik was a rarity in Estonia. He was a communist and because of this, his views were immediately discounted. "Stalin is simply moving to protect his western flank. Our weakness makes Russia vulnerable. There'll be no changes in the way we live with Stalin in charge. Look," Salu continued, "at how prosperous the Soviet people have become. There is, under Stalin, plenty of food, plenty of drink, plenty of everything."

Big Peeter had objected. "Where in the hell do you get your information?" the giant, bangs of shaggy black hair concealing his thick face like forest underbrush, roared. "Have you not heard of what happened to the North American immigrants to Karelia? Folks who, I might add, believed in *Marxist theory,* just as *you* do. And what about the generals in Stalin's own army? And the intellectuals. And the priests. And the teachers. And all the others. Where have they gone off to, Brother Salu? They've *vanished*, is what the people are told. But a cruel life in a labor camp or the silence of an unmarked grave is their reality!"

Miik had shaken his head with violence. "Nonsense," he said. "A few agitators who opposed Stalin may have suffered. But the vast majority of the people? They have what they need and they thank Stalin for it. You are all being deceived by the politicians in Tallinn as to how bad things will be under Stalin's protection."

The discussion had reminded me of my father and what he and other men of Estonia sacrificed to ensure our freedom. I knew little of Stalin, little of the details of his reign of terror at the time. But I knew this: Father would have stood with Big Peeter, I am certain, in the discussion held on the docks of Tallinn.

France had fallen quickly to the Germans and Stalin believed that Hitler was, despite the Molotov-Ribbentrop accord, about to embark on a Napoleonic quest against Mother Russia. To shore up the Soviet Union's western border, Lithuania was given eight hours to agree to Soviet occupation or face extinction. Similar messages were conveyed to the leaders of Latvia and Estonia. With Soviet military bases already established on Estonian soil, and with additional Soviet armor and troops poised to east, Tallinn had, in the barest of political terms, no choice. 90,000 additional Red Army soldiers marched into Estonia, bringing the total Soviet contingent quartered in the country to over 100,000 men—

one-tenth the population of Estonia. This capitulation had effectively ended the Republic of Estonia without a shot being fired!

The wooden door to the café opened. Big Peeter Saul cast a shadow over the room. The man spotted me and wasted little time closing the distance between the door and my table.

"Kristian," Peeter said, as he sat on the chair across from me. "The shit has hit the fan."

"What are you talking about?"

"The damned Russians."

I lowered my newspaper so that the headline faced Saul and pointed at the headline with my left index finger. "I know about the 'agreement' to 'allow' the Russians to bring in more troops," I said.

He shook his head. Ropes of thick, black hair flew from side to side. "No, no," he corrected. "I'm talking about the shipyard. The bastards have taken over the shipyard and abolished the unions! Miik Salu is now a supervisor in the electrical division. They walked in, looked around, found a guy who thinks Marx walks on water, and put him in charge!"

I stared hard at the older man. "Miik's not so bad. At least he knows his stuff. He's the best of us, a master electrician. He's forgotten more about the craft than I'll ever learn."

"That's not the point. With Salu being installed as our lord and master comes the end, the end of our union. By decree of the new regime, our union is kaput. We're at the mercy of committees for wages, vacations, where and when we work. No more bargaining for fair treatment. It is what they say it is."

I thought further on the topic. "It could be worse."

Big Peeter frowned. "How in the hell could it be worse?"

The edges of my mouth turned into a sardonic grin. "President Päts could still be in charge."

One of my father's greatest disappointments was watching Konstantin Päts dismantle Estonian democracy. Though the title "Republic of Estonia" remained in place until Stalin occupied the country, in reality, the Estonian Republic ceased to exist a decade after the nation gained independence. And Konstantin Päts, to my father's way of thinking, was a major cause of Estonia's demise.

Päts started his career as a journalist. He left Estonia for Finland during the 1905 uprising. Czar Nicholas II put a price on his head and death awaited Päts if he returned to Estonia. But when the Czar vacated the death sentence, Päts returned, was arrested, and served a short term in prison. Upon his release, the future Estonian president entered politics.

Päts was re-arrested when, towards the end of the Great War, Germany briefly installed a pro-German government in Tallinn. After the Kaiser capitulated, Päts was again freed. He established himself as the head of a new conservative party, the Farmer's Assemblies, which propelled him into the *Riigikogu* (Estonia's legislature). A constitutional crisis ensued during the Great Depression and Päts accepted the presidency of Estonia under a new constitution meant to thwart right wing extremism.

From March 12, 1934 until January 1, 1938, Päts ruled Estonia without a functioning legislature. He was, in essence, a dictator. Opposition parties were forbidden. Power was consolidated and Päts's supporters dominated the bicameral legislature. Some Estonians derisively viewed this period of Estonian history as the "Era of Silence". Others claim Päts was justified in seizing power to prevent the Vaps Party from turning Estonia into a Fascist state.

Despite being a veteran, Father did not share the Nazi-like views of Artur Sirk, a lawyer and head of the Vaps movement: an Estonian political force that embraced militarism, nationalism, and anti-Semitism. Based upon the Lapua movement in Finland, Germany's Nazis, and Italy's Fascists, the Vaps possessed only one attribute Father admired: a hatred of communism. Propelled onto the political stage because of the harsh economics of the Great Depression, the Vaps posed a threat, much as Hitler's Nazi Party did in Germany, to democratic rule in Estonia. And though no direct link between Vaps and the Nazis was ever shown, the imprint of fear, hatred, and reliance upon extreme rhetoric was clear in the public statements of Sirk and his adherents, one of whom was fellow lawyer and veteran, Ernest Raun. Päts's ability to galvanize power in opposition to Sirk rested in the near-unanimity of Estonian voters: they did not want the rise of an Estonian Hitler.

One would expect that Father supported Päts's moves to shore up Estonian democracy, which Father did at first. But when the "Era of Silence" dragged on, Father's view became: "Enough is enough". He believed Päts had overstayed his welcome.

"That would be better than what has happened," Big Peeter said quietly as he sat across from me and ordered coffee from a passing waitress. "Even if Päts sold out, gave up too easily, he's far better for the country than Stalin will prove to be."

"But you're forgetting one crucial thing," I said, watching the waitress place a chipped mug of coffee in front of my friend.

"What's that?"

"Päts is the asshole, as you so aptly pointed out on the docks, who *let* the Soviet Army into our country."

Big Peeter Saul was taken in by my argument. Päts had indeed let the Russians occupy Estonia. And I, in turn, had to agree with Big Peeter's premise that Estonia *should* have mounted a defense against the incursion. And if, like Poland, Estonia was crushed, then so be it. At least we would be considered to be brave and fearless. Instead, Estonians were now viewed as a timid people by the outside world.

Peeter closed his eyes as he sipped hot coffee. The big man appeared to be searching his mind for a clever retort. But none came because what I had said was indeed what he had once argued. "You're right, you little shit. How can one so young be so clever?"

Had Päts not signed the Mutual Assistance Treaty with Stalin, the concession that allowed Soviet troops into Estonia, perhaps resistance to the invasion would have been possible. Some say that Konstantin Päts did what he did because he had no spine. I believe that, for all his faults, Päts knew that resistance would likely bring the total destruction of Estonia. We had few airplanes. We had few tanks. Our navy was small and outdated. We were—and still are—a nation one-fifth the size of our kindred, Finland, in population. We possessed a limited supply of able-bodied men from which to form an army. And we did not have the benefit of Finnish-Karelian geography that would, as the drama involving our Finnish brethren unfolded, prove to be a key in stopping the Russians.

Whereas much of eastern Finland is marshy, lake-filled, and forested, making mass assaults with tanks and mechanized troops problematic, the Estonian border with Russia is not nearly as difficult for invaders. Cross a river or two and the path is clear to Tallinn. Historians still debate Konstantin Päts's decision to capitulate to Stalin. I decided long ago, despite my enmity towards the man, that his decision saved, rather than cost, Estonian lives.

"What the hell do we do now?" I asked Big Peeter, as we finished our coffee and stood up from the table.

"Show up for work," Peeter Saul replied, leaving coins on the table to pay for his coffee, "and hope they don't force us to work on any goddamned Russian ships!"

CHAPTER 6

With the arrival of Soviet soldiers, sailors, and airmen, so too came ordinary Soviet citizens: men and women brought into Estonia to begin the process of "Sovietization."

Stalin's intent was clear. He wanted to stamp out dissent and end democracy in Estonia. The Soviet leader believed that the best way to achieve this goal was to pour Russians across the border and to round up any Estonians who looked like trouble. This two-pronged approach began immediately after Soviet forces were "welcomed" into my country and it was the influx of foreigners into Estonia that ended my time with Liisu Koidula.

There was no warning that our relationship was passé. One evening, after a hard day running electrical cable through the filthy bilge of the *Ladoga,* a Soviet troop transport—Big Peeter's fears had come to fruition and we *were* working on Russian naval ships—I walked into the Water's Edge, intent upon downing a stiff shot of vodka to be followed by a quick romp with the corpulent woman. But as I stepped into the dark bar and my eyes adjusted to crackling electric light, I saw that the stool next to the bar owner was already taken. A skinny Russian sailor about my age, his face disrupted by acne, his greasy blond hair swept into sticky bangs framing his narrow face, his uniform crisply perfect, sat in *my* place, his left arm draped around *my* woman's shoulders. At least eight other Russians stood or sat along the bar rail, chortling in their native tongue.

I searched the room for friends. I didn't recognize anyone other than Miik Salu, whose thin lips twisted with appreciation when he noticed me from a booth in the furthest corner of the speakeasy. Miik was alone. The Russians were not his friends, despite his politics, and he'd lost any sort of credibility he once had with his Estonian co-workers. He was, in essence, a man without a country.

"Friend Kristian," Salu bellowed, as he rose to his feet, obviously drunk. "Come join me," he urged, raising a tumbler of beer.

Liisu heard Salu's invitation to me, removed the skinny sailor's arm from her shoulder, and walked towards Miik's booth. Liisu's movements caused her hair to shift unnaturally. There were so many hair pins holding her artificially blond bouffant in place, the fibers moved as one solid piece, like a toupee shifting on a bald man's head in a windstorm.

"What would you like tonight, *kallike*?" Liisu whispered suggestively, as I took a seat in the booth across from my boss.

The scent of cheap perfume wafted from the woman's powdered jowls. I fixed my eyes straight ahead, wondering what in the hell she was up to by coming on to me when things had clearly changed.

"A beer."

"A beer?" she said quizzically. "But you always drink vodka."

I couldn't help myself. I stared at her pink bosom as she continued to bend over in a suggestive manner. "You don't know everything about me."

She giggled like a young girl. "Oh, but I think I do."

Salu tilted his head and studied the woman draped over me. "I see you two know each other."

Liisu stood up, adjusted her breasts, and nodded. "Yes. We know each other. Or used to, in the Biblical sense…"

I had no idea what her game was. I stared at my hands. Liisu looked at me with her painted face and squinty brown eyes. I kept my gaze focused on my hands, on the tabletop, on anything but her exposed cleavage. She leaned over again, as if to kiss me. Instead, she whispered in my ear.

"You should have moved in with me when I asked you to," the woman purred, her voice soft and inviting. "I could have taught you so much more. But you had your chance. I've found someone else," she said, gesturing with her head towards the sailor at the bar.

I looked at the Russian. I didn't want trouble but I sensed trouble was about to find me.

"I'll get you that beer."

I nodded and watched Liisu's big bottom sashay inside her tent-like dress as she moved away. The skinny Russian stared at me, his black eyes fairly burning with hatred as he considered whether to advance, whether to stake his claim.

"What the hell was that about?" Miik Salu asked, his voice slurred, his eyes narrowed by beer to mere slits.

"Nothing."

Salu leaned back and studied my face with drunken appreciation. "You little bastard. You've been fucking her, haven't you? How long? How long have you been with Liisu?"

I kept my mouth shut.

"Come on, man. I hear she's a tigress in bed, does things that even whores won't do. Out with it, Kristian. What's it like to sleep with a woman who's as big as a cow and as hot as a birch fire?"

"Shut up," I mouthed, watching the Russian out of a corner of my eye.

"*Shut up*? Why you little pipsqueak! A boy with barely any hair on his balls and you tell me to *shut up*?"

"Listen," I said, maintaining calm. "She's moved on. She's with the Russian," I said, jerking my head in the direction of the bar. "Let's just drop it."

Salu focused his bleary eyes on the sailor across the room. "I'd say she got a meager bargain there, my friend. But tell me, what is she like? How sweet is her skin, how nimble her thighs? I need to know these things. I'm doing research, research into the women of Tallinn. I've been in a long dry spell myself—not that I haven't had offers," he added. "But *you*," Salu continued, the sarcasm clear in his words, "*you* seem to be able to find women to fuck," he said, through a broad grin.

I fingered the long bladed knife sheathed on my belt. There was a limit to my patience and Salu had exceeded it. "Fuck you."

I stood up, intent upon leaving.

"Sit down," Salu said, his voice softening. "I offered to buy you a beer."

I hesitated. Though Salu was much smaller in stature, he was built of sinew. If we got into a fight in the bar, I would likely win. But I would also likely find my face bloodied and my clothes torn. I wasn't in the mood for an altercation. I relented and sat down.

"Good. You know how to listen," Miik said quietly. "I apologize. I was out of line to criticize your choice in women and to ask intimate questions," he said, patting the back of my hand like a father. "Besides," the drunk continued, "it's bygones, right? She's moved on. To the *Russian*."

Liisu brought my beer. There was no further dialogue between us. Miik paid the woman. She sauntered back to her lover, exaggerating her hips and pelvis as she walked, strutting like a fashion model depicted in the women's clothing catalogs Mother always confiscated from Karl and me when we hid them beneath our beds.

"Mmm," the communist murmured as he watched the fat woman leave. "I think I know what you see in her."

I took a swig of beer. It was flat but at least it was cold. Outside the bar, humidity clung to the city like sweat on an overworked horse. The sun had set but the day's heat remained trapped between city and sea. No wind stirred. Perspiration beaded on my forehead and dripped from my nose onto the table as I thought about Miik and his politics.

When Soviet forces moved into Tallinn in June of 1939, the machinery of communism wasn't far behind. By the time the main force of Soviet troops occupied Estonia in the summer of 1940 there were fewer than 200 Estonian communists left in the country. Most of the leadership of the Estonian Communist Party (EPC) had fled Estonia when the party was banned in the early 1930s. The EPC's leaders sought safe harbor in nearby Soviet Karelia. But, as with the American and Canadian Finns who immigrated to Karelia to experience communism under Joseph Stalin, Estonian communists who immigrated to the U.S.S.R. found little solace and much sorrow in their decision. Stalin imprisoned or executed nearly all the former leaders of the EPC in his effort to purge foreign influences from the Party. By the time Miik Salu was anointed as my supervisor at the Kinnunen Shipyard, there were few communists left in Estonia. He was one of the lucky ones. His skill as an electrician saved his life.

"Comrade Kristian, you seem very pensive tonight," Miik said, interrupting my thoughts.

I remained silent, watching Russians come and go from the bar. Two whores, their faces gaudy with makeup, the seams of their black stockings provocative against their milky white calves, worked a pair of Soviet Marines in a far corner. The men were drunk. Laughter tittered from the couples as they downed their drinks and headed up narrow stairs leading to the rental rooms Liisu kept on the second floor for such purposes. Her flat was a floor above the rooms set aside for trysts. There were many nights, as I lay panting, my head buried in the quivering flesh of the fat woman's bosom listening to the pounding of her heart, that the sounds of love-making from the whores below accentuated my melancholy.

"What are *you* staring at, Finlander?"

Miik Salu and I looked up. I'd been so preoccupied by visions of the past I hadn't seen the Russian leave the bar and approach our booth. The skinny sailor stood over us and spoke Russian with an unfamiliar accent made more difficult by the thickness of his drunken tongue.

"He's no Finn," Salu replied. "He's Estonian."

One of the sailor's companions, a man with biceps the size of anvils, hovered nearby. The man's shadow engulfed me, made me fairly disappear in its bulk.

"He looks like a Finlander to me," the big Russian murmured.

"I'm Estonian," I said quietly, placing sufficient calm and firmness behind the words to make it *seem* that I was in control. In reality, my legs were shaking.

"I say he's a stinking Finlander. And he's been insulting my friend's woman," another sailor said disdainfully, as he moved into our corner of the bar.

Miik Salu attempted to defuse the situation. "Friends, why not pull up a chair and let me buy you a beer,' Miik offered. "It's too hot to argue and there's little to be gained by impugning a man's birthplace. I tell you, I work with this boy. I know him to be from Puhja. His father is a farmer and his mother has the most beautiful voice in all of Estonia."

"You mother's a whore and you were staring at my girl," the young Russian declared.

I looked into the sailor's small eyes.

He's terrified. This isn't his idea.

I ignored the insult to Mother, though it pained me to do so.

We're outnumbered. Let it pass.

"Liisu was my girlfriend. I meant no disrespect. Seeing her with someone else surprised me."

There was no warning. The big Russian had me on my feet and flying through the musty air of the bar in one motion. My head struck the floor, as I landed in a heap near the door. In a flash, Miik was on the other big sailor, riding the broad-backed Russian like a crazy American cowboy on a bronco. I knew that if I stayed on the floor, my attacker would put the boots to me. I bounced from the floor into a fighting crouch.

"Stop this nonsense!" Liisu screamed in Russian. "I'll not have you brawling in my place!"

The bartender moved out from behind the bar with a maple baton in hand. He gave no warning as he struck the skinny Russian on the head with the stick. The blow crumpled the sailor to the floor.

"You heard the woman!" the barkeep roared. "Stop fighting or the next man who raises a fist gets a busted skull!"

But there were eight Russians in the bar, not counting the two Marines who were upstairs and otherwise occupied, and only Miik Salu, the bartender, and me. We were outnumbered.

The big Russian clenched his fists. I was not a trained boxer and though I was ten centimeters taller than the Russian, he outweighed me by at least twenty-five kilos. And then there were his friends. Two nearly identical Russian sailors, their crew cut heads bobbing in unison as they flanked me and sought to force me into a corner. I didn't think about the consequences. I didn't mull over what my actions would mean. I simply extended my right hand to my belt, unsheathed the long bladed *nuga* given to me by my father, and held it in front of me as a warning.

"He's got a knife!" the big man bellowed in Russian. "The son-of-a-bitch has a knife!"

The sudden appearance of the blade, its steel shiny in the dim light of the bar, forced the sailors to make space. Miik stopped fighting. The bartender stopped fighting. Everyone in the room was riveted on the dance I was caught up in with the three Russians.

"Are you crazy?" Miik yelled, trying to make his way to my side.

The Russians would not part. They kept Miik away from the fight. The barkeep tried to make his way to me but sailors barred his path. The bartender's threats—that he would bring down his maple baton on the heads of those who blocked him—fell upon deaf ears. I was alone. I would receive no aid. My destiny was in my hands and in the steel of my father's hunting knife.

BOOK THREE: THE WINTER WAR

CHAPTER 1

Elin Goldfarb survived her confinement on Kalajoki Island. Camp manager Urho Metsä managed to keep Elin supplied with insulin through Captain Vladislav Karashvili, the Red Army officer charged with oversight of the logging operation. Karashvili also came to appreciate the woman's office skills and assigned his personal cook, Olga Kelikov, a Russian speaking Karelian giantess whose skin was covered with so many warts it appeared that her closest relative was the Karelian common toad, to prepare Elin's meals whenever the captain was on the island. Elin Goldfarb had regained her weight and her health. But there was a price to be paid for Elin's recovery. The privileges attained by the woman in the face of the poor food and never-ending labor experienced by other prisoners encouraged whispers. Elin's relationships with Metsä and Karashvili became the subject of endless tongue wagging. Gossip against the American increased as harsh weather drove the internees indoors. Idle time gave the women of Kalajoki Island ample opportunity to speculate as to just *what* Elin Goldfarb *did* behind the closed doors of Urho Metsä's and Captain Karashvili's offices to curry such favor.

The Red Army moved into position along the border. Concentrations of Soviet troops extended from Petsamo in the far north to Viipuri in the south on the Karelian side of the imaginary line dividing Finland from the U.S.S.R. Negotiations for a peaceful resolution of Stalin's demands, including the Soviet leader's insistence that the border between the two nations be moved towards Helsinki and that Finnish defenses on the Karelian Isthmus be dismantled, were rejected by the Finns.

An excuse—the Soviets claimed an "unknown party" shelled a Soviet border patrol location near Manilla—would eventually lead to war. Finland would refuse to apologize for the attack, an attack that was orchestrated by the NKVD, and on November 30, 1939 the Soviet Union would invade Finland. The conflagration would come to be known as "The Winter War" because the conflict was fought and decided during the coldest season of the year.

Elin Goldfarb was not privy to the details of the forthcoming invasion, though she was, as the secretary to the highest-ranking officials on Kalajoki Island, a witness to much activity during the days leading up to war. Bits and pieces of information leaked through to her, information she wished to share with Matti Peltomaa. But due to changed circumstances Elin had little chance to interact with the quiet American.

After restoring Kalajoki's sawmill to full capacity, Peltomaa was transferred by Captain Karashvili to nearby Lime Island to supervise the repair of rock cutting equipment. Lake barges loaded with lime extracted from Lime Island steamed south via the canals and rivers connecting Lake Onega to the Baltic Sea. The lime mined on the island was a key ingredient in the concrete used to fortify Leningrad. While Peltomaa's reassignment was said to be temporary, he spent much of the summer and fall of 1939 living and working on Lime Island, a place far less hospitable than Kalajoki Island.

When Matti Peltomaa arrived on Lime Island in late June of 1939, the prisoners living there lacked adequate shelter. The only structures available to house the internees were uninsulated stables. The prisoners were also being worked to death, extracting lime by pick and shovel from open pit mines with limited mechanical assistance. With Karashvili's approval, Peltomaa reorganized the labor force on Lime Island. He removed invalid men and all women and children from the mines and reassigned them to revamp the dilapidated stables and to dig fresh wells and latrines to improve the island's sanitation. The work, while not as taxing as laboring in the pits, remained physical but was Peltomaa's attempt to keep the most vulnerable islanders alive. In spite of Peltomaa's best intentions, old men, women, and children continued to die from disease and starvation, even as the island's rations of gruel and black bread were increased and conditions improved. The interior of the rocky, desolate place—the trees long having been lost to mine excavation, the landscape barren and exposed to the elements—became littered with unmarked graves. By the end of October, Peltomaa had restored order to Lime Island but he could not bring the dead back to life. Nor could he prevent, even if he had wanted to, the occasional escape of miners and their families.

As boats bearing lime left Lime Island, miners—and on occasion, their wives and children—hid amongst the rocks piled high in the holds of boats and sailed off the island. Many escapees died, crushed by the weight of shifting rock as the boats chugged south towards the Svir River. Others were apprehended when their boat docked at the mouth of the Svir to take on fuel and supplies. A handful of stowaways safely made their way to Finland. But with the surge of Russian military activity in Karelia, what had once been a dangerous game became a fool's errand.

Elin Goldfarb knew about the escapes. She knew, for example, that the Tomas Huttila family had been moved at Peltomaa's request from Kalajoki Island to Lime Island because Tomas was a master welder and Peltomaa needed Tomas's skills to repair equipment. Elin learned that the Huttilas—Tomas, Betta, and their two children—had left Lime Island and that Karashvili blamed Peltomaa for their escape. Only

Metsä's intervention saved the American from disappearing into the Soviet gulag. But the Huttila episode meant that no other Kalajoki internees would be transferred to Lime Island. This prohibition posed a problem for Elin Goldfarb as she planned her own escape.

CHAPTER 2

"How goes your day, Mrs. Goldfarb?"

Captain Karashvili asked the question as Elin tidied up the camp commander's office, a dust rag in hand, sweat pouring off her face.

"Very well, captain. Very well."

Karashvili was a native of the Georgian S.S.R. and a childhood acquaintance of Joseph Stalin. Despite his pedigree, the captain was relegated to a backwater command due to his mediocre brain and slight abilities.

The Georgian sat in a swivel chair behind his desk and watched the prisoner clean.

As attractive a woman as I've seen in a long while.

Karashvili's wife was sickly. They had been married twenty-five years, a union that had produced little physicality and no children. Lena Karashvili spent much of their marriage bouncing from doctor to doctor in hopes of solving the malaise that routinely blanketed her spirit like a shroud. She sought answers for the ups and downs in her psyche, ultimately being diagnosed as manic-depressive and being placed on sedatives. Lena accepted medications briefly, only to discover that she did not appreciate the limitations drugs imposed on her creative mania. She was a composer and it was during periods of heightened awareness that Lena was able to write her best scores. When she understood that the sedatives ended her flights of productive fancy, she discontinued the drugs and returned to the wild and unpredictable roller coaster ride of her disease.

His wife's unpredictability caused Vladislav Karashvili to give up on his marriage. He would not divorce Lena but there was a mistress, a Russian speaking Karelian girl of eighteen, Galina Ostrov from Kondopoga, who shared the captain's bed whenever the opportunity arose. Lena knew of the girl and though it disgusted her to learn of her husband's weakness, Lena chose to ignore the insult and trudge through marriage, content to write her music and dream her dreams when not locked in the hell of depression.

She is so much more poised, so much more intelligent and worldly than Galina.

Elin suspected what Karashvili was thinking as he ogled her. Granted, she didn't know the *exact* words forming in the captain's mind as she removed dust and grime from the bookshelves, file cabinets, and other furniture in the camp commander's office. But she recognized desire even if she did not know the precise order of the words in the man's subconscious. She had grown accustomed to Karashvili's leering, though he had not touched her or made an untoward comment about her, despite the obvious longing etched on his face. And that, in Elin Goldfarb's view, was enough reason to hold her tongue and let the man think his dirty thoughts.

Elin stood and stretched the muscles in her calves as the captain averted his gaze and pretended to study a document on his desk.

"Will there be anything else?"

The Georgian looked up, loneliness clear in his eyes. "No, I think that takes care of it for now, Mrs. Goldfarb. Thank you. You may return to your duties with Mr. Metsä."

As she made ready to exit, Elin glanced at a map of Karelia located on the far end of Karashvili's desk. The map depicted Soviet troop concentrations in red pencil.

I'll come back when he's at lunch and study the map.

Her delay in responding caused the officer to frown.

"Is there something I can help you with, Mrs. Goldfarb?" Karashvili asked, shifting papers to cover the map.

I need to be more careful. I can't stare, can't give away my interest in the map.

"No, Comrade Captain. I was simply lost in my thoughts about the coming winter," she lied. "I fear it will be another cold season on the island."

Karashvili smiled. "I am thankful that I only spend a few days a month here. I pity you, Mrs. Goldfarb, pity that you have been forced to make this place your home. But what can be done? We are sorting things out, trying to find the proper place for foreigners who have settled in Karelia. One day, we will have an answer to your unfortunate situation. Hopefully, it will be an answer that allows you to go about being a productive citizen, no?"

The man sat up to his full height.

The answer the Soviet nation had for Hiram was a bullet and an unmarked grave! Is that the sort of answer that awaits me? I don't think I shall sit patiently on Kalajoki Island waiting for your kind to come up with an answer to a question that should never have been asked.

Elin didn't respond. She simply backed out of the office, leaving the captain to ponder the woman's interest in the movement of Soviet troops.

CHAPTER 3

A hand-drawn map was hidden beneath Elin Goldfarb's clothing piled on her bunk in the barracks she shared with seventy-five other detainees. As Elin sat on the edge of the rough-hewn planks of the wooden bed, the air near the floor cold and infiltrating, she removed the map from beneath the clothing and placed it next to Hiram's rucksack. The canvas satchel rested on a wool blanket next to a hand-me-down coat. Her own winter coat had lost its buttons and sustained so many rips and tears, its ineffectiveness against the escalating October chill was made manifest to Matti upon his return from Lime Island. Though Peltomaa possessed no wealth, he was the owner of one significant character trait: adaptability. No matter the situation, Matti Peltomaa made things happen. He saw, at first glance upon his return to Kalajoki Island, that Elin Goldfarb's coat would not survive another winter. There were no great stockpiles of clothing, no shops, no storehouses of goods from which Peltomaa could select a replacement, and yet he found her a suitable replacement—a thick green and black wool Mackinaw stout enough to withstand the bitterest Karelian wind.

The woman emptied the rucksack onto the blanket and commenced an inventory.

One battered copy of Leaves of Grass
Three vials of insulin, two steel needles, a pumice stone, and one syringe
Two pairs of wool socks
Two pairs of long underpants
One bra
One gray sweater
One pair of wool mittens
Two men's undershirts
One toothbrush (the handle carved for her out of birch by Matti; the bristles purloined from brushes used in the machine shop on the island)
Tooth powder
One bar of pumice soap
One pair of Red Army wool fatigue slacks
One hairbrush
One tablet of lined paper
Two completed journals
Two pencils
One jack knife
One pound salted and dried pork

One half-pound cheese
One box of strike anywhere matches
One small pair of scissors
Assorted cotton compresses
One hand drawn map

My treasures, Elin thought, carefully restoring the items to the rucksack. *All my possessions.*

She picked up the book, opened it, and studied the author's image. Carefully, so as not to tear the fragile parchment—it was a second edition and over seventy years old, a gift to Elin from her mother as a young girl—she arrived at her favorite verse.

To her children the words of the eloquent dumb great
mother never fail,
The true words do not fail, for motion does not fail and
reflection does not fail,
Also the day and night do not fail, and the voyage we
pursue does not fail.
Of the interminable sisters,
Of the ceaseless cotillions of sisters,
Of the centripetal and centrifugal sisters, the elder and
younger sisters,
The beautiful sister we know dances on with the rest.
With her ample back towards every beholder,
With the fascinations of youth and the equal fascinations
of age,
Sits she whom I too love like the rest, sits undisturb'd,
Holding up in her hand what has the character of a mirror,
while her eyes glance back from it,
Glance as she sits, inviting none, denying none,
Holding a mirror day and night tirelessly before her own
face.

Elin could not help but dwell on "A Song of the Rolling Earth." Her own mother, Laina Gustafson, had been Elin's Mother Earth: *the* grounding, guiding, sustaining force in Elin's life. And Elin had tried to fulfill that role for the half-sister she considered to be her own daughter. Differences in their personalities made such a connection difficult. Alexis was so stubborn, so headstrong (traits Elin was once accused by her own father of exhibiting!) that Elin had convinced herself that she'd failed as a mother.

Where is Alexis at this very moment? I have not heard from her in over a year. Does she know I am on this island, in this camp? Does she know—does she appreciate that Hiram is dead? What sort of woman has my daughter become?

The anxiety of not knowing and of being poised on the edge of a precipice caused Elin to remember that she was due for an injection. She opened the rucksack, dug into the bottom of the bag, and removed a needle, syringe, vial, and the pumice stone. It was so cold in the room that Elin could see her breath. The grating of steel being drawn across stone was the only sound in the building. The other internees were at work. Wandering air agitated the pages of the poetry book. The rustling was subtle, like a whisper, as the woman tapped the insulin vial, inserted the needle into the container, and drew medicine into the syringe. With a practiced hand, Elin rolled up the edge of her blouse, pulled down the waistbands of her skirt and union suit, pinched the skin of her tummy, and eased the tip of the needle through flesh. She grimaced at the initial prick but relaxed as she pushed the plunger of the syringe.

I have enough insulin to last until I cross the Finnish border, she thought. *If everything goes right, I should make Sortavala before the medicine is gone. There are doctors in Sortavala. There should be an apothecary there as well.*

Her plan, one decided after many hours of studying her crude map, required being assigned to Lime Island. According to Matti Peltomaa, the office on Lime Island needed organizing. Elin had been subtly lobbying Urho Metsä to allow her to spend a week on Lime Island to accomplish the task. Metsä had balked at losing her for even a day but, with input from Peltomaa, Metsä seemed to be softening. The final hurdle would be Karashvili. The captain had decreed that no Kalajoki detainee other than Peltomaa would be allowed to visit Lime Island. Captain Karashvili would be the thornier of the two men to convince.

CHAPTER 4

The barge carrying Elin Goldfarb and Matti Peltomaa plowed through rolling waves. The escapees huddled in the vessel's hold, concealed from discovery by a tarp and empty wooden crates. There was, as with any such crossing, the possibility of being buried by the crates if the ship encountered a rogue wave. A late October wind brought unending rain. Though the deluge meant that Matti and Elin would arrive at their destination soaked to the skin, the foul weather kept nosey sailors from looking for stowaways.

A sudden pitch to port threatened the escapees as they sat on the cold steel floor of the hold, their backs rigid against the rusted hull of the old scow, their legs curled against their chests in an attempt to retain body heat. But the old boat righted in the storm and the crates remained in place. The man and the woman were not lovers. They did not entwine as they sought warmth. They merely sat next to each other, an appropriate distance apart, as the boat fought the weather.

"God, it's cold," Peltomaa whispered through chattering teeth.

"It is. I don't believe I have ever been *this* cold. Not even when we lived at *Hyvämetsä*. Winter in that god-forsaken, bedbug-infested logging camp was as cold as I've ever experienced—until now."

"Bedbugs. God, how I hate bedbugs," the logger muttered.

"Nothing worse for ruining a night's sleep," Elin agreed, eyes closed, words leaking over clicking teeth.

"Do you think this is a wise decision?" Peltomaa asked after a pause.

"You have doubts? It is a bit late for that, don't you think?" Elin asked.

"You're likely right. It's too late to cry over spilled milk."

Elin considered Peltomaa's use of the familiar expression before answering. "It is."

Elin Goldfarb knew. She had known, for some time after reconnecting with Matti Peltomaa in Petroskoi, that the man was in love with her.

That has probably always been the case, she had decided as she formed her plan to escape. *His feelings cannot be new, something that just developed. Because he was Andrew's friend, I never gave it a thought, never considered him in that way. He is a good man. His appearance, at first glance, is not striking, does not cause one's heart to skip a beat. But Matti Peltomaa is an honest, hardworking man. I may have used him to get to this point. But I will not lead him on. I do not love him. I must make this point abundantly clear.*

It had not taken as much persuading as she first thought to gain Captain Karashvili's permission to accompany Matti Peltomaa to Lime Island. Karashvili was charged with running operations on both Lime Island and Kalajoki Island for the Red Army. The civilian superintendent in charge of the lime mines had made a mess of things. The man's record keeping was a disaster. There was no way for Karashvili, given the shabby paperwork, to rebuff suspicion from Moscow that *his* management style was inefficient. Inefficiency, given the critical need for lime, would likely be used as a reason, perhaps *the* reason, to snatch Karashvili away from the comfort of his Lake Onega dacha, his wife, and his mistress and send him away. Karashvili had no intention of leading Russian soldiers against German or Finnish troops or of being exiled to Siberia to oversee another labor camp. When Matti Peltomaa suggested to Urho Metsä, and Metsä in turn passed the request on to Karashvili, that the American woman "assist" in organizing the office on Lime Island, there was little hesitation from the Georgian. Elin Goldfarb was given a week to put the Lime Island mining records in order. Karashvili had no fear of granting the request. After all, where could a diabetic, forty-something-year-old woman go?

Matti Peltomaa took great care to select the appropriate vessel for their escape.

At first, Elin believed that she—and she alone—would be making the voyage. But from the very beginning, when Elin had first asked Peltomaa about being assigned to the mining operation, Matti had known her intentions and knew he must accompany her. Peltomaa's unassuming nature led him to avoid revealing his own plans until the *Kiev,* the vessel he selected for their escape, had left the mainland and was headed towards Lime Island.

"Your plan. What is your plan, Mrs. Goldfarb?" Peltomaa had asked the question as he worked to secure passage on the *Kiev.*

They had been alone in Karashvili's office. The logger had been keeping tabs on the woman. She had been clever in the way she gathered necessities for her journey but not clever enough to conceal her duplicity from the fellow American.

"Whatever do you mean, Mr. Peltomaa?"

Her tone, meant to come off as flippant, came off as edgy instead.

Peltomaa had crossed the room, placed a rough hand on the woman's bare left wrist, and ushered her into an empty chair next to Karashvili's desk. "I know what you're up to. You're ready to try to make a break for it, am I right?"

The woman had looked at Peltomaa with pleading eyes. "I don't see how you—"

"—could know?" Peltomaa said, finishing her thought.

She had nodded.

"You're adept at hiding it, if that's your concern. I doubt anyone suspects a thing. But I know, Elin," he said, converting their conversation to the familiar.

Elin Goldfarb had stared hard at the man.

"You think stowing away on a lime boat headed south, towards Lake Ladoga, is the best way off this shit covered rock. Correct?"

Elin nodded.

"That's a mistake others have made. First, the voyage down the lake is a far longer journey than simply going back to Petroskoi. Second, where did you think you would go, once you landed at the Svir?"

The woman had swallowed. "I was planning to make my way to Sortavala."

Peltomaa had shaken his head. "Bad idea. The Russians are concentrating their forces in southern Karelia and around Lake Ladoga."

Elin's eyebrows arched. "I hadn't heard that."

Peltomaa had smiled. "I know. Even with your ability to eavesdrop, some things are simply not said publicly."

"How do you know this?"

Peltomaa flicked the lobe of his right ear with his right index finger. "You're not the only one with big ears."

The woman had smiled weakly and touched the lobe of her right ear. "Are they so obvious? I try to conceal them with my hair."

They are beautiful like the rest of you.

Matti Peltomaa had ignored his thought and continued. "I know you've been tracing Karashvili's map. Do you have your copy with you?"

Elin pointed to a satchel resting beneath a chair across the room. The logger had covered the distance, opened the flap of the rucksack, removed the hand drawn map, walked back to Karashvili's desk, and unfolded the intricate drawing, a map of Eastern Finland and Western Karelia copied in painstaking detail by the woman in pencil.

"Here is where the Red Army will be concentrating," he said, pointing to the Karelian Isthmus. "And here as well, between Pilkäranta and Petroskoi. And here," he had continued, "between Karhumäki and Ilomantsi."

"So my plan to travel by foot to Sortavala is—"

"—foolhardy," the old man had interrupted. "There will be over one hundred thousand Russians pushing northwest between Lake Ladoga and Lake Onega. You would have no chance, no chance at all, of reaching Sortavala."

Elin had sighed. "But taking a boat to Petroskoi brings us in contact with the same soldiers, does it not?" she asked.

"Yes and no. The troops at Petroskoi will move towards Lake Ladoga and also towards Joensuu to capture the railroad line. That second column must first pass through Ilomantsi. The Finnish Home Guard is defending Ilomantsi, which will cause delay. We have the opportunity, if we leave from Petroskoi and head directly to Joensuu, to beat the Russians to the border."

Elin had nodded. "And from Joensuu, I could take the train to Helsinki."

Matti Peltomaa had smiled. "Exactly."

Peltomaa had folded the map and returned it to Elin's rucksack.

"I still have one question," the woman had said quietly as she stood up and faced the logger.

"Which is…?"

"You said 'we"."

The man had nodded.

"You mean to accompany me?"

"I do. At least as far as Joensuu."

The woman had considered the statement. "You are tired of running a logging camp?"

Peltomaa smiled. "Your first love, Andrew, fought in a war against an enemy he had no quarrel with."

Elin had tilted her head. "And?"

"This war will be different, far different, from the Great War."

"How so?"

"Finland is a little country without dreams of being a world power. It seeks nothing but peace. No major powers will take Finland's part. Finland will stand alone against Russia. Sweden will claim neutrality. The United States will seek redress through the League of Nations—an entity that it doesn't even belong to—but do nothing more. Great Britain and France will wring their hands and worry that Germany will join the fight on the side of the Russians. I want to be there, on the front lines, when Finland needs me."

"You surprise me, Matti. I didn't know you were a patriot," Elin had whispered.

The logger's eyes had fallen to the dirty floor of the office. "I'm not. Russians are the reason—their czar is the reason I left Finland for America in the first place. Stalin is nothing more than another czar. He's no Romanov, I'll grant you that, but he's a czar nonetheless."

Matti Peltomaa had walked to the door before turning to face Elin. "My reason for going with you, Mrs. Goldfarb," he said, "is quite simple: I hate czars. I hate kings. And I hate Russians. I want to kill as many of them as I can," he had confided before leaving the woman to her work.

Ismo Salo, the captain of the *Kiev* and a Finn who had piloted tramp steamers for the better part of three decades, was a man known to Matti Peltomaa. Salo had the reputation of being able to hold his tongue and his vodka. These attributes made Salo the logical choice to ferry them to freedom. Peltomaa had no money—nothing of value to use as a bribe. The only payment Peltomaa could offer Salo was satisfaction—the personal satisfaction of one Finn helping others escape and spitting, as it were, in the face of the Russians.

Having served in the Finnish Navy during the Civil War on the side of the Whites, and with full knowledge of Matti Peltomaa's communist leanings, Salo was wary of the logger's politics. But as the men watched foodstuffs and other supplies being unloaded from the *Kiev* under a low hanging October sky, Peltomaa had been able to convince Salo of the true nature of the logger's intentions—that Peltomaa wanted to escape the island and join the Finnish Army. The ship captain's enmity towards Stalin had overcome his skepticism. A deal was struck: Ismo Salo agreed to carry Peltomaa and his friend, whose identity was unknown to Salo, away from Lime Island.

"No!" Salo had said when Matti Peltomaa and Elin Goldfarb appeared on the pier alongside the *Kiev*. "No women!"

Matti Peltomaa stood on the concrete dock next to the boat, darkness cloaking his presence, a slight wind rising in the west, the flat blackness of Lake Onega beginning to dance.

"She's a good soul," Peltomaa had replied quietly.

Salo had been on midnight watch. His sailors were fast asleep in their berths aboard the barge, subdued by the vodka they had swilled in the mining camp's office with the inept manager Elin had been assisting. Salo would not drink with the Karelian. He had no time for Russian speakers. But his crew was not so deferential. Free booze was free booze, no matter who was pouring. The crew had slumbered on, oblivious to the debate being held outside their quarters.

"I know she's a Red but I don't care about her politics; I care that she's a woman. Women on ships bring bad luck."

Salo, a short, stocky man endowed with an aura of power and strength, had spat tobacco into the churning lake.

"Look, Ismo. She's lost her husband. She hasn't heard from her daughter. She's sick, diabetic. She will die if I don't get her away from this place."

The boat captain had looked towards Elin. "A woman. Sick. A communist. And you want me to risk my neck for her? I said I would take you, Peltomaa, you and one other. I did not agree to take a woman!"

Time had been crucial. The longer the men stood jawing in the open night air, the greater the chance that one of the kapos on his rounds would stumble upon their conversation.

Elin had understood, without hearing the words being spoken, that the argument was about her. Taking the initiative, she closed the distance between her and the men.

"I understand your concerns, Captain Salo," Elin had said quietly as she stood next to Matti. "If I were you, I wouldn't be too keen about to taking a sickly woman—whose discovery would mean your execution—on your ship. But I need to find my daughter. The last I knew, she was in Leningrad. With my husband dead, she is all I have left. I must find her. And to do that, I must get to Finland. You're the only hope I have of seeing her again."

Salo had studied the woman.

What the hell? I have no children of my own. But if I did, I would want to see them, to know for certain of their safety. The damn Russians. Damn Stalin. Damn his purges. If I could, if the communists would let me, I would sail this barge to Helsinki and rig her to fight. I'm old. Maybe too old to command a warship but not too old to put a shell through the hull of a Russian destroyer!

"Goddamn you, Peltomaa."

Matti Peltomaa had known, upon hearing the invective that Captain Ismo Salo was conceding; that the woman would be allowed aboard the *Kiev.*

The crossing left them seasick and fatigued. Elin was down to two vials of insulin when the *Kiev* pulled into Petroskoi. Captain Salo timed the boat's arrival so that it docked after dark.

"I will live to regret this day," Salo whispered, as he ushered Peltomaa and the woman onto the wharf. "My good luck is ruined."

The rain had stopped. Peltomaa shook the captain's hand as they stood in milky fog, the boat silent, the crew ashore in search of more liquor and compliant whores. In the morning, its coal hopper full, the *Kiev* would return to Lime Island where it would take on a load of lime rock before steaming to Leningrad. No lights illumined the dock. The captain had difficulty seeing Peltomaa's face as they spoke.

"I disagree. I think," Peltomaa continued through a smile, "that your good luck will increase due to your good deeds."

Salo dismissed the compliment with a wave of his hand. "You'd best be down the road. It won't be easy, making your way through this country with Stalin's army trying to beat you to the border," he muttered. "You armed?"

Peltomaa placed his right hand on a sheath dangling from his belt. A long-bladed *puukko*—the perpetual friend of Finnish loggers—rested in worn leather.

"You'll need more than a sharp blade to keep Mrs. Goldfarb's hair away from the Russians," the sailor said plainly. "And, with all due respect, ma'am, I'm not talking about the hair on your head!"

Before Elin could object to the man's coarseness, Ismo Salo pulled a Luger from inside his winter coat and handed the pistol, grip first, to Matti Peltomaa.

"Take it—you'll need it more than I will," the captain said, as Peltomaa accepted the Luger. "Here's a full clip and a box of cartridges as well," Salo added, pulling a magazine and a box of ammunition from the depths of his coat pocket.

Peltomaa considered the gun. "I can't accept this. It's too generous."

Salo smiled, exposing decaying teeth, the result of too much strong coffee and an affinity for his wife's *pulla*. "The German Marine who caught a bullet standing the line with me during the Great War didn't complain when I took it as a souvenir. I'm sure he won't mind if the Luger finds its way back to Finland."

Peltomaa tucked the pistol into the waistband of his trousers, accepted the magazine and the box of cartridges, slid the ammunition into a pocket of his red and black Mackinaw, and hoisted a gray canvas pack onto his left shoulder.

Elin Goldfarb raised her rucksack from the cement, slid her narrow shoulders between the pack's leather straps, and snugged the rigging.

"*Kiitos*," Peltomaa said, shaking the ship captain's bare hand with vigor.

"*Jumalan siunausta*," the old sailor said softly, as he watched Matti and Elin disappear in the fog.

CHAPTER 5

The man and the woman slipped out of Petroskoi. The ground beneath their boots was frozen. A trace of snow had settled on the lane they traveled. Sounds of diesel and gasoline engines cranking beneath the slowly advancing dawn made it clear to Matti Peltomaa that the Red Army was hell-bent on crossing the border before winter. The clank of tank treads against hardened ground, the sounds of truck engines being revved, and the noises of other machinery echoed in the distance as Matti and Elin walked towards Finland.

As the two made their way across the rough and uneven terrain between Lake Onega and Suojärvi—the last town of any size before the Finnish border—they left the road and traveled forest trails to avoid soldiers.

"I am sorry to burden you," the woman said, as the two sat in the shade of a pine, the warmth of the rising sun blocked by the snowy boughs of the dense forest. "You should have never agreed to do this."

Matti Peltomaa balanced on his haunches and observed the terrain through the trees, his right hand on the grip of the Luger as he sipped cold water from a canteen. The logger's deep brown eyes surveyed the landscape with intensity.

"I thought I heard something," Peltomaa whispered, removing his right hand from the pistol, placing his index finger to his lips.

They sat in silence. The occasional flit of songbirds' wings or the caw of ravens interrupted the quiet. But Elin heard nothing that indicated human presence in the surrounding wilderness.

Satisfied, Peltomaa sat on his rump, leaned against the harsh bark of the tree, and nodded. "You still have some of that bread left? And cheese?"

Elin sat Indian style as she opened the flap of her rucksack. She reached inside the pack and withdrew two squares wrapped in oilcloth. Her fingers worked the parcels and revealed a brick of cheese and a lump of black bread. It was the only food they had left. Though ample wild game—in the form of moose and roe deer and hares and black grouse—abounded in the forests west of Lake Onega, there was too much danger inherent in taking an animal. The noise of Matti's Luger would draw attention. The making of a fire in the deep woods to cook would draw the curious. Peltomaa's pistol remained unfired and they made do with cold food Elin had purloined from Lime Island.

"Here," Elin said quietly, her hair hanging long and free and shifting across the shoulders of her Mackinaw as she handed her companion chunks of bread and cheese.

Peltomaa glanced at the empty oilskin that had covered the bread. "You need food, to keep up your strength," he said, breaking the skimpy portion in two and handing a piece of stale bread back to the woman.

Elin shook her head. Though her disease demanded starch, her stomach was upset from monthly cramps—not diabetes—and she did not feel like eating. "I'll stick with water. Perhaps I can keep down a bit of bread later. For now, water will have to do."

The logger placed a piece of bread on his tongue and swallowed. "Here,' Peltomaa said, handing Elin the second portion of bread. "For later."

The woman accepted the food without comment, wrapped it in the oilskin, and returned it to the rucksack.

Peltomaa took a deep swig of water before offering his canteen to the woman.

Elin accepted the steel container and drank greedily. "How much further to Suojärvi?" she asked, as she wiped a dribble from her chin with a sleeve of her Mackinaw.

They had been walking for the better part of a week. Their pace, so far as Peltomaa could discern, was about twenty kilometers a day. *Too slow*, in the Finn's estimation. *We don't have enough food.* The logger removed Elin's map from his coat pocket and studied his compass. "A day."

"And then?"

Peltomaa looked up from the compass.

Despite it all—the dirt, the absence of make-up and other niceties—she remains striking.

"Matti?"

Elin's voice caused Peltomaa to return to her question.

"Twenty to thirty kilometers to the border. A day if we can move with a bit more purpose."

He knew his estimate was on the optimistic side. His stomach growled. His dark eyes focused on the small lump of depleting cheese on the dirty square of oilcloth sitting between the woman's legs on the humus-covered ground. A *närhi* flew above them, flitting between overhanging limbs, making no sound save for the whisper of air beneath its wings. Elin's eyes followed the path of the bird as it headed west, the direction of their own trek.

"Pretty."

Peltomaa grunted, retrieved the canteen, and took another swig of water. "Damn things. In the States, I've spent time watching blue jays and Canadian jays—whiskey jacks we call them. They drive you crazy when you're hunting. Noisy and curious, they won't leave a man alone," the logger concluded, stroking the salt and pepper stubble of his face.

"That one seems intent on making the border," the woman observed through a tired smile. "He doesn't seem interested in us."

The logger nodded and studied the map with greater concentration. "Nothing between Petroskoi and the border but forest, swamp, and lakes. Lake upon lake upon lake. Reminds me of Minnesota."

The woman nodded.

Peltomaa folded the map, tucked it into the pocket of his Mackinaw, and stood up. "The land of the *Kalevala. Maahiset* and magic and legends of great deeds," he continued.

"And in the summertime, the land of mosquitoes…" Elin added.

The logger suppressed a laugh. "Just like Minnesota! Up, young lady. Time to be on our way."

Elin Goldfarb covered the cheese and put the small bundle in her rucksack. Closing the flap, she stood up and slid the straps of the pack over her arms and wiggled her shoulders until the pack rode evenly across her back.

"Ready?"

The woman nodded.

"We'll stay off the road. I thought I heard trucks. We need to stay out of their way."

The pair began walking down the single-lane logging trail.

"This path will take us south of town, south of a big lake. I don't know the name of the lake but this path should keep us away from traffic."

"Traffic, like in New York City?"

The logger chuckled. "No, traffic like in western Soviet Karelia. Anyone we meet on the road will not be friendly," Peltomaa said. "The Russians are moving up to the front and there's no telling when the ground will be covered by deep snow, snow that will cause no end of hell for trucks, personnel carriers, and tanks. There's an urgency to the Russians moving up now."

"Winter here is worse than in Minnesota," Elin observed between breaths. "Just as cold, but with more snow."

"It's not a burden if you know how to ski. That may well be the secret to beating the Russians: Men on skis and impenetrable snow."

"Maybe. But there are so many of them; the Russians are like ants swarming over crumbs."

Matti Peltomaa turned and touched his index finger to his lips. Their pace became second nature as they found a familiar rhythm.

CHAPTER 6

Lake Syam's frozen plain stretched out before the travelers like an endless white desert. The man and the woman knelt behind spruce trees hugging the lake's shoreline. Snow fell gently from a pewter sky. The flakes were big and wet as they settled over the shoulders of the land. They were alone. There were no sounds of loggers working the backwoods; no voices, no noises of Russian troops, tanks, or equipment moving towards war. But such solitude, Matti Peltomaa knew, was only temporary.

"We need to avoid the villages; Lakhta and Kudama, here and here," Peltomaa said as he crouched out of the wind. He held Elin's homemade map in his left hand and pointed to the locations of the small Karelian settlements with his right index finger. "There are Russians on the move everywhere. By keeping to the forest, we can avoid the soldiers. But the last thing we need is for some Karelian hunter to stumble upon us and turn us in."

Matti Peltomaa and Elin Goldfarb were traveling the north shore of Lake Syam. Matti had selected the route in hopes of avoiding enemy soldiers using the road leading from Petroskoi to Suojärvi.

Elin looked up from the map and took in Matti Peltomaa's scraggly beard and scrutinized his ragged face.

He doesn't think we'll survive.

The woman rested against the uneven trunk of a large spruce. The boughs of the tree sheltered her from the wind and the snow. Elin's monthly had arrived the previous night. For decades, her cycle had been a useless inconvenience. Since being infected with gonorrhea by her first husband, Elin had endured the monthly inconvenience without purpose. What most fertile women accept as a prelude to motherhood was simply a reminder to Elin of all that she had lost due to Horace Ellison's infidelity.

When she felt the first cramps in the middle of the night, she had pardoned herself, grabbed her rucksack, and sought seclusion. She abated embarrassment by use of a medical compress before returning to her blanket on the cold ground. But the surge of hormones accompanying her monthly made sleep impossible. By daybreak, she had slept only an hour or two and, as Matti Peltomaa studied the map and expressed his views, her head was pounding. With each beat of her heart, she felt as if vessels in her brain were going to burst, killing her in a massive aneurism of blood, her blood, the same blood leaking slowly from her body.

And then there was the diabetes. She was down to one vial of insulin after she injected herself that morning. Matti had come to anticipate her need for privacy. Despite his obvious affection for Elin, he remained physically distant. If not a gentleman by status, Matti Peltomaa was surely, in the eyes of his female companion, a gentleman by all other measures.

"Ready to go?" he asked. He folded the map, placed it in a pocket of his jacket, threw his canvas pack over his left shoulder, and stood up in the squall.

Elin didn't reply. She simply lifted her rucksack from the ground, looped the straps over her shoulders, and snugged the leather straps to her chest.

Peltomaa looked at his companion. "You don't look well. Is it the diabetes?"

Elin shook her head.

"What then?"

"Female issues."

"Ah," Peltomaa replied. "You OK to push on? We can't stay here. The longer we remain in one place, the more likely we'll be found."

Elin nodded.

What the hell did I get myself into? the logger thought as they began moving through the spruce forest.

Lake Syam is one-half the distance from Petroskoi to the Finnish border and one-third of the distance from Petroskoi to Joensuu. Though the man and woman skirted the villages located along the north shore of the lake, their trek brought them to the outskirts of the town of Khautavaara, a circumstance that could not be avoided.

"There, along the roadway," the man whispered, pointing to a column of Red Army soldiers marching towards Suojärvi. Peltomaa and Elin lay on muddy ground created by melting snow as they watched the enemy move west. "We'd best stay put. We can cross the road after dark."

Elin nodded without conviction. Her teeth were chattering and she was near the end of her physical reserves.

I should have stayed on Kalajoki Island and waited for a change in the government's philosophy, she thought. *I am of little use to Matti and I will be of no use to Alexis if I die of exposure.*

Peltomaa noted the woman's shivering and moved close to add his body heat to her own. "Here," he said, reaching into a pocket of his Mackinaw and retrieving a small corner of foil. "My last piece."

Chocolate.

"I can't."

Peltomaa realized his *faux pas*. "Shit," he murmured, withdrawing the offering. "I am so stupid sometimes."

The woman smiled meekly. "Apology accepted. It's not nice to tempt a diabetic with chocolate," she whispered.

Peltomaa slid the foil back into his pocket and fixed his attention on the marching troops. "Tartars," he said.

"How's that?"

"Stalin is so desperate for soldiers, he's brought in foreigners. Tartars can take the cold but, from all accounts, they're not anxious to die for Mother Russia."

Elin considered the revelation. "How can you tell they're Tartars?"

"I've seen them before, in Petroskoi, when they arrived by train."

She nodded and closed her eyes, seeking respite in a brief nap.

They crossed the gravel highway after dusk, skirted Khautavaara, and made for the pine forest to the west of town. A few kilometers beyond Khautavaara, Peltomaa and the woman stopped. Breath vapor curled against the descending evening cold as they stood in silence.

"Wait here," the logger whispered. "I need to do my business."

As Peltomaa wandered off, Elin removed her pack from her shoulders, brushed snow from a fallen spruce log with a gloved hand, and sat down. The wilderness remained still. There was no wind. There were no birds flitting about or wolves howling in the distance. There was only the deep despondency of aloneness. And then she heard them: boots shuffling through snow and the rapid breathing of effort. The enemy soldiers came at Elin so quickly she had no time to cry out, no time to alert Matti Peltomaa.

There were three of them: two short, emaciated Tartars with long thin moustaches, thin black hair, and leather caps set atop their narrow heads and one larger, square shouldered man—a Russian officer by the markings on his uniform—who seemed to be in charge of the detail. One of the Tartars, his arms strong, his face streaked by sweat, wrapped a dirty palm around Elin's mouth to close off protest. The other Tartar stood over her, discarded his thin summer coat, the garment evidence of Stalin's ill prepared invasion in the face of Karelian winter, and tore at the buttons of his trousers.

The Tartars said nothing. The Russian stood to one side, his left hand holding a revolver, his eyes searching the woods.

"Where is he?" the officer asked calmly. The question was rhetorical, unanswerable because a boney hand covered the woman's mouth.

The Russian maintained a vigilant eye, his revolver leveled at seemingly empty forest.

They must have followed us, Elin thought in panic. *Matti is better off leaving me. It will be over soon. They will have what they will have and I will be dead. That is how it will be. Better me than both of us.*

The Tartar standing over Elin tore her Mackinaw open, lifted her sweater, and forced his hands beneath wool. His fingers were rough and the stink of horse imbedded in his soiled clothing nearly gagged Elin. The other Tartar forced her to the ground. The back of her head struck wood. Elin tried to bite the hand covering her mouth. The Tartar standing over her punched her face in response. She snapped her teeth. Fist struck flesh again and stunned her.

It is over.

Elin Goldfarb looked away, towards the Russian officer who was standing in shadows cast by a newly revealed quarter moon. Thin clouds drifted over the moon's abbreviated face. She closed her eyes. Buttons were undone. Her dirty long johns were yanked to her knees. The bloody compress fell aside. Elin kicked at the man on top of her but her clumped underwear and trousers restricted her from landing any blows. Her head slammed against the log again in reply. Blood oozed from a gash in her scalp and matted her hair. The rapist pressed himself onto Elin's body.

"Get on with it," the Russian muttered, his pistol at the ready, his eyes focused on the forest. "Finish with her so we can find her companion. We need to bring him in alive so the Commissar can interrogate him. He's likely a spy, a Finnish operative with much to say. Get on with it."

Elin closed her eyes.

God have mercy on my soul.

Despite her lapsed faith, she prayed to the God she once knew as a child. She was numb and near unconsciousness and she did not feel the man's violent thrusts. It was over in seconds. The man fumbled with the buttons to his barn door and whispered in Russian: "Ivan, you want some?"

The Tartar holding Elin down shook his head. The rapist regained his feet, pulled up his trousers, buttoned his fly, and retrieved a bayonet from his right boot.

He means to kill me.

There was a sudden calm, an understanding that Matti Peltomaa had escaped and left her to fate. She did not lament his choice. There was no anger in her soul. Matti would live to kill Russian soldiers. She was a woman, sick, exhausted, defiled, and ill equipped to fight. In weighing who should live, who should die, she was expendable.

The rapist knelt down, and touched the tip of the knife blade to Elin's thigh. In a moment of clarity, she understood. The Tartar meant to violate her a second time, to open her with his knife like a hunter opens a deer. Before she could react, before she could initiate one last effort of resistance, the Russian officer collapsed at her feet. Crimson sprayed from the man's neck like water from an uncontrolled fire hose and the officer's cocked revolver dropped to the ground.

Matti.

Peltomaa's silhouette manifested against the slender moon. The Tartar pinning Elin down released his hold on her as the rapist stood and pivoted on his heels. The Tartar's sudden movement caused the tip of the bayonet to nick Elin's thigh. Blood leaked from the shallow wound. Peltomaa's knife rose. The blade caught the rapist in the center of his chest. The other Tartar scrambled on all fours towards his rifle. Elin's fingers dug through snow. Flesh touched steel. The woman blinked tears. The pistol was heavy in Elin Goldfarb's hands as she raised the barrel, squeezed the trigger, and fired six rounds into the Tartar's back.

CHAPTER 7
November 13, 1939

The forest was intensely cold. The man and the woman rested in a pine grove overlooking an open meadow a few kilometers west of Korali Lake. Matti Peltomaa lay prone on the snowy ground, binoculars he had purloined from the dead Russian lieutenant pressed to his eyes as he scanned gently waving grass. A Tokarev automatic rifle taken from one of the dead Tartars rested on the snow next to the logger. Elin lay next to Peltomaa, her eyes also searching the woods across the meadow for movement.

When Elin reclaimed clarity after the assault, her thigh bandaged and her clothing restored to order, the back of her head felt like she'd been hit by a frying pan. Her cheeks and jaw were sore from repeated blows. Her left eye was closed, the eyelid puffed and distended due to an ugly black and blue bruise. Once she regained her senses following the attack, she saw that Matti Peltomaa was sitting on cold ground, his back propped against a spruce trunk, a strip of the dead Russian's uniform blouse covering a hole in his trousers. The Tartar's bayonet had cut the logger's thigh and the wound left Matti in a precarious state. But despite her aching head and the wound to her own leg, Elin had pulled herself together.

"We best be on the move," Matti had finally said. "The friends of the dead will wonder what happened to their comrades. More Tartars are likely on the way."

The sun had climbed and they had resumed their quest. It was hours and many kilometers later before Peltomaa had obliquely broached what had taken place. "How's that nick on your leg?"

"Fine."

Matti had considered how best to delve into the events of the past evening. "Are you sure?"

Elin nodded and patted the revolver she had claimed from the dead Russian. The pistol rested in a holster on the dead man's belt pulled snug around Elin's Mackinaw. The gesture was Elin's way of communicating that everything was indeed *fine*. Silence had resumed. Considerable time passed before Matti broached the topic again.

"Did those bastards touch you?"

How much should I tell him? Elin Goldfarb had thought, recalling the terror. *I was raped. But why are you asking me this? What value, what good can come from this talk? Nothing can change what happened. You saved my life. For that, I am forever grateful. But nothing positive can come from you asking me these things. Nothing.*

She had shaken her head.

There is nothing wrong with a lie in such circumstances.

Matti Peltomaa had noted the tension between them and continued walking.

Why did I ask her that? She has been through more than most women can endure. Stupid Finlander, that's what I am. Stupid.

Peltomaa had abandoned the topic. They increased their pace despite their injuries and had been breathless when they arrived at the meadow.

"From your map," Matti Peltomaa said, reviewing the wrinkled paper in his hand, the pencil drawing smudged from use and weather, "there's no way to avoid this open ground. The only road is to the south. That's no good as the Russians are surely using it. And there's a Russian camp to the north, just inside the border. Patrols are likely being sent out from there as well. It looks like the only way to Finland lies directly ahead."

Elin studied the map. "Wouldn't it be better to cross at night?"

"My leg is stiffening. If we wait too much longer, I won't be able to move. I see no signs of anyone about. I say let's take a chance and get across now."

Matti maintained a steady gaze. He did not look at the woman as he replied. Elin stared at the inviting woods across the meadow. Golden stalks of wild grass interrupted the snowy terrain and shifted in the slight breeze. The sun cast shadowy tendrils across the flat, white landscape as the woman scrutinized the conifer forest on the other side of the meadow.

"If you think it's the right thing to do, then let's go," Elin said.

Peltomaa raised the binoculars to his eyes. Satisfied that there were no surprises lurking in the trees, he lowered the field glasses, grabbed the Tokarev, and, using the rifle as a crutch, regained his feet.

The woman stood up, brushed snow from her fatigue trousers, and arranged her dirty hair beneath the stocking cap she'd reclaimed from her pack.

Matti Peltomaa took a deep breath and began a cautious trudge.

Crash.

Halfway across the open country, the man and the woman were startled by something moving through the forest behind them. They crouched. The noise grew louder.

A squad of Tartars hot on our heels!

Peltomaa slid the Tokarev from his shoulder, pointed the barrel in the direction of the noise, flipped off the safety, and slid his gloved right index finger into the trigger guard.

The woman unsnapped the flap of the holster on her belt, jerked steel free of leather, and took unsteady aim with the pistol. Elin's heart pounded as she forced her injured eye open. She was unnerved that they'd been discovered, that at any moment a cadre of enemy troops would be upon them with bad intent.

"Steady," the logger whispered. "Don't fire until I tell you to."

The hubbub increased. Peltomaa wondered if the cacophony wasn't the sound of a T-26 tank, the staple light armor of the Soviet army, moving through forest.

But that makes no sense, the logger thought, as he considered the notion. *There's no room in these woods for a tank. And the snow is too deep. What the hell is making that racket?*

A cow moose burst from shadow into light and trotted into the open, its hooves spraying snow, its nostrils wide from effort. Matti smiled and lowered his rifle. A second moose, a mature bull, his antler spread nearly two meters across, followed the cow into the meadow.

"The rut."

Elin lowered the pistol. The animals passed within a stone's throw of the humans.

"How's that?"

Matti Peltomaa smiled, pulled out a crushed cigarette from a pocket of his Mackinaw, struck a match, and lighted the tobacco. The American had given up on chewing tobacco and become a cigarette smoker after being interned on Kalajoki Island. He inhaled deeply before releasing a faint cloud of gray against the blue sky.

"Mating season," Peltomaa observed as the ungulates disappeared in dense brush. "Don't want to be anywhere near a bull moose during the rut. They've been known to destroy an entire dog team on the trail in order to get at a cow."

The woman nodded.

"We best follow their lead," Peltomaa said as he flicked the cigarette aside. "The border is only an hour away."

Peltomaa studied his compass beneath a thick canopy of Karelian pines. His sense of direction was disoriented. The sun had disappeared behind thick clouds. Snow was again in the air.

"By the looks of things," the logger thought aloud, "this is going to be one of hell of a winter."

"Which way to the border?" the woman asked.

When Peltomaa turned to reply, he heard a noise, placed his right index finger to his lips, returned the compass to an upper pocket in his jacket, unslung his rifle, and pointed its barrel towards the sound. Elin stood behind her protector. Her right hand groped but she was unable to retrieve the pistol in time.

Apparitions in white sheets looking very much like images of the KKK Elin had seen on American newsreels manifested from the wood and surrounded them.

"Put down the rifle," a voice commanded in Russian.

Matti Peltomaa gauged the situation.

"Put down the rifle!" the voice said again with more insistence.

Peltomaa placed the Tokarev on the ground and raised his hands in submission.

CHAPTER 8
November 30th, 1939
Leningrad

Alexis Gustafson stood on the bank of the wide and resolutely churning Bolshaya Neva River and watched wave after wave of Soviet bombers and fighter escorts drone overhead. She stared into the blue void as the warplanes darkened the Russian sky like migrating swans. Other students stopped to gawk. No one spoke. The sight was ominous, a clear indication that Stalin meant what he said: He would not rest until Finland was part of the Soviet Union.

The headlines in the papers will not proclaim this truth, Alexis thought. *Instead, the papers will say that Finland, a country the size of a grain of sand next to the Russian beach, "provoked" the assault—that Finland fired the first shot. Maybe that is true. But I doubt it. I doubt many things I hear from Soviet politicians and read in the Soviet press.*

It was near the end of November. Ice danced in the Bolshaya Neva as the river flowed towards the sea. Alexis averted her gaze from the parade of destruction crowding the high ceiling of the winter sky. Her neck ached and there was no further point, in her view, in continuing her vigil.

Stalin will do whatever Stalin wants to do, she reasoned, *just like he did in Poland.*

She did not know the whole truth of her thoughts. She did not know the details of Stalin's brutality towards the people of places he coveted. Such knowledge would be unknowable for years. Alexis, and the rest of the world, would one day learn of the Katyn Massacre—the mass execution of twenty thousand Polish military officers carried out under Comrade Beria's (the head of the NKVD's) direction. Only after the Germans occupied territory formerly controlled by the Red Army were the mass graves discovered. And even then, Stalin would discount evidence of the atrocity as another of Hitler's "Big Lies."

After the war, Alexis would also learn the fate of her adopted father. She would never know the who, the how, nor the why of Hiram Goldfarb's death—only that he had perished in a purge. Secrets, it seemed, would always be part of her life.

"An impressive sight, don't you think?"

Yuri Godenov stood next to Alexis, his right hand shading his eyes, heavy textbooks cradled in the crook of his left arm.

Alexis had grown weary of her relationship with the Russian. Though their intimacy retained power, his politics and his unfettered support of Stalinism strained her patience. And because of the times, she was not free to verbalize her opinion that Stalin had desecrated the utopian ideals of Marx, Engels, and Lenin.

"They're headed for Finland to bomb Helsinki, to kill innocent women and children. *Impressive* is not an adjective I would use to describe such a thing."

Yuri fixed stern eyes on the woman. "Actually, they aren't."

"What do you mean?"

"Those planes are headed for Tallinn."

"The bastard."

"Who are you talking about?"

"Stalin. Using little Estonia to do his dirty work, to launch air strikes against Finland."

"Be careful, my love, be careful of what you say," Yuri whispered, his eyes shifting towards a distant group of students. "You never know who works for Comrade Beria."

Alexis studied the gaggle of young people, their arms stuffed with textbooks, their faces fresh and youthful, as the crowd watched the departing airplanes.

"You're right," she said. "*You* are always right."

Yuri noted the sarcasm but did not engage in argument. He simply nodded towards the river. "The Neva will freeze soon enough," he said, changing the subject. "Do you ice skate?"

Alexis shook her head. "Father tried to teach me on the rink in Central Park when I was young. It was a disaster."

"You ski well enough," Yuri continued, walking with the woman towards her next class. "I should think skating would come easy."

"Weak ankles," Alexis explained, trying to be polite despite her mood.

"You have lovely ankles. Attached to lovely calves. Attached to lovely thighs. Attached to…"

Her eyes flashed anger. "Don't."

"Don't what?"

"Don't treat me like some common tramp. These things you speak of, or try to speak of, they are private, between you and me. They are not for public discussion."

Yuri laughed lightly. "So now you're inhibited? What game are you playing, 'Lexis? Why this sudden bit of outrage over a simple compliment?"

They arrived at the biology building, where the woman was to attend a dissection class. Yuri was headed across campus to do research in the university library. They stood facing each other. The Russian's question hung between them. There was no wind. The sun warmed the sidewalks and the lawns and melted snow that had fallen overnight. To Alexis, it felt like a fine spring day instead of the onset of the long Russian winter.

"I am tired."

Yuri studied the woman. His dark eyes scrutinized her demeanor.

She is lying. There is more between us then exhaustion. Now is not the time to push the issue. And she is starting to think and speak in dangerous ways. I need to get her to see the truth. Stalin is doing what needs to be done to secure Lenin's vision. For us. For the young people of this country. She does not see that to make an omelet a few eggs must be broken. Her parents' disappearance prevents her from taking the long view, the appropriate view, of current events. I will leave her to her pain. Later, I will try to make her understand the truth in subtle and gentle ways.

"Go to your class and then take a long, restful nap in your dorm," Yuri said quietly, his bare right hand touching the back of Alexis's neck in tenderness. "You *do* look tired."

The woman took her leave and began climbing the stairs into the biology building where the preserved carcass of a pig awaited her.

CHAPTER 9
Finland

The train lumbered south along tracks running from Joensuu to Helsinki. Elin Goldfarb sat in the crowded passenger car as sunlight flitted through dirty glass. The woman next to Elin, a mother of four children, her husband recently dead from an accident in the western forest, moaned softly. Children, three boys and a girl, their rosy cheeks blemished from dirt, their clothes barely covering skin, and their eyes wide with apprehension, sat in seats behind their mother. The children were, despite the circumstances and their meager upbringing, well behaved and presented no trouble.

Elin surmised that the guttural sound coming from the woman served a purpose. It was the only way the widow could dispense grief. And so, Elin did not pry. She simply looked away, training her eyes on close forest and passing farms as the train chugged south under a plume of black pine smoke thrown skyward by the locomotive's boiler.

It was an amazing thing, Elin `mused as she considered her good fortune, as her thoughts turned to her own circumstances, *to have been rescued by friends.*

"You are spies, no?" one of their captors had asked gruffly in Russian.

Matti Peltomaa, his leg bandaged, his hands raised in capitulation, the borrowed Luger removed from his belt, had protested.

"We're not spies. We're Finns, just like you."

The towering leader of the squad of the Finnish Home Guard had removed his white hood to reveal a handsome face covered in week-old golden stubble.

There's something familiar about that young man, Elin had thought.

The other Finns had followed their leader's example and the removal of their hoods revealed an assortment of faces. As Elin focused on the Finn's features he, in turn considered her.

"You don't remember me, do you?" he asked, moving closer.

She had shaken her head.

"Juha. Juha Rintala. I was acquainted with your daughter. We knew each other in Kontupohja, when I worked the docks, before I returned to Joensuu, my parents' home."

"Oh my!" Elin had replied in English, forgetting her surroundings.

"What did she say?" another Finn had asked.

"Oh my," she repeated in Finnish.

"Who is this?" Juha interjected, gesturing towards Matti Peltomaa.

"A friend."

Elin sensed that Rintala thought the statement implied more than it did. But the situation had not lent itself to correction so she held her tongue.

"How did you come by such a weapon?" one of the other Finns had asked Peltomaa, pointing to the Tokarev.

The question came from a middle-aged, fat faced, ruddy-complected short barrel of a man standing next to Rintala. The Finn aimed his ancient rifle, a relic from the Great War, in Peltomaa's general direction as he spoke.

"A very good question, Salminen," Juha Rintala said. "Where did you get such a weapon?"

"I killed a Tartar and took it from him."

Elin opened her mouth. "Actually, he killed a Tartar *and* a Russian officer, a lieutenant."

Rintala's attention had been drawn to the leather holster with the faded red star imprinted on its flap riding on the woman's hip.

"And you, what did *you* do to earn an officer's pistol?" Rintala asked, skepticism in his voice.

"She took care of the last Tartar, the one who stabbed me in the leg," Peltomaa had replied.

Rintala grunted, removed a white handkerchief from somewhere, and blew his nose. "Mikkel, take the Tokarev from the Finn," he had said with authority, "from Mister…What is your name?"

"Peltomaa. Matti Peltomaa."

"From Mr. Peltomaa. Your Finnish is very good, Mr. Peltomaa, but I detect an accent," the Home Guard leader said, as he directed another soldier to confiscate Elin's pistol. "American?"

Peltomaa had nodded.

"Ah. Things, they are certainly complex, no? A Canadian Finn leading a Home Guard patrol in Karelia stumbles upon two American Finns in the forest, one of whom he knows from his days on Lake Onega. These are indeed strange times," Rintala had mused, as he motioned for the two captives to fall in line.

There had been talk of Elin and Matti being interned in a refugee camp. Arguments had ensued between Juha Rintala and his superiors regarding whether or not the woman, whose communist beliefs and writings were well known, should be confined or should be allowed to travel from Joensuu to Helsinki in search of her daughter. In the end, Rintala had obtained a travel permit for Elin Goldfarb and she left one cold, clear morning on a train bound for the Finnish capital: a few Finnish marks in her pocket, an assortment of hand-me-down clothing obtained for her by Juha Rintala from women he knew in his ancestral town stuffed in an old suitcase, new vials of insulin wrapped tightly in her underthings, a small paper sack of cheese and rye bread and a bottle of spring water, and her cherished Whitman stored in her rucksack.

Peltomaa, his loyalty to the Finnish cause established by his actions in the forest, had reclaimed the automatic rifle and joined the Home Guard. There was no pay for the privilege: only a warm bed, hot food, and the promise of a fight. Matti Peltomaa did not fear the specter of dying in battle. He was a pragmatist, a man given to change, to adapting to circumstances. There was an element of fatalism to him, the same inbred grasp of unavoidable suffering that had compelled Peltomaa to leave Minnesota for Russian Karelia.

It is destiny, Peltomaa had thought, *that I fight for my parent's homeland against the communists, despite my politics.*

The only complicating factor had been Elin. Matti Peltomaa was in love with her, though he knew that she was not in love with him. Indeed, he was concerned, not for himself but for the woman's psyche, that, after the assault in the forest, Elin Goldfarb might never love again.

What really happened? Christ, had I not been off pissing in the snow, I might have stopped them. Maybe I did, he had thought as he stood on the railroad platform of the station in Joensuu watching Elin's train chug slowly away. *Maybe I arrived in time. No: Something unspeakable and dirty and evil happened. The details I do not need to know. But if she would only talk to me, only let me take up some of her burden. She's not built that way. Proud. Stubborn. Like her mother: She is just like her mother.*

Peltomaa had sighed as black soot from the locomotive settled on the wool collar of his Mackinaw. His eyes had squinted as the rumbling caboose disappeared around a bend in the tracks.

Time to get some breakfast, he had thought, his disappointment that Elin only hugged him lightly before she boarded the train rising within him anew. Peltomaa had longed for a kiss: A kiss on the cheek, if not the lips. Such was not the case. He had settled for a slight, less than passionate, sisterly hug.

Elin had completed the arduous journey from Kontupohja to Joensuu without significant symptoms of disease. Before boarding the train, she had injected herself with insulin in the privacy of the railway station lavatory. The first few hours on the train, her attention was captivated by the hustle and bustle of troops on the move: Columns of cavalry and infantry, the occasional clanking tank, convoys of trucks—both military and civilian—packed with fresh-faced, pensive men, and the hasty shouts of their leaders urging speed, filled the landscape as the train rolled south. But exhaustion compelled Elin to close her eyes. She fell asleep in the hard wooden seat as the train moved through desolate country.

How long she slept, her head wedged against the young widow's shoulder, her mouth open in a snore, drool wicking onto the widow's coat, she did not know. But when Elin awoke, the train was idling, waiting to be switched onto the track running to Viipuri where thousands of other Finns were clamoring for transportation. In Viipuri, more passenger cars would be added to the locomotive to carry more refugees. Overburdened by its load, the train would labor towards Helsinki. Two days: Two days until the woman and the others were dispatched onto the streets of the Finnish capital from the great edifice—the Helsinki rail station. Two days until Elin was safely within the protection of Finnish armed forces, units of the army, navy, Marines, air force, reserves, and Home Guard hastily thrown around the city to stop the Russians.

"Where are we?" Elin asked.

The young widow was staring vacantly out a grimy window. A thick necked and broad lapped woman, only thirty years old but aged by anxiety and loss beyond her years, the widow did not face Elin to reply.

"Viipuri."

Elin yawned, opened her rucksack, removed a paper bag, pulled out a small brick of cheese covered in newspaper, broke off a hunk, and offered it to the woman.

"Cheese?"

The woman glanced at Elin and then glanced at her children. There was not enough food for the six of them. The widow shook her head. Elin understood the woman's refusal.

"I wish I had more to share," Elin said quietly. "But I am diabetic. If I don't eat…"

"There's no need to explain," the young mother said flatly. "It was my fault for taking the children from our village without adequate preparations."

Just as Elin was about to reply, a locomotive pulling a string of boxcars roared past. Cheers rose from weary civilians. The boxcars were filled with Finnish soldiers bound for the vaunted Mannerheim Line, a system of shallow trenches and concrete machine gun emplacements running from Lake Ladoga to the Gulf of Finland, the only fortification along the border between the Soviet Union and Finland. North of Lake Ladoga there was only the terrain—swampy, forested, snow covered and wind swept—to stop the invaders. North of the Karelian Isthmus there were few permanent gun emplacements and few big guns—only Finnish men carrying small arms to thwart the Russian onslaught. North of Lake

Ladoga, beyond the slight protection of the Mannerheim Line all the way to Petsamo on the Barents Sea there were only men on skis—no tanks or airplanes—only infantry, a few odd pieces of ancient artillery, and the occasional anti-tank gun to stop the Russians.

Only men on skis, Elin Goldfarb considered. *Like Matti Peltomaa and Juha Rintala.*

"What day is it?" the young widow asked a passing conductor.

The woman's question interrupted Elin's melancholy.

"It is Thursday, ma'am. Thursday, November 30th."

"Thank you, sir," the widow replied without emotion.

The children slept on, despite the glare of daylight streaming into the car.

Elin glanced at her companion and noticed the widow's cheeks were streaked with tears. "What's wrong, Mrs. Kemi?"

Though the woman had been recalcitrant, Elin had been able to coax bits and pieces of information from the widow. Her name was Helmi Kemi. She was traveling from Lieksa in eastern Finland, though she had originally been born and raised in Pietarsaari, a Swedish-speaking city on the Gulf of Bothnia. Despite her roots, Kemi was a Finnish speaker. Her dead husband's name was Axel. Axel had worked as a logger in the forests of eastern Finland. He was only thirty-one years old when his head was crushed by a pine tree felled by another member of his crew.

"It is his birthday."

"Whose?"

More tears. "Axel's."

"Oh, dear," was all Elin could think to say.

She, like myself, is widowed, has lost the man she shared her bed with. But she, unlike me, has the fruit of his loins: four lovely children to cherish from their time together. Me, Elin thought selfishly, *all I have left of Hiram and our love is memory. Memory slowly fading in the gauzy afterglow of time. That I could not have children with Hiram because of Horace's infidelity was a cruel trick of fate, or worse, of God. Ghost children*, the woman sadly contemplated, *children of my dreams. Ghost children, as I approach fifty years old, as I recover from being raped by a filthy Tartar on the frozen ground of Soviet Karelia, is what I carry with me.*

Images of floating children in utero entered Elin Goldfarb's consciousness. She visualized tiny arms, legs, heads, and torsos as if seen by x-ray growing in her uterus. But the images were, like the fading images of Hiram, indistinct. She could not perceive details. She could not appreciate the gender or the hair or eye color of the fetuses of her mind. But they were there, occupying her selfish thoughts when the noise of airplanes overhead disrupted her melancholy.

"Out of the car!" screamed the conductor, the same one who had just walked through the passenger car with such quiet confidence. "The Russians are going to strafe the train!"

The Soviet invasion of Finland arrived, very real and personal, to the men, women, and children on that train. War did not appear as a headline in *Helsingin Sanomat* opened casually over coffee and *pulla* before work; for those on that train, war burst into their lives as sudden reality.

Elin heard the propellers of the Soviet fighter planes, a sound reminiscent of mosquitoes buzzing, as she scrambled out of her seat and helped Helmi Kemi gather the children and herd them towards the door. The passengers, despite the urgency of the conductor's plea, did not rush to escape. The evacuation was orderly and Elin Goldfarb and the Kemis were already outside the train, moving as best they could through ankle deep snow towards the woods lining the tracks, when bullets began to strike the wood and steel canopies of the train cars. Splinters flew. Windows shattered. Bombs fell—the explosions deafening and terrible—as hundreds of Finnish civilians scrambled to make the protection of adjacent trees.

A squadron of four snub-nosed monoplanes—*siipioravas*, "flying squirrels"—swooped down and opened fire with their machine guns.

"Oh my God," Helmi screamed as she scooped up the two youngest children, a boy and a girl, and ran towards brush lining the railroad right-of-way. "They mean to kill us all!"

The two eldest boys, identical twins Eino and Ernst, moved as fast as their small legs could carry them but soon fell behind their mother.

"Faster, boys, faster," Elin Goldfarb urged as the children's threadbare shoes slapped snow.

The airplanes leveled their wings and fired short bursts. Bodies fell like rows of corn sheared at harvest. There was no justice to the assault. The passengers on the train were not military targets. The men, women, and children on the ground were defenseless civilians who had nothing to do with politics or the manufactured grievances of Joseph Stalin. Still, bullets flew. Still, people fell. Eino and Ernst Kemi were twenty meters from their mother's arms when they were hit.

"They are gone, Helmi. They are gone," Elin whispered, as she restrained the stricken woman beneath the forest's canopy. "If you go out there, into that slaughter, you will leave your youngest children without a mother. Stay here. Stay here for your other children."

The squirrels pulled up and disappeared.

Thank God they have left.

Elin's perception was wishful thinking. In reality, the Soviet fighter planes were realigning themselves for a final assault. The pilots planned to drop their remaining bombs upon the Finns cowering in the trees. As the planes roared back into view, Elin Goldfarb gleaned the enemy's intent and pulled Helmi and the two remaining Kemi children to her bosom.

CHAPTER 10

Finland *attacks Western Border…*

Alexis Gustafson studied the headline of *Izvestia*, the official foreign affairs newspaper of the Soviet Union, as she sipped thick coffee in a small café at the intersection of Bol'shoy Prospekt and Neva Street. Wind lashed. Rain cascaded. Snowdrifts melted from the uncharacteristic weather, reduced to quicksilver flowing towards the Neva.

She had been right. Stalin was blaming the Finns. The border incident, where an installation on the Soviet side of the imaginary line dividing the two countries was allegedly shelled by Finnish artillery, had been recounted in the Soviet press until the average Soviet citizen could recite the "facts" as easily as a child recalls "Mary had a Little Lamb." 'Lexis sighed, folded the newspaper, placed it on her dirty plate, and studied the passage of students, university employees, professors, and citizens outside the café.

The young woman was concerned. There had been no word from her mother. Alexis had learned, through gossip emanating from the Finns of Leningrad, that Hiram Goldfarb was dead. The details were murky. Inquiries into Hiram's disappearance revealed nothing definitive. But it was also rumored that Elin was alive and working in a labor camp, though her exact location remained a mystery. Whispers and vague disclosures gave no clue as to Elin Goldfarb's precise whereabouts. It was difficult for Alexis to discern what she knew for certain and what she merely believed. And, with Yuri gone—their relationship having splintered as she became more and more vocal in her railing against Stalin's actions—Alexis had no one to confide in, no one to discuss the plan formulating in her mind.

I can search for Mother once the fighting in Finland is over. To bide my time, I can seek a transfer to Tallinn Pedagogical University by claiming I want to become a teacher. It means giving up medical school until I find Mother and we find safety. Where might that be? the young woman thought, as she sipped coffee. *What part of Europe is safe for us, for women born and raised in America but who claim Karelia as their home?*

Alexis stood up from her table, slipped into her winter coat—a gift from Yuri, a luxury that she could not afford on her meager student's stipend—and buttoned up against the cold. She had no umbrella. She had no slicker. There was nothing beyond the wool of her new coat to protect her from the rain.

"You wish to transfer to a *teacher's school* in Tallinn?"

Alexis's advisor, Professor Irina Nabokov, a thin, athletic woman in her late forties, with graying brown hair drawn into a bun, the tension of the hair style pulling her already gaunt cheeks flat against her skull, stared hard at the young student, incredulity clear in the question.

"Yes."

"That," the professor said slowly, studying a transcript of Alexis's grades, "would be a serious mistake. You are gifted, Miss Gustafson: truly gifted in the sciences and mathematics. What happened to your plan to become a physician?"

Alexis struggled to meet the woman's ebony eyes—irises so black they formed spheres of floating eternity against the professor's milky white skin.

She knows me too well. She will ferret out the lie, call me on the deception I am about to utter. Still, I cannot be forthright. I cannot be open with Professor Nabokov. I can trust no one with the true purpose behind my request.

Alexis fidgeted with the sleeve of her blouse. "I have become disillusioned," the young woman lied. "I want to be done with school. I have enough credits to earn my instructional certificate in less than a year."

The professor pressed her thin body against the back of her chair and grimaced. "A teacher…"

Alexis nodded.

"And there is nothing I can do or say to dissuade you from this folly?"

Alexis shook her head.

Irina Nabokov pursed nearly invisible lips. "Well. I cannot prohibit you from leaving here and going to Tallinn. But Alexis…" There was a short pause as the professor considered the younger woman. "May I call you by your familiar name?"

"Yes."

The change in the professor's approach made the student nervous.

What is she trying to do, softening her tone, making it appear that we are equals?

"Good. We have known each other, what, three years? I am glad you allow me this privilege. Alexis, I must know the answer to one question."

"Which *is*?" Because they were conversing as familiars, Alexis allowed a hint of disrespect to color her question.

"Why in Stalin's name would you ever consider giving up a chance to live in Moscow, the capital of our nation and the place of advanced learning—for Tallinn—a backwater of ignorance?"

Alexis sighed. The weight of creating fiction was tiring. "The truth?"

"Yes, that would be refreshing, don't you think?"

The student considered the best line of fabrication. "There's a man…"

Nabokov's eyes arched. "Ah."

"…an officer in the Red Army."

The professor touched her right index finger to her chin. "And this, this 'connection,' if you will, is serious?"

"It is."

There was a slight pause. "But I thought you already had a 'friend,' a young man who was also studying to be a physician…"

"Yuri. Yuri Godenov. That," Alexis said quietly, as if she was still lamenting the breakup, which she was not, "has been over for a while."

"And this soldier, he is willing to make an honest woman of you? He is not married. He is of suitable age?"

"Thirty," Alexis lied. "He is thirty. A lieutenant in the artillery. An honest man. A good man. And unmarried."

"He is a career soldier?"

Alexis nodded.

"Doesn't sound like the vision you came here to fulfill."

"Will you send a transcript of my grades to the school in Tallinn?"

Irina Nabokov concentrated on the girl's eyes and noted their contradictory irises, a condition the professor had marveled at the first time she observed it.

"I will. Tomorrow. By air post."

The young woman stood up. "Thank you, Professor. I know you don't agree with my decision but this is what I want. My life will be less stressful if I can begin working with children and begin forgetting."

The older woman nodded. There was no need for the student to verbalize what she meant. Alexis Gustafson was not the only young woman attending the university whose family had vanished. The key was not to ignore the emptiness caused by such events but to avoid publicly questioning decisions made in Moscow and move on with life.

Maybe, the professor thought as Alexis turned and walked out the door, *that is exactly what she is trying to do.*

CHAPTER 11
Viipuri, Finland

Two Fokker D-XXI's plunged, the blue swastikas of the Finnish Air Force visible on their fuselages. Elin clutched Helmi Kemi and the surviving Kemi children as the Russian "squirrels" re-appeared and dove on the civilians hiding in forest. The enemy pilots seemed unaware of the Finnish fighter planes seeking advantage and made no attempt to abort their bombing runs.

"Our boys!" a male voice shouted from the crowd on the ground. "Our boys are here!"

Elin's eyes locked on the Finnish monoplanes diving on the Russian fighters. She saw flashes from the lead Fokker's wings. The flares were visible long before she heard the rat-a-tat-tat sound of machine guns. As the Finnish planes attacked, the Russian pilots finally realized the danger and attempted to pull up.

"They'll not let the bastards get away!" another male voice cried out.

"God speed our boys," a woman standing next to Helmi Kemi said, in a stage whisper.

Helmi paid little mind to the ballet above the forest. Her eyes were riveted on the snowy field where her two sons lay, their bodies lost in a heap of civilians who had fallen in the open country between train and trees. Helmi Kemi wanted desperately to make her way to her sons but Elin held her fast.

"We will go to them when it's safe," Elin said firmly, as the lead Fokker emptied its guns on a climbing squirrel.

Smoke billowed from the engine of the Russian airplane. The snub-nosed fighter stalled and then, after a moment of hesitation, tipped towards the ground. The Finnish pilot wasted little time pursuing dead prey. The drone of accelerating propellers echoed through the air. Machine gun bursts drew cheers from the civilians. A second Russian plane disintegrated. The lead Fokker's wingman caught a third Russian fighter as it tried to escape and sent it plummeting to earth. Of the four squirrels that had attacked the train, one survived. Though its tail had been hit, the last enemy airplane was still faster than its pursuers, which allowed the squirrel to evade the Fokkers and limp back to the nearest Russian airfield.

"Too bad they didn't get them all," another woman lamented.

The Finnish fighters came in low and wagged their wings. Surviving passengers from the train cheered. Elin Goldfarb held the youngest Kemi boy's hand and cradled the toddler's little sister in the crook of her arm as Helmi Kemi ran to the dead.

CHAPTER 12
Tallinn, Estonia

The new student sat in the front row of the composition class scribbling intently. Marina Ostov, a tall and business-like teacher, stood stork-like over the young woman, thinking critical thoughts about the student's penmanship but marveling at the language skills of the storyteller.

"Your Russian is very good," Ostov said. "But your handwriting is…" The teacher searched for the right adjective.

"…sloppy?" the young woman offered, looking up from the lined pages of her writing journal.

"Yes, that's the perfect word—'sloppy'. You are concise in your composition. But your penmanship? Yes, 'sloppy' is a good description for the scrawls you've placed across the paper!"

Alexis Gustafson smiled.

Since coming to the Tallinn Pedagogical University, Alexis's angst had lessened. Not that she was any less strident or stubborn in her ways. She had not changed *everything* about her personality in the six months she had been in Tallinn. But a significant calm had descended over the young woman.

Gone also was the inherent contradiction of being in a relationship with a Stalinist. Alexis had taken no man into her confidence since shedding Yuri Godenov and leaving Leningrad. She had ignored the catcalls from Russian soldiers and sailors milling around Tallinn as she walked past them going about her business and she had rebuffed more respectable offers of companionship from Estonian men. Her focus was on completing school, waiting for the war to end, and securing passage from Tallinn to Finland, where, if she made the right connections, she hoped to find her mother. Finnish-speakers from Soviet Karelia had swarmed across the Finnish-Karelian border in the days leading up to the Winter War, a reality that prompted Alexis to be hopeful.

Someone must know. Someone living in the refugee camps must know something of Mother's fate.

The Finnish government did not welcome Finnish-speaking refugees from the Soviet Union. Many who entered Finland from Karelia were communists. Finnish politicians believed that the refugees could not be trusted. They were believed, despite contrary appearances, to be in sympathy with the Russians. And so, the refugees were relegated to internment camps located far from the Russian border so as not to pose a security threat. It was in these camps that Alexis Gustafson hoped to find information about her mother, if not, by some great stroke of luck, Elin Goldfarb herself.

The Winter War appeared to be a costly mistake for the Soviet Union. Alexis gleaned this opinion, not from reading *Izvestia*, which claimed that a great Soviet victory was nigh at hand, but from clandestine discussions with other Finnish speakers in Tallinn. She was careful to conceal her personal opinions about the war. She maintained friendships with a few men and women she trusted, but devoted the majority of her energy to her studies, not the discussion of world politics.

I have no control over what Stalin will do tomorrow, she thought, *but I can control what I am doing, what I am learning, how I am perceived by my teachers.*

Her goal was to attain a teaching position in a Russian language school on the Estonian island of Hiiumaa.

There are teaching positions posted for the schools in Kärdla. It will take some planning to carry out my mission, to travel to Helsinki and find Mother once the fighting has ceased. I have no desire to follow Mother into slavery and I have every intention of finding her and rescuing her from such a fate, God willing!

The issue of God had embedded itself in Alexis's mind, in her being, after reading a Finnish language Bible during her stay in Leningrad. It was during this casual, self-guided study of scripture that Alexis arrived at a place of reverent acceptance. Her conversion was not rooted in Saint Paul's version of Christianity, which Alexis believed unwisely supplemented rules pronounced in Leviticus with more rules, but of the pure, easily understood, less onerous language of Saint Matthew.

Blessed are the poor in spirit,
for theirs is the kingdom of heaven.
Blessed are they who mourn,
for they shall be comforted.
Blessed are the meek,
for they shall possess the earth.
Blessed are they who hunger and thirst for justice,
for they shall be satisfied.
Blessed are the merciful,
for they shall obtain mercy.
Blessed are the pure of heart,
for they shall see God.
Blessed are the peacemakers,
for they shall be called sons of God.

Blessed are they who suffer persecution for justice's sake,
for theirs is the kingdom of heaven.

These are simple ideals to live by, Alexis had decided, after discovering Matthew 5:3-10 in the quiet of her dorm room at St. Petersburg State University. Her anger at something Yuri had said or done had left her seething and near the breaking point until she embraced the Beatitudes.

Some of the young Finnish men and women she encountered in Leningrad were Laestadians. Though prevalent in some rural areas of America (in the form of the Apostolic Lutheran Church) the Laestadian movement had not been represented in the circles Alexis and her parents frequented in New York. And there had been no discernible Laestadian influence in Karelia, at least not amongst the immigrants who came there in response to Oscar Corgan's battle cry. It was only in Leningrad, where the strict rules of the Lutheran sect bubbled beneath the surface in some young folks seeking answers, answers that communism did not provide, where Alexis Gustafson came face to face with Laestadian doctrine. She knew in an instant that the conservative faith was not for her. But the fervor of the fundamentalists she encountered did have a positive aspect: Martina Hultula was a Laestadian and it was her Bible that Alexis borrowed and read in hopes of finding a faith, a belief system, to replace communism. In the end, it had been Saint Matthew's reporting of the Sermon on the Mount that brought Alexis to her knees in prayer.

A mechanical bell rang in the classroom.

"Do not forget to work on your verbs, your possessives, and your tenses," Madam Ostov said, as she towered above the scurrying young women, the students' intent upon packing away their composition books and pencils and escaping the classroom for the spring weather outside. "You have much to learn before your matriculation in June."

Because of Alexis's prior schooling, she'd been placed in a section of prospective teachers nearing the culmination of their instruction. The courses Alexis had completed in Leningrad served her well. She was slated to become a secondary school science teacher upon graduation from the Tallinn Pedagogical University in June of 1940. It was March of that year and the only portion of Alexis's training that remained to be completed was a stint as a student teacher. Her Russian had improved to the point where she was no longer nervous about the challenge of instructing children in that language. And her knowledge of Estonian, a tongue closely related to Finnish, was increasing daily as she worked shifts at *Rohke Söökla* near the school where she was posted as an apprentice teacher.

Alexis's apartment, a one-room efficiency she shared with another student, Marikka Parming, a twenty-four-year-old Estonian woman on the cusp of her own graduation as a social science teacher, was only a block from the school and a two minute stroll from Alexis's work. The wages Alexis earned waiting tables were barely enough to pay her share of the rent for the third-floor flat that she and Marikka occupied, allow for groceries, and some small luxuries such as real coffee when it was available in the poorly stocked communal stores run by the E.S.S.R. Alexis had, in an effort to calm her nerves as she formulated her plans, taken up smoking. She found herself, as she studied in the dim gas light of the flat late into the night, lighting up Russian cigarette after cigarette, drawing stale smoke into her lungs in an unsuccessful attempt to steady her countenance.

• • •

"Why do you read that gibberish?" Marikka had asked one evening not long after Alexis responded to the young Estonian's posting on the university bulletin board for a roommate.

The reference was to Alexis having purchased her own Finnish Bible from a second-hand bookstore. The bookseller told Alexis in broken Finnish that she was lucky to find a copy of the Good Book at all. Most copies of the Bible available in Estonian second hand shops had been confiscated after the capitulation. "To find such a beautiful version of the Bible in your language," the old man had said, "is truly a miracle."

Alexis had not corrected the man. Few people she spent time with or encountered in Tallinn knew the truth: that she was not a native of Karelia, as she claimed, but an American. Her identification and travel papers indicated that she was from Kondopoga, which supported her deception. Of her friends in Estonia, only her roommate knew the truth: that Alexis had been born in Duluth, Minnesota, lived as a child in New York City, and immigrated to Karelia. Marikka was not privy to all the details of Alexis's past, only bits and pieces of the story sufficient to satisfy her curiosity, a curiosity fueled by her recognition that Alexis's Estonian and Finnish carried an unusual lilt betraying something foreign, something exotic.

"I find reading the Gospels, particularly the Gospels of Matthew and Mark, to be comforting," Alexis had replied to Marikka's criticism. "I am struggling to understand what it all means. But I am intrigued."

Marikka had inhaled smoke from her own cigarette as Alexis stubbed out a butt on a cracked saucer serving as their mutual ashtray. Marikka's eyes had locked on the Finnish print inside the book before continuing.

"I tried reading the Bible once. On a dare. I don't remember who dared me," the young Estonian woman had said, tousling her thick blond hair off her forehead, revealing blue green eyes and a round face, "but I couldn't get past 'Numbers'."

Alexis had smiled. "The Old Testament is, outside of 'The Song of Solomon,' a challenge," she had agreed. "So many 'begats,' followed by so many rules. Rules such as the one decreeing that farmers who plant two crops in the same field be stoned to death. Seems fairly harsh, as penalties go, don't you agree?"

Marikka had smiled but made no reply.

Alexis found she enjoyed Marikka's company. Though tired to her bones from working at the diner and mentally drained from having to fend off suggestions of intimacy from men who took their meals in the café, Alexis was not too tired to discuss religion with her roommate. Such evenings distracted Alexis from her decision regarding men. She had sworn off male companionship after Yuri Godenov and had vowed to remain celibate until she found her mother.

"Still," Marikka had finally said, "I don't understand your dedication to an old book of fables. You would be better served, in my view, spending your time at your studies, getting ready for your final examinations." The Estonian woman paused. "They are coming up very quickly and I know you want to pass them so that you can fulfill your dream of living on an Estonian Island teaching science to little communists."

Alexis had struggled mightily to maintain her composure. She had no interest in disrupting her relationship with Marikka by getting involved in an argument. Before she found the calm of the Beatitudes, Alexis's natural inclination when confronted had been to invoke a quick tongue and a sharp retort. But that part of her personality had been undeniably altered by her newfound faith.

Nothing will be accomplished by sparring with Marikka. I need her, need to keep living with her, to make it to graduation. There is no point in trying to change her views. She will believe what she will believe. And I am free, at least in the privacy of my mind and heart, to do the same.

"It's late," Alexis had said at last, closing the Bible, bookmarking the "Parable of the Sower" in Mark, her favorite passage after the Beatitudes. "I have to work early in the morning."

Marikka, who had never known the "old" Alexis, the feisty, argumentative, strident young girl who took a Finnish dockworker to bed over the objections of her parents, stood up from the table, walked to the room's only closet, lifted her cot from the enclosure, opened the canvas and wood bed, and began smoothing a sheet across its length. Alexis followed suit. When both girls had changed into their nightgowns,

Marikka turned off the room's solitary gas light, plummeting the space into darkness. The city's night sounds migrated into the room as an accompaniment to Alexis's recitation of the Lord's Prayer:

Isä meidän, joka olet taivaissa,
Pyhitetty olkoon sinun nimesi.
Tulkoon sinun valtakuntasi.
Tapahtukoon sinun tahtosi,
myös maan päällä niin kuin taivaassa.
Anna meille tänä päivänä
meidän jokapäiväinen leipämme.
Ja anna meille meidän syntimme anteeksi,
niin kuin mekin anteeksi annamme niille,
jotka ovat meitä vastaan rikkoneet.
Äläkä saata meitä kiusaukseen,
vaan päästä meidät pahasta.
Sillä sinun on valtakunta
ja voima ja kunnia iankaikkisesti.
Aamen.

Sleep had overtaken Alexis that night as she dreamed of the sea, of sand dunes, and a little white and green cottage overlooking an Estonian beach.

CHAPTER 13
Helsinki

They waited in a bomb shelter. Helmi Kemi's youngest children snuggled against their world-weary mother. Elin Goldfarb and Helmi Kemi held hands as bomb after bomb descended upon the city above them.

The Russian attack continued. Ilyushin BD-3 and Tupolev bombers, part of the 3,000-plane Soviet Air Force, flew sortie after sortie against Helsinki. In contrast to the vast Soviet air armada, Finland possessed an air force of 162 antiquated aircraft. The best of the lot were Fokker D-XXIs (like those that had appeared above the idling train in Viipuri). The Finns possessed but thirty-one of these slow, fixed-landing-gear monoplanes; planes whose design was outmoded before their purchase by the Finnish government from the Dutch in the mid-1930s. They were the best the Finns had and, in the hands of good pilots, caused modest damage to incoming Soviet bombers but the Fokkers were too few in number to have any real impact.

Forty-four Brewster B-239s, surplus fighter planes donated by the United States, would eventually arrive in Finland. Nicknamed the "Buffalo," the Brewsters were a step up for the Finnish pilots, despite their relative obsolescence. But the Brewsters weren't deployed until after the Winter War and there were too few Finnish fighter planes to dent the onslaught of Soviet flying machines, which day after day after day dropped ordinance on the civilian populations of Helsinki and other Finnish cities.

"God, I wish the Russians would go away and leave us in peace," an elderly woman moaned, as she rocked to and fro on a wooden bench next to Elin.

With sounds of crying, farting, coughing, the blowing of noses, and whispered prayers to the Almighty reverberating through the cold subterranean space, Elin shut her eyes and thought back to a period in her life when she was not tired, afraid, or anxious.

On the train from St. Petersburg to Petroskoi: That was the last time I felt safe. I felt optimistic. I felt truly blessed.

She refused to call the former Russian capital by its communist name, "Leningrad." She was done with communism, done with the secular faith she had acquired from her husband and adhered to for more than a decade.

What did communism give to me? Hiram's death? Separation from my country, from my people, from my daughter? Communism led to the destruction of my dignity at the hands of those filthy animals on the way to Joensuu. Gylling's dream died for me the day I stepped off the train in Petroskoi. I was just too much in love with Hiram, too deeply enamored with communist doctrine, to see the blight, to comprehend the cancer.

She watched the Kemi children slumber, their heads resting in their mother's lap, their soft snores echoing off the cement walls of the shelter.

And Helmi's loss? Incalculable. Again, caused by the edicts of a madman. Strafing civilians? Bombing cathedrals and train stations and fish markets? What has that to do with military tactics? Stalin and Hitler are two peas in a pod: two "heads" of the same coin. There are rumors of what Hitler intends towards the Jews. There are stories about the Ukrainians Stalin starved to death. These men are leaders? These men are saviors?

Explosions shook the shelter. Dust drifted down on the civilians like dirty snow. The tunnel walls vibrated and, even seven meters below the destruction of Helsinki, the sound was deafening.

"Why are they doing this?" Helmi moaned the words.

Elin patted the back of the woman's hand. "There is no answer to that question other than, 'because they can'."

"I wish to God someone would put a bullet in Stalin's brain," the old woman muttered.

"Hitler's too," another woman, a mother of two teenaged girls sitting on the far side of the bomb shelter, added.

"Amen," an old man, his cigarette stub flaring in the poor light, whispered.

The shaking and shifting of the ground above them went on for an hour. And then, as quickly as it began, the raid was over.

It was night when Elin and Helmi and the children climbed the concrete stairs leading from below the ground onto Fredrikinkatu. The scene that greeted them was surreal, as if a framed by a director on a motion picture set attempting to recreate the havoc of war. Firefighters in turnout gear and steel helmets wrestled with hoses and poured water onto burning steel, wood, and concrete heaps that had once been apartments, shops, and offices. The moon was clouded over. Ash contaminated snow covered the sidewalks and streets, but no new snow fell as Elin, Helmi, and the children emerged from Helsinki's underworld.

Flames waxed and waned as fire fighters scurried from emergency to emergency. Here and there, muffled voices cried out from beneath collapsed buildings. Soldiers on leave threw off their gray winter coats and joined in the search for survivors. Retired policemen, pressed into service due to a shortage of able-bodied men, tried their best to establish order and assign volunteers to the most emergent tasks. Off-duty nurses stepped out of the wide-eyed crowd to work alongside off-duty doctors, dentists, chiropractors, and ambulance attendants. The streets were clogged: No traffic could negotiate the crushed and burned out cars and trucks and horse-drawn wagons blocking the thoroughfares. Acrid smoke curled into the fresh winter air and made breathing difficult. Folks scurried away, handkerchiefs over their mouths and noses, intent upon inspecting their homes, or what was left of their homes, for damage.

"Oh my," Elin whispered as she stood next to Helmi and the children on the wet sidewalk as snow melted from the heat of the surrounding fires.

"If they can do this to Helsinki," Helmi Kemi observed sadly, "there is no hope."

A column of the Home Guard marched smartly around smoldering hulks in the street and stopped in front of a demolished apartment complex. An officer barked. Men fell out of formation, stacked their rifles, and began to assist the civilians already at work. Shovels, picks, and sledgehammers materialized. The men and women lending aid seemed to know their roles. There was no bickering, no conflict: the people of Helsinki simply rolled up their sleeves and did what needed doing.

"We'd best see if the Woman's and Orphan's building is still standing," Elin said, touching her companion's hand again.

They had been in the city for a month, living as refugees in a shelter sponsored by the Red Cross in the Kamppi neighborhood two blocks from the air raid shelter. Helmi and her children shared a large room with five other displaced women and their children. Elin had a cot and a military footlocker in a room with thirty other single, childless women of all shapes, sizes, and ages: their only commonality was that they were female refugees—women made homeless by war. Elin's belongings fit easily in the wooden box on the floor. Her distressed copy of *Leaves of Grass* was hidden beneath her pillow; Whitman's poems being Elin's only comfort amidst the unceasing sadness and desolation she felt amongst strangers.

They had buried the Kemi boys in an unmarked grave in the Johanneksenkirkko graveyard. The minister had prayed old Lutheran prayers over the tiny coffins. The only adults in attendance other than the pastor and the gravediggers were Helmi and Elin. Eeva, Helmi's infant daughter, and Juhani, her three-year-old son, were not present. Helmi Kemi was determined to save her surviving children further trauma. She carried the burden of her boys' deaths on her shoulders, as weak as they were, and was unwilling to share her burden with anyone. Helmi had been subdued during the committal. She had not cried as the coffins were covered in snow-moistened earth. She had simply looked on as if she was a spectator.

The Red Cross came to the shelter and handed out Christmas presents for the children: an apple and a rubber ball for each boy, a pear and a rag doll for each girl. It wasn't much, in Elin Goldfarb's estimation, a paltry Christmas for the Kemi children in the aftermath of tragedy. With the few Finnish marks remaining in her pocketbook, Elin visited a bakery near the shelter and bought caramel rolls to share with Helmi and the children. She was gone only a few moments. She asked Helmi to accompany her but the younger woman declined. There was something distant, almost disconnected, in the manner of Helmi's reply.

Christmas is hard enough, what with all the anticipation and expectations. Imagine, Elin thought, as she hugged Helmi and left the woman washing clothes in the basement laundry room of the shelter, the Kemi children upstairs playing with newfound friends, *what it must be like to confront Christmas after burying your children?*

The day was sunny and bright as Elin Goldfarb walked to the bakery. New snow had fallen during the night but ever-efficient Helsinkians had cleared the sidewalks of the city as if they were Santa's elves working on deadline. A tentative sun embraced the reporter's face. The morning's warmth brought a sense of life, an aspect of new beginning to Elin Goldfarb despite her overall malaise.

Elin lingered inside the bakery relishing the odor of fresh pastries and breads after making her purchase. Her mood had improved. A smile overtook her as she stepped outside. As Elin walked back to the shelter, she greeted folks she had met during her brief stay in Helsinki, folks who lived and worked in the vicinity of the Woman's and Orphan's Building. The sun melted carefully arranged snow banks. Water pooled on the sidewalks and streets before forming rivulets that flowed into street drains that emptied into the sea.

It is a good day to be alive.

"Helmi," Elin called out as she walked into the large room occupied by the Kemi family and other mothers and their children.

"She hasn't returned from the laundry," one of the mothers said quietly, her six-year-old daughter holding Eeva Kemi in her lap on the cold maple floor, the girls stacking wooden blocks that Juhani Kemi joyfully knocked down.

"I brought treats," Elin said happily. "You're welcome to some while I go find Helmi," she added, placing the paper sack of pastries on a nearby table.

Elin descended the basement staircase. An electric light bulb cast shadows against the stone walls and the cement floor of the cellar.

"Helmi?"

There was no answer.

"I brought sweets for you and the little ones," Elin called out.

That's odd, Elin thought as she approached the washtub. Cold water ran from the tap over clothing piled in the basin. *Maybe she needed to use the restroom.*

Elin turned off the faucet and looked about the dank basement. Sunbeams entered the space through small windows along the opposite wall. The daylight illumed a wooden chair tipped on its side and resting on the floor. Helmi Kemi's body dangled above the spilled chair, her lifeless form suspended by a freshly laundered dress tied to a wooden beam.

CHAPTER 14
Tallinn

Alexis Gustafson waited tables, working feverishly under the scrutiny of the diner's owner, Margit Köiv, a slip of an old woman. Though Alexis's face wore a perpetual smile for customers, her cheery demeanor was a ruse. Her hair, once magnificently golden, was braided into a dull, yellow rope. Her disparate eyes, once bright and expressive, were clouded with doubt. In contrast to Alexis's deflated persona, Margit flitted from table to table like a honeybee—her voice syrupy, her manner intimate and friendly—as she made sure patrons knew how much she appreciated their trade.

Two weeks, Alexis thought, as she bused a stack of dirty dishes off a recently vacated table, *two weeks and I will be done with college and on my way to Hiiumaa Island. I want to move to Kärdla, find a place to live, and be settled in before the children come back to school.*

The weight of the plates and cups and saucers in her arms slowed Alexis as she skirted tables filled with dinner customers, smoke from cigarettes and pipes lazily curling in the still, hot air of the diner. Voices rose and fell in earnest discussion. Alexis eavesdropped as she moved towards the kitchen with her load. Most of the discussions concerned the Winter War and the terrible, terrible price Finland was paying to maintain its freedom. But one conversation, a subdued dialogue between three shipbuilders—a giant in his early thirties, a smaller, more intense man of about the same age, and a tall, handsome, blade-like adolescent on the cusp of manhood—sitting at the table closest to the door to the kitchen, caught her ear.

She stopped at the roller system used to send dirty dishes into the kitchen to a lone dishwasher trying to keep pace. Alexis's interest was piqued, not by the content of the discussion, but by the profile of the youngest customer. Though she had sworn off men, she was not blind.

It does no harm to look.

"Shit," the smallest man in the group said despondently.

"You can say that again," the young one, the one Alexis was interested in, said as he stabbed gristle.

"Why in God's name did you pull a knife?" Alexis heard the giant ask.

The young man leaned back in his chair, wiped gravy from a corner of his mouth with a linen napkin, and placed the napkin on his empty plate. "I had no choice."

"He's right, Big Peeter," the smaller man said. "Damned Russians outnumbered us and the bartender wasn't able to break it up. In fact, the bartender never even made it through the crowd once he conked the skinny little bastard who started it all on the noggin. Some bouncer he is," the man lamented.

"Barkeeps aren't bouncers," Big Peeter corrected. "They're only cashiers with *kepps*. You can't expect a barkeep to save you from communists." The big man added, grinning sheepishly as he considered his hands before continuing. "No choice, you say?"

The gangly youth surveyed the entrance to the café while removing a box from his front shirt pocket. He selected a Russian cigarette, held it to his mouth between his right index and middle fingers, flicked a match, and took a drag before answering.

"Liisu was the cause of it all."

The small man shook his head vigorously. "Not really. When the skinny sailor and his buddies were surrounding us and I jumped the one guy and rode him like a bull, Liisu was screaming for us to stop. She didn't encourage the fracas, Kristian. She tried to prevent it."

The one called "Kristian" blew a smoke ring. Alexis watched his handsome face out of a corner of her eye as she slid plates along rollers. The boy didn't look like he'd been in a fight. His face bore no bruises, no black eyes as evidence of a scuffle.

"You might be right, Miik." Kristian replied, after a significant pause. "Big Peeter, you asked why I pulled my knife. What was I supposed to do? We were outnumbered eight to two. Three, if you count the bartender. Miik and I were in danger of being beat to shit by those goddamned Bolsheviks."

"Being Bolshevik had nothing to do with their behavior," Miik corrected.

"You're right," the young man agreed, drawing on his cigarette. "They were just assholes. I didn't discuss politics with them," the boy added, through a wry smile.

"You stabbed one of them?" Big Peeter asked.

Miik responded before the boy could. "Damn right. The biggest one tried to back him into a corner. The kid was so fast, like the sting of a hornet, with that blade. Had the sailor's arm bleeding like a virgin after her first time…" The master electrician stopped, looked in Alexis's direction, and lowered his voice deferentially. "Anyway, Kristian cut the guy and the rest of the Russians backed off. I rode my sailor to the ground and smashed his skull on the floor until he was out cold. Two down and the other six wanted no part of us."

"The police will be looking for you. You know that, don't you?" Big Peeter asked, before sipping water from a glass tumbler. "You assaulted a Russian sailor. That's not something the captain of the guy's ship is likely to let pass."

Kristian felt Alexis's gaze and returned her stare. "Would you like to join us?" he asked sarcastically.

"No thank you," the waitress said, embarrassment clear in her voice.

Kristian couldn't place the woman's accent but knew she was not a native Estonian speaker.

Big Peeter grinned. "Oh shit! Not this again," the big electrician said. "You just got done defending yourself because of the last woman you slept with."

Alexis fled to her work.

"I'd fight a hundred Russians for one night with that," Miik Salu murmured, as he watched Alexis move across the room to wait on another table.

She has the most unusual eyes I've ever seen.

Nigul Kristian did not voice his observation. The young electrician kept his own counsel as he raised the cigarette to his lips and drew smoke.

"She is striking," Big Peeter finally admitted, placing his empty water glass back on the greasy surface of the table. "Well, I'd best be getting back to the missus," he said, standing up from his chair. "She's likely into her second glass of vodka."

Peeter's wife, Ingrid, had been a closet alcoholic until he discovered her stash of liquor hidden in their flat. They had five children, all under the age of ten, children whose behavior was, as observed by Nigul Kristian on the occasions he'd been at the Saul residence, akin to that of wild baboons. The problem was, with Ingrid completely sauced and Big Peeter being so docile, no one undertook the role of disciplinarian with the Saul brood.

As a consequence, the Saul apartment was a war zone, a dangerous place for visitors. Big Peeter had tried to cajole and argue with his long-suffering wife about her tippling. His remonstrations had accomplished one thing and one thing only: Ingrid Saul's drinking was now public, out of the shadows of shame and into the bright light of scrutiny.

Nigul knew the extent of Ingrid Saul's addiction and knew how it afflicted his friend. He stood up and placed a hand on the big man's broad back. "Maybe she will stop."

Peeter nodded. "When she's dead," the big man whispered. "When the vodka kills her."

Miik Salu wasn't a close enough friend to add commentary. The conversation remained solely between the young man and his mentor.

Kristian tried to think of something compassionate, something intelligent, by way of a response to his friend's lament. As Kristian struggled to respond, the door to the restaurant opened and before anyone at the table could react, five Estonian policemen were in their space.

"Which one of you is Nigul Kristian?"

Silence greeted the question.

"Out with it or we'll take the whole lot of you in. Which of you is Nigul Kristian?"

Every head in the place turned towards the encounter. Alexis stood off to one side, her hands clasped in front of her apron, her eyes riveted on the tall young man and his friends.

"See here now," Margit said in a commanding voice as she re-entered the dining room, "what's this all about?"

A door slammed behind the café owner. She moved quickly and with purpose, positioning her waif-like body between the police and the electricians.

"Move aside," one of the policemen, the biggest of the five, said in a firm voice. "We have a job to do."

The woman shook her head. "Not before you tell me what this is all about."

The leader of the contingent nodded. "Fair enough, Margit. You know me. I know you. This man," the officer continued, pointing the business end of his baton at Kristian, "meets the description of someone who pulled a knife on a Russian last night. Word is: it was an unprovoked attack. The blade severed a nerve and a tendon in the Russian's arm. Surgery was required. This man needs to answer for his crime."

Margit looked at Kristian. "Is this true?"

"No," Kristian mumbled.

Miik offered his version of the altercation: "It was the Russians who started it. Over a woman. Someone thought this boy was making eyes at her. They attacked us. It was eight against two, simple as that. The boy was only defending himself. The bartender will vouch for us."

The policeman studied Kristian, taking in the scabbard on the boy's belt. "That the knife you used?

Nigul nodded.

"An admission, sergeant," one of the smaller cops said excitedly. "He's just admitted to assault and battery!"

The policeman leading the investigation removed handcuffs from his belt. "Turn around, son. We have to take you in."

Kristian obliged and put his hands behind his back. The policeman clamped the handcuffs in place.

The officer removed Nigul's knife from its sheath. "Evidence," he said, handing it to one of his companions.

"You're making a mistake," Miik Salu said quietly. "I told you: he didn't do anything wrong. I know people in the Party, in the government. You're making a big mistake."

The sergeant didn't respond. Margit and Big Peeter stepped aside as the policemen led the taciturn youth through the café. Patrons watched with great interest.

Alexis Gustafson's eyes followed the strapping young man and his captors until the group stopped at the restaurant's exit. And as Nigul Kristian waited for someone to open the door, he looked back at Alexis Gustafson and smiled.

CHAPTER 15
December 23rd, 1939
Tolvajärvi, Finland

He thought of her often as he worked birch skis across sticky, early winter snow. That Matti Peltomaa was in love with Elin Goldfarb was a given. But the war—the war brought an intensity to his feelings that made it difficult to put Elin's image out of his mind. Emotions—stirrings he had been able to overcome and relegate to the recesses of his psyche—bubbled to the surface like sulfur water at a hot spring. As Peltomaa skied through the wilderness surrounding Tolvajärvi, a small village west of Joensuu—gliding through silent forest, the Tokarev strapped to his back, bandoliers of Russian bullets crisscrossing his Mackinaw beneath the white sheet he'd draped over himself as camouflage, grenades hanging from the equipment belt snugged around his waist—Elin's face, the vivid edges of her jaw, her hazel eyes, her sturdy body, travelled every stride of his journey with him.

I should have told her how I felt at the train station in Joensuu before she left for Helsinki. Stupid. No, weak kneed. That's it. I was afraid—afraid she would reject me. She has loved two men in her life: Andrew Maki and Hiram Goldfarb. Can she love yet another? Can she find a way to love me? I was unwilling—during the instant we embraced—to find out. Despite what they say about me in the field, I am not so brave. I am afraid of a woman.

Carl Gustav Mannerheim, Commander-in-Chief of the Finnish Armed Forces, had miscalculated. He believed that Stalin would throw only three infantry divisions at the Finns north of Lake Ladoga. The Finnish commander assumed that Stalin's main push, the largest concentration of effort, would come on the Karelian Isthmus. This assessment proved partially correct: The main Soviet force *did* attack on the Isthmus. But instead of only three Soviet divisions being deployed north of Lake Ladoga, there were seven, which left Finnish forces at Tolvajärvi, where Matti Peltomaa and Juha Rintala were posted, woefully under strength.

Mannerheim also miscalculated the improvements the Russians had made on the Murmansk to Leningrad rail line, improvements that allowed for the easy redistribution of troops and equipment. The speed with which the Red Army could adapt because of the railroad was something that Mannerheim did not appreciate until the enemy was on the brink of taking Ägläjärvi. Before the arrival of Lieutenant Colonel Aaro Pajari, the rag-tag defensive force protecting Tolvajärvi (including the Home Guard unit Peltomaa and Rintala were assigned to) was undisciplined. When Pajari assumed his new command, the Red Army was close to taking Tolvajärvi. By reorganizing his men and impressing upon them the discipline to not only stand their ground but to push back against the Russian invaders, Pajari stemmed the tide at Tolvajärvi and ultimately claimed the first major victory for the Finnish Defense Forces. By the end of December, as Peltomaa and his squad skied through snow covered trees east of town, the front had stabilized and the enemy advance had stalled. An isolated element of the Red Army remained over-extended and it was this enemy position that Peltomaa's unit, led by Sergeant Juha Rintala, was about to engage.

"How do you know so much about the area?" Juha Rintala asked Marko Erkkilä, as the two Finnish soldiers lay on frozen, snowy ground, their white sheets concealing them from the enemy.

Erkkilä—whose intelligence regarding the local terrain had brought the platoon to the edge of an open farmyard, the sky foreboding above them, the wind gentle as a baby's sleeping breath, deep cold penetrating the soldiers' jackets, long underwear, and wool socks—studied the farmhouse in front of the Finns with nostalgic eyes. "See the birch and pine stacked along the back wall of the house?" he asked.

Rintala considered the tidy rows of firewood. "Ya."

"I cut every damn piece. The smoke that's curling from the chimney? It's coming from my hearth. The goddamned Russians are using *my* house as their command post!"

"Shit."

"You've got that right, sergeant. It is, as you say, 'shit'."

A horse neighed, evidence that the Russians had stabled their mounts in Erkkilä's barn.

"Goddamn it!" the Finnish farmer exclaimed, slamming his gloved fist against the stock of his rifle. "Their horses grow fat on my hay!"

"Shush. All in good time, Marko, all in good time," Rintala said.

Matti Peltomaa and the rest of the squad slid their boots out of leather ski harnesses and belly crawled to the line. Forty-five Finns surrounded the farm. The Russian sentries loafing around a fire burning in a barrel outside Erkkilä's barn had no idea of what was to come.

"Pass out extra grenades," Juha Rintala whispered to a youth crouched behind the men.

The boy—a lad of no more than fifteen—opened a wooden crate and handed out grenades.

"Erkkilä, Peltomaa, Johnson, and Pekkala: Take care of those guards," Rintala whispered. "Do it quietly before tossing your grenades into the house."

Erkkilä's mouth opened, but knowing that his sergeant would not retract the order, suppressed his protest. The soldiers removed their sheets and began crawling towards the barn. Lieutenant Laurila, the hood of his winter camouflage jacket removed, his brown eyes following the progress of his men, pulled a revolver out of a holster and cocked the hammer.

"His place," Rintala said softly, nodding towards Erkkilä.

"Damned communists," the officer muttered. "You sent The Old Man?"

Laurila's question referred to Matti Peltomaa, who, at sixty-one, was the oldest soldier in the platoon.

"He's up for it. As fit as you or me. Besides," Rintala said through a grin, "when he aims that Russian rifle at Russians, he never misses!"

The officer nodded and turned his head to watch his men advance. Across the open land, Erkkilä rose from snowy ground and attacked a sentry making water on the barn. Erkkilä's knife sliced through the Russian's coat as the Finn clamped his hand tight over the enemy soldier's mouth. Peltomaa and the others rushed the remaining guards, attacking before the enemy had a chance to react, the butts of their rifles knocking the beejeebers out of the Russian sentries before they could raise alarm.

The Finns continued towards the farmhouse. Erkkilä removed his right glove, held it between clamped teeth, and yanked a hand grenade free of his belt. Pulling the grenade's pin, Erkkilä waited for Johnson, Pekkala, and Peltomaa to do the same. The farmer counted down softly from "three." When his count reached "zero," all four men tossed their bombs through the glass windows of the home.

Boom. Boom. Boom. Boom.

Debris showered the men. The door was torn from its hinges. The explosion killed Russians playing whist at the kitchen table. A fire started. Enemy soldiers who had been lounging about or asleep scrambled to escape the burning building.

"Steady, boys," Sergeant Rintala yelled. "Here they come."

The four attackers scrambled back to the Finnish line, rolled onto their stomachs, and aimed their rifles. Russians streaming through the home's only door were gunned down. Enemy soldiers who tried to escape through the windows met similar fates. It was, in the end, a slaughter.

Marko Erkkilä stood on ash-covered snow. Fire had destroyed the tinder dry log house. Across the farmyard, Russian horses snorted and neighed in Erkkilä's barn.

"This was my home," the farmer said quietly as he and Juha Rintala surveyed the smoking debris and the charred bodies of the dead enemy. "The bastards had no right to be here."

CHAPTER 16

Kollaa, Finnish Karelia

March 10th, 1940

For months, Matti Peltomaa and the other ski soldiers under the command of Colonel Pajari (who had been promoted after the battle of Tolvajärvi from lieutenant colonel to full colonel) harassed Red Army units north of Lake Ladoga. But the hostilities, beyond the occasional Finnish victory, such as Suomussalmi, where the Finns encircled and destroyed several Russian divisions, had stalemated. The Red Army was content to maintain its position and the Finns were content to maintain theirs. The weather—inhospitable cold and near constant snow—made a Soviet advance problematic. But the lack of Finnish manpower and artillery made a sustained counter-attack by the Finns similarly impossible. And so, the men led by Lieutenant Laurila and Sergeant Rintala had to be content with skirmishing.

Peltomaa made many sorties with his fellow ski soldiers under the cover of darkness. Despite efforts by the Russians to tighten their defenses against sabotage, Finnish ghosts on birch skis whisked into Soviet-held territory and blew up supplies, killed sentries, and wreaked havoc. Rintala's Raiders, as they came to be known, were a fearless and dedicated band of marauders sanctioned by Colonel Pajari. The Raiders had no formal orders but were allowed to improvise and mete out their own brand of Finnish justice.

By March 1940, the Finns were exhausted. Constant bombardment of the Finnish positions by Russian artillery and, when the skies were clear, the ever-present strafing and bombing of the Finnish line by the Soviet Air Force, as well as a lack of hot water, decent food, and acceptable living conditions, left the Finnish defenders despondent. This was true even for Rintala's Raiders, a platoon not bogged down in the greasy mud of the narrow trench system that was Finland's only line of defense against the Russians, but who had the freedom to strike out against the enemy.

"We've received orders," Colonel Pajari told his men.

"Where to now?" a ski soldier Matti Peltomaa did not know—a new man who had transferred into the unit after losing his platoon—asked boldly.

The man's directness wasn't unique. The Finnish common soldier did not shy away from questioning his superiors. So long as the questions were posed with deference, Finnish soldiers had the freedom to inquire. Pajari looked the enlisted man straight in the eye.

"We're being sent to Kollaa," the colonel said gravely. "Svensson's in danger of being overrun. The Russians are trying to take the main road with hopes of swinging south around Lake Ladoga so they can attack our boys from the rear."

"Kollaa. Isn't that where 'Killer Hill' is?" Juha Rintala asked.

The commander nodded. "General Hägglund sent what men he could spare from Ulismainen. A counterattack was raised. The Russians sent, and continue to send, more tanks and infantry. Our recent counterattack was an attempt to stop the enemy from encircling Kollaa. One Finnish platoon held Killer Hill against an entire regiment of the Red Army. But the hill's been abandoned. Svensson's in danger and we've been assigned the task of reinforcing him."

Dirty, worn, and tired faces stared at the colonel under a claustrophobic sky, the sun hidden behind thick, low, snowless clouds.

"How many?" Lieutenant Laurila asked.

"What's that?"

"How many men are going to Kollaa?"

"Two battalions. It's all I can spare. I send more and I risk our own position. I'm not about to give up territory gained and held by Finnish blood. You'll leave at once."

Juha Rintala frowned. "In daylight?"

The colonel bit his lip. "I understand your concern, sergeant. There's a chance the clouds will break and you'll be spotted. If that happens, you'll be at the mercy of the Russian bombers and fighters. We have no planes, no pilots to send up. But time is of the essence. Kollaa won't hold another day. And if Kollaa falls, so too goes the road and an open route to the south."

"We'll be ready," another officer stated plainly. "We'll be ready as soon as you give the order."

"Now," Pajari said without emotion. "You are to move out now."

The Finns skied over old snow beneath clouds that did not break. No Russian planes discovered the column. Near the end of their trek, the Finns happened upon a column of enemy tanks and soldiers struggling across an open marsh. The Russians were laying pine logs over soft, mushy peat to support their armor. The Finns watched as enemy troops cut trees with axes and saws and used the timber to shore up the thawing earth. The Russians worked without sentries: they were unconcerned because Kollaa was surrounded. The town was under constant artillery bombardment and the Russians did not notice Pajari's men on quick birch skis concealed by white camouflage, their rifles leveled, their heavy machine guns planted behind hedgerows, their grenades and Molotovs ready to assail the enemy laboring in the swamp.

"Hold steady," Juha Rintala whispered as the Raiders took up positions on a slight rise overlooking the enemy. "Wait until Laurila gives the order."

Rintala's platoon lay in slushy spring snow, their garments soaked to the bone, their teeth chattering, and their stomachs empty. Each man carried a canteen of drinking water on his utility belt and two slices of rye bread in his pocket. They would not have a proper meal until they were safely inside the defenses at Kollaa.

Up and down the Finnish perimeter, the ski soldiers flicked off the safeties of their M28-30 rifles and Suomi submachine guns. If they could defeat the Soviet force in front of them, the way to Kollaa would be clear. The new arrivals would remain in Kollaa until Colonel Pajari recalled them, though there was a good chance that they would stay put through the end of the war. There were rumors of a cease-fire circulating: wild speculation that the Finnish government was close to giving away much of Finnish Karelia to end the Winter War.

The Finns waiting to do battle didn't like it, didn't like it a bit that the blood and sweat and toil of the past four months might be for naught. But they had a job to do. Politics could wait for another day, a day when bullets ceased flying and rifle barrels cooled. The rightness or wrongness of capitulation was something to be debated and discussed over coffee around hot wood stoves. On the day of battle, Colonel Pajari's men were not interested in debating policy: They were interested in killing Russians.

An eerie birdcall echoed.

"There's the signal," Laurila said. "Open fire!" the lieutenant shouted, his voice changing in pitch and volume as adrenaline took over, as he leveled his pistol on a seemingly unconcerned enemy soldier not thirty yards away.

Crack.

The Russian crumpled.

Crack.

Rat-a-tat-tat.

Boom. Boom. Boom.

Small arms fire. Machine gun fire. Grenade detonations. Mortar explosions: All erupted from the forest at the edge of the marsh. The Russians wielding axes and saws and carrying logs were sitting ducks. Soviet tanks waiting on the log road rotated their turrets to provide covering fire for the exposed soldiers. Finnish soldiers rose from the snow, shed their white sheets like caterpillars leaving cocoons, and charged.

Machine-gunners zeroed in on enemy soldiers trying to lock, load, and aim their rifles. Russian soldiers danced eerily, their breasts pierced by Finnish bullets, and fell like sheared wheat, until piles of dead men were stacked around the lightly armored tanks.

Juha Rintala reached the closest T-28, lit a Molotov, and slid it down the monster's breathing hatch. Flames erupted. Russian crewmen scrambled out the tank's main hatch but Matti Peltomaa was waiting for them with the Tokarev. The scene was repeated a half-dozen times. Russian armor in the distant woods—T-28s that were waiting to begin the crossing—pivoted on their treads and retreated without engaging. Soviet soldiers bolted for the trees. Most of the fleeing men did not look back, did not provide fire in support of their exposed comrades.

A few Soviet officers tried to organize a defense. Using the burning hulks of tanks and the ruined skeletons of transport trucks for protection, the Russians fought back. During the stiff fighting, Peltomaa narrowly missed death. A bullet struck the steel carcass of an overturned Russian command car inches from his head.

"Keep your goddamned American head down!" Rintala barked.

The sergeant aimed his Suomi, fired a short burst, and cut down the offending Russian. Peltomaa tossed a grenade in the direction of the enemy fire and took out three more enemy soldiers. Acrid smoke wafted from the firefight, curled upward, and merged with the steely sky. Cries and moans from the dying echoed across the killing field as Peltomaa watched the last of the able-bodied Russian soldiers desert their fallen kin and scramble towards the trees.

Rintala's Raiders made Kollaa later that day. Matti Peltomaa caught a few moments of sleep, ate some cold food, and waited in a waterlogged trench for the inevitable counterattack. But the Finns defending Kollaa faced no further hardship. The next day—the day after the battle in the swamp—up and down the weary Finnish line, from the Gulf of Finland to Barents Sea, Finnish soldiers in every unit, under every command, heard the same news: The Winter War was over.

CHAPTER 17
August 1940
Estonia

The sun warmed Alexis Gustafson's face. The woman's feet dug into the hot sand of Lehtma Beach, a stretch of solitude at the north end of Hiiumaa Island jutting into the Baltic Sea. The beach was located outside Kärdla where Alexis had been posted as a teacher. She had yet to instruct a single student. Classes were set to begin the following week.

I am ready for the children, the blond woman thought, as she sat in the canvas seat of a camp chair. *But are they ready for me?*

Lehtma was her favorite place on the island because it allowed Alexis to look north.

With a fragile peace between Finland and Russia in place following the Winter War, there is hope, hope that relations will stabilize and travel restrictions will be lifted so that ferries will once again travel from Helsinki to Tallinn and back on a daily basis. Until then, I will bide my time. Mother taught me that attribute—patience—something that is not part of my given nature. But I have learned to curb my impulsivity and think things through before I act. I am twenty-two years old. A grown woman. A professional. I have learned to be steadfast, to be level headed. I can wait.

A gull drifted into view. It was Wednesday and the narrow stretch of sand was empty. The families who normally crowded Lehtma Beach on weekends were absent. The white bird's flight was hesitant. Alexis watched it struggle against a Norwegian wind. The bird's effort was anything but random. The gull was pursuing an osprey that had snatched a fish from the gull's beak. The raptor intermittently flapped its wings, the fish eagle's size and strength a distinct advantage, as the gull struggled to keep up.

"Good luck, little bird," Alexis said, returning her eyes to the book in her lap.

She held the Russian language copy of *War and Peace* in her right hand and adjusted military-issue sunglasses she had purchased in Kärdla at a second-hand shop, the same shop where she found the Tolstoy novel, with her left. The early afternoon sun stood high against the aqua sky. The straps of her one-piece bathing suit (another purchase from the second hand store) rested on her upper arms. The arcs of her small breasts were golden. Her face, legs, and arms were also tan. Despite her apprehension regarding her mother's fate, Alexis Gustafson was momentarily at peace with herself and the world.

The Germans will have what they will have. The Russians too. Eventually, the gluttons for power will eat their fill and the war will cease. When? That's the difficult question. Tomorrow? The next day? Next month? Who knows? But the world can only endure, as we learned from the Great War, so much loss, so much suffering. Eventually, men will come to their senses and peace will be secured. Eventually, the ship pitching and rolling in this sea of loss and devastation will be righted.

She smiled at the metaphor as her eyes scanned the salt water stretching as an endless gray-blue plain to the north. She tilted her head and began to read.

There were Soviet soldiers and sailors and Marines on the island and there were Russian gunships stationed in Kärdla whose job it was to patrol the narrow straight between Hiiumaa Island and Haapsalu on the mainland. She had seen the small, quick vessels, their diesel engines coughing oily black smoke, their bows crashing through waves in hot pursuit. She had heard the staccato rat-tat-tat of machine guns when the gunboats' demands were ignored. She had not seen the results of Soviet Marines boarding offending ships but, having witnessed encounters on the streets of Tallinn between the occupiers and the occupied, she could guess the likely outcome of such episodes.

As a handsome single woman, Alexis had been accosted any number of times by Russian sailors and Marines bent on infiltrating her strictly professional demeanor, the façade she had adopted since leaving Yuri Godenov. She had suppressed physical desire to focus on teaching and her quest to find her mother. Alexis had made a decision to leave men out of her life. But in the sun-warmed confines of her rented flat in downtown Kärdla, she could not escape a singular vision, an apparition that plagued her and tested her resolve.

The young Estonian at the diner…there was something about his eyes, his look, his bearing. Something I have longed for in a man, despite the obvious disparity in our ages. I wonder, she had thought on several occasions during that period of repose between being wide awake and fast asleep, the lovely, soft glow of nightfall entering her room from windows overlooking the town, *whatever happened to that boy.*

Her brief interaction with the young man, as he was placed under arrest and taken from *Rohke Söökla* by the police, was fixed in her mind like a still photograph. She retrieved the scene, the portion of the incident where he turned and smiled at her, over and over and over in her mind as she sought sleep. There was something about an Estonian boy willing to stand up to Russian sailors that appealed to Alexis Gustafson, something about his bravery and *sisu* that made it hard for her to forget what she had witnessed that night in the diner.

The French were beaten. The Russians pursued Napoleon's defeated army across wintery land. Tolstoy's prose brought the scene alive for the young teacher as she reveled in the sun and tried to connect Napoleon's folly with the present.

During The Winter War, the Finns killed tens of thousands of invading Soviet soldiers, destroyed countless Red Army tanks, shot down squadrons of Soviet airplanes, and earned the respect of Franklin D. Roosevelt, Winston Churchill, and a host of other foreign leaders. Still, in the end, Finland lost the Winter War by at least one measure; from Petsamo in the north to Viipuri in the south, Joseph Stalin forced the annexation of Finnish territory where half a million Finns lived and worked and raised families. This seizure of land unleashed a flood of refugees. The number of expatriates crossing the border into Finland was one-tenth the total population of the country.

As Alexis Gustafson sat in the canvas chair in the hot sun, she hoped that the worst was over for her adopted corner of the world.

We learn from history, Alexis observed hopefully.

Lifting her eyes from *War and Peace*, the teacher considered the plight of emaciated French troops retreating through waist deep snow in threadbare uniforms and rag-wrapped feet. Casting her eyes to the furthest point of land, where beach ended and sea began, she digested the rumors she'd heard about the discord between the Germans and the Russians and the inevitable conclusion expressed by many that a larger, fiercer conflict was about to begin. Despite her optimism, the notion plagued her that the two powers who had commenced the second European war of the 20th century might one day stand toe to toe like punch drunk heavyweights trading blows in the center of a prizefighting ring. But the idea was so shocking, so untoward, she dismissed it as folly.

Hitler would never be so stupid as to attack the Soviet Union, Alexis thought, closing the Tolstoy novel as her eyes followed the gull's futile chase of the osprey until the birds disappeared from view.

CHAPTER 18
Hiiumaa, Estonia
December 1940

Alexis Gustafson tromped through mushy snow—the result of a storm blown in from Scandinavia—snow that, had it fallen in Sweden, would have been light and fluffy, but, due to the temperate influences of the Baltic, fell as sludge upon the small town at the edge of the sea. The teacher was depressed. It was Christmas Day and Alexis had not heard from her mother.

Though the Winter War was over, the tensions between Finland and the Soviet Union remained unabated. It grated Stalin to no end that Finland had not capitulated. The resolve of the Finns was, to Joseph Stalin, unnerving, given the cozy ties the NKVD had uncovered between Carl Mannerheim, the Finnish military leader, and the German High Command. If the Finns allowed the Germans to move troops through Finland as part of an offensive against the U.S.S.R., or if, as Stalin believed might happen, Finland joined Germany in an alliance and sent battle-hardened troops to lay siege to Leningrad, such an attack would be crippling, perhaps regime ending. Stalin was nervous about the Finns—nervous to the point of paranoia.

But the answer to the question in Stalin's mind *What is Hitler's game?* would not manifest for six months, until long after the snow melted from Kärdla's streets and Alexis's first year as a science teacher in the local school was completed.

The young woman splashed through pools of water and kicked at ridges of slush. The air was warm, seemingly too warm for snow. And yet, there it was, falling from the pewter sky, descending in thick, gluey flakes, and coating the town in a mantle of white. Alexis's blond hair was flecked with snowy residue and her blue wool coat and matching wool skirt gathered oversized snowflakes as she walked. She looked to the western sky, to where gray was fast turning to black, to where night was quickly claiming day, but she was not thinking of nature or the progression of seasons: She was thinking about the Estonian.

It was remarkable, the coincidence of the young man being on the island. Alexis had seen him once, in a group of prisoners working along the highway running from Kärdla to Pühalepa, when she had been out riding horses with another teacher, Anna Tooms, during a vacation week in early December. The horses they rode, a mixture of Estonian pony and Arabian, the animals golden flanked and mild of spirit, clambered down the gravel highway on iron-shod hooves as the two women conversed. The horses had whinnied at the sight of the work crew, ten convicts in prison garb breaking rocks with sledge hammers alongside the roadway a dozen meters outside Kärdla. Four Estonian guards watching the workers, their rifles resting across their uniformed arms, had grinned as the women approached.

"Hey," the boldest of the guards, a spectral, lanky Estonian had said loud enough for the teachers to hear, "there's a couple of fillies I wouldn't mind mounting!"

Alexis and Anna had reined the horses to a stop a few meters from the prisoners. Alexis avoided chastising the guard. Instead, she had taken a superior tone, one similar to that of an officer dressing down his troops, in response. "Ignore him, Anna. He's likely a gelding," Alexis had observed, loud enough for all to hear.

The guard's face had reddened. His companions had guffawed. The prisoners had sniggered.

"Come down off that horse," the guard said, hiding his embarrassment with bravado, "and I'll show you who's a gelding and who's a stallion!"

Anna Tooms blushed but the man's retort had no effect on Alexis Gustafson.

"I think it's clear from my vantage point," Alexis had replied with impertinence, her old personality surfacing, her eyes looking out over the flat countryside in feigned boredom, "which of you measure up and which of you do not. Let's leave it at that."

As Alexis flicked the reins of her horse with the intention of taking her leave, she saw him. Even dressed in clothing indistinguishable from that of his fellow prisoners, Nigul Kristian was hard to miss. Though the guard addressing the women was a tall man, Nigul Kristian towered over everyone in the group.

His shoulders have broadened since I last saw him, Alexis thought. *He's become a man. God, he is a fine one. I can't stop staring at his face. Especially his eyes: Intelligent, knowing, not unlike Juha's eyes, though with a touch more kindness, I should think.*

Alexis's gloved hands had drawn the reins taut and kept the prancing horse in place.

"I know him," Alexis had whispered to Anna out of the side of her delicate mouth. "I saw him once, in Tallinn."

Anna Tooms scanned the prisoners standing idly in the ditch, picks and shovels mere props in the prisoners' hands as they watched the women.

"Which one?"

"The tallest one."

Anna had nodded. "Handsome," she had whispered nervously. "We should be on our way."

Alexis had smiled at Nigul Kristian and he had grinned subtly in reply.

"Indeed," Alexis had whispered. "I'd wager *he* is a stallion," she added, as the two women and their horses moved down the road.

CHAPTER 19
Pietarsaari, Ostrobothnia
January 1941

***Dear** Elin:*

This letter means that I have done what I did not have the courage to do back in Lieksa when the forest took my beloved. I know from our conversations that you have loved a man as I loved Axel. You spoke often of Hiram and the tragedy that took place. You seem to be able, despite your loss, to carry on. There is much strength in you, even after what you experienced at the hands of the Tartars. You didn't share the details of that horror, only that something evil occurred. But even after that, you still have the courage to carry your head high and seek a place in this terrible, terrible world for yourself and your daughter. I hope one day you find her. Alexis seems, from your description of her, to be a remarkable young woman.

Now to the point of this letter. My people, as I have told you, live in Pietarsaari. My father and mother, Ismo and Kaisa Numila, as well as my brother, Henri, still live in town. While Axel's family is wonderful, I would prefer if Eeva and Juhani were raised where I was raised; amongst the people who loved me. So this is what I am asking: That you take my children to Pietarsaari and ensure that they are placed in the hands of my parents. You are the only person I can entrust my children to until they are safely in their grandparent's arms. Helsinki is no place for little ones.

Please forgive me for what I am asking of you. And please forgive me for what I have done. I see no other way. I am content, in these final moments, to reflect that I love my children but unlike you, I am not strong enough to raise them without a father.

Peace to you.
Helmi Kemi

The train to Kokkola had rumbled north. Due to her immigrant status, Elin Goldfarb was required to obtain permission from the Finnish State Police, the Valpo (*ValtiOllinene poliisi)* to travel from Helsinki, where she lived, to Ostrobothnia. Elin had two strikes against her, so far as the Valpo was concerned, as it considered her request.

First, she had been, up until Hiram's disappearance, a communist. Her participation in the Karelian Fever experiment, along with her journalism in support of that cause, aroused suspicion amongst state police hierarchy.

Second, she was an American and, at least by surname, a Jew. Though the Valpo had no indication that Elin (or Hiram, for that matter) were practicing Jews, her surname labeled her, along with her political beliefs, as a potential agitator.

On the positive side of the ledger, the Valpo, after closely monitoring Elin's activities in Helsinki, uncovered no evidence of disloyalty. In addition, Elin Goldfarb had support within the Finnish military. Juha Rintala had vouched for her integrity, which, in turn, caused his superiors to do the same. Such support made scrutinizing the American woman's actions delicate.

Elin's story, that she had befriended Helmi Kemi, that she had been the unfortunate young mother's confidant in Helmi's last days, and that the dead woman had entrusted Elin with the task of returning Helmi's son and daughter to the Numila family, seemed too tightly wrapped and convenient in the Valpo's view. But absent proof of a contrary narrative, and with the support of the military, Elin was allowed to make the journey to Pietarsaari.

The war had ended badly. Despite the fact that the Finns battled the Red Army to a standstill, the treaty concluding the war devastated Finnish pride. Much of Finnish Karelia (including Viipuri) became part of the Soviet Union. Despite this insult, a fragile and delicate peace ensued between the belligerents, a peace that allowed Elin Goldfarb to settle into a quiet and unassuming life in Pietarsaari as she searched for her daughter.

One letter from Kärdla made it to Finland. Given that the message was written in English, the letter was forwarded to the U.S. Legation in Helsinki. From there, Alexis Gustafson's message found its way to Elin Goldfarb in the small apartment Elin rented above Dr. Walter Cohen's flat in downtown Pietarsaari.

June 30th, 1940
Dear Mother:

I have been advised by the authorities in Tallinn that you escaped from a labor camp and now live in Finland. I trust this letter finds you well. There is much I would like to say in this letter about what I have been doing, where I have been, and how it is I came to Hiiumaa Island, but given the nature of censorship here in Estonia, I will save that discussion for one that we can have in person.

How is your diabetes? It cannot be easy finding medicine in the midst of a war. I trust you were able to do so and keep in good health. I know about Hiram. I feel your pain and your loss: He was a good man, a good father. I miss him, as I miss you, every day.

I am currently teaching science here in Kärdla, the largest town on the island. It was my hope, by securing a post here, that I would have an opportunity to take a ferry to Helsinki and find you. But, with the war and the tense peace following the armistice, no such opportunity has presented itself. I have inquired repeatedly about obtaining a travel permit but I have been refused each time, without explanation. I will continue to inquire so that one day we can meet, share an embrace, and remember.

I trust this letter finds you in good health and good spirits. Please write if you are able.

Love.

'Lexis

The letter arrived months after it was written: the first information Elin Goldfarb was privy to regarding her daughter in nearly three years. That Alexis had survived in Soviet Russia was not surprising to Elin, given the young woman's adaptable nature. But that Alexis had given up her dream of becoming a physician to teach science—that bit of information had shocked Elin.

She says she took a job on the island to find a way to me. I hope my disappearance is not the cause of her giving up on her plan to become a doctor.

Elin read and re-read the letter many times after the Finnish postman placed the rumpled envelope marked "postage due" in her hands, the letter carrier refusing Elin's insistence to pay for the missing stamps, claiming it was "his duty" to make up the difference given all that Mrs. Goldfarb, whose story was well known in Pietarsaari, had gone through. And though she wrote to the address listed on the envelope, telling her daughter that she had survived and including her address in hopes that Alexis would find her, the Valpo, which did not entirely trust the American woman, intercepted her letters and prevented Alexis from knowing where her mother was living.

Ignorant of the Valpo's actions, Elin remained optimistic and kept 'Lexis's letter and envelope in her black clutch purse, the purse she carried with her to her job. Despite her college education and considerable language and writing skills, there were no professional jobs open to Elin Goldfarb in Pietarsaari. As a Finnish-speaking immigrant living in a city where Swedish-speakers controlled power, the best position, the only position Elin Goldfarb could find, was that of hotel maid.

"How goes it today, Mrs. Goldfarb?" Ernst Larsson, the day manager of the *Hotellet Jacobstad* asked as Elin entered the hotel's lobby.

"*Bäter*," she replied in Swedish, a language she was struggling to learn.

Larsson nodded and handed her a typewritten list of rooms needing attention.

"A full day's work," Elin observed.

Larsson, a short, blond headed man with a pasty complexion, smiled, exposing perfectly straight, white teeth. "For a full day's wage."

Elin nodded and moved to the coatroom to hang up her coat, a red, wool, full-length garment she had purchased to replace the green and black Mackinaw Matti Peltomaa had given her. The Mackinaw had seen better days. She'd given it to a homeless man who begged daily on the street corner near her flat. The man had been coatless and, once she had purchased the new coat, she had no need of the Mackinaw. The mentally disturbed man did not thank her for the gift. He simply threw his arms into the sleeves, buttoned his new coat, and returned to reciting the entirety of the Constitution of the Republic of Finland from memory to anyone passing his corner of the world.

Elin retrieved her cart of cleaning supplies and pushed it towards the service elevator. Her work was confined to the top four floors of the eight-story hotel. Another maid, Lahja Lindstrom, took care of the four lower floors. The women worked together to clean the lobby, the public restrooms, the coatroom, the small bistro, and the bar on the hotel's main level. But that work was saved for last.

Elin Goldfarb scoured the tile floor around the toilet in Room 810.

"Filthy pigs," she said aloud in Finnish as she chipped old piss from the white porcelain pedestal of the toilet. "Men can't ever seem to hit the target. Why they don't sit down and pee like a woman is beyond me," she muttered, scrubbing the cool white fixture with a rag soaked in cleaning solvent.

As she worked, Elin reflected upon the long, slow train journey she had made with Eeva and Juhani Kemi. Juhani was old enough to miss his mother and to convey his upset in crying jags and tears. Eeva was too young to comprehend what had happened, how her life and that of her brother had been turned upside down by her mother's selfish death. When the grieving grandparents approached their grandchildren in the Kokkola train station, Juhani had hidden behind Elin and the little girl had wailed. Nothing seemed to be right about what Elin Goldfarb was required to do. And yet, she handed both children off with a clear understanding that, for the children's sake, she would never see them again.

Elin's thoughts turned to consideration of Matti Peltomaa. She had not heard a word from the soldier since she left him at the station in Joensuu. There had been no letters, no messages through returning veterans who might have served with Peltomaa.

The war is over. It has been more than nine months since the men were released to go home, and still I have heard nothing.

Not that she had a claim on the man. They had endured a harrowing ordeal. He had saved her from certain death. She had done the same for him, though, upon reflection, Elin Goldfarb had to admit that her killing of the Tartar was more rooted in hatred for the Tartar than in any desire to protect Matti Peltomaa. She had fired shot after shot after shot from the Russian officer's revolver until the chamber was empty and the trigger was firing dry, and in the process of killing the Tartar, she had saved Matti Peltomaa.

But did I save myself? I wake up to the smell of horse and Tartar in my bed. I feel the rough hands, and then, worse. I see the blade of a bayonet raised, a glint of steel. And even though it never happened, I can feel my body being split in two by the knife as those black eyes laugh at me. Thank God, she thought as she polished the chrome of the sink faucet and the taps, *I am unable to become pregnant. Imagine what sort of monster would be created from the sperm of the Tartar!*

Elin realized she had no claim on Matti Peltomaa beyond that of their connected journey. Her reluctance to allow a deeper relationship with Matti was grounded in Hiram's death and the guilt she felt as a survivor.

I know, from our time together and the look of longing on Matti's face when he stood on the platform of the railroad station watching my train depart, he is in love with me. If only I could find some way to repay that love. I don't know how. I can't see a way to it. I've never held those sorts of feelings for Matti, not even as a young woman.

Her face flushed from effort. Her skirt was tight around her waist and thighs and made kneeling on the hard tile floor of the bathroom uncomfortable. Perspiration leaked from her hairline and slid down Elin Goldfarb's smooth cheeks and dripped onto the crisp fabric of her white blouse as her strong hands worked the hard bristles of a scrub brush over ceramic tile. She was lost in her work, as mundane and trivial as it was, and did not see the shadow looming behind her as she pushed a galvanized bucket of cleaning solution ahead of her.

"You've always been a hard worker."

The voice startled Elin. In her surprise, she nearly knocked over the cleaning bucket. A strong arm reached around the woman and righted the pail before it spilled. Elin Goldfarb did not rise to her feet to greet the visitor. She simply turned her head towards the familiar voice and smiled, full in the knowledge that Matti Peltomaa had found her.

CHAPTER 20
Kärdla, Estonia
March 1941

Alexis Gustafson saw the Estonian again. She was walking near the Soviet naval yard in Kärdla when she chanced upon him. He was no longer in prisoner's garb: He was dressed in blue dungarees and a light blue denim shirt—the sort of clothing any tradesman might wear. At first, Alexis did not recognize him. It had been six months since she'd seen him breaking rocks as a prisoner. But something about the way the tall, angular man securing Kuhlo wiring to a cement block building near the entrance gate to the Soviet naval yard caught the teacher's attention as she walked alone on that misty spring day.

It's him.

She stopped and fixed her uncommon eyes on the muscular young man at work, his shirtsleeves rolled to the elbows as he tugged and pulled stubborn wires through pipe, his blond hair matted to the high crown of his prominent forehead. Alexis stood in fog studying the Estonian for what seemed to her to be an eternity before his gaze caught hers.

"*Tere*," the electrician said in greeting, a puzzled look forming over his features as he stood to his full height.

He doesn't remember me.

"Hello, yourself," Alexis replied in Estonian.

"It is not such a nice day to be out walking," the young man replied awkwardly.

Alexis smiled. "You don't remember me, do you?"

True, she had changed her hairstyle, cutting her previously shoulder-length blond hair to a shorter, more contemporary style. She'd also gained a bit of weight. Not much, just enough to soften the edges of her jaw, to round out her face, her meager chest, and narrow hips. Still, she had hoped he would remember her.

"Certainly I do." His answer seemed tentative.

"Oh you do, do you? Where do you remember me *from*?"

"You were there when the *politsei* arrested me. For stabbing that goddamned Russian sailor," the young man replied, returning her smile and making no apology for the curse.

She frowned at the language but held her tongue.

I doubt he's a believer but that's something one can work on.

"The diner is the only time you remember meeting me?"

He laughed. "I wouldn't call a wink and a smile while I was working off my sentence at hard labor 'meeting' someone, would you?"

He remembers that as well. God, she thought, as she gauged the measure of his intelligent hazel eyes, *he is one handsome man.* "You're no longer in prisoner's clothes," she said.

Nigul Kristian stopped working and moved towards the woman. The shyness that had been apparent in his initial response had vanished, replaced by a quiet confidence that Alexis found appealing.

"Served my sentence. Didn't kill the bastard," he said calmly, again, making no apology for his choice of words. "If I had, I wouldn't be standing here, a reasonably free man, or at least," he said in a lower tone of voice, "as reasonably free as a man can be under the thumb of the Russians."

"I see."

There was a pause in the conversation while Nigul took inventory of the woman. "And you? What are you doing on Hiiumaa Island? You're not Estonian. Finn or American, I'd wager, by your accent."

He's more perceptive, despite being a tradesman, than most men who attended university with me!

She glanced over his shoulder and nodded in the direction of a Soviet naval officer, likely a *politruk*—a political officer assigned to a military unit—by deportment. The Russian was staring at them.

"Ah," Kristian said. "That's just Vedyetev. He's harmless. Scowls and swears and threatens me with Siberia nearly every day. But I'm the only electrician on the base. The base commander keeps Vedyetev in line. Still, I best get back to work or the commander himself will be displeased."

The man began his retreat.

You're not that shy, Alexis thought. *Come on. Introduce yourself.*

As if reading her mind, the man stopped, turned, and offered Alexis his hand. "Nigul Kristian."

She accepted the gesture. "Alexis Gustafson."

"Ah," he said, through an open smile. "A Swede."

She laughed. "No, you were correct the first time. My *natural* father was a Swede-Finn, from the Åland Islands. But he became an American citizen. My *natural* mother was Finnish. She too, lived in America."

"I see," the Estonian replied.

Though curious about the woman's personal history, Nigul did not press for an explanation of the woman's use of the adjective "natural" to describe her parents.

I've said too much about my family, Alexis thought. *He's concerned about my origins.*

She sighed. "It's, as we Americans say, 'complicated'."

Nigul Kristian nodded and returned to fastening metal tubing to cement block. As he worked, the electrician considered how to broach his interest in Alexis Gustafson.

"Would you like to go to dinner with me, sometime when you are free? That is, if you are not otherwise spoken for," Kristian finally said after glancing furtively at the woman's left hand.

Alexis smoothed her skirt. She let the silence between them extend so as not appear to be too desperate, too eager. She had made the mistake once, of leaping into a man's arms and then into his bed. She was not about to make the same unforced error again, especially given the transitory nature of her time on Hiiumaa Island.

Finding Mother must be my primary goal. This, Alexis thought, considering the pleasant evening she might spend with the strapping Estonian, *is but an interlude. Still, a diversion from the sameness of my day, from dealing with children and their parents, would be a welcome change. He may not ask again. He needs to know my interest.*

"I would."

BOOK FOUR: UNDER THE BLUE SWASTIKA

CHAPTER 1
Kärdla, Estonia
May 1941
(Nigul's Story)

When I first glimpsed Alexis in the diner in Tallinn, I fell hard for her. On first seeing Alexis in the *Rohke Söökla,* I was bowled over, plain and simple. That we met again, some months later, well, my dear departed wife would likely ascribe that to God. But I've never delegated to the Creator such mundane duties. I believe that I met Alexis Gustafson that day in Tallinn, and later, on the island of Hiiumaa, because of simple chance: A cosmic roll of the dice, if you will.

After Alexis and I were reintroduced, things progressed slowly. We did not fall into each other's arms. Our courtship was a slow, delicate waltz rather than a frenzied jitterbug. Alexis was cautious of being entangled with a young Estonian five years her junior. We began our relationship, despite the curious acceleration that seems omnipresent between men and women during war, in traditional fashion. Our first official outing was a bicycle trip from Kärdla to Kõrgessaare and back. Both Alexis and I wished to visit the Kõpu *tuletorn*. Kõpu light is the oldest working lighthouse in the world. I rented bicycles from a local vendor. Alexis packed a modest picnic lunch: two herring sandwiches on rye bread, two apples, a chocolate bar to share, and a bottle of cheap black currant wine from Põltsamaa. It became clear to me immediately, from the ragged cuts Alexis made through the sandwiches, that the woman I was about to embark on a bike ride with lacked domestic skills. But what did that matter? With her unevenly colored eyes, her short stature, her cropped golden hair, and her exquisitely delicate face, her looks were such that she could have put dog shit between two pieces of birch bark, called it a sandwich, and I would have eaten it!

"This is a longer trip than I expected," Alexis said, between gasps as we climbed a rise east of Kõrgessaare. "I knew I should have paid attention to how far we were going before accepting your invitation."

We had eaten our sandwiches and drained the bottle of wine. We had engaged in small talk. We had stopped at the lighthouse and marveled at its stamina. And, on the return trip, we were racing, as best we could, against weather. Thunderheads roiled above us as we pedaled furiously with the wind at our backs. We didn't make it. Somewhere between Rootsi and Kidaste, the sky let loose.

"Hurry," I said, my best blue short-sleeved dress shirt and khaki slacks soaking up heavy rain, "there's a bridge up ahead where we can wait out the storm."

We pedaled like maniacs, a measure that, given Alexis was wearing a blouse and skirt, proved her mettle. In short order, we arrived at the overpass and found refuge. As we waited out the storm under the bridge, Alexis glared at me. Her blouse was soaked through and implied details of intimacy that caused me to stare.

"Stop looking at my chest," Alexis scolded as we stood under the concrete bridge, rain pummeling the roadway above us, walls of silver blocking our view.

"But…"

Alexis shook her head and looked back to the west, towards the lighthouse.

"*Men.*"

The word was tinged with contempt.

"But…"

Her hair was sodden. Rainwater slipped down her cheeks. She wore no lipstick and yet her lips, pursed as they were, held the color of blood, the color of life. I looked away.

"You better turn your eyes from me, Mr. Nigul Kristian. You better…"

The temptation to look again, to study her body, revealed as it was by the wet clothing, was excruciating. But I obeyed. I did not want to upset Alexis more than I already had. An interval of silence passed as I studied the low hanging storm.

"Tell me about your farm," Alexis finally said, as she leaned her bicycle against the cement wall of the bridge and sat down on a large boulder—one rock among many rocks holding back the slope of the land.

I looked in Alexis's direction but took great care not to leer. Her delicate right hand swept an errant strand of damp yellow hair away from her blue eye. I thought a moment before answering.

How much should I say? She might be NKVD. Unlikely, given what she's told me about her parents and how she came to be in Estonia. The purges. The upset. Her mother surviving a labor camp and living somewhere in Finland. Her father killed by the Russians. Fucking Russians. They've ruined Estonia. Stolen my family's farm. But Alexis is OK. I can trust her. Besides, if she turns out to be a spy, well, at least the best-looking NKVD agent in the entire Russian security service will have done me in!

"Our farm was small by American standards," I said. "Sixty hectares adjacent to Kalevipoeg Creek in central Estonia."

"*Was?*"

"Fucking Stalin," I blurted out. "I apologize. I shouldn't have cursed," I added quickly.

We were speaking Estonian. Though not Alexis's native language and not the language she used when teaching, it was a language she had come to master.

"Nigul," Alexis said plainly, "it's not like I haven't heard *that* word before."

The rain enclosed us in quicksilver. There was no traffic: The weather kept folks with any common sense indoors. Thunder boomed and lightning arched across the heavy sky.

"Every farm of more than 30 hectares was taken, without compensation. Every piece of property belonging to churches, charitable organizations, counties, towns, and cities was seized," I said, with bitterness. "The stolen land was given to new emigrants from the Soviet Union. But that theft, I am afraid, is only the beginning."

Alexis stood up and walked to the rain's edge. She craned her swan-like neck, tilted her head, opened her mouth, and caught water on her tongue. "Why do you say that?" she asked, upon returning to her rocky perch.

I lowered my eyes. Desire was beginning to manifest within me and I did not want Alexis to witness the involuntary crassness of my body. I concentrated on what was being asked and tried to ignore the person doing the asking.

"Collectivization: Stalin and his thugs have made certain that there is no private farmland left in the Soviet Union. Even the smallest family plots in Russia are being merged into collectives. That's where Estonia is headed; that will be the fate of all the farmers, orchard men, and herdsmen. Their stake in life will be no different than that of a factory worker or tradesman. Men like my father don't work well for others. They need to be their own masters. These changes will cause men like my father no end of hardship; they will be unable to adjust."

Alexis looked at me with a reflective gaze.

One can tell, Ms. Gustafson, just by how you furrow your brow, that you are more intelligent than I am, than most anyone I have ever known.

"Where are your parents now?"

I sighed. The rain continued to pound the roadway above us.

"In Puhja. They have a little house on the main street. I haven't been home since I was arrested, though I have written them and they have written me—such as they can, given the NKVD."

"Don't you have a brother?"

I smiled. "I do. A year younger. Karl. He's at university. In Tartu. Wants to be a professor of literature. You would like him. He's read most everything there is to read."

"Jane Austen?"

The reference was lost on me. I was an electrician—someone whose reading habits ended with the morning newspaper. An unexpected crack of thunder startled us.

"That was close," Alexis said.

"Jane Austen?"

Alexis smiled. "An English writer of romantic novels. She's very well known. If your brother knows anything about fiction, he knows about Jane Austen."

"What are some of her books?"

Alexis frowned. "*You* are interested in reading her work?"

She was teasing me. I hadn't finished secondary school and I didn't read fiction, though my reading skills, even with my limited education, were more than adequate.

"Not really," I replied.

"Just making conversation?"

"To pass time," I admitted. "And to endear myself to you."

The last phrase sounded awkward.

"Well," Alexis replied coyly, apparently not disturbed by my candor. "Austen is *one* way to a girl's heart," she added, batting her eyelashes.

There was a sustained pause in our banter. Another lightning bolt seared the black sky. Thunder clapped. The rain kept coming. A truck approached from the east and slowed to a stop under the bridge. The driver, a Hiiumaa Island sheep farmer by the look of the equipment piled in the bed of the pickup, rolled down his window, adjusted his rumpled felt hat to see better, and smiled.

"Nice day for a bike ride," the old man teased. "You and the Misses need a lift someplace?"

I shook my head. "I'm afraid we're going in the opposite direction."

The farmer's eyes were red. Age and gravity had taken a toll on his face.

"We're not married," Alexis interjected, as she stood up from the boulder and smoothed her wet skirt against her thighs. "It's our first outing together."

The old man squinted, took in my companion's shape as revealed by her saturated clothing, and nodded.

"I've got plenty of petrol to make it back to Kärdla and still get to where I need to go," the old man said with authority. "Seems like you young folks could use some help," he added, softening his words. "And I sure as hell don't want to be responsible for the two of you dropping dead of exposure before your second date," the old man deadpanned.

I shook my head. "That's too much to ask of you. The Russians…"

The old man grimaced. "Goddamned Russians," he muttered improvidently, unaware of whether or not we were allied with or stood against the enemy. "I've got my connections. I can get all the goddamned petrol I want. But the bastards took my sheep farm. Broke it up into little plots and handed them out like communion wafers to no-good immigrants. Took my sheep too! Paid me less than I had in them. I'm on the way to sell off my shearing equipment. Now, I work in Kärdla on the docks. Night watchman. Pay's for shit but at least I'm still my own boss." The man's pale green eyes darted. "Sorry about the cursing, ma'am."

"No need to apologize," Alexis said. "It's not like I haven't heard it before."

I smiled. "I work in the naval yard as an electrician. I thought I recognized you. Nigul Kristian," I said, shaking the man's hand through the window.

"Kolt Pelke," he replied as our hands met.

Pelke's grip evinced years of farm work.

"Put your bikes in the back and get in. Plenty of room. No sense being stubborn about it. I won't leave until you say 'yes.' I'm not about to leave a pretty lady stuck out in the rain with a boyfriend who doesn't have enough sense to check the weather before planning a bicycle ride."

Alexis laughed.

I held my tongue, lifted the bikes, and laid them in the bed of the pickup. We climbed into the warm cab, the truck's heater fan squealing from effort, the interior smelling of sheep dung and cigarette smoke. Alexis slid across the dirty cloth seat of the old Ford and squeezed in between the old man and me. Kolt Pelke had a hell of a time getting the truck out of neutral with the shapely legs of a beautiful woman in the way of the old clunker's gearshift. It was an interesting ride back to Kärdla.

CHAPTER 2
Pietarsaari, Finland
June 10th, 1941

Elin Goldfarb did not immediately embrace Matti Peltomaa and allow him into her bed. In fact, at the beginning of their renewed friendship, Elin was convinced that the veteran of the Winter War was wasting his time on her.

Matti has no chance. He is too sweet, too kind, to have any idea of how senseless his ardor towards me is. I can't encourage him. I can't lead him on. I must refuse even the slightest hint of anything beyond friendship. I owe him that. I owe him more, but more I cannot give. The debt I owe him can only be satisfied by a platonic friendship. He must know this. I must insist upon this.

Matti Peltomaa rented a room in the same apartment building Elin Goldfarb called home. Matti lived on the fourth floor, the very top floor, and Elin lived on the third, one floor above the Cohen family's apartment.

It was curious to Elin how Dr. Walter Cohen would leave his wife, Rosi, and their newborn son William, alone in the apartment for weeks at a time. Elin heard whispers that Cohen, a baptized Christian who maintained his secular Jewish heritage, wandered about Finland despite the legal constraints placed upon him as an illegal immigrant. The mystery to Elin wasn't why the Cohens left Nazi Germany but why Dr. Cohen was absent from Pietarsaari for extended periods of time.

Is he, as the Valpo suppose, a communist agitator?

Is he, as some Jewish neighbors suggest, merely providing free medical care to Jews throughout Finland?

The answer to what the good doctor was doing while away from home was uncertain but the rumors were many.

It's none of my damn business, Elin finally concluded. *I'm done trying to understand the motivations and comings and goings of someone I've never even been introduced to.*

Elin developed a connection to the doctor's wife, despite the fact that Rosi Cohen was reclusive. The tiny Jewish community had no real center, no real place for gathering. Prayers, religious services, and social occasions took place in the apartments or homes of Pietarsaari's Jews, but due to her husband's conversion, Rosi Cohen did not attend such events. Though she generally avoided others of her kind, the doctor's wife *had* become friendly with Elin Goldfarb.

William Cohen was born on May 5, 1941. Mrs. Cohen traveled to Helsinki to be with friends during her confinement and the child's birth. Why the good doctor did not stick around and deliver his own son was, like so many things regarding Dr. Cohen, enigmatic. But shortly after William's birth, Rosi and the newborn were back in the family's apartment. The infant did not disturb Elin. She heard no crying jags, no evidence of colicky behavior from the Cohen flat.

Does she breast-feed the child? Elin mused one day as she left the Turvallisuus Apartment Building on her way to the market. *She should really breast feed the baby if she can.*

There was envy in Elin's thinking. Elin resented the fact that her first husband's infidelity had cost her not only the ability to conceive but all the attendant circumstances that flow from giving birth.

That ass.

It had been decades since Elin had divorced Horace Ellison and yet her resentment against the man lingered as fresh and as hurtful and as painful as the incident in the Karelian woods.

That bastard Tartar.

A tear formed and slid down the woman's cheek as she walked.

It takes time, Elin thought.

Her attention shifted to the lack of food on the shelves in the local markets. Despite the end of the Winter War, Finland's economy remained stagnant. Stores throughout the country were sparsely stocked.

Nothing positive happens overnight. It takes time and patience to recover from...

Elin's thought ended there. She stopped at a street corner and waited for a red Mercedes sedan to rumble past. She saw Matti Peltomaa standing across the street, his head down, his eyes riveted on the latest edition of the *Helsingin Sanomat*.

Matti: I can't avoid him. I've turned him down so many times. We are friends, yes. But we cannot become involved. "No movies at the Pietarsaari Cinema, Matti. Friends only. No dinners. No dates." She had said that at least a dozen times. Oh, she had allowed a casual lunch or two at an inexpensive diner down the street. But they paid for their own meals. Friends can eat together without causing a stir, without it meaning something else. "You understand this, don't you Matti? Lunch is permitted, provided we both pay. But no dates. No walks in the park. No movies. No drinks. No dancing. Platonic, Matti. Strictly platonic. OK?"

The kind, quiet man had never argued, never harangued. He had accepted the limits Elin Goldfarb placed on their relationship. But he would not yield, would not allow her to win. In the battle of wills between them, she felt that he was stronger. Though she did not want to give in, every time she looked into his honest, piercingly brown eyes, every time she considered where the two of them had come from and what they had witnessed, a small chink in her armor fell away. There was a way around her constant refusals to be had if Matti kept at it—a path to her heart that Elin Goldfarb did not want to admit existed. But he would have to win. She would not capitulate.

"Good morning, Mrs. Goldfarb," Matti Peltomaa said cheerily, glancing up from his newspaper as the woman approached.

She stopped by his side. "Good morning, Mr. Peltomaa."

He nodded. "You're as striking as always," Matti observed. "A fine summer day, don't you think? Not long until Midsummer's Eve. How are things going at the hotel?"

Elin frowned. "It's a struggle. Whatever the pharmacy is doing to my insulin is making me less able, less strong. I'm injecting more frequently but still, the malaise persists. But what options do I have? I must keep working at the hotel. The Valpo is not about to let me write for the newspaper," she said, tapping his copy of the *Sanomat* for affect. "No, that isn't something they'll allow."

"So the Valpo thinks you're a Red? Do they think that because of the color of your hair?"

She couldn't help but laugh. "You tease me, Matti Peltomaa. There aren't many auburn hairs left on this gray head," she replied, wiping a wayward strand of hair away from her forehead. "And you know I gave up politics when Hiram was taken. I am no longer a believer…in much of anything, I'm afraid."

He folded the newspaper. "Not even in love?"

The words fell softly in the windless air. Elin's face flushed.

"Matti. What have I said? None of that, all right? Haven't we agreed to be friends? Friends for life, but only friends."

"No."

"What are you saying? That if we can't be lovers, we can't be friends?"

The man smiled. "'No.' As in *'No, I haven't agreed to stop loving you.'*"

She felt her resolve soften.

He's unattractive. He's a decade older than I am. What is the point? What is the use in all of this? But he has something: There's some spark inside him that I need to yield to. Love? I don't know if that's it. Physical closeness? Perhaps. Maybe it's the simple touch of another human being: the fragility of intimacy that calls out to me, that assails my resistance. Who can say?

"Elin, I know the answer to this question. But I have to ask, as I will until you either tell me to go to hell, or one of us is no longer around: Will you have dinner with me?"

Damn you, Matti.

A garbage truck rattled past, the odor of rotting trash incongruous with their discussion. Horns honked as traffic on a main thoroughfare a few blocks away became snarled. Children's voices rang out from a nearby schoolyard. A woman passed by pushing a baby carriage. Elin thought she knew the woman but quickly changed her mind.

That's not Rosi Cohen.

The siren at city hall declared that it was lunchtime. Elin Goldfarb felt her heart thump, thump, thumping. She felt blood course into her face. She felt her fingers and toes tingle in a way that she hadn't believed possible. She looked at the man and he looked at her. There was no deception, no lust, and no baseness in Matti Peltomaa's small eyes.

"All right, Mr. Peltomaa. I'll have dinner with you."

CHAPTER 3
Tallinn, Estonia
June 15, 1941
(Nigul's Story)

When I returned to the mainland, I was shocked by what I found. The sidewalks of Tallinn were free of pedestrians. The city's stores, shops, taverns, and cafés were empty. Despite the high sun, no citizens seemed to be out enjoying the day. No businessmen negotiated deals in the alcoves of downtown buildings. No country folk gawked at the walls and towers of Old Tallinn. The only people on the move were Soviet soldiers and sailors who appeared, to my untrained eye, to be in a great deal of hurry.

Throughout the city, streets and avenues were clogged with Soviet tanks, transport trucks, tracked vehicles, and command cars boasting the bright red star of communism. Columns of soldiers wheeled and marched across hot pavement, their helmets and rifles glinting in the noon sun.

This makes no sense, no sense at all.

What I was to learn, as I made my way through the city, as I reconnected here and there with old friends was this: Nearly 20,000 Estonians had been rounded up and deported during the first two weeks of June. This information was not shouted by my friends nor screamed across the headlines of the newspapers; it was provided in whispered confidence with the understanding that, everywhere about us, the NKVD and the pro-communist Tallinn police were listening.

The missing included folks deemed "counterrevolutionary" by the communists—former police officials, prison wardens, military officers, clergy, teachers—as well as an assortment of other folks thought to be dangerous. The deportations were not limited to the perceived offenders but also included the extended families of the damned.

"Come over to my flat," Big Peeter Saul urged when I chanced upon him near our old stomping grounds. "Ingrid has gone to the country, to a sanitarium for the cure. The children are staying with her parents until she sobers up."

It was a chance meeting. I was unprepared for the changes that had taken place in my friend. The big man's shoulders sagged. His face was lined with worry. But it was Big Peeter's eyes that told me something was up, that something deeply disturbing was at work in the man.

"All right. I have two hours until my train leaves," I replied. "But I'll only come if you've got some hot coffee: real coffee and not that rye shit Ingrid is always trying to pawn off on your unwanted guests," I added, trying to lighten the mood.

"There's enough left for a pot," Peeter said agreeably, though his demeanor didn't change. "Care for a smoke?" he asked, pulling a pack of Russian cigarettes from the pocket of his dirty work shirt, removing a match and a cigarette, hanging the butt from his chapped lips, and lighting it.

"No thanks. I made a promise to try and quit."

My reply, delivered with just a hint of mystery, caused a change to come over Big Peeter. A hint of my friend's former gregarious nature emerged.

"A girl got *you* to quit smoking?" he said. "Must be quite a catch if she can get *you* to give it up. Let me guess. Some fat girl from a sheep farm outside Kärdla with big titties has let you into her drawers and now you think you're in love. Am I right?"

I laughed. "Far from it."

We walked on. I didn't reveal to my friend that it was indeed a woman, Alexis (who had stopped smoking herself), who urged me to give up the habit.

"Out with it, man. Who the hell is she? The curiosity is killing me."

I chuckled, marveling at the coincidence of having first met Alexis in Tallinn and then having bumped into her again on Hiiumaa Island. Since our outing in the rain, we'd been out to dinner twice, taken a number of casual walks, and talked for hours about life, religion, politics, and our families. But we had not engaged in anything close to what my friend was envisioning.

Big Peeter and I arrived at the doorway to the Saul flat. The distressed fir entry door demanded varnish. Sunlight bathed the faded wood. Big Peeter pulled a ring of keys from a pocket, his dungarees worn so thin that the blue fabric leaked white, and slid a key into the door lock. The big man opened the door, stepped aside, and bid me to enter. My friend followed me into the foyer, flicked a light switch, and led me up a set of narrow stairs.

"You gonna answer me, Kristian, or am I supposed to guess at what you've been up to?"

Big Peeter opened an interior door. We crossed the threshold into the Saul apartment. It was a marvel inside.

When Ingrid Saul was in charge of the household, there were dirty dishes piled in the sink, soiled laundry draped from the furniture, moldy food scattered across the kitchen counter, dust everywhere, cobwebs in the corners and on every light fixture in the place, and children's toys randomly spilled across the wooden floor. There had been no question that Ingrid valued her vodka more than she valued housekeeping. With the woman of the house gone, the place had been transformed.

"This is really something," I said reverently, as I stood on the newly mopped hardwood floor and gazed across the living room, a glorious afternoon sun casting pleasant shadows across the space through freshly cleaned windows. "I take it you hired someone to do this?"

"Nope. Did it myself," Peeter replied, pouring water from a ceramic pitcher into a white porcelain coffee pot on the gas stove. He spooned coffee into the pot's strainer, lit the burner, and motioned for me to take a seat in the living room of the three-room flat. There was no bathroom in the apartment. The Sauls shared a community bath down the hall with two other families. There was a kitchen/living room and two bedrooms: one for the parents, one for the children. "And you haven't answered my question, Kristian. Who is she?"

I sat on an upholstered chair and looked out the nearest window in an attempt to avoid answering.

"No details, no coffee," Big Peeter said, as he sat heavily on a davenport, a piece of furniture normally covered in crumbs and soiled by stains but now cloaked in a freshly laundered bed sheet.

I stalled a bit longer. "What the hell has happened to all the people?"

Big Peeter sighed. "Fucking Russians sent them away. In boxcars, packed like cattle. Men, women, children: it doesn't seem to matter or make any sense who or what you are or you believe. Stalin's orders. Men to labor camps, the women and children transported for "resettlement" on goddamned Russian communes."

"How long has this been going on?"

"Since the takeover. The numbers are staggering. That's why you see only Russian troops out and about. Folks believe 'out of sight, out of mind.' They think that if they stay indoors the NKVD and the goddamned traitor police won't find them," Big Peeter said, as he approached the stove. Steam chugged from the coffee pot's spout. "Coffee's ready," he said, pulling two ceramic cups with his big right hand towards him and filling them. "Here," Peeter continued, reaching towards me with a saucer and a white cup brimming with black coffee. But just as my fingers touched the saucer, he withdrew the offering. "No confession, no coffee," he repeated, with a wink.

I blew air through my nose and mouth. "All right. I'll tell you what you want to know."

He handed me the cup and saucer. "Now. Tell me now: Your train won't wait all day for you."

I nodded. "Remember the waitress at the diner, the night the police dragged me away?"

The big man's brow furrowed. "You should've killed the sonofabitch. A *real* man would've killed the sonofabitch."

"You're missing the point of my story. And if I *had* killed the Russian, I'd either be dead or in prison. But my story isn't about whether I should have killed someone or not. It's about the waitress. You remember her?"

Big Peeter sipped coffee and thought. After a moment, he shook his head.

"Describe her."

"Short, blond, and pretty: The most striking face I've ever seen."

"Still doesn't ring a bell."

I considered how I to describe Alexis in a way that would spark Peeter's memory. More time passed.

"Well, she does have unusual eyes," I finally said.

Big Peeter frowned. "Unusual Eyes? What, is one of them made of glass?"

I sniggered. "No, not glass. She has one blue eye, her left, and one brown, her right. She's also American. Came to Karelia in the Fever."

Big Peeter's expression lightened. "Ah! *That* waitress. Why you dog!"

I grinned and took a big swig from my cup. The coffee was so hot it scalded my tongue. "How can you drink this shit? I burned my fucking mouth!"

"The difference between being a boy and a man, my friend. Despite whatever you and…What the hell is the girl's name?"

"Alexis. Like the Finnish poet. Her name is Alexis Gustafson," I mumbled, my tongue not working right after the trauma of the coffee.

"Well, despite whatever you and your little woman have cooking, you're still just a young buck. Hot coffee is a real man's drink. You'll learn how to handle it someday, just like you'll learn how to handle that knife your father gave you. Wound a Russian? Bah. Kill the bastard, is what I say."

Silence claimed the room. The gas burner on the stove under the coffee pot hissed.

I glanced at the clock on the living room wall. "I best get moving. The train for Tartu leaves in an hour."

Big Peeter smiled. "Finish your coffee. You've got plenty of time," he said quietly. "Your brother still at the university?"

"Studying literature—wants to be a professor."

"Doctor Karl Kristian. Has a nice ring to it, don't you think?"

I nodded but didn't reply.

"He meeting you at the Tartu station?"

I nodded again and drained my cup.

My friend sighed. "I miss you on the crew. Goddamned apprentice they brought in when you went to jail is a fucking communist, worse than Miik Salu."

I stood up. "How is Miik?"

"As ignorant as ever. Despite the purges and folks vanishing in the night, he still thinks Stalin will get it right in the end. Stupid bastard."

"But a good electrician."

"Not as good as me," Big Peeter said through a smile.

I walked to the door.

My friend got up from the couch and placed the palm of his right hand on my shoulder. "You're a clever lad," Peeter said quietly. "And, as it turns out, a bit of a gentleman."

I was puzzled. "How so?"

Peeter's devilish smile exposed tobacco stained teeth. "You never told me what your young lady is like in bed…"

I shook my head and walked out the door.

CHAPTER 4
Helsinki, Finland
June 21, 1941

Rain pummeled them as they scurried along a sidewalk adjacent to a park. They had arrived after a laborious journey. Their train had acquired Finnish soldiers at every stop. War was again in the air and all of Finland was engaged in preparing for the inevitable. Their destination stood on the north side of Esplanade Park. Despite the near constant light of Midsummer, the Hotel Kämp glowed yellow in the mist. The lights of the historic building blazed against the weather and were welcome beacons for the weary travelers from Ostrobothnia. The visitors were dressed in matching yellow rain slickers: garments the man had purchased for their journey. Each carried a valise. In addition, the man held an umbrella. The fabric of the umbrella rippled in the wind and threatened to fail.

"There it is," the man said to the woman.

She looked up. Rain dripped from the umbrella's brim onto her slicker. She nodded and returned her eyes to the wet sidewalk.

In the year since the Winter War's conclusion, events in Europe had changed the relationship between Finland and its neighbors. Tensions were again heightened. Germany, Finland's informal ally, had, through its agenda of expansion, become a source of anxiety. As the ink on the armistice ending the Winter War dried, Germany invaded Denmark and Norway. Hitler followed this surprise move with a blitzkrieg into France. During the same timeframe, the Germans also entered into the Tripartite Pact with Italy and Japan. This agreement was later amended to include Yugoslavia and Bulgaria, though in the case of Yugoslavia, Hitler's promise of mutual assistance meant nothing: Germany invaded Yugoslavia as a prelude to invading Greece and occupied Yugoslavia for the remainder of the war.

Finland was left in a precarious position. Though only a minority of Finns looked to Nazi Germany with approval, the military choices for the Finns were limited: Go it alone if the Soviet Union attacked a second time or form an alliance with Hitler for the limited purpose of defending Finland. Despite previous discussions in Finnish circles of attaining a "Greater Finland," there is no evidence that the Finnish government desired to annex Russian Karelia, Estonia, or other kindred lands and append them to Finland. There was, however, significant interest amongst Finnish politicians in reclaiming areas taken by the U.S.S.R. as part of the Winter War settlement.

Unknown to the man and the woman making their way to the Hotel Kämp, Finland had entered into a secret accord with Nazi Germany. The agreement allowed the Germans to use Finnish ports and airfields as bases of operation for what Hitler termed Operation Barbarossa: the invasion of the U.S.S.R. As part of this accommodation with Germany, Finland also agreed to participate in the upcoming war to a limited degree. The Finnish Army would invade the Karelian Isthmus and push towards Leningrad. A second wave of Finnish troops would attack Petroskoi. Elements of the German Army stationed in Norway would be allowed to cross from Sweden into northern Finland to attack Soviet positions near Salla. Finally, elite German forces would strike from Norway in hopes of securing Petsamo and Murmansk above the Arctic Circle.

The man and the woman entered the hotel's lobby. Neither of them had ever been in the building before. Their visit was an extravagance that the man insisted upon: A gift to the woman, to honor her, to repay her for what she was about to do.

"This is too expensive, Matti. Isn't there a cheaper hotel we can find?"

Elin Goldfarb stood on the marble floor of the foyer, rain dripping from her slicker, her eyes elevated in appreciation of the soaring ceiling.

"Tonight justifies the expense."

There was much about Matti Peltomaa's statement that caused Elin anxiety. Though she had intended their courtship to be lengthy, patient, and slow, in reality, they had only been out to dinner a handful of times; danced once—cheek to cheek waltzing that had made her heart flutter as if she were a hummingbird—kissed and petted with deliberation, and attended one movie and one play. In her state of mind, Elin couldn't recall what the plot of the movie had been, or what the lead character's name in the play was, despite the fact that both outings had taken place only a week ago.

While Matti Peltomaa made arrangements with the desk clerk for a room under the name "Mr. and Mrs. Hintala," Elin tried to curb her nervousness.

Too quickly: It's happening too quickly. When he kissed me that first time, when his lips opened and his tongue sought mine, I refused. Refused to be drawn into passion. He did not complain. He did not object. He is, as I've always known him to be, a patient man. Then why this—so soon, so insistent? Because I agreed to do it! I agreed to come to Helsinki. War is coming. Again. Damn, fucking war. That word: it's not like me to say that word. But it feels good to think it. Fuck, fuck, fuck, fuck.

The curse word became wedged in her mind, like a seed stuck between teeth, as she considered her motivation for accompanying Matti to the hotel.

I felt something rising inside me where nothing has arisen in over a year. When his hand touched my blouse. When his thin, long fingers undid the buttons. When he found my bare skin. I felt it. Needed it. "Not here. Not in some little bed in some little flat in some little town," he had said, withdrawing his fingers, despite the obvious desire on his face. I was ready. I was ready to give in, to let Matti Peltomaa do what he wanted to do. From the way he touched me, from the tender way his fingers explored me, I know he knows how to love a woman. But do I remember how to love a man? That is the ultimate question we are here to answer.

"Something bothering you, Mrs. Hintala?"

Matti stood by Elin's side with a room key in his right hand, his suitcase and the folded umbrella in his left.

She smiled faintly. "Not really, Mr. Hintala."

"Are you ready to find our room?"

Matti Peltomaa's brown eyes shone brightly. He placed the hand holding the room key on her arm and urged her forward. It was a subtle gesture, though Elin felt a sense of urgency, an emotion she had never appreciated in Matti Peltomaa before, as she began to walk, the weight of her suitcase heavy as she moved. They entered an elevator. The doors shut. The lift operator kept his eyes to himself as the car began to climb.

"Here for a while?" the operator, a man about Peltomaa's age and stature, asked, his thick brown beard moving as he spoke.

"Just one night."

The man smiled. The smile was such that it caused Elin to understand that the man was recalling images of other men and women doing things that men and women have been doing since the dawn of humanity. The man's reaction wasn't a smirk—the gesture wasn't that obvious. But all the same, Elin knew what the man was thinking.

"Splendid. You could have asked for assistance with your bags," the operator added, as the car clanked upward. "Our bellhops are good guys, very discrete."

Matti Peltomaa frowned. "We can carry own bags."

The words were curt: As if to say succinctly, but without rancor, *Keep out of our business.*

"I see," the operator said, his eyes glancing at Elin's left hand to discern if she wore a wedding ring. She did. Elin had never removed the simple gold band Hiram had placed on her finger. Cables whined. Gears clanked. The car stopped. "Here's your floor," the operator added. The exterior door opened automatically. The operator pulled a lever and the car's interior door also opened. "Have a good stay," the man said judiciously.

They exited the elevator car. The interior door closed. The main door shut. Cables whined. Gears clanked. The car descended.

"There's our room," Elin said, with a nod.

They walked down the carpeted hallway in silence. If the woman expected some gallant reassurance, wherein the man would express something akin to "Nothing has to happen, Elin. Simply say the word, and I will sleep on the floor," she was mistaken. Matti Peltomaa said nothing of the sort as he turned the key in the lock, pulled hard on the doorknob, and opened the smoothly painted wooden door to their room.

He slept like a man who hadn't slept in years. His seed was inside her. She could feel the wetness where, had she been fertile, and perhaps a few years younger, life is made.

When he had exited the bathroom, the first naked man Elin had seen since Horace—Hiram never allowed her to see his nude body and the Tartar did not disrobe before he raped her—Matti's manhood prominent and ready, his abundant black body hair luxurious in the glow of a bedside lamp, the starchy sheets of the rented bed in the finest hotel in Helsinki wrapped tightly around her body, the man's eyes looking at her with a mixture of angst, longing, and love, she felt familiar stirrings. And, as Matti had climbed under the sheets, the blanket in the hot room having been tossed aside, and his fingers and mouth began their search, their inventory of her, her body responded. The nerve endings of intimacy had recognized Matti's touch and fired in response. And so, the thing that she believed would never be completed—was.

Elin left the bed. She did not cover herself demurely as a schoolgirl might. She walked to the only window in the room, threw back the drapes, and stood naked before the window overlooking the park across the street. The grass was green. The birches and maples were in full leaf. People in summer attire hurried up and down the sidewalks. Cars and trucks puttered. Horns honked. A flock of pigeons took flight.

"God, you are beautiful," Matti Peltomaa said in a sleepy voice, as he scratched his scraggly beard and looked at her from across the room.

She turned towards him, her body accented by sunlight streaming through the window. Her once striking auburn hair, now gray and lacking the luster of youth, was backlit like a saint's halo in an Orthodox icon. Elin Goldfarb smiled but did not reply. She was not embarrassed or ashamed. She was in her natural state and she knew that Matti Peltomaa loved her.

CHAPTER 5
Puhja, Estonia
June 19th, 1941
(Nigul's Story)

In the interval since I'd last seen my brother Karl, he'd taken to wearing wire-rimmed spectacles like those worn by the professors he aspired to be. When we met at the Tartu station after my long, slow, hot ride from Tallinn, the train stopping at every village and town along the way, I was tired and ready to complain about Soviet ineptitude. The Russians were now running things. Or not running things, as in the case of the railroads. Beyond their military capabilities, very little about the Russians or their communist theories impressed me. Inefficiency, rather than equality of brethren, seemed to be the hallmark of Soviet administration. The train ride from Tallinn to Tartu was but one small example of this truth. But instead of complaining, I noted Karl's newfound maturity.

"Brother, you've grown taller," I observed.

I was traveling light. I had left most of my things in Kärdla because I was uncertain whether I would be staying in Puhja, returning to my old job at the shipyard in Tallinn, or going back to the naval yard on Hiiumaa Island. I had a week to consider my options. My heart, of course, was on the island. As I stood on the platform in Tartu, I smiled as my "little" brother, who was just five centimeters shorter than I was, approached. A surplus store duffle bag—a purchase I'd made in Kärdla—hung from my right shoulder. Before Karl could reply, I reached out and slapped his tummy.

"And some weight," I added.

My brother chuckled. "84 kilos," he replied. "But I see I have a ways to go to catch up!"

I glanced down at my waist. It was true. Life at the naval yard had given me an advantage over ordinary Estonians. I was eating well. I had reached my full adult height by then, my eighteenth year, and was 198 centimeters tall and 95 kilos. I patted my belly, which wasn't distended but was firm to the point of snugness in my trousers.

"All muscle," I quipped. "Care to try me?"

Karl laughed again. "I'll pass, brother. I'll pass. We'd best get a move on. With Jaak pulling that old wreck of a wagon, it'll be slow journey back to Puhja."

We began to walk.

"How are they?"

Karl shook his head and muttered a curse, something about "damned communists."

"I meant in terms of their health. Too late to lament what happened to the farm."

Karl's eyes flashed. There was anger, a passion in his look that I'd never seen from him when he was younger.

The university has changed my brother.

"They're doing as well as could be expected. Father's *kannel*s keep him busy. Even though the Reds don't allow folk music to be performed in public, he's got enough of a following to keep bread on the table."

"And Mother?"

"Working as a seamstress in a collective the Russians established in town. Sews children's clothing and has a steady income."

I nodded. We arrived at the four-wheeled wagon. Jaak, who was getting on in years, stood patiently, his ears twitching and his tail switching flies. The horse turned his head at our approach.

"Hello, Jaak," I said, throwing my duffle into the bed of the wagon before standing next to the horse's withers and stroking his velvety hide.

The golden flanks of the horse reflected the sunrise. I stared into the horse's black eyes and encountered my reflection.

"Enough already with the horse," Karl remonstrated. "Time to get moving."

My brother removed the reins from a pine hitching board and clambered onto the wagon's wooden seat. I climbed up alongside him. With a flick of leather, the spoked wheels of the old buckboard began to move.

Once we cleared the city, we resumed our conversation.

"How goes the university?" I asked.

My brother frowned, shifted the reins to his left hand, and lifted the bill of his rumpled cap so as to look me in the eye. "Damned Russians."

I was puzzled. "What?"

"As soon as I started school, they gathered up anyone on the faculty or in the administration who stood with Päts, stood for independence, and carted them off to God-knows-where."

"Stood with Päts? That wouldn't be standing for much. That asshole let the Russians into the country in the first place!"

"Yes, yes. I know. Poor judgment, that. But he at least was an Estonian, believed in Estonia. Most faculty members who thought like him have vanished. The communists also closed the theology department, which, since I wasn't thinking of the ministry," Karl said wryly, "didn't affect me. But then they liquidated the Academy of Sciences," Karl continued, his somber mood returning, "which had just formed. They also purged tens of thousands of 'objectionable' books from the university library."

"Shit."

Jaak stumbled over a stone in the road but regained his balance. A flock of crows cawed in the mild, warm air and flew off to a nearby pasture in fallow to peck at empty soil.

"I'll say," Karl muttered.

The wagon rumbled on. We didn't speak for a while. We passed villages and individual farmhouses, many of them boarded up and unoccupied as the result of collectivization. But despite the abandoned dwellings, there were men and women working the fields and tending herds of cattle and sheep on nearly every hectare of land we passed. An overwhelming feeling of loss manifested as I traveled. I was burdened by the knowledge that the government owned our family's ancestral home on Kalevipoeg Creek and that an end had come to generations of Kristians living off the land. This feeling of loss prevailed, even though I had expressed no inclination to continue the family tradition and Karl—who clearly had no desire to farm—wasn't about to take over from Father in that regard.

"Could it get any worse?" my brother asked.

"Yes," I said quietly. "There will be war."

Karl nodded. "Yes, there will be," he agreed. "The Germans are coming. They will not let the Russians stay here," Karl observed, pulling the wagon off to the side of the dusty road to take a piss.

My brother climbed down from the wagon and found a thicket of brush. I joined him. We did not talk as we did our business. We only resumed our conversation when the wagon was once again rolling.

"And they won't let Stalin take Finland. No way in hell will Hitler let that happen," I continued. "Besides, the Finns showed what they're made of during the Winter War. I doubt Stalin has the stomach for another round in the ring with Mannerheim."

Karl shook his head. "Don't be too sure. Stalin's xenophobia requires that Finland be brought back to the fold."

"*Xenophobia?* Don't use university words on an electrician, little brother," I said, slapping Karl's knee.

"It means 'a fear of strangers or other nationalities'."

"Oh."

The linguistics lesson stalled our discussion for a bit.

"Well," I finally said, "if Stalin is that stupid, he deserves what he gets. Russian blood will flow again. The Finns will not go down without taking tens of thousands of Russians with them. And even then, if Stalin is able to annex Finland, he'll face years of guerilla warfare."

Karl frowned. "It happened here," he observed.

A black fly landed on the crown of my head where my hair was thinning. I swatted at the insect but it flew away without injury. "Damned flies."

"It's been dry. They're out in force. We need rain," Karl said.

What Karl said was true. The road was dusty. In the tilled fields, where the shoots of rye and wheat and barley should have been tall and green, there was withered evidence of my brother's observation. The thirsty lakes and ponds we passed provided additional proof of the need for rain. Creeks trickling beneath the road through culverts ran thin and shallow.

"Yes, it happened here," I finally replied. "But we *let* it happen here. My friend, Big Peeter Saul, he had it right: Päts should have mobilized the army and the navy. Giving in was cowardice, plain and simple."

My brother did not reply immediately. When he spoke, he changed the subject. "I'm hungry. How about you?"

I nodded.

"I packed sandwiches and two bottles of beer. The beer's warm but beer is still beer," Karl said.

My brother found a grove of birch alongside the road and pulled the wagon into shade. Jaak stood out of the sun and away from pesky flies. We sat on hard, dry ground and ate pork sandwiches on Mother's rye bread. Karl had managed to find two pears—two good, firm pears at the market. Fruit was generally the first food subject to shortage. Finding two quality pears was miraculous. The beer was tepid but refreshing against the hot day. Sweat that had formed in my armpits and along the back of my shirt collar chilled me as we ate in the shade. Karl's face was red from the sun but I saw no sweat marks on his shirt.

"How's the love life?" I asked, watching a line of geese move across the clear sky in search of water.

"Nonexistent. I've been concentrating on my studies. No time for socializing."

I smiled. "Well," I said, "it's summer. Time to find a girl and see what happens."

Karl snickered. "What happens is babies are made, that's what happens. No thank you, big brother. I'll keep mine in my pants until I've got my education behind me."

I looked up from the lip of the brown beer bottle. "A firm right hand is a man's best friend," I offered.

Karl laughed. "And less expensive than a baby."

I nodded as I sipped beer. "True enough. True enough."

A truck, its wooden cargo deck stacked with lumber, rattled past our picnic spot on its way to Puhja.

"And you?"

"I have one too," I answered proudly, lewdly gesturing with my right hand.

Karl grinned. "No, I mean, have you found someone?"

Alexis Gustafson's dimpled chin and exquisite face came to mind. Time passed.

Karl stood up and crumpled the paper bag and newspaper wrapping from his lunch into a ball and tossed it in the back of the wagon. "Nigul?"

I smiled sheepishly as I followed suit and tossed crumpled paper into the buckboard.

"You dog," Karl said. "You *have* found someone. I thought you were through with women after that German girl, what was her name?"

"Ellisabet. Ellisabet Raun."

Karl led Jaak and the wagon out into the sun by the horse's leather harness. Jaak stood patiently as my brother straightened the reins and climbed into the wagon seat.

"Yes," Karl said gaily, "Ellisabet. The girl in the barn—a true roll in the hay! Whatever happened to her?"

I clambered into the wagon. "Last I heard she was in Germany, going to university."

Karl clicked his tongue. Jaak began to walk. "Isn't she a Nazi?"

"Her Father. Her Father's a Nazi."

"Oh."

We were only a few kilometers from Puhja when Karl brought up my love life again. "Who is she?"

I was lost in thought. I was considering how Estonia would react if the Germans invaded.

It could be a godsend. The Germans might, so long as we stand with them against Stalin, give us back our country. Self-rule under their protection. That's one possibility. Or, I thought, *we could be trading one master for another. Hard to say what will happen when they come. Not 'if'. It's not a question of 'if' but 'when'.*

"Damn it, Nigul. I asked you a question."

"Sorry. An American Finn. Came to Karelia in the Fever and then went to Leningrad. To university. To become a doctor."

"St. Petersburg," Karl corrected, disdaining the Soviet name for the Russian city.

"Yes, St. Petersburg. She ended up becoming a teacher. Came to Kärdla in hopes of getting to Finland. Her mother is supposedly in Finland. Her father, really her stepfather, disappeared. No one knows for certain what happened to him, though Alexis—that's her name—is certain he's dead."

"Where the hell did you meet an American woman?"

"Tallinn. In a diner. She was waitressing. She was there the night they came to take me to jail."

Karl whistled. "Should have killed the bastard."

I smiled. "Big Peeter Saul said the same thing."

Karl nodded. "Never met the man and already I like him."

The horse worked hard. Sweat glistened on his yellow flanks. The white steeple of Puhja's Lutheran church announced itself on the horizon.

"Nearly there," I said.

"Stop changing the subject. So this 'Alexis': Is she beautiful, like Ellisabet?"

I hesitated. My mind sought images for comparison. "More beautiful."

Karl whistled again.

The gelding strained in his harness at the prospect of home. With Jaak's renewed vigor, we made Puhja before dark.

"There's the house," Karl said softly, as dusk settled over the village.

Puhja's buildings appeared as silhouettes against the setting sun. Shadows lengthened and enveloped the road.

The wagon rolled to a stop in front of a modest frame house. A white picket fence enclosed a drought-stricken front lawn. The fence was newly painted. Two apple trees, the blossoms gone, apples beginning to form from the fallen flowers, stood at opposite ends of the front yard. The home was newly painted to match the fence: white with blue trim. The leaves of the apple trees were fragile from drought. Behind the house, a small garden plot flowed towards empty pasture, the adjoining fields unworked due to the lack of rain. In my parent's vegetable garden, cabbage, carrots, potatoes, and beans had germinated but seemed destined to fail. A familiar profile appeared in a front window of the modest house. Mother's face pressed against the glass and made me realize that, though the farm on Kalevipoeg Creek was no longer ours, I still had a home.

CHAPTER 6
Joensuu, Finland
June 22, 1941

"Go home, old man," a young sergeant said to the veteran. "Sit this one out."

Matti Peltomaa had traveled by train, in cars overburdened with Finnish men, from Helsinki to Joensuu, where he hoped to reunite with his mates. Rintala's Raiders were to be attached to Unit P of the 18th Division, a special operations battalion under the leadership of Major General Aaro Pajari. Juha Rintala had telegraphed Peltomaa in Pietarsaari, advising him to hurry to Joensuu, which, other than a slight detour to the Hotel Kämp, Peltomaa managed to accomplish.

Matti had traveled in uniform. He had kept his gray trousers and blouse, the Tokarev, two bandoliers of ammunition, as well as his canteen, boots, the Luger, and other assorted gear after the Winter War. He wore no medals. Peltomaa's service had been rewarded with pendants and ribbons, but he was uneasy with such honors. The commendations and finery were stored in a wooden box in Juha Rintala's home. Rintala was saving them for the day when Matti Peltomaa would accept the medals honoring his service but that day would never come.

Medals? I need no medals to reward me for what has been done or what will be done. We'll sweep the Russian trash back to Russia. We'll reclaim Karelia. That's what's important—not pieces of tin and ribbon hanging from my shirt.

"I served during the Winter War. I am here to serve again."

Peltomaa displayed no emotion as he replied. He remained steadfast in the face of the sergeant's insolence. It was clear, from the recruiter's age and demeanor that he had not served in the Winter War, that he had no experience regarding the wet and mud and snow and blood that bonded one man, one soldier, to the next.

The recruiter wore his blond hair in a stiff pompadour and was but a slip of a man, barely present, in a physical sense. He had a thin face, razor sharp cheekbones and weak hazel eyes. A large, red birthmark discolored the right side of the man's face. Peltomaa had all he could do to refrain from staring at the blemish.

"How old are you, anyway?" the youth asked.

"Sixty-three."

"You're a grandfather, for chrissake."

Matti smiled a Cheshire smile. "Not that I know of."

"How's that?"

Peltomaa took a breath. "Well, sonny, though I've slept with many women, so far as I know, I've never made a one of them pregnant. Either good luck or bad swimmers. You decide."

Peltomaa's attempt at humor did not break the sergeant's demeanor.

"Doesn't change the fact that you're too old to fight."

"No he's not."

Lieutenant Laurila—now Captain Laurila after a battlefield promotion—strode through the milling crowd of impatient men and stood next to Matti Peltomaa. The officer looked down his nose, a black handlebar mustache drooping off his cheeks as he bent close to the young sergeant.

"Sir?"

"This man is not too old to serve with *me*," Laurila repeated. "Assign him to my company in Unit P. Rintala's platoon."

The sergeant stared blankly.

"Did you not hear me, sergeant? Assign *Corporal* Peltomaa to Rintala's platoon."

Matti smiled at his instant elevation in rank. "Thank you, sir," he said.

Laurila grunted, said nothing, and walked away.

The sergeant drew the necessary paperwork. Peltomaa signed.

"Looks like you're already equipped," the young man observed, his tone more respectful, as he nodded at the Tokarev resting against the wooden desk. "Russian?"

"Taken from Tartars in the Karelian woods..." Juha Rintala responded unexpectedly from behind the old man, "...while you, sergeant, were still nuzzling your mama's teat!"

The young man's face reddened. Peltomaa picked up his rifle and followed Rintala towards the exit.

"It's good to see you, Matti," Juha Rintala said, as the two men went outside. A mist was falling. Cold Arctic wind blew in from the north. It had rained for two days and another storm was on the way. "I trust the trip from Pietarsaari was slow and boring?"

Peltomaa smiled. "All of that."

Except, of course, for the night I spent with the loveliest woman in all of Finland. I felt Elin awaken as we met in the bed of our hotel room. Did I complete her? Matti silently considered this question as he reflected on the brief, wondrous exchange their bodies had succumbed to. *I don't honestly know. But if I did, then hopefully, she has put the past away. Forever. If not, we have time. I will, on the very first chance I get, marry that woman. Whether she knows it yet or not, she will become the first Mrs. Peltomaa. I am, as that young whippersnapper just observed, an old man. But an old man who can still fight…and love!*

"You're lost in thought," Rintala observed, as they walked towards a café. "Nervous about the war?"

Peltomaa shook his head.

"Then what?"

Peltomaa looked down the street.

"It's a woman, isn't it?"

Matti nodded.

"From Pietarsaari?"

"Indirectly."

A pause. Rintala opened the door to the restaurant. The smell of fried meat greeted them as they entered.

"Damn! It's that American woman, isn't it? I should have known!" Rintala said.

Peltomaa smiled.

"You're not going to tell me, are you?"

They sat down at an empty table.

Peltomaa leaned the automatic rifle against a cracked plaster wall before responding. "No, I am not."

"Asshole."

They considered the menu. The waitress, a small girl, no more than ten years old, on summer break from school, appeared. She wasn't a stereotypical Finnish girl. She was black haired, brown eyed, and darkly complected. The men both ordered fish stew with rye bread, butter, and coffee. The girl wrote down the order on a notepad and walked away, never having said a word.

"Quiet kid."

Peltomaa nodded. "Sami."

They sipped cold water from glass tumblers. They did not speak until after their bowls of stew, plates of bread, pads of butter, and cups of hot coffee arrived. Again, the girl remained silent as she served them.

"Strange little girl."

Peltomaa smiled. "Sami."

"I heard you before," Rintala grunted, sipping hot broth off a spoon. "Good stew."

Peltomaa broke off a piece of rye bread and buttered it. Another period of quiet ensued.

"Think we can take back Karelia?" Rintala finally said.

Matti Peltomaa thought about the question. "Ya. But we can't hold it."

Juha Rintala leaned away from the table. "A half a million Finns will return to their homes in Karelia. How can you say we can't hold it?"

Peltomaa slurped.

"Out with it, man," Rintala said impatiently.

Matti put down his spoon and looked at his friend. "The Germans won't win," he said quietly, so as not to be overheard. "This whole alliance, this whole campaign, this whole new war, it's…wrongheaded. That's what it is. The Germans will come in, blitzkrieg is what they say, and roll across Russia. They have better men, better tanks, better air support, better leaders. Hell, Stalin killed any Russian officer worth his salt before the war ever started. But…."

The American paused.

"Yes? I am interested to hear what it is you have to say, *corporal*."

Peltomaa ignored the pejorative inflection affixed to his new rank. "In the end, the Russians will throw them out. They are simply too many for the Germans to handle so far from home, so far from their petrol and food supplies. From a military standpoint, it's wrongheaded. And it's wrongheaded because we'll be asked to join the Germans. We already have, in fact, done just that by allowing them to cross our country to put troops on the Russian border, by allowing German planes to use our airfields and airspace, and by allowing German ships to patrol our seas. The Allies, Britain, France, and eventually, if it's drawn into the mess, America, well, they won't take kindly to Finland siding with the Nazis. Because, regardless of *why* President Ryti and Prime Minister Rangell believe it's our only option, we are still, in the end, my young friend, joining the fucking Nazis."

Juha Rintala nodded. "But what other choice is there?"

Peltomaa picked up his bowl and slurped down the last of the broth. "None," he said, placing the empty bowl on the table. "Absolutely none. But when the allies see our warplanes and tanks displaying blue swastikas and fighting on the same side of the question as the Germans, who are no better—and in fact, may be worse—than the communists in terms of rounding up innocent non-combatants and murdering them, well, the conclusion, though it will be wrong, that the allies will draw, is that we are now Nazis."

Rintala took a sip of coffee. "The swastika was *our* symbol before Hitler hijacked it," he observed.

"I know that. You know that. But the allies don't. The symbolism is but a small thing. Allowing the Nazis free rein over our country, to come and go as they wish, to use our ports, to land planes on our soil, will prove to be far greater wrongs in the eyes of the allies. We will be seen, to use an American legal term, as 'conspirators' in Hitler's hatred towards the Jews and others. Is that a label Finland wants to be stamped with?"

Juha Rintala shook his head. "But there aren't many Jews *in* Finland. What has happened to the Jews in Poland and Lithuania won't happen here."

"You're probably right. But Finland's reputation isn't enhanced by siding with Adolph Hitler."

The men stood up, drew money from their pockets, and paid their tabs. The girl reappeared, cleared the dishes, took the money to the cashier, pocketed her tip, but never said a word.

"Strange girl," Rintala said again, and, before Matti Peltomaa could reply, quickly added, "I know, I know: She's Sami."

CHAPTER 7
Puhja, Estonia
June 24th, 1941
(Nigul's Story)

Hitler *Attacks the Fatherland! All Loyal Estonians Called to Arms!*

I read the lead article in the *Eesti Päevaleht* with interest, though I knew the premise of the headline was a lie. The Germans were coming not to destroy Estonia; they were coming to destroy Stalin. But I also knew that the issue of whether the Germans would allow Eesti its independence was an open question.

I doubt Hitler is willing to allow Estonia to be self-governing. No, it's more likely the Germans are coming to replace the Russians as our masters. Which will be the worse? Who can say?

"This is shit," I whispered, as I turned the page to read the rest of the article.

"Nigul, watch your language," Father said, his weary look accentuated by the low glow of the electric lamp across the room. The confiscation of our farm, *his* farm, had taken an immense toll on the old man. I could see it his stooped frame, shuffled gait, and heavily lined face. "Your mother is listening."

Mother sat in the claustrophobic living room of the small frame house on Viljanditee, the main east-west thoroughfare through Puhja, her feet propped on an ottoman, her eyes closed, enjoying a symphony on the radio. Between bits of propaganda, the station would play "approved" symphony and brass music. No folk songs or popular tunes, nothing with lyrics was allowed to "contaminate" the People. Still, with my mother's love of music being so fervent, so ingrained in her being, even poor music was better, in her view, than no music.

"The man who must curse to express himself," Mother said quietly, her eyes remaining shut as she spoke, "is a man with nothing to say."

Father nodded, as he whittled a new walking stick. The maple was white, having not been exposed to the air long enough to turn. Strips of bark fell from the blade of Father's folding knife and cluttered the pine floor around his stocking feet.

"I am sorry, Mother, but this piece, this story in the newspaper, well, it's so damned biased, it serves no purpose to print it."

Father frowned at my second curse but said nothing.

Mother's eyes opened slightly. "I know you're upset," she said, with steadiness. "I know you think that, at eighteen years old, you should be doing something brave and heroic. That somehow you need to strike out, to lend a hand, maybe join the Germans when they come. *If* they come."

"Oh, they will come, Hele; they are already on their way," Father said sternly. Despite Father's physical decline, his voice maintained vigor. "And nothing good will come of it. True, they helped us against the Russians in the civil war. But to what end? Estonia is too small, too isolated, too weak to continue as it has been. The Germans will come, my darling wife, and they will never leave!"

I sighed. "Perhaps. But what good has transpired with the goddamned Russians being in charge? Deportations? Hunger? Loss of rights? Are these good things, things that you wish to continue?"

My father rested the blade of the knife on his knee. He held the staff in front of him to inspect his work. "Watch your mouth," he repeated evenly. "Do not take God's name in vain in this house."

I smiled, put down the newspaper, and tilted my head like that famous RCA dog. "Since when did you become a churchman?" I asked.

Mother opened her eyes. "Nigul, your father *is* a godly man. He may not attend services much, but he is a godly man. Apologize."

I looked at my mother. Though her blue Finnish eyes did not reveal the same weariness as Father's, it was clear from the age lines that had recently appeared across her forehead and around her mouth that the loss of the farm, the loss of my parent's good life in the country, had taken a toll on her as well.

This is not the time for an argument.

"I'm sorry."

Father grunted, lowered the maple walking stick, and resumed his work. I opened the paper and finished the article. Mother's eyes closed again.

"Where's Karl?" Father asked, after I moved on to another section of the newspaper.

"At the tavern," I replied.

"He's not eighteen."

"Riki Laak is bartending tonight. Karl went to school with his sister. Took her to a dance or two. Karl won't have any problems buying beer from Riki."

Father put down his knife again. "Too young. It starts too young with you two."

I shook my head but there was no point in debating my love for vodka with my old man. No point at all.

"Boys will always be boys, Andres," Mother said. "Seems to me, you're not shy around a bottle yourself."

Father opened his mouth to protest, but yielded to truth and said nothing. He stood up from the wooden chair, leaned the maple stick, the bark completely removed, against a wall, and shuffled over to a closet. He opened a door, retrieved a broom and dustpan, walked back to his chair, stooped over, and pushed maple shavings into the dustpan with the broom.

"You missed some," Mother observed through a partially opened eye.

Father grunted again, found the wayward piece of curled bark, picked it up with his fingers, and dropped it in the dustpan.

"Satisfied?"

"Quite," Mother replied with a grin, as she closed the eye.

Father walked to the woodstove, opened the door, and shook the shavings from the metal dustpan into the inert firebox. He returned the broom and dustpan to the closet, shut the door, and stood in fragile light, considering what his next chore should be.

"Think I'll go down to the *Halb Perse* (Bad Ass) and join Karl," I said quietly, as I uncoiled my legs and stood. "You want the paper?"

Father shook his head. "Damned rag isn't worth using to wipe my ass," he muttered.

I smiled. "I guess I'm not the only one with a cursing problem," I quipped.

Mother was snoring softly and made no reply.

Karl and I sat at the bar drinking Saku beer from bottles. It was Tuesday and we were Riki Laak's only customers.

"How goes it, Riki?" I asked, when Karl and I had exhausted topics between us.

Riki was tall and thin, nearly my height but at least twenty kilos lighter. He had a shaved head—the result of a scalp condition that left his blond hair patchy. He shaved his skull to the skin, so that, under the Estonian sun, it had browned to the color of a light skinned African. He had brown eyes and a nasty knife scar on his left forearm, a reminder of an altercation between Riki and the husband of a married woman in the village, a woman Riki had the misfortune of convincing into his bed. Riki had been lucky. Other patrons in the Bad Ass were present when the jealous husband showed up, swinging a knife. Customers subdued the crazed lunatic shortly after he sliced Riki's arm and before the pissed off husband could carry out his threat of cutting off Riki's balls and stuffing them down the bartender's throat.

"My last day."

"Been reading *Revelations* again, Riki?" Karl asked through a slur.

The biblical reference was completely lost on Riki, who was an atheist. "What the fuck are you talking about?"

"I thought you were talking about the rapture," Karl added, with deliberation. My brother was on his seventh beer and his effort to appear sober wasn't successful. "You know, 'the last day'," Karl added.

Riki shook his head. "You're crazy, you know that, Karl? That university bullshit has gone to your head."

I drew another mouthful of beer, swallowed it, and motioned for Riki to bring me another Saku. He walked over to the cooler, opened it, pulled out a frosted bottle, popped the top, and slid the bottle down the bar. Riki's aim and pace were perfect. The bottle stopped directly in front of me without hitting the empty.

"What do you mean, 'your last day'?" I asked.

"I'm joining the Forest Brothers."

"Whatareyoutalkin' about?" Karl asked.

Riki shook his head. "No more beer for your little brother."

I nodded. "But answer Karl's question? What's this about the 'Forest Brothers'? You joining the Orthodox Church? Converting? Becoming a monk?"

Riki grinned widely, exposing ugly teeth, the enamel black from rot.

Only a matter of time and he'll be down to gums, I thought.

"Major Kurg is organizing a battalion of veterans," Riki explained. "Estonians who were impressed into the Soviet Army are deserting in droves now that the Germans are on the way. Kurg wants to take Tartu back from the Russians before the Germans get here."

"To hell you say!"

The bartender eyeballed me. "You'd fit in well, Nigul. You shoot straight. You run like a deer and ski like the wind. Kurg would take you in a heartbeat," Riki said quietly, placing both hands on the bar. "And he'd probably even take this one," he added, nodding towards Karl who had succumbed to the beer and was now sleeping, his head on the bar, his mouth open and drooling, "if you can keep him away from beer."

I laughed. "Where do we sign up?"

"Village hall. At first light. Action's already started up in the Harju District. The Forest Brothers attacked a Soviet convoy and killed dozens of Russians. It's begun, Nigul. Liberation is at hand."

Liberation? Maybe. Maybe not. But, despite my concerns about Hitler, I'd rather fight alongside the Germans than continue kowtowing to the Russians.

"At first light, Nigul. Be there at first light."

I nodded, lifted Karl's head from the bar, and brought him to his feet. My brother wobbled so I draped his arm around my neck and propped him up as we walked through the bar's front door. It was dark outside except for the soft glow of an electric street lamp at the end of the block and the neon sign announcing the *Halb Perse*. The sign jutted out from the tavern on a wrought iron standard and crackled in the heat.

A tavern with more class, I thought, as we turned towards home, *would animate that donkey.*

But the neon ass didn't kick: It just flickered occasionally until Riki shut the sign off and closed down the bar shortly after Karl and I took our leave. Mosquitoes buzzed us as we lumbered home. I couldn't swat the pests because I was propping Karl up. I let the insects stab me and drink their fill. Puhja was asleep. Light leaked through drawn curtains onto the vacant street. As we passed a two-story house, the biggest house in town, I heard a voice, a woman's voice, tittering behind glass. The voice triggered memories of bicycles and rain.

I wonder if Alexis will understand? I'll write her. I won't ask her to wait for me—we don't have that kind of bond. But I'll explain what I've decided. I'll have her pack my things from my flat and send them to my parents. Maybe we can rekindle what we've started after the war, after the Russians are gone.

Our folks were asleep when we arrived home. I helped Karl up a steep, narrow stairway. The attic was heavy with summer heat as I stripped Karl to his undershorts and laid his limp body on a quilt covering a single bed. My brother never stirred as I propped his head with a pillow. I opened a dormer window in search of fresh air, but there was no breeze. With my brother snoring like a hibernating bear, I undressed to my undershorts, pulled a wool blanket back, and slid beneath a freshly laundered sheet.

CHAPTER 8
Kärdla, Estonia
November 1, 1941

Alexis Gustafson no longer taught in Russian. She had returned to educating Estonian students in their native tongue. This change was made possible because German soldiers occupied Estonia.

Alexis had received Nigul Kristian's letter in early September of 1941. By then, Nigul and his brother had participated in the fighting as members of the Forest Brothers. Major Kurg and his men reclaimed Tartu after a pitched siege of the city lasting more than two weeks, during which the medieval city was reduced to rubble by Stalin's "scorched earth" policy as the Russians retreated. The Germans had invaded Estonia in early July but the Wehrmacht had been content to allow Kurg's men to do the dirty work at Tartu. After that city fell, the Germans joined the partisans in retaking Narva and Tallinn. And, by October 21, 1941, the Soviet occupiers of Hiiumaa Island had also been dislodged.

Dear Alexis:

I hope this letter finds you in good health. I have left my job in Kärdla. Please understand that this is no reflection on you. I chose to sign up with Major Kurg to fight the Russians. Given your history and the history of your mother and father in Karelia, I am certain you'll understand. My brother Karl, whom I spoke to you about at some length, has also joined up. In his case, the choice was very easy. The university in Tartu is now a pile of bricks. So, at least for now, his education will have to wait.

I am writing this letter to ask that you pack my belongings and send them to my parents. Send them in care of Andres Kristian. Tell the landlord that I will mail him a money order for my rent as soon as I am able. He should understand this if you explain that I am now a Forest Brother, as I believe him to be a patriot.

There are personal things I would like to write, words between us that should be said. However, the time grows short and the words I am thinking of are best delivered in person. Once the fighting is over and the Russians have been pushed back, the Germans will likely launch an offensive. When that occurs, Estonia will be left alone and I will be free to come to Hiiumaa and tell you how I feel.

You can write me in care of my parents. The post is very slow but eventually I will get whatever letters you send.

Yours,
Nigul Kristian

Alexis had done as Nigul asked. She had met with the landlord, gained access to Nigul's apartment, and retrieved Nigul's belongings, which she dutifully packaged and brought to the Estonian mainland on the ferry for mailing to Puhja. Alexis had also, out of her own meager savings, taken care of Nigul's past due rent. This was not a gesture she shared with Nigul in any letter or note: It was simply done.

In addition to the restoration of Estonian as the official language of the country, the invasion—though feared by Estonian Communists who retreated with the Red Army only to find their fate under Stalin to be no better than what Hitler would have accorded—allowed Estonians the freedom to move about the country. This freedom prompted Alexis Gustafson to plan a journey from Hiiumaa Island to Tallinn and then to Helsinki in search of her mother.

Though travel restrictions had eased, it was no simple matter for Alexis, an American citizen who had lived in Karelia and Leningrad, to convince the authorities that her trip to Finland was as a dutiful daughter and not as a spy. Her mother's reputation did not curry favor with those in power. It took months of wrangling and begging and solicitous patience for Alexis to receive approval from the Estonian government for permission to travel. She was to exercise this privilege during the first week of January1942. Despite her good fortune, there remained a significant and complicating factor to Alexis's quest: She had no idea where her mother was.

Alexis tried to determine her mother's whereabouts before leaving Kärdla. There was some evidence that Elin Goldfarb had been in Helsinki. Records from the Woman's and Orphan's Building placed Elin at that facility. According to the United States Legation in Finland, Elin had briefly lived at the shelter during the bombings at the onset of the Winter War. But after that, there was only confusion as to Elin Goldfarb's whereabouts.

To find Mother, the young teacher thought, *will require my own effort, my own investigation. I will start by talking to those at the shelter who knew Mother. Perhaps they have information as to where she went. If that doesn't lead me to her, I will inquire of the Finnish authorities, including the Valpo if necessary, to determine if she has been placed in a resettlement camp. That's a distinct possibility given Mother is an American without documentation. Though Finland is a big country, it is a small place: Most everyone knows someone who knows someone. I will find her. I have a week. I will find her.*

The trip across the Gulf of Finland on a Finnish ferry was uneventful. Despite the onset of winter, the sky was clear and the slight southerly wind was warm. The sea was calm. The *Tampere*, an old tub that plied the waters between Tallinn and Helsinki, rode the sea with steadiness. Alexis, who had been prone to seasickness during her family's long voyage from America, did not experience nausea. She was steady on her feet and yearning to find her mother when the *Tampere* docked in Finland and disgorged its passengers.

"There is little I can tell you, Miss Gustafson."

Alexis Gustafson sat on a hard oak chair in the office of Lahja Jussila, the executive director of the Woman's and Orphan's Building. Alexis was dressed for traveling in knit trousers, a heavy sweater, blue blouse, and boots. Her overcoat was draped across the back of her chair. A matching scarf remained wrapped around her throat as she sipped hot coffee and listened intently to the older woman.

"Your mother was here, that is true. She came from Joensuu, after crossing into Finland from Soviet Karelia, was processed by the authorities, and cleared for travel. She arrived in Helsinki and stayed with us for a brief time. But then, as best I can tell, she simply left. The records should be more complete in this regard—they should indicate where she went. But unfortunately, there is nothing more."

"Could you look more closely to see if anyone else arrived with Mother? That might give me a name of someone I can contact."

The director studied the folder of official documents on the desk in front of her. The woman was in her early sixties. Her formerly blond hair had turned silver and formed a thick, tightly woven bun on the back of her head. Square eyeglasses sat low on her long nose. Despite her age, age that was revealed as folds in the skin of her neck and as lines around her mouth and eyes, Miss Jussila (she wore no ring) remained attractive. Her hazel eyes displayed intelligence and concern.

"I'm sorry, Miss Gustafson, but that would be nearly impossible. Many women and children were displaced by the Soviet attack. There was so much turmoil, I don't see how we could begin to honor your request."

Alexis frowned. The two women faced each other and remained silent for a considerable period. A radio in the corner played soft music.

Sibelius. The Seventh Symphony.

Alexis forgot her situation for a moment and hummed a few bars of the movement along with the orchestra.

Lahja Jussila smiled. "You're a Sibelius fan?"

Alexis shook her head. "Not really. Mother is. She's also partial, as strange as it might seem, to the Russian composers. The old music. Before Stalin," she added hastily. "I recognized the tune and hummed it out of habit."

Jussila nodded.

"Can you think of nothing that we can do to find out who may have had contact with my mother, who might know where she went?"

The older woman considered the question. "Perhaps someone on my staff might recall something."

"It's worth a try," Alexis said after consideration. "Where would I find someone like that to talk to?"

Miss Jussila donned her winter coat and accompanied Alexis Gustafson to another building in the complex. The director introduced Alexis to staff members who had been at the facility when Elin Goldfarb arrived during the Winter War. The third woman the pair interviewed recalled Elin Goldfarb.

"Lovely woman. Striking," the young worker said, as they stood in the hallway of the building that had once housed Elin, Helmi Kemi, and the two youngest Kemi children. "She was very close to that woman who committed suicide in the laundry room. I can't recall that unfortunate woman's name..."

Lahja Jussila thought a moment.

"Helmi Kemi...Of course! Now I remember your mother," Miss Jussila exclaimed. "Very strong-willed and loyal to her young friend, Mrs. Kemi. They came here from Joensuu. That young woman lost two sons during an air attack on the train. A daughter and another son arrived here with Mrs. Kemi and your mother. Your description—that your mother had auburn hair—threw me a bit. She's lost most of that color, you know. To age, like we all do," Miss Jussila said with a smile, patting the taut bun of silver resting atop her head. "Of course I knew your mother!"

Alexis felt hope, colored by angst, well up inside her.

Three years. I haven't seen Mother in three years. She's gone gray in that time. What other changes have there been?

"Do you know what happened to her?" Alexis asked.

The other woman nodded.

"Well, out with it," Miss Jussila demanded. "Can't you see this woman is in a hurry?"

The aid worker, a homely faced, large girl about Alexis's age, paused to collect her thoughts.

"Your mother was to escort the children back to Mrs. Kemi's hometown," the woman finally said. "Mrs. Kemi left your mother a note—with instructions."

"And?"

"Joensuu?" Alexis interrupted. "Did Mother return to Joensuu?"

The woman shook her head. "No, that wasn't it. Somewhere in Ostrobothnia, I believe."

Miss Jussila lost her patience. "Think, damn it, think! Miss Gustafson only has a week to find her mother, not a year!"

The aide worker's pie-shaped face contorted from effort. "Pietarsaari! That's where your mother went. We got a postcard from her some months later. She turned the children over to their grandparents and stayed on in Pietarsaari. I still have the postcard. It has a picture of a hotel on it. She also wrote her return address on the card. I'll get it for you."

The woman retrieved the postcard from her room and handed it to Alexis.

Mother's handwriting. Mother's address. God be praised.

Miss Jussila nodded. "Thank you, Henna. I'll see Ms. Gustafson back to the office and on her way."

Alexis tucked the postcard into the front pocket of her coat and the women made their way back to the main building.

"I hope you find your mother," Miss Jussila said with concern, as the women stood outside Miss Jussila's office.

"Thank you for your help," Alexis replied, shaking the woman's blue veined hand. "It's in God's hands now."

The older woman nodded but said nothing further as she watched Alexis Gustafson walk out the door.

CHAPTER 9
August 1941
Karelian Isthmus

The mosquitoes were incessant. The sun was high and the day was hot. The soldiers were adept at fighting in the cold and snow that had defined the Winter War: They were not accustomed to the heat and insects of Karelian summer.

Corporal Matti Peltomaa marched along a dusty country lane with his mates. Above the Finnish column, Brewster Buffalos flew in formation, providing protection against the seemingly infinite Soviet Air Force. Sergeant Rintala strode at the head of the platoon. The young Finn's legs were long and his pace was difficult to emulate but no man lagged behind. No man failed to keep up because the Finns were engaged in a hastily conceived flanking maneuver engineered by General Pajari, which, if successful, would place the entire division behind the enemy. If the general could out-think the Russians, his men would be able to strike at the enemy's soft underbelly and route them from the field. But there was risk inherent in Pajari's move. If the general's plan was detected *before* the Finns were in place to launch their strike, the Finns would be encircled, and Pajari—not the Russians—would be the one raising the white flag.

"Damn it, Juha, you move too fast," Peltomaa muttered as he walked next to Rintala, the late summer sun glaring in his eyes.

Juha Rintala did not turn his head as he replied. "Captain Laurila and I both stood for you in Joensuu when that pup called you an 'old man.' Your whining makes me think the recruiter was right," Juha Rintala said firmly.

Peltomaa frowned. "If we keep up this pace, we'll be so damned tired by the time we take up our positions, we won't have any energy to fight," the older man said between breaths.

The sergeant nodded and softened his words. "There is that. But I have faith in your powers of recuperation."

Dust settled over the column as the Finns hurried forward. There was no way to completely conceal the presence of so many men, though, as he would do throughout the Continuation War, General Pajari was a master of the "special project": clandestine operations that relied upon surprise. The 18th Division's rushed advance was the first of many such strategies employed by the general during Finland's second conflict with the Red Army.

Soviet T-26 medium tanks, captured by the Finns during the Winter War, made up the majority of the armor the Finnish Army could muster for an attack. But to avoid detection, the Finns advanced without tank support. A few of the platoons were now outfitted with the Lahti: an anti-tank rifle produced in Finland and nicknamed "the elephant gun." But the heavy weapon, while effective against older Soviet tanks like the T-26 and T-28, had little impact against newer Soviet tanks. Projectiles fired by the Lahti simply bounced off the armor of T-34s. Corporal Peltomaa was charged with manning his platoon's Lahti, knew the weapon's limitations, and was thankful that Rintala had purloined a draft horse from the artillery to pull the heavy rig.

The cumbersome Lahti rolled along behind Peltomaa on steel wheels. The nag pulling the heavy gun swished its tail against flies. A young private walked alongside the tired black horse leading it by a leather halter. Buffaloes roared overhead. After a full day of marching the Finns arrived at their destination: a long gash in the flat terrain from which the division would launch its assault.

"They have no idea we're here," Captain Laurila said quietly as he studied the Russian position through binoculars.

The Finnish troops waited behind the natural berm of a creek hollow. Peltomaa's Lahti was positioned in a thicket, its muzzle aimed at a cluster of tanks parked at the rear of the Russian position and facing west, away from the hidden Finns and towards the expected fight. A box magazine holding ten rounds was affixed to the Lahti. Additional magazines rested on the ground on a tarp next to the anti-tank gun. The air was still. The Russians were too distant to be overheard. The quiet was unnerving even to veterans like Rintala and Peltomaa. A radio crackled. A corporal assigned as Laurila's communication specialist picked up the receiver and handed it to the captain. Laurila said a few words and then handed the receiver back to the radio operator.

"Our guns will open up in five minutes. A ten minute barrage and then we go," Laurila said quietly. A flock of long-tailed ducks landed in the creek behind the Finns. "A good sign," Laurila said to Juha Rintala who was kneeling next to his commander behind the cover of birch trees. "Even the ducks don't know we're here."

Rintala nodded.

"Make sure the Old Man takes out those tanks," Laurila added. "I don't want those bastards turning on us when we break across open ground."

"He'll take them out. He's got as good an eye as any man in my platoon," Rintala replied, "despite his age."

Laurila tipped back his officer's cap and looked at the sergeant. The pressure of command, of being on the cusp of his first major engagement of the Continuation War, was clear in the captain's expression. Laurila said nothing. He returned to watching the enemy through his binoculars.

Five minutes after the radio transmission, the Finnish guns opened up. Explosions rocked the enemy position. Dirt and men and supplies and equipment were blown to bits as the Finnish gunners honed their aim. The Soviet tanks spun their turrets in the direction of the cannon fire.

"Take out those goddamned tanks!" Laurila roared.

Peltomaa aimed the Lahti at the metallic rump of a T-26 and squeezed the anti-tank rifle's trigger.

Crack.

Dirt spit behind the tank.

"Raise the barrel one click," Peltomaa ordered.

The private adjusted the gun. Peltomaa squeezed off another round.

Crack.

The 20mm slug slammed into the tank. Flames erupted. The crew scrambled to escape out the tank's main hatch.

"Take out the next one!" Rintala yelled at the top of his lungs over the Finnish artillery.

Peltomaa aimed and fired the Lahti. The round found its target and disabled a second T-26. The remaining Russian tanks rotated their turrets and returned fire but failed to hit the Lahti. Peltomaa calmly aimed the anti-tank rifle, squeezed the Lahti's trigger, and took out two more Russian tanks.

"Leave the Lahti!" Rintala yelled above the barrage. "We're a minute away from going over the top."

Peltomaa nodded. The gunner and his assistant picked up their submachine guns and joined their mates below the crest of the creek berm. Peltomaa had given up the Tokarev despite its sentimental connection to his escape from Karelia. He was now outfitted with the workhorse of the Finnish Army, the Suomi KP-31. Lighter, easier to maintain, and nearly indestructible, the Suomi would prove to be a better choice for the old Finn than the Tokarev.

The bombardment continued. Russian troops, the rear of their entrenched position exposed to the Finns, scrambled for cover. Bodies were tossed into the air. Carts and horses and trucks and tents went flying. And then, the big guns fell silent.

"Now, men! For Finland! For Karelia!"

All across the front, Finnish troops climbed out of the creek bottom and swarmed across the flat terrain like hungry ants at a picnic. Free of the thickets and birches and willows lining the creek, the Finns were exposed. But the element of surprise and the rapidity of the Finnish charge made it difficult for the enemy to concentrate fire.

Peltomaa's sturdy legs carried him along in the surging wave of Finnish soldiers. His heart pounded from excitement and exertion as he ran forward while aiming his Suomi at enemy soldiers taking up defensive positions behind the burning tanks.

Rat-a-tat-tat.

Crack.

Boom.

Machine gun fire from the Russians mowed down Finnish soldiers to the right and left of Rintala's Raiders but did not strike the sergeant's men. It seemed like an eternity to the advancing Finns before they were inside the Russian lines, fighting hand to hand with the enemy.

A young Russian soldier stood up, his rifle jammed, his face pinched from fear, intent upon retreating. Peltomaa leveled his Suomi and fired a burst. The man spun and collapsed on sun-hardened ground. Another Russian stood up from his prone firing position and took aim.

Crack.

The bullet caught Peltomaa's gunner in the forehead and toppled the teenager. Peltomaa's heart raced faster.

Dead. Patu Panula is dead.

There was no time to mourn his comrade. Peltomaa was too close to the Russian to fire. Instead, he swept the butt of the Suomi through the air and caught the man on the jaw. The enemy soldier stumbled but did not fall. The interlude created distance.

Rat-a-tat-tat.

Bullets struck the Russian from his thighs to his chest. Blood soaked the man's uniform. The stricken soldier dropped his rifle and tried to stem the bleeding with his hands.

Rat-a-tat-tat.

Peltomaa finished the Russian off.

The 18th Division pushed hard as other Finnish units simultaneously attacked the front of the Red Army line. Pajari's intent was to surround the enemy. But the lack of Finnish armor supporting the attack was a serious deficit: Just as the pincers of the assault seemed poised to encircle the Russians, a division of elite assault troops accompanied by T-34 tanks broke out from the Soviet reserves. The weight of the counteroffensive and the lack of sufficient armor in the

Finnish force caused the offensive to be blunted and then, after fierce fighting, to be turned back.

"Retreat!" Rintala urged his men. "They have won the day. Back to the draw!" he yelled above the din.

Men fell all around Matti Peltomaa. Bullets whistled through the heavy, still air. Smoke curled. Grenades exploded. Heavy machine guns from fixed emplacements and from advancing Soviet tanks raked the Finns. There was no cover, no forgiveness in the terrain.

"Matti!" Rintala called out, his face smeared with dirt, his Suomi firing without aim as he ran towards the creek, "Keep that goddamned American head of yours down!"

Juha Rintala's warning came too late. A bullet slammed into Peltomaa's right shoulder, spun the Finn around like a pinwheel, and drove him to the ground.

CHAPTER 10
Tartu, Estonia
July 30th, 1941
(Nigul's Story)

Karl was the better soldier. This surprised me. I was the more active, the more athletic Kristian boy. I had been the better hunter, the better skier. I was fleeter of foot. But Karl had the proper attitude. Despite his intellect and his bookish ways, he was able to stifle his natural inclination to debate folks whose opinions were not aligned with his. In short, he was better at listening to our commanders and following orders than I was. He was also able to kill without remorse.

After joining the partisans in June of 1941, Karl and I were given a week of training under Major Kurg, the former Estonian cavalry officer leading the Forest Brothers against the Soviet forces at Tartu. We were handed Mosin Nagnant rifles, cartridges, grenades, bayonets, and ill-fitting uniforms left over from the War of Independence and assigned to a unit. As kin, we were placed in the same squad where it was presumed I, the elder brother, would look after Karl, the younger brother. That's not how it worked out.

The battle for Tartu was brutal. As an inexperienced soldier, I was terror-stricken during the fight. Try as I might, I could not shake a feeling of impending death as the stark realities of combat replaced my romantic notions of heroism.

Father was right: There is nothing glorious about war.

I managed to keep my head down and my eyes forward as our platoon, a unit of thirty Estonian farmers, shopkeepers, and tradesman led by Jüri Lapin, a former Tallinn policeman who had been commissioned lieutenant, advanced. A few men under Lapin's command were veterans of the War of Independence. But most of my comrades-in-arms were as green and wide-eyed as Karl and I were as we marched at the double-quick towards a fight that had been raging for a week by the time we made the front lines.

Understand what we were up against. In the entirety of the country, there were fewer than two hundred thousand Estonian males of suitable age to bear arms. Of these, approximately 35,000 had already been impressed into the Red Army to fight *for* Mother Russia. The conscription of Estonians was the precipitating cause for the formation of the Forest Brothers. Major Kurg, and others like him, took to the forests and marshes of Estonia to avoid being impressed into the Red Army.

Taking into account the needs of farming and industry, my tiny homeland had the resources to gather an army, navy, and air force of a little over 100,000 men. By way of contrast, the Soviet Union had, at various times during the war, over thirty *million* men in uniform. Indeed, the Russians lost over eleven *million* men in the fighting, ten times the entire population of Estonia!

It's like a gnat biting the ass of an elephant.

This is what I thought as I scurried between the bombed out buildings on the outskirts of Tartu, my rifle held tightly to my chest, my brother close at hand, both of us willing to die for Estonia. By the third day of combat, we had already lost seven of our platoon: two were dead and five were wounded so severely they were removed to hospital. Karl had shot and killed two Soviet soldiers and I had yet to fire my weapon. Oh, there were occasions, as our platoon pressed forward as one, our hands sweating against the hot wood stocks and the warm steel barrels of our Mosin Nagants, bullets flying, grenades exploding, pungent smoke and the cries of the dying filling the air, that I had the chance to stop, aim, and fire my rifle. But each time I had the opportunity to make such a statement, I lacked the nerve to pull the trigger. Sweat poured off my face as I held the Mosin to my right eye and took aim, my arms trembling at the prospect of taking a human life. At least once, Karl was standing next to me, his rifle aimed, his finger squeezing off a round. When he was done firing, his breathing calm, his blue eyes clear and without anxiety, he lowered his rifle and looked at me. He could have said something as I stood there, still as a statue, my rifle poised for action but never fired, but he did not. He simply placed his free hand on the barrel of my Mosin and pressed it towards the ground, ending my pose.

"We need to move forwards or we'll be left behind," was all he said.

I nodded, cradled my rifle to my chest, and ran along the disrupted streets and past the exploded buildings of my brother's former home. Tartu was a disaster. Stalin had ordered the retreating NKVD Destroyer units and the Red Army to level the city. The devastation was apocalyptic: virtually every building was either damaged or destroyed as the Soviet Army escaped across the Emajõgi and entrenched itself along the river's east bank.

"The fucking Russians," Karl whispered, as we stood near a burned out building. All that remained of a structure that had once been a part of Tartu University was two walls of fire-scarred brick. The building had collapsed on itself, burying its contents in rubble.

We were ordered to dig in along the west bank of the river where we endured a never-ending artillery barrage from Russian guns located on high ground across the Emajõgi. What were we doing? We were waiting—waiting on the Germans.

On July 12th, the Germans finally arrived. Led by anti-tank platoons, the Wehrmacht appeared triumphantly in Tartu. Task Force Burdach quickly took up supportive positions behind us. Counterattacks by the Soviets demanded additional German troops be sent and by July 20th, as we waited instructions, the Germans had changed the focus of their efforts to include the liberation of Tartu.

Capturing bridges at Põltsmaa to the north of our position allowed the Germans to slip behind the Soviet defenses. Major Kurg ordered us to cross the wide Emajõgi on temporary pontoon bridges erected by German engineers. At the same time, German forces were floated across Lake Peipsi behind the Soviet position to out-flank the enemy. The Russians were thus trapped between Estonians in the west and Germans in the east.

Throughout all of this fighting, my Mosin remained silent. Karl killed another Soviet soldier after we crossed the river. The Russian Karl shot had been operating an entrenched heavy machine gun. Another enemy soldier knelt next to Karl's victim, ready to feed a cartridge belt into the gun. The two men, no older than my brother and me, had been left behind to cover the Russian retreat.

Sacrificial lambs.

But rather than mow down our platoon, which, given the Russians' strategic advantage (they were positioned above us on the river bluff) should have been an easy task, the gunner had slammed his fist against the barrel of his machine gun and cursed. The man's upset with the malfunctioning gun caused him to waive caution. As the Russian gunner stood up to struggle with the gun's breech, his mistake had provided Karl with opportunity.

Crack.

I had watched disbelief spread over the young soldier's face as he grasped his chest with both hands. The man's reaction brought him no solace, only an additional bullet to his forehead. Another Forest Brother had taken out the machine gun tender. My rifle had remained mute.

That night, as we stood guard in what had once been Soviet trenches, Karl broached the unspoken.

"Nigul."

It was a moonless night, though stars were shining in the summer sky. Mosquitoes, thick and active along the marshy shore of the river, were insistent. Between swats, I prayed that my brother was not about to ask me questions regarding my behavior.

"Yes?"

Behind us, fires crackled as off-duty comrades cooked supper over open flames. There was little danger of Soviet artillery taking aim on the campfires: The Russian guns were pointed east, towards the 93rd and 61st Divisions of the German Army. The Forest Brothers were no longer the enemy's main concern. Hitler's invading army was a far more serious threat to the survival of the 11th Soviet Rifle Corps than the ragged partisan army encamped to the west of the Russian position.

"Why do you hesitate?"

There was a long silence as I considered how to answer my brother. A star shell erupted over the Soviet position. German guns commenced pounding the enemy.

"How's that?" I asked, pretending not to understand Karl's question.

I couldn't see my brother's face but I knew his intelligent eyes were bearing down upon me.

"You know what I mean. Why won't you kill Russians?"

I gulped air and thought for a reason that made sense but discovered none. "I have no idea," I finally said.

I sensed Karl thinking. "You're no coward, Nigul. You've never backed down from a fight before. I just don't understand—"

I interrupted his thought. "I know, I know," I sighed. "But there's something about trading blows with a foe, standing face to face and fighting a man with one's fists that's different from shooting someone I've never met, that I have no personal quarrel with. I can't really express it. But that's what stops me. Oh, I aim. I level my sights on the enemy every time we're in a fight. But I can't pull the trigger. I just can't."

Though I couldn't see my brother, I sensed he nodded.

"You need to find a way to pull the trigger, brother. Someone will die if you don't."

The implication was clear. *Karl* might die because I couldn't see my way clear to do my duty.

"Do the others know?"

Another pause.

"Not yet. But I've heard grumbling from them about men like you who've been found out. You need to change your thinking. If you don't, well, it won't go well for you. When you need the help of others, it won't be there. I don't want to see you sacrificed to your fear."

I thought further. "I don't know if it's fear so much as, like I said, the notion that I can't take a life of a man I've never had a personal disagreement with."

Another barrage lit up the eastern sky.

"Well," Karl finally said, "you need to get over it or you won't make it out of this fight."

The following day, our platoon advanced from our trenches onto the demolished streets of East Tartu. We deployed in a single file and joined other units moving through positions abandoned by the Russians. Wary eyes scanned the burned out hulks of office and apartment buildings lining the streets as we moved.

Snipers.

Soviet soldiers who had failed to evacuate might be lurking in the shadows, their rifles steady, their eyes watching us as we marched towards the front. One man in a protected setting could take out an entire squad before he was dispatched. But no shots rang out as we advanced. The Russians who had once occupied Tartu had moved east and were now encircled by the Germans.

CHAPTER 11
Pietarsaari, Finland
November 1941

Though the bullet that found him did considerable damage to his right shoulder, Matti Peltomaa did not die. A surgeon in a field hospital outside Viipuri pried shards of lead from muscle, the cure doing more damage than the initial insult. But the surgery was a necessary invasion: the old man had bled like a stuck pig from the wound, and, had the bullet remained where it was lodged, Matti Peltomaa would have surely died.

"Good morning, Mr. Peltomaa."

A voice called the old soldier back from a long and languid dream.

My parents are walking hand in hand behind me down the road. We are intent upon visiting the sea. It is a bright summer day. I am a boy, maybe four or five years old, dressed in short pants that were once my cousin Esa's, a short sleeved shirt, and worn-out shoes, my only shoes. Reetta has already died. She was a year younger than me. Born sickly and into a poor family, she had no chance when the influenza came. It struck me as well. It touched my parents too. But we were healthy when the curse descended upon our log cabin. My sister was not so lucky. She paid for her infirmity with her young life.

In the dream, I turn towards my parents. They are still young and remarkably in love despite the loss of their child. But the weight of that event is clear in their eyes and by how they are hesitant and protective of me in ways they hadn't been before Reetta passed.

"Keep close to us, Matti," my mother calls out in her sweet, trilling voice. "Don't run ahead."

"Yes, Momma." I say but I don't slow down.

"Son." My father, a short, squat farmer working someone else's land, a circumstance that will eventually cause my parents to send me to America, joins in. "Listen to your mother."

"Yes, Poppa," I say, though my pace does not slow.

We avoid the city where our tattered clothes might subject us to derision. We are poor, as poor as any family living in our parish. It is a rare thing for Poppa to tithe. When he puts money in the collection plate on Sunday, it is generally only a pittance, a small offering to the Lord that, quite frankly, if I had been older, would have been an embarrassment.

We arrive at the Gulf of Bothnia. I find a stone and throw it at the churning sea. Hiekkasärkät Beach, the most popular beach in the area, is deserted because a storm is brewing over the blue-green water of the Gulf. Birds draft on the wind, their wings set against oncoming weather. I rush to the water's edge to find another stone to skip.

"Be careful," Momma cries out above the din of the surf. "You don't know how to swim."

"Do so, Momma," I shout back as I select a rock worn smooth by water and sand and toss it towards the sea. "Onni (a reference to my best friend, Onni Rikala) "taught me how. In the creek by his house. I can even hold my breath under water and float!"

I can't recall my parents' reaction to my disclosure. I am certain that they mulled over the dangers and risks attendant to a five-year-old taking swimming lessons from a seven-year-old. All I remember of that day is a feeling of being lost in the memory of my sister as I removed my shoes and dug my toes, the skin browned by the Finnish summer sun because I was nearly always barefoot, into the cold, golden sand of Hiekkasärkät Beach. It is one of the few memories I have of growing up in Finland. Whether it is an accurate recollection of one day spent with my parents or a composite of multiple visits to the seashore, I cannot say. But despite the sadness of these recalled images, the love that surges over me at the thought of my parents is very real.

A ray of morning sunlight touched the old man's haggard face. Despite being unconscious and in the throes of fever, the result of an infection in the shoulder wound—morphine pills and prontosil having been prescribed for the patient for the pain and the infection respectively—Matti Peltomaa thought he recognized the lovely voice that called to him.

"Elin?"

Peltomaa's eyes opened. The image of the woman in front of him was distorted by narcotics: Elin appeared younger and slimmer than he remembered. The woman smiled.

"No. I'm Alexis, her daughter. I have brought you some tea. Mother is out."

The old man sat up and propped his head and neck with the pillows of the small bed. The room was unfamiliar. "Where am I?"

"Pietarsaari. In Mother's apartment, in her bedroom," the young woman said, a blush starting across her cheeks but disappearing as quickly as it began.

"How did I get here?"

"I wasn't here for that part," Alexis said, holding a tray of steaming coffee, warm toast with lingonberry jelly, two poached eggs, and a glass of thick whole milk.

The woman placed the food tray on a nightstand next to the small bed. Without hesitation, Alexis touched Peltomaa's forehead with the back of her right hand.

"Fever's down. The sulfa's working," she observed, removing her hand and sitting on a varnished pine chair near a window across the room. The shades were not drawn and the sun brought gaiety into the forlorn space.

"How long have I been here?" Peltomaa asked.

Alexis scrutinized the patient.

Interesting eyes, the old man thought.

"Mother brought you here on the train over a month ago. You were conscious, able to sit up in the train car. You were on the mend. But infection took over. You've been in and out of it for the better part of—"

Matti cut the woman short.

"I remember nothing after the sound of a rifle being fired. I don't remember being hit. Or being in hospital. Or taking the train."

"As I said," Alexis replied, somewhat more assuredly, "you were at the hospital, in Viipuri. Then you were furloughed home to mend. Things looked like they were headed for a quick recovery but the infection struck. You really don't remember anything of this? That must be due to the morphine. Though from the looks of things, you likely don't need it anymore."

Peltomaa turned his head towards the bandage on his shoulder. He tried to raise his right arm. Pain seared through his mind like the warning one receives when attempting to grasp the handle of a hot skillet. "Goddamn, that hurts," he muttered.

Alexis frowned. "Maybe you *do* need the morphine," she said quietly. "In any event, I brought you breakfast. Do you feel like eating?"

The sound of a key turning in a lock interrupted the soldier's reply. A door creaked on its hinges. The noise of heels striking wood echoed outside the bedroom.

"'Lexis?"

"In here Mother."

Elin Goldfarb placed a paper bag filled with fruit and freshly baked rye bread on a kitchen counter, pulled off her coat, tossed the garment over the back of a chair, and walked towards the bedroom.

"Hello, old man," Elin quipped as she stood in the open doorway. "How's the shoulder?"

Peltomaa marveled at the woman. Her face was still the most striking he'd ever laid eyes upon. Her calves, exposed as they were by her modest dress, retained the shapeliness of youth. He was dumbfounded and didn't reply.

"Matti?"

"He just tried to move and winced in pain," Alexis said. "But the fever is almost gone."

Elin walked across the hardwood floor and placed the fingers of her left hand on the man's temples. "You're cool to the touch. Another day of the sulfa and I think you're out of the woods."

Matti smiled. As she retracted her hand, he lifted his right arm. The gesture sent another surge of pain through his body but he insisted on grasping her forearm with his dominant hand.

"Careful, Mr. Peltomaa. You may undo all the good work of the doctors," Elin teased.

She sat on the comforter covering the small bed. Her rump, confined as it was in her skirt, spilled over the edge of the mattress. He kept his hand on her wrist, the grip intense yet tender.

"I'll leave you two alone," Alexis said coyly, her eyes riveted on the intimacy of Peltomaa's touch.

Alexis rose from the chair, left the room, and closed the door quietly upon exit.

"I think you embarrassed my daughter," Elin said softly, her lips curling into a smile.

"Didn't mean to. She could have stayed. I'm in no condition to…"

Elin let loose a small laugh. "Oh, I doubt that a little thing like a Russian bullet is going to limit your interest," the woman teased.

Matti smiled, despite the pain in his shoulder. He removed his hand and rested his arm on the soft down comforter. His eyes were touched by sunlight and their deep brown irises revealed hints of floating green.

"How did Alexis get here?"

Elin looked out the window. On the street below the apartment, the Cohen family, the doctor, his wife, and their infant son, secure in a baby carriage, were leaving their flat for a late morning stroll.

Doctor Cohen is the most unusual man I've ever met, Elin thought distractedly. *Despite his status, being an illegal immigrant under suspicion by the Valpo, he still vanishes for long stretches of time, leaving Rosi to tend to their affairs and the child. Now that the Germans are here, what does that mean for the Jews of Finland? Will the Valpo round up the Jews? Who can say? There are only a few thousand Jews here. What if Hitler refuses to assist Finland against the Russians unless we follow his social policies? I was married to a Jew. I have a Jewish surname. I am not a Finnish citizen. Am I any different than Walter Cohen? Rosi Cohen? Or the others who have come here to escape? I wonder…*

"Did you hear me?"

Matti's question called Elin back to the room.

"What?"

"How did Alexis get here?"

Elin's eyes narrowed. Her hands dropped and folded in her lap. She shifted her weight to bring her rump firmly onto the mattress.

"Well," she said softly, her blue eyes locked on Matti's cleanly shaven face, the result of her handiwork. "She's living on Hiiumaa Island, in Estonia. I think you knew that. I received a letter…"

"Yes, yes. She's a teacher there, right?"

Elin nodded. "She's on leave. Followed me to Helsinki and then to here."

"A resourceful young lady."

Elin smiled. "Very."

"And?"

"She's leaving tomorrow: On the train to Helsinki and then, by ferry to Tallinn. From there, she'll go take *another* train and *another* ferry back to Kärdla."

"She won't stay in Finland?"

Elin shook her head. "Doesn't want to. She's applied for Estonian citizenship. She only has time for a visit and then, it's back to work."

"I see."

Elin looked at the cracked plaster of the bedroom's ceiling. It seemed to Peltomaa that she was fighting back tears.

"And me, how did I get here?" he asked to break the mood.

"Ah. Juha sent me a telegram at the hotel. I'm back working there, though now, I am the night clerk. I finally convinced the Swede-Finn in charge that I have a brain and the talent for something more than housekeeping!"

Peltomaa grinned sheepishly. "You have many talents…"

Elin slapped his left forearm playfully. "Mr. Peltomaa! I thought you were too ill for such thoughts."

"Not likely."

An image from their night in Helsinki emerged from Elin's memory.

I felt something with this man.

"Back to my question," he insisted.

Peltomaa's voice startled Elin but she immediately regained her composure.

"I came to Viipuri by train. You were furloughed to recover from your wound. I told Captain Laurila that I would 'nurse' you back to health…"

Peltomaa smiled more broadly. "I like that term, 'nurse'…"

The comment was eerily close to Elin's unspoken remembrance of the intimacy they had shared.

Can he read my mind?

Her cheeks flashed color. Matti's left hand slid to the buttons on her blouse.

"Stop it. My daughter is in the next room!" Elin whispered.

Matti's hand dropped.

"Anyway, with the morphine, you were able to tolerate the trip. Do you remember none of it?"

He shook his head. "Nothing after the sound of the Russian's rifle. The next thing I remember is waking up here, this morning, to a beautiful woman bringing me breakfast."

The old man stopped and considered what he'd said. "I thought, when I heard her voice, that Alexis was you."

Elin frowned. "We don't even sound alike. But you really remember nothing? Not even arriving on the train and coming to the apartment?"

Matti Peltomaa shook his head.

"The doctors said that might be the case. With the fever and the narcotics, they said you might lose some memory."

"That appears to be what's happened."

Elin paused and looked towards the closed door. "She is, isn't she?"

Matti was puzzled by Elin's off-hand question. "How's that?"

"Beautiful. My daughter is beautiful."

The old man smiled. "The second-most beautiful woman in the building.

CHAPTER 12
Tallinn, Estonia
February 1942
(Nigul's Story)

192 Estonian civilians held in Tartu prison murdered as the Red Army retreated: all executed—shot without trial. 8,000 Estonian politicians, police, civic and military leaders arrested—2,200 of that number murdered by the NKVD on Estonian soil—again, without trial. The remaining 5,800? Shipped off to die in labor camps in the Soviet Union. 10,000 ordinary Estonians deported to Siberia or other distant places inside the U.S.S.R. The confiscation of nearly every horse, cow, pig, and sheep in the country: the livestock and most of the nation's stored grain sent to Russia. 33,000 Estonian men conscripted into the Red Army where they were forced to fight the Germans—at least until the Russians deemed them unreliable—at which time they too were sent to labor camps, where 10,000 died of disease and starvation. The Jews who fled Estonia believing that Stalin was a better alternative than Hitler? 500 of them perished in Siberia. President Konstanin Päts, our leader, the man who capitulated rather than fight? Päts was arrested and deported to the U.S.S.R. He died in a psychiatric hospital in 1956 after years of abuse at the hands of his Soviet captors. As much as I disagreed with the man's policies, he too was an undeserving victim of Stalin's terror.

These are the calculations one must take into account when critiquing the actions of Estonia during the Second World War. Where were we to turn? From where was our help to come if not from Germany? Nearly one-tenth of our population was murdered, used as cannon fodder, or starved to death by the Russians. What were we to do in the face of such degradation, of such destruction?

Yes, I lament the Jews. I lament that we allowed Colonel Martin Sandberger of the SS to operate with impunity inside Estonia. It was men like Sandberger, with assistance from Estonian collaborators like Alfred Rosenberg, who rounded up over one thousand Estonian Jews, Roma, and other "undesirables" and sent them to their deaths. I lament that, after the war, when Sandberger was sentenced to die for his crimes, American politicians of German ancestry intervened to save his miserable life. Such actions I surely do regret. For, as I have said, I knew a Jewish family in Puhja. The Friedmans did not leave Puhja at the onset of war. They did not evacuate and follow the Red Army to Russia. They stayed put, apprehensive of what the Germans were up to, but convinced that their status as leaders of the village would save them. Such was not the case. They were sent to Auschwitz, where Greta was immediately gassed and the man and the boy worked until they were skin and bones. Then they too were sent to the showers.

Of course, I did not know these things when they were happening. There were whispers and murmurs throughout Estonia about what the Germans were up to. There were only a *few* Jews remaining in Estonia when the Germans arrived. Because of their small numbers, they did not seem to be of consequence. But the truth cannot be hidden: there were *no* Jews alive when the Germans left Estonia. I share the blame for the disappearance of our Jewish brothers and sisters with my kindred: We did nothing to stop what was happening. This is the legacy of Estonia and the Estonians. We failed to resist the Russians and when faced with annihilation by our communist occupiers, we chose, in our view, the lesser of two evils. Let history be the judge of our decision.

I did not redeem myself as a soldier during the Battle of Narva. Karl, as he had done during the taking of Tartu, fired his Mosin Nagnant accurately at the enemy. He killed another Red Army soldier during the long and heated battle to retake Estonia's eastern-most city. Oh, I raised my rifle once again at the enemy charging towards our trenches outside Narva. I put my finger on the trigger. I controlled my breathing, just as I did when hunting with my father's .22. But I did not fire. I did not consummate my duty. Karl watched over me, protected me during the fighting. He took on the role I, as the older brother, was supposed to take on. Why others in our unit did not uncover this deception, I cannot say.

After Narva, we moved against Tallinn. Again, we fought. Or I should say, Karl fought. Bravely. With distinction. My rifle remained cold and the capital city was liberated without a shot being fired by the eldest son of Andres and Hele Kristian.

On August 28, 1941, the Soviet flag flying above the *Toompea* was torn from the flagpole and replaced by the Estonian flag. Jüri Ulots was installed as our new president. But the Germans took exception to Ulots's elevation to power. They immediately removed Ulots from office and my homeland once again became a province of a foreign government. Estonia was decreed part of "Ostland," part of the German Reich.

After the Russians were vanquished, I went back to my job as an electrician at the Kinnunen Shipyard in Tallinn alongside Big Peeter Saul. Miik Salu no longer worked with us, having fled to Russia where he thought he would fare better. Salu's belief in communism proved to be ill advised. He died in a Russian labor camp, imprisoned for his politics. I do not know why Stalin had such a distrust of foreign communists, but he did. Most of them vanished in anonymity just like Miik Salu.

Karl took a teaching position at a local elementary school, instructing Estonian children in the nuances of their native language. He was fond of reading classic novels, works written in Russian, German, or English to his students. He'd simultaneously translate the words into Estonian for the children. He was a marvel, a genius, at such things. His favorite author, despite the bitter hatred he felt for the Russians, was Tolstoy. His favorite story? "The Kreutzer Sonata," which, of course, isn't a tale suitable for children.

The job of teacher was not Karl's vocational choice. He longed to finish university and become a writer. He was, at age 18, already a fine poet. I know this only because others told me so. I did not read any of my brother's poetry: not for years, not until I was old enough to appreciate his work. I was more interested in making a living and having a good time than reading.

You might be curious why we did not join our liberators in chasing the Red Army back to Russia. Well, the truth is, the Germans didn't trust us any more than the Russians did. Once Estonia was free of communists, the Germans had no further need of us. Our rifles were confiscated, our units disbanded, and we returned to civilian life.

"What was it like?" Big Peeter asked, as we toiled in the bowels of a Finnish tanker.

"What?" I said, as I drilled holes into a steel beam to affix a hanger for the cabling we were running.

Big Peeter loomed behind me, a spool of wire in his big hands, the far end of the wire anchored to a junction box. We stood on a platform suspended above the innards of the ship, the walkway devoid of railings or other safety precautions to prevent us from spilling into the void. I didn't look at my friend as we talked. But I didn't have to. The topic was not a new one, but one that Big Peeter had been nipping at the edges of whenever we were alone: *What was it like to go to war, to kill another human being?*

Of course, I knew and could respond about the war part. That, I surely could do. But the other? I had no experience in the thing and by admitting as such, my take on what it was like to face an enemy in combat would lose veracity. So I tried like hell to avoid the topic. But Peeter Saul was a relentless man. He would not be denied.

"You know what I mean, Nigul. What was it like to go to war, to face the enemy, to shoot straight and kill Russians?"

I muttered under my breath. Not words—just nonsensical syllables so as to give Big Peeter the impression my work was frustrating me. But he knew better. He knew I had, in all things electrical, an abundance of patience. The ruse did not work.

"Come on, Kristian. Give me a taste of what it was like being under arms with the Germans, fighting side by side with your little brother."

I backed away from my work as if I was trying to solve a problem. My actions were a feint, an attempt to get the big man to move on to some other topic, which, uncharacteristically for his stubborn nature, he finally did.

"Alright then, what about this American girl, this Alexis? What is going on between you two?"

Little, unfortunately. Little has been going on now that she is back on Hiiumaa Island and I am stuck here in Tallinn. I've seen her once since she's been back from visiting her mother in Finland. A quick dinner at our old common stomping grounds, the Rohke Söökla.

The food had been plentiful but the conversation, well, it seemed to lack intimacy; that is, until my brother happened to stumble upon us. Or did he really? He knew I was meeting Alexis that night. We were sharing a room two blocks from the diner, a place close to both my work and the elementary school where Karl was teaching. He knew very well that, on that Sunday afternoon, as Alexis killed time waiting for the train to Haapsalu, I would be having dinner with her at the Plenty Diner. I'm convinced it was no accident my brother showed up. I had, of course, told him about Alexis, even revealing that she was a devoted fan of Jane Austen. This last revelation was likely a mistake on my part but once said, I could not unsay it.

So, there we were, on a dreary early winter Sunday, fierce rain sliding down the big plate glass windows overlooking Sauna Street, quietly sipping our coffee and considering each other. We'd exhausted the news between us. Alexis explained the circumstances of her mother's situation: How the Valpo was watching her, how her mother's "friend," an American from the same town in Minnesota, had fought with the Finns on the Isthmus and sustained a near mortal wound. How the mother and the soldier looked at each other with love. I searched for something similar in Alexis's eyes when we spoke. I knew it was much to expect, given her education, given the differences in our ages. But I felt that we had shared something in our brief time together: nothing physical but a prelude to such a connection. But whatever had once been there—or I had once imagined was there—had vanished. Oh, Alexis was pleasant enough. But her thoughts and her heart were elsewhere. That was clear to me even before Karl arrived.

"Miss Gustafson, this is my brother, Karl," I had said when my imprudent younger brother walked through the doors of the diner, his hair plastered to his scalp from rain, his face drawn from cold. "Karl, this is Alexis Gustafson."

They had exchanged formal handshakes. Though I did not want to interrupt my time with Alexis, I offered to buy Karl a bowl of soup. He accepted and took up a chair across the table from me. Alexis sat to the right of Karl and I was able to watch the woman I hoped to love immediately be transformed by the presence of my brother.

"So I hear you were going to be a doctor?"

Karl became enthralled by Alexis's description of the time she spent in St. Petersburg. I was mortified. I felt certain that Alexis would protest, or, at the least, would re-direct the conversation to something less personal. But I was wrong. She seemed to relish the interest Karl displayed in her past. There had been a swift and sudden change in her mood. From the somber discussions she and I had been engaged in regarding her mother and the American soldier, the exchange between Karl and Alexis gained intensity and I knew in an instant that I was sunk.

Alexis had been immediately taken with Karl. And when the conversation moved onto literature, specifically a discussion of *Pride and Prejudice*, which, in turn, prompted Karl to dig into the pocket of his trench coat and remove a damp handwritten copy of a new poem he had written, well, the jig was up, as they say in America.

"It's unusual to find a man who reads, let alone appreciates, Austen," Alexis had said after complimenting Karl on his poetry.

"She's not my favorite English writer," Karl offered. "That would be Hemingway."

Alexis frowned.

"You take me wrong," Karl quickly interjected. "I know he's American. I meant, my favorite author writing *in* English."

"Oh."

"Didn't he fight with the communists in Spain?" I said, trying to join the conversation.

"He did," Karl had replied. "And he wrote a great book about the experience: *For Whom the Bell Tolls*."

Before I could add my own thoughts, Alexis replied. "I haven't read Hemingway," she admitted. "What is his style?"

"Terse. Manly. Far different from Austen, or Tolstoy, for that matter. But still very literary, in a minimalist way."

"You're a fan of Tolstoy?" Alexis asked.

Karl had smiled. "Immensely so."

Alexis had nodded. "I am as well. Especially his shorter works. He has a way of crystallizing an idea, distilling it down into a shorter format than a novel, but still retaining depth."

Karl put his soupspoon down on the plate holding his bowl. "The 'Kreutzer Sonata'..."

Alexis smiled. "Oh you men," she whispered, touching her hand to the bare skin of Karl's right wrist in a manner that was too familiar for their brief acquaintance. "Always intrigued by sex."

Karl had grinned. "And the topic," he knew he was on dangerous ground as far as I was concerned but he did not desist, "is of no interest to the feminine gender?"

Alexis had furrowed her brow. "I shall not answer that, Mr. Kristian. It is an impertinent and personal question."

Karl had laughed. "Fair enough. I apologize. What do you think of *Anna Karenina*?"

Karl's apology apparently satisfied Alexis. The discussion between the two resumed and became an in-depth discourse regarding the literary techniques Tolstoy employed to tell the story of a doomed woman. I was lost. The conversation was beyond me.

"I doubt, given that he sided with the communists, the Germans would allow Hemingway's work to be sold here," Alexis had added, when there was a lull in their conversation. "The Germans seem very clear on eliminating traces of Marxism from the arts."

Karl had tilted his head, likely to appear more intelligent and to give *my* woman the opportunity to experience his handsome profile. Or perhaps he was just thinking. Perhaps my reflections upon that day are too jaded.

In any event, after considerable silence, Karl responded. "You can borrow mine. I have *For Whom the Bell Tolls* and *A Farewell to Arms*. In Russian."

Alexis had appeared puzzled. "Stalin allowed a Western writer to be translated and published?"

Karl smiled.

I bit the inside of my mouth in silent protest over my brother's insensitivity to *my* situation.

"Not only allowed but encouraged," Karl replied. "Hemingway's been a best-selling author in Russia since 1937."

The walk to the Tallinn train station had been very quiet. The few words spoken between Alexis and me were not words I wanted to hear.

"Your brother is a well-read man," Alexis observed, as we waited for traffic to clear so we could cross a street.

"He is that," I had muttered. "But he's not a man; he's just a boy."

Alexis perceived my pique. I think it amused her to know that she could spark competition between brothers. "Oh Nigul," she had continued through a devilish grin, "are you jealous?"

I had wanted to reply, "Yes," but I simply muttered something under my breath and stepped out into the street. The rain had stopped. Water gushed along cement curbs and into grated gutters in torrents.

"Boys. Men. What does it matter?" Alexis had finally said as she stood in front of the ticket window inside the Tallinn train station. "You are all so transparent in your emotions."

I had murmured something about betrayal. The words tumbled out, one over another, forming a nonsensical diatribe under my breath.

"What was that?"

I had shaken my head. We walked to the platform where the train to Haapsalu was waiting, its boilers fired, black coal smoke curling from the locomotive's stack, and steam hissing intermittently against the cold air. German soldiers stood about the station, their dove-colored uniforms immaculate, Mausers slung across their backs, their expressions nonchalant as they watched passengers board. We had remained silent until Alexis stepped onto the first steel rung of the passenger car, turned towards me, and said: "I'm sorry, Nigul."

How was I to explain this unfortunate change in circumstances to Big Peeter Saul as we worked inside a Finnish ship in an Estonian shipyard?

CHAPTER 13
Pietarsaari, Finland
December 25, 1941

A Christmas tree stood in the center of living room of the two-room flat. There were no candles on the tree because, despite being elevated to the position of night manager at the *Hotellet Jacobstad*, Elin Goldfarb could not afford candles for decoration. Matti Peltomaa was living with her, nursing his right shoulder, and money was tight. But that was a temporary circumstance. Matti was due to leave Pietarsaari and return to the Karelian front.

Though the tree was devoid of candles, the tall, slender, nearly branchless pine draped with colorful ribbons and glass bulbs dominated the small room. Most of the decorations had been purchased at secondhand shops in Pietarsaari. Theirs was the only Christmas tree in the apartment building, given that Jews occupied the other flats.

Early morning light edged its way into the apartment through dirty glass. The windows overlooking the street outside the apartment building had not been cleaned since Elin moved in. The rent was higher than it should have been considering the neighborhood and the condition of the building. The landlord, a Swede-Finn who owned a half-dozen tenements throughout the city, charged Jews more than he charged his Gentile customers. Oskar Staffansson was not a Jew and saw no reason to be fair towards the people who controlled the finances of Europe.

Their kind gives those who borrow from them little leeway when a note comes due. Why should I be any different in my treatment of them?

Had Staffansson been a church-going man, he might have been inclined to be equitable. But he wasn't religious in any sense of the word, unless his fervent devotion to commerce qualified as a sort of faith.

Sunlight struck the ends of Elin's hair, which, after a night of renewal in the arms of Matti Peltomaa, fell across her shoulders and upper back without restraint and shifted as she moved across the tiled floor of the kitchen in her stocking feet. She was naked beneath the flannel bathrobe she wore, the fabric belt of the robe tight across her stomach. She filled a blue porcelain coffee pot with cold water from the tap, placed two scoops of rye and coffee in the pot's steel basket, lit a gas burner on the two burner stove, and set the pot down to perk. An aroma of sweetness circulated through the kitchen. Elin was re-heating rice porridge left over from Christmas Eve dinner and baking fresh sweet rolls filled with bilberries given to her by Rosi Cohen. Rosi had picked the berries in the summer and Elin had stored several quart containers of the tart gems in the freezer of the hotel kitchen for use throughout the year. The gift of the berries had been the gesture that solidified the women's friendship. Their connection had advanced to the point where Rosi felt comfortable leaving young William to toddle around Elin's apartment under Elin's watchful eye whenever the Jewish woman ran errands. But though the two women trusted each other and shared frank and open discussions about their respective circumstances, Elin had little connection with Mrs. Cohen's husband. Her only real link to the physician was the fact that both she and Dr. Walter Cohen were subjects of the Valpo's curiosity.

Despite the watchfulness of the police, the situation in Finland did not mirror the new reality in Estonia concerning Jews. The Finns retained their independence and political integrity despite their alliance with Germany. In contrast, the Estonians were a captive people forced to comply with edicts from Berlin. Headlines in the *Pietarsaaren Sanomat* made this distinction very clear. Once the Germans stabilized their position in Estonia, their brand of National Socialism became imprinted upon the tiny Baltic nation. As a result, the Ostland High Command proclaimed that the draconian Nuremburg laws applied in Estonia. Under these laws, Estonian Jews were required to display yellow stars of David on their clothing. In addition, Alfred Rosenburg, an Estonian of German descent born and raised in Tallinn who held a prominent position in the puppet regime governing Estonia, decreed that it was the occupiers' goal to "Germanize" Estonians capable of being "improved" in culture and ethnicity, to allow increased immigration from Germany to accelerate that process, and finally, to deport "undesirables."

When Elin Goldfarb read articles in Finnish newspapers describing the new racial "policies" being implemented in Estonia, it sent a chill down her spine.

Is not President Ryti headed towards the same capitulation of Finnish values? Great Britain has declared war on Finland because of its alliance with Hitler. Is there not, because of Finnish ties to Germany, suspicion amongst some Finnish politicians as to whom the loyalties of the Jews of Finland are directed? Jewishness has always been linked to communism. And the powers-that-be despise communism. It is the philosophy embraced by the hated Russians. Though Hiram's belief in communism had nothing to do with his Jewish origins, I'm not sure the Finnish government understands this. I bear his name. Might not I be the target of similar suspicion? I was, after all, once a communist. Communism brought me to Karelia. But my former political beliefs had nothing to do with Hiram's Jewish heritage. Will those in power here understand this? Will they?

Elin had gone to the local immigration office during Matti Peltomaa's recuperation. She had completed an application seeking residency status with an eye towards citizenship. Matti had completed his own application for residency during his convalescence. Given his war service, Peltomaa's request had been quickly approved. But Elin's application languished. Waiting for an answer from Helsinki was excruciating to Elin Goldfarb in light of what was happening to the Jews of Estonia.

The old man ambled into view in his skivvies, his long underwear drooping in the rear, his narrow feet bare against the cold hardwood of the floor. Peltomaa's hair stood on end as he stopped in the middle of the living room, smoothed stubbly whiskers with his right hand, and admired the Christmas tree.

"You've done quite a job making that ugly stick into something even Santa Claus would love."

Elin smiled, stirred porridge with a wooden spoon, reached across her body, picked up a container of cinnamon and sugar, and added brown and white specs to the mixture of milk and rice. There were no raisins, but Elin did have bilberries left over from the rolls with which to decorate the crust of the porridge.

"The porridge's nearly reheated. Would you like a sweet roll and a cup of coffee while you wait?" she asked casually, the presence of Matti Peltomaa in her life now an accepted circumstance.

The woman smiled as she spoke. Matti was a sight as he admired the Christmas tree. With his skinny torso, his legs and arms covered in white wool, his wild hair, and the beginnings of a new beard, Matti Peltomaa bore no resemblance to the ideal man of Elin's dreams. And yet, she did dream about Matti when they were apart.

War makes for curious bedfellows, she thought, as she slowly stirred the thick goo in the pot. *Who can predict love?*

"Ya. Coffee and something sweet would be good. I'd take sugar but I know you used up what you had to make the rolls."

"Sugar's hard to come by," Elin admitted, her eyes looking at the empty jar sitting on the kitchen counter.

The woman walked with slow elegance into the kitchen, selected a cup and saucer from the cupboard, and poured coffee from the porcelain pot into the cup. She selected the fattest of the sweet rolls, placed it on a separate plate, and carried the cup, saucer, and pastry to Matti. The old man's eyes widened with greed at the prospect of hot coffee and sweets. He accepted the cup and saucer and, without hesitation, took a swig of the steaming coffee.

"How can you do that?"

"Do what?"

"Drink coffee like that? It must scald your mouth something terribly."

The soldier leaned against the counter and studied the woman.

"You look lovely this morning."

Elin dropped partially thawed berries into the porridge. Her eyes furrowed at the remark. "You obviously need glasses, Mr. Peltomaa."

Elin had taken to wearing reading glasses when she was doing detailed work of any kind, including the time she spent writing in her daily journal. She used this casual scribbling, the jotting down of daily events, to fill the void left by her inability to work as a journalist. Matti, despite being over sixty years old, did not need glasses. His eyesight was that of a child.

"I don't think so," he remarked, drawing another mouthful of coffee. "I can see just fine."

The sunlight was bright enough to display the silhouette of Elin's body beneath the flannel robe.

Elin knew what Matti meant by his comment and shook her head. "Stop that. It's Christmas morning."

She removed the porridge from the stove and carried it to the kitchen table where the rolls, butter, a pitcher of buttermilk, bowls, plates, and utensils were waiting. "Come eat."

She returned to the counter and retrieved another cup of coffee and a saucer. Steam escaped from the cup into the close air of the warm room. A radiator hissed beneath one of the windows overlooking the street. They sat in silence, a bit apprehensive of the protocol they should observe when spending their first Christmas together.

"Would you say grace?"

Matti's eyebrows rose. "Me?"

The question was a serious one. Matti was not an atheist but he most certainly was not a man a faith. Baptized Lutheran, he had fallen away from the church while living the hardscrabble life of a laborer, logger, factory worker, and soldier.

"It's tradition for the man of the house to say grace."

Matti signed deeply. He thought for a considerable period of time. Opening his eyes, he began:

Come, Lord Jesus, be our guest;
And bless what you have bestowed.

"Ah," Elin said, "the Table Prayer."

She lifted a roll from the platter and buttered it as Matti dug into his porridge.

"It was the only one I could remember."

Elin bit into the soft pastry. A bilberry met her tongue. The tartness of the fruit contrasted with the sweetness of the roll. She considered the man across the table from her and the prayer he had reluctantly offered. "You don't pray before battle?"

The old man put his spoon down on bare wood, reached for the pitcher, and filled a tumbler with cold buttermilk. He lifted the glass to his lips and drained the buttermilk before responding. "Some do. I don't."

Elin's eyes softened. "Why not?"

Matti leaned away from the table. Sunlight struck the crown of his head. Dust motes floated like tiny worlds within the light. Peltomaa looked away from the woman but did not anger. His countenance was one of great patience as he considered his answer. "I have seen," he said softly, "too many Finnish soldiers: boys, men in the prime of their lives, and old men like me, raise prayers to the Almighty when the fighting begins. Their words, while they may offer solace, do not stop Russian bullets."

Elin nodded. She understood that her question made Matti Peltomaa uneasy. He was away from the war and she had caused unpleasant memories to intrude upon the quiet peace of Christmas in Pietarsaari. "I'm sorry. I shouldn't have asked you about what you've experienced."

He shook his head. "It's alright. It's just, well, something that one lives through and then hopes to forget."

As they sat in silence, sipping their coffee, a thought struck the woman.

"Matti?"

The old man raised his brown eyes from his now empty plate. There was weariness in his expression. "Ya?"

"Could we go to service this morning? After all, it is Christmas Day."

Matti nodded. "We could. But first, you must open your present."

The man stood up and walked to the tree. His right arm reached into the scratchy depths of the pine to retrieve a small jeweler's box. He carried the gift in his large weathered hands with delicacy back to the woman and handed it to her. Elin Goldfarb knew, without opening the container, what was inside.

CHAPTER 14
Tallinn, Estonia
February 1942
(Nigul's Story)

I lost Alexis Gustafson to my brother. That's about as simple as I can tell the tale. I tried to stake a claim to her but my effort failed. Once Alexis got to talking to Karl about literature and books and writing and poetry, there was nothing I could do, short of killing the man, to prevent the inevitable. As much as I admired the American woman who had taken Estonian citizenship, I couldn't do that. Karl was my only sibling and, whatever the circumstances between us, I wasn't about to make myself an only child.

Their relationship began, as I have said, with a "chance" meeting at the *Rohke Söökla* over soup. To be sure, my connection with Alexis didn't end immediately. But the earlier tension, the beginnings of romance that I believed were percolating just below the surface of pleasant courtship, dissipated like rain evaporating off asphalt under a hot sun. There was nothing left between us other than a shallow sort of friendship—a casual connection not at all like the one I had envisioned.

"You're reading Tolstoy again?" I had asked on my last visit to her apartment.

I picked up a hardcover copy of *The Death of Ivan Ilych and Other Stories* resting on the wooden counter in the kitchen of Alexis's flat. She had never moved from the first place she rented in Kärdla. When the Nazis invaded, she stayed put and greeted them as liberators. She didn't follow the mass exodus of Soviet soldiers, sailors, aviators, and workers across the water to the Estonian mainland. She had no reason to run: she was an elementary school teacher, not a warrior or politician. The pro-German authorities allowed islanders like Alexis to resume their day-to-day lives with little constraint or interruption. There were no Jews or undesirables on Hiiumaa. Such people fled with the Russians. An illusion of peace and harmony between the German occupiers and the islanders was maintained, a sort of unspoken truce that suited Alexis Gustafson's desire to live her life without turmoil or controversy.

"I am."

I knew the inspiration behind Alexis reading the book. I didn't mention Karl.

"And the teaching?"

We claimed seats at the kitchen table and looked at our hands, a quiet, ungainly distance between us. In retrospect, I think we both sensed this would be our last visit. Alexis had been as lovely as ever that day with the winter sun behind her, casting low yellow light into the room through a window. A half-empty bottle of Estonian apple wine stood on the pine table. Two glasses of honey colored liquor shimmered in the sunlight. My glass was nearly empty. I drank for fortitude but Alexis merely sipped her wine as we talked.

"It goes well," she had finally answered.

I studied Alexis's face: the dimpled chin, the graceful cheeks, the shiny flaxen hair cropped in the boyishly short style she favored. And I considered her body. I am certain my lewdness was obvious but if it was, Alexis had not voiced objection.

"Well," I said with hesitation. "What do you feel like doing tonight?"

I had hoped, by coming to the island unannounced, a bouquet of dried flowers in hand, a box of Swiss chocolates under my arm, that I could rekindle something. I was determined not to allow my younger brother to best me. He had never been my equal with girls growing up and I was not about to let him snare the woman I was courting. And yet, deep inside my heart, I knew my brother had, during one seemingly inconsequential meeting, captivated Alexis beyond any measure I could duplicate.

"Nigul..."

The elongated phrase had made me understand the futility of my journey.

"Yes?"

My hands had trembled as I snapped up the slender stem of my wine glass and downed the last of my wine.

"This isn't working."

I placed the glass on the tabletop and stared at my hands. "What do you mean?"

A man of courage, a real man, would have engaged Alexis's disparate eyes and challenged her outright. I did not, at that young age, possess such courage. I did, however, feel my anger rise as we advanced to the visit's inevitable conclusion.

She sighed. "I have been thinking about our relationship. We are at the point of advancing to...." She had stopped, considered the right choice of words, and then continued. "...a place of intimacy. I am not comfortable with that. You are a nice young man. But I want more than bike rides and picnics and walks on the beach. I just don't think we have enough in common to satisfy my needs for a deeper connection."

My hands had clenched. I wanted to make a dramatic statement, some last ditch pronouncement of my love, my desire, my need for the woman sitting across from me in the cool winter air of the little kitchen. "How can you say that? We've only been on a handful of outings. We've kissed but once or twice. How can you measure me with such scant evidence?"

She wasn't interested in a debate. She had made a decision and there was no changing her mind.

"Perhaps," Alexis had whispered, "it does seem unfair, like I haven't given us enough time."

She sipped wine from her glass as she studied me. Her aquiline nose tilted upward, creating a slight note of superiority about her as she swallowed. I don't think the posturing was intentional but it was there, all the same.

"It's my goddamned brother, isn't it?"

Alexis hadn't responded.

"Damn it, woman! You've only just met him. He's a boy, a year younger than I am. Barely out of school and in his first job. He lacks…" I knew to be careful as I touched the edges of intimacy, "…experience. What can he possibly give you that I can't, other than some vague understanding of words written by dead men?" I asked, my eyes landing on the volume of Tolstoy behind Alexis.

Her brow had furrowed. "He knows Austen and the Brontës. He understands women, Nigul, in ways that you can never hope to."

The last remark exited Alexis's mournful lips in a manner that convinced me it was over.

Over? It never really began. We've never made love, never fallen into each other's arms. Over? For something to be over, it must have started. At best, we were sizing each other up, negotiating which path to take. She has clearly decided to strike out in a direction that doesn't include me.

"And that's how you've decided? Based upon one conversation with a boy over dinner?"

She had reached behind her, located a cardboard box on the kitchen counter, lifted the box, and placed it on the table in front of her. Opening the box, she removed several envelopes and held them up for me to consider.

"That bastard…" I muttered. "…he's been writing to you behind my back?"

Alexis had replaced the envelopes in the box and closed the lid. We stared at each other in silence. When Alexis finally spoke, her words were nuanced, a failed attempt to spare me further degradation.

"I wrote to him…after that night in the diner. He replied to me. He didn't initiate the contact."

I am not proud of what happened next. Even years later, as I tell this story, as my life turns its final page, I regret what I did that afternoon in the little flat on Hiiumaa Island.

I threw my empty wine glass across the room. It shattered into a million crystalline shards against the white plaster wall. Without another word, I rose to my feet, reached across the table, and slapped Alexis's lovely face with the callused palm of my workman's hand, before walking out the door.

CHAPTER 15
The Karelian Isthmus

The insulin Elin Goldfarb obtained from the pharmacy in her neighborhood in Pietarsaari seemed inferior to the insulin she had acquired in Karelia. Relying upon her portable chemistry kit and felt strips to test her blood sugar levels, Elin fastidiously injected herself through her abdominal wall whenever a test strip indicated the need to do so, or whenever insatiable hunger or thirst manifested, or whenever she found herself urinating with increased frequency. Many times, she simply guessed at the level of insulin her body required; the control of her disease was an inexact science. With experience, she was able to approximate the amount of the hormone needed to counteract the two extremes of her disease. Too much insulin, and Elin became *hypoglycemic* or sugar depleted. She had experienced the symptoms of this condition many times during her internment on Kalajoki Island when she was not able to eat enough bread or other forms of carbohydrates and her sugar levels dropped precipitously. Too little insulin and she became *hyperglycemic*: too much sugar accumulated in her blood because her pancreas was an ineffective producer of the enzyme.

Even before entering into sexual intimacy with Matti, Elin had taken the steadfast, taciturn man into her confidence with respect to her disease. He had, on at least two occasions, found Elin Goldfarb on Kalajoki Island in the throes of a diabetic reaction that necessitated Matti injecting insulin into her soft belly. In a more lucid moment, Elin explained the process and the approximate dose needed to bring her around and Matti Peltomaa had not failed the woman he loved.

The wedding was set for December. Though there was much urgency in their love, maturity demanded that Elin and Matti wait to stand in front of the justice of the peace in Pietarsaari to say their vows. In the interim, Elin continued her work at the hotel as the night manager and Matti returned to Karelia where a stalemate between the Finns, their German allies, and the Russians stretched from the Gulf of Finland to Barents Sea. Elin Goldfarb was fifty-three years old and on their last night together, she finally reached exaltation in the arms of Matti Peltomaa. It was the first time since Hiram's death that she felt physically complete and she cried for joy as Matti slept. There had been more tears the following morning when the train carrying her lover left the railroad station.

Walking back to her apartment after Matti departed, Elin was overcome by a premonition.

He will die in Karelia.

No evidence buttressed Elin's fear. Hers was an irrational, unfounded dread that caused dark thoughts and reflections to manifest. Memories of their lovemaking kindled an abnormal level of angst in her soul. Elin found herself sinking into an unrelenting depression triggered by visions of spectral Tartars leering at her. Try as she might, the faces of her rapists and a horrific image of Matti collapsing in battle could not be repressed as she went through the motions of living life in Pietarsaari, while the man she loved fought for their adopted country.

• • •

Fighting was at a lull. The Russians had concentrated their forces to fend off the German Army as it pushed out of Estonia towards Leningrad. Mannerheim decided to wait and see: If Leningrad fell to the Germans *and* it appeared that Hitler would win the war; the Finns *might* advance. But the Finnish leader was circumspect. The German attack had been blunted. Hitler's boys had been unable to take Leningrad or Stalingrad or Moscow. To Field Marshall Carl Mannerheim, Operation Barbarossa was beginning to look a lot like Napoleonic folly. And Mannerheim was no fool; he was not about to gamble his country's future by advancing towards Leningrad if retreat was inevitable.

"It's damned cold," Matti Peltomaa muttered as he pressed against the frozen wall of the shallow trench he and his mates manned. "I can't seem to keep my hands warm."

Juha Rintala nodded. The soldiers were wearing thin wool mittens that, over time, had become so threadbare they were nearly transparent. Matti carefully leaned his Suomi on the frozen ground in front of him and tucked his hands into the waist of his gray wool campaign trousers. Rintala did the same.

"I'm just happy I don't have to deal with that goddamned Lahti anymore," Peltomaa said quietly, referencing the anti-tank rifle he had been assigned before being wounded. "I'd much rather be able to move quickly, without worrying whether that stone around my neck will get me killed."

"Faster is better," Rintala agreed, as he pulled a pack of cigarettes he'd "liberated" from an enemy soldier foolish enough to be captured snooping around their lines, opened the pack, and removed two fags. "Smoke?"

Peltomaa nodded. Rintala struck a match, lit the cigarette, and passed the burning match to his companion. The old man touched the match to the stale cigarette and inhaled. The tobacco flared. He blew out the match before dropping it onto the hurly burly confusion of frozen boot prints defining the ground beneath their feet.

"Hey," the sergeant said as the two sat pondering. "What happened to the Luger?"

Rintala nodded towards Peltomaa's utility belt where the German pistol had once been secured as he raised the question.

"Traded it."

There had been, up to that point, no disclosure by Peltomaa to his fellow soldiers that he was a marked man. The missing Luger was part of an untold story.

"How so?"

Peltomaa didn't look at Rintala. The old man focused his small eyes on Russians moving into position.

"Out with it, man. What happened to the Luger?"

Matti didn't reply.

"Peltomaa..."

There was an extended period of silence.

"I traded it for a ring."

Rintala stared at his mate. Matti Peltomaa refused to return his friend's gaze. Juha Rintala pulled hard on his cigarette, exhaled, and sent smoke towards low, dreary clouds.

"A ring? What sort of ring?"

Peltomaa tossed the remnant of his cigarette onto the frozen ground. "An engagement ring."

Juha Rintala smiled. "That Goldfarb woman—the Jew who came out of Karelia with you?"

"She's no Jew," Matti corrected, "she was just married to one."

Rintala slapped the smaller man on his back. "You old dog! Jew or not, she's a fine looking woman."

The sergeant paused as he recalled his own connection to the woman's daughter.

"Congratulations," Rintala added after a moment of contemplation.

Peltomaa nodded but said nothing. Silence returned to the line.

Two days later, Captain Laurila approached as men under his command washed pots and pans in a kettle of hot water. Camp life had fallen into a routine that included hot food and the occasional sauna. An engineering platoon had erected a crude log building to serve as a bathhouse. Unable to fabricate an appropriate stove, the engineers had relied upon Rintala's Raiders to locate a proper heat source for the sauna.

Toivo Tyynelä, a beast of a man and a former ironworker, had *acquired* a stove from a very surprised teamster driving a single horse sledge in the direction of the general's headquarters.

"There are others where this came from," Tyynelä quipped, as he muscled the stove off the back of the sledge. "Tell the general to use plenty of perfume while he waits for another stove!"

"Better yet," Juha Rintala had added, holding the bridle of the horse as the stunned teamster watched his cargo disappear, "tell the general he's welcome to stop by anytime to sauna with us!"

When Captain Laurila appeared by his company's campfire, dusk was settling over the pockmarked landscape and shell-stunted trees. His men had just returned from the bathhouse and had, at least on a temporary basis, defeated the lice digging away beneath their filthy uniforms.

"Sir," Rintala said, as the Laurila entered firelight.

Rintala stood to greet his superior but did not offer a salute because such a gesture would be a cue to Russian snipers. Killing officers, "cutting off the head of the snake," so to speak, was a tactic favored by the Red Army and Rintala made certain he did nothing to hasten his captain's death.

"You boys sauna?"

"Yes, sir," Peltomaa replied, scouring the last pot and tipping it upside down on a log drying rack. "The steam did my shoulder wonders."

The captain nodded. "How *is* your shoulder?"

Peltomaa rotated his right arm to show that he had regained full movement.

"Like a young buck," Juha Rintala teased.

The captain lifted a tin cup from the drying rack and poured himself a cup of rye coffee from a pot simmering on the edge of the pine fueled fire.

"Tomorrow," Laurila said quietly.

"Yes?" Sergeant Rintala asked.

"The general has been given an assignment that will take us off the line."

Rintala frowned. "Just the Raiders?"

"No, the whole brigade."

Peltomaa winced. "Shit."

"I know, I know. We all could use a little more rest. There's no question that, if the Germans fail to take Leningrad, we're going to be in for it. But this gives us a chance to do something, to make a difference."

Juha Rintala moved closer to his commander. "Where?"

Laurila smiled. "You'll need your skis."

Peltomaa tilted his head. "Laatokka-Karelia?"

The captain shook his head.

"Then where? Not the fuckin' Arctic. It's cold enough here. I don't want to be shipped to the fuckin' Arctic," Rintala muttered.

Laurila shook his head again. "Four in the morning."

Peltomaa grew puzzled. "What?"

"We're moving out at four. We'll be taken by truck to Kotka."

Juha Rintala frowned. "There's no fighting at Kotka."

Laurila smiled. "We're going to re-take Suursaari Island. Across the ice. Make sure your skis are waxed and ready to go."

Laurila drained the last bit of liquid from his cup and returned it to the drying rack before moving off to talk to the next platoon.

"There's not much cover skiing across ice," Peltomaa observed as the captain disappeared.

"None whatsoever," Juha Rintala agreed. "None whatsoever."

CHAPTER 16
Hiiumaa Island, Estonia
August 1942

***Of** all passions, the most powerful and vicious and obstinate is sexual, carnal love; and so if passions are annihilated and with them the last and most powerful, carnal love, then the prophecy will be fulfilled, men will be united together, the aim of mankind will have been attained, and there would be no longer any reason for existence. As long as humanity exists, this ideal will be before it, and of course this is not the ideal of rabbits or of pigs, which is to propagate as rapidly as possible, and it is not the ideal of monkeys or Parisians, which is to enjoy all the refinements of sexual passion, but it is the ideal of goodness attained by self-restraint and chastity, Toward this, men are now striving, and always have striven. And see what results.*

It results that sexual love is the safety-valve. If the human race does not yet attain this aim, it is simply because there are passions, and the strongest of them the sexual. But since there is sexual passion, a new generation comes along, and of course, there is always the possibility that the aim may be attained by some succeeding generation. But as long as it is not attained, then there will be other generations until the aim is attained, until the prophecies are fulfilled, until all men are joined in unity. And then what would be the result?

Will the human race come to an end? Can anyone who looks at the world as it is have the slightest doubt of it? Why, it is just as certain as death is certain. We find the end of the world inculcated in all the teachings of the Church, and in all the teachings of Science it is likewise shown to be inevitable.

Karl Kristian read aloud from a tattered copy of Tolstoy's *The Death of Ivan Ilych and Other Stories.* The Estonian was propped up in Alexis Gustafson's bed, his narrow chest lacking the blond hair that draped from his head over his spectacles, the book held between his long fingers, the words from "The Kreutzer Sonata" echoing in the still, tight air of the room. It was dark outside but they had made love for the first time and could not sleep. Alexis lay sprawled beside the younger man, her short blond hair splayed to the sides of her face, her fine features staring at the ceiling, her exposed breasts sagging beneath her unshaven armpits as she listened.

"What a lot of stuff and nonsense," Alexis observed. "Life without passion, without romance, without sexual satisfaction? What was Tolstoy thinking?"

Karl closed the book on a leather bookmark and placed the cloth bound volume on a nightstand next to the bed. His eyes were drawn to the woman next to him. "Still," he said softly, as he removed his eyeglasses, placed them on a nearby nightstand, shifted his body, and rolled onto the woman's warm body, "he makes a point. How much of the pain and suffering and upset we experience as human beings is related to jealousy and envy instilled by the pursuit of romantic love? Would mankind not be better off if there was no such emotion, no such driving force behind our existence? Could not the Tolstoys and the Sibeliuses and the Picassos of the world create even more art if they were not constrained by need, by longing, by passion for another human being?"

"You have bad breath," Alexis said with a slight grin as she stared into Karl's face as he hovered above her.

He laughed. "You're changing the subject."

"It's hard to have a serious discussion with a naked man whose breath smells of garlic."

Karl Kristian lingered for a moment before pushing himself away. He repositioned an overstuffed goose down pillow behind his head. "My breath? That would be your fault. You're the one who insisted on using garlic on the leg of lamb you cooked last night."

"Can you go down to the corner for eggs and the newspaper? It would give me a chance to bathe."

His blue eyes stared at Alexis's naked body. "I thought we were going to spend Sunday in bed, wasting our time and energy on copulation to spite Leo Tolstoy."

She frowned. "There'll be plenty of time for *that* after church."

It was Karl's turn to frown. "You know I'm no churchman."

Alexis sat up and pulled a white cotton sheet to her chin. Karl's disclosure did not come as a surprise. They had talked at length about her renewal of faith and his disdain for religion. "But you *will* go to church with me, won't you?"

Karl sighed. "What's the point? Oh, I'll grant you that the hymns are touching. And prayer, while naive, does no harm. But the institution behind your little church, behind the good wishes and sincerity of its parishioners? Therein lies the problem. Organized religion has been the bane of peace and tranquility since David smote Goliath."

She shook her head. "There's nothing religious about the present world conflict. It's political—fueled by nationalism—not by religious discord."

Karl stood in the warm summer air of the apartment. He retrieved his boxer shorts, slid them over his long muscular legs, pulled his trousers up to his waist, wove a thin leather belt through the pant loops, and pulled a T-shirt over his upper body. He covered the T-shirt with a loose fitting casual shirt, swept his right hand through his blond hair, retrieved his glasses, affixed the frames on his face, and pulled a pair of black stockings over his feet.

"You're wrong about that."

Alexis blinked. "How so?"

"It may be true that Hitler isn't a religious fanatic, that his megalomania isn't fueled by Christianity. But consider this: He was raised Catholic. His views about Jews and communists were forged from his upbringing in the Church and from his time at a monastery school. I am not saying the Church sanctions what he's doing. I am simply pointing out that, at the bottom of his beliefs, are notions of Christian justification."

"I'm not sure you're correct on that point, Mr. Kristian. Seems to me that National Socialism has very little to do with Catholicism or any other brand of Christianity."

Karl opened his wallet and removed a distressed scrap of newsprint that he had saved from *Eesti Paevleht*.

"Listen to this:

My feelings as a Christian point me to my Lord and Savior as a fighter. It points me to the man who once in loneliness, surrounded by a few followers, recognized these Jews for what they were and summoned men to fight against them and who, God's truth! was greatest not as a sufferer but as a fighter. In boundless love as a Christian and as a man, I read through the passage which tells us how the Lord at last rose in His might and seized the scourge to drive out of the Temple the brood of vipers and adders.

How terrific was His fight for the world against the Jewish poison. Today, after two thousand years, with deepest emotion I recognize more profoundly than ever before the fact that it was for this that He had to shed His blood upon the Cross.

As a Christian, I have no duty to allow myself to be cheated, but I have the duty to be a fighter for truth and justice... And if there is anything, which could demonstrate that we are acting rightly, it is the distress that daily grows.
For as a Christian I have also a duty to my own people.

"That," Karl said quietly, as he replaced the article in his wallet and bent to tie his shoes, "is Hitler in his own words."

"Why would you keep *that* in your wallet?"

Karl strode over to the door leading from the bedroom to the living area of the apartment, placed his hand on the door handle, stopped, turned, and answered before leaving. "I knew that, one day, I'd end up debating religion, politics, and love with an intelligent naked woman in her bedroom on Hiiumaa Island," Karl said mischievously.

"Still," Alexis called out as he left the room, "you will go to service with me?"

There was pronounced silence as she listened to footfalls across the bare wood floor of the living room.

"Karl?"

"Alright," came the distant reply. "I'll go. It's been a long while since I enjoyed a good hymn."

CHAPTER 17
Tallinn, Estonia
September 1942
(Nigul's Story)

"**The** Germans want us to fight," Big Peeter Saul said, looking at the headlines in *Eesti Paevleht* as we bought hot coffee from a sidewalk newsstand outside the Kinnunen Shipyard. "They're forming something called the 'Estonian Legion'," he added, as he squinted to read the paper up without picking it up.

"Why don't you buy the damn paper instead of tiring your old eyes?"

My friend claimed his full height and sipped coffee from a waxed paper cup. "Damn this is hot," he complained.

"Patience is a virtue."

"Ya. You're such a patient man, Nigul."

We walked away from the newsstand. It was early evening. We had worked a twelve-hour shift. I was bone tired and craved sleep. My brother and I no longer shared an apartment. When I realized what Karl was up to, I filled a suitcase with his clothes, books, and toiletry items and tossed the luggage out the second floor window of our flat. The suitcase was still there, on the sidewalk, intact and unopened, when Karl came home from teaching. I did not tell him why I had done what I had done and he didn't ask. We parted company that day and had not spoken since.

"What do you mean?"

Big Peeter tried another sip of coffee. "You don't even have patience for your own brother."

I shook my head. "Patience has nothing to do with it. He went behind my back, took Alexis from me. What sort of brother does that?"

Big Peeter laughed. "*Took* Alexis from you? What, were you engaged? Had you proposed? Were you ready to 'pop the question'? You are so full of bullshit sometimes, Nigul."

I fumed but did not answer.

"You hadn't even slept with the woman. Yes, she is striking. And brilliant. And all the rest. But Karl 'took' her from you? Please…"

I drew a mouthful of hot coffee. I wanted to spit it in the big man's face. But I knew I was no match for Peeter Saul.

"You know what you're problem is?"

I sighed. "I'm sure you're going to tell me."

We matched strides as we walked.

"You're a romantic man in a pragmatic world."

"Big words from someone who left school at age twelve."

Big Peeter laughed again. "Right. A man can't keep learning outside school? Maybe that's your problem, Nigul. Maybe you've stopped learning life's lessons. Get over Alexis Gustafson. Sit down and talk to your brother. It will do you good."

I shook my head. "Not now. Maybe in a while but not now. I am still upset that he sent her poems and love letters all the while knowing what she meant to me."

We arrived at Big Peeter's flat. The sounds of children at play inside the apartment greeted us.

"That's another one of your problems," the big man said as he stood at the threshold of his building.

"How's that?"

"You were so confident of what Alexis meant to *you*. Did you ever stop to consider what, if anything, *you* meant to *her*?"

I saw Big Peeter's point but I didn't like where our discussion was headed so I didn't reply.

"What do you think about the headlines, about the Estonian Legion?" my friend asked, changing the subject.

I knew that eventually the Russians and the Germans would bring their dispute back to Estonia. And though I hadn't acquitted myself as a soldier, I would not dodge serving my country again if called.

"I have no interest in fighting under German officers," I said plainly. "If and when I can fight the Russians again under Estonian command, that I will surely do."

Big Peeter nodded. "There may be fighting to be done before the Russians come back," he said slyly.

"Against the Germans?" I whispered. I knew that such talk could get a man arrested by the Gestapo.

"You misunderstand. Some folks have been talking about another fight, the fight in Finland."

My eyebrows rose. "You're kidding me. You would actually consider fighting for the Finns?"

The big man nodded. "If it looks like they need my help. They're our cousins, after all, a kindred people. If they need help stopping the Russians from trampling through their country, then yes, so long as Estonia is safe, I might go to Finland."

I thought for a moment. "You're serious, aren't you?"

"I am. Think about it. There's no urgency to it. The Finns haven't asked for our help and the Karelian front is quiet right now. But the Germans don't seem to be making any headway. If the Russians break out of St. Petersburg, we may be needed."

I shook my head. "That's crazy talk, Peeter," I said, walking away from the cement stoop in front of the Saul apartment. "And as the father of five children, you're crazy for even considering it."

"We'll see who's crazy and who's sane," Big Peeter called out as I left him. "I have my feeling that you'll be on a ferry to Helsinki when the time comes."

CHAPTER 18
Suursaari Island, U.S.S.R
March 1942

Lieutenant Kai Järvinen stood behind two ancient Ford trucks as steam rose from the radiators of the vehicles. The personnel carriers had been delivery trucks in another life before the war. A motley column of military and civilian trucks rumbled past the disabled Fords. There was no room in the passing vehicles for soldiers who had been riding in the hand-me-downs so the convoy moved on.

"Damned pieces of crap," Järvinen, the leader of Rintala's Raiders now that Laurila had been promoted, muttered as he adjusted leather bindings over his boots. "We're going to have to ski the rest of the way."

Juha Rintala and Matti Peltomaa stood next to the lieutenant at the head of the platoon ready to move out on skis across crusted snow to the north and west of Suursaari Island. Thick, gray clouds hung like pillows above the Finnish column. Across the frozen sea, other vehicles of General Pajari's assault team waited. The force assigned to breach this sector of the Soviet defenses on the island was small and could not proceed without Järvinen's men.

Noisy Buffaloes flew low over the straights between Kotka and Suursaari Island. German Stuka dive-bombers followed the Finnish fighters, their telltale screams echoing as they dove from concealment. Wave after wave of German and Finnish planes attacked from Immola where the main air wing of the Army of Karelia was based. There was no opposition to these flights: the closest Soviet warplanes were engaged in protecting the besieged city of Leningrad.

The attacks on the Soviet Union had led to four distinct theaters of operation requiring cooperation between Nazi Germany and the Republic of Finland. In the far north, the Army of Norway had tried to take Murmansk. But this German drive to secure Russia's only all-weather port ended in failure. Due to the inhospitable climate, inadequate manpower, and horrific geography that favored the entrenched Russians, the Army of Norway never came close to achieving its goal. A second German force bogged down near Salla. Finnish contingents involved in that operation had gained ground, at one point reaching the tracks of the most important north/south railroad in the Soviet Union. But elite German SS units involved in the attack retreated at the first sounds of conflict. The offensive lost traction and the Salla front settled into a defensive "wait and see" contest. In the sectors assigned solely to the Finns: Laatokka-Karelia (the territory between Lake Ladoga and Lake Onega) and the Karelian Isthmus, the Finns accomplished their *political* objective by recapturing territory ceded to the Soviet Union at the close of the Winter War. But Mannerheim refused to take the offensive against Leningrad (the fourth theater of operation) as Hitler demanded. Mannerheim's reluctance in this regard was a major point of contention and became one of the linchpins of failure for the northern war.

In the doldrums of stalemate, Mannerheim approved the assault on Suursaari Island in hopes of buttressing Finnish patriotism. But the operation was not purely for show. There was a strategic component to the assault across the ice. Suursaari sits in the middle of the Gulf of Finland and offers a convenient steppingstone between Finland and Estonia. Beyond the tactical importance of the island, Mannerheim deemed the morale value of a Finnish victory worth the operation's inherent risks. In a season of bad news from the front, taking the island would have significant propaganda value for the beleaguered Finnish commander.

"At the double quick," Järvinen shouted.

The lieutenant was a tall, thin, athletic man who moved well on skis. Though experienced skiers, Juha Rintala and Matti Peltomaa found it difficult to keep up with their commander.

"Christ, he's fast," Rintala muttered.

"Too fast for a man as old as me!" Peltomaa complained.

A spring thaw had threatened the attack by reducing previously frozen salt water to ankle deep slush. But a cold front had swept in from the north just in time to re-freeze the ice, allowing Rintala's Raiders to make quick work of the distance between the stalled truck and their waiting comrades.

"What was the hold-up?" Captain Laurila asked when the platoon rejoined the rest of the command.

"Damned pieces of shit stalled again. I think the engines are hatched," Järvinen disclosed. "We had to ski the last five kilometers."

"Get your breath quickly. The barrage won't last long."

The booming of Finnish guns, artillery that had been ferried across the ice under the cover of darkness, interrupted the cold quiet. Shells whistled and whined as they passed overhead. Explosions rocked fortifications on the island, sending spirals of flame and debris into the frozen air.

The guns stopped as suddenly as they had commenced.

"Time to move," Laurila said plainly, pulling his revolver from his holster. "Let's go!" he shouted.

The two hundred men under Laurila's command sprinted across the ice as Buffaloes strafed the entrenched Russians. Battle Group P (named after its overall strategic commander, Major General Pajari), a force of nearly 4,000 men, confronted a Soviet defensive force one-sixth that size.

"We're in for it now," Rintala said as his platoon approached a concrete wall. "Pajari gave our company the worst possible line against the most fortified position on the island."

Machine guns chattered as Finns rushed towards outcroppings and tall pines framing the beach. Cries rang out as men fell and moved no more. A Buffalo left its companions and swung to the aid of the exposed soldiers. The airplane's machine guns sent Red Army soldiers sprawling before the Buffalo exhausted its ammunition. The Finnish fighter's three companions joined the fray. An errant Russian squirrel, the only Red Air Force fighter in the area, dove from concealment and attacked a Buffalo as the Finnish pilot strafed the ground.

"Sippola!" Juha Rintala shouted as his men crouched behind boulders, "turn your gun on that Russian bastard and get him off our friend's ass!"

Arvo Sippola unfolded the bipod of his light machine gun, adjusted the sights, and sent a burst towards the Russian plane.

"The bastard's too fast," Sippola said.

"Wait until he's broadside and aim in front of him, like you would hunting ducks," Peltomaa urged.

The Russian fighter pulled up. Smoke wafted from the Buffalo's engine. The enemy pilot had scored a direct hit and was coming around for the kill. The other Finnish planes were nowhere to be seen. As the Russian turned his plane to issue the coup de grace, Sippola followed the enemy fighter with his machine gun.

"Now," Peltomaa urged. "He's slowed to make the turn. Take him now!"

Rat-a-tat-tat.

Bullets hit the fuselage of the Russian plane. Fearing another Buffalo was on him, the Russian pilot abandoned the chase and vanished into the clouds.

"Nice work," Rintala said. "Nice work."

The Buffalo wagged its wings in appreciation before limping home.

Enemy fire pinned the Raiders behind a rocky hedgerow marking the end of frozen sea and the beginning of land.

"This won't be easy," Rintala said to Peltomaa as they lay on their bellies studying the Russian fortifications. "They're dug in."

The old man nodded. Fear gripped his gut but did not show on his face.

I don't want to die on this piece-of-shit-rock, he thought. *I wouldn't even be leaving a widow behind. I need to survive, to get back to Elin. I have a wedding to attend!*

"Ready?"

Peltomaa glanced at the flat stretch of sand between the Finnish position and the Russian fortifications.

"As ready as I'll ever be."

"Juttinen," Lieutenant Järvinen shouted as he crawled into the safe haven occupied by Rintala and Peltomaa, "fix your mortar on that concrete pillbox. Drop a few rounds on top of it and see what happens."

Jaako Juttinen gauged the distance to the enemy and adjusted the weapon. His tender dropped a shell into the tube.

Whoosh.

Boom.

The tender fed a second round into the tube

Whoosh.

Boom.

Black smoke curled above the enemy emplacement.

"Now, sergeant. Take that bunker now!" Järvinen shouted over the din.

Rintala waved his men forward. The platoon rose from the beach and rushed headlong into the fight.

CHAPTER 19
June 1, 1942
Pietarsaari, Finland

Dear *Elin:*

As I write you, I am in one of the "senile battalions" away from the Karelian Front. I am unable to reveal my location but understand that I have now been, after three major battles (including the defense of the Isthmus where we beat back a fierce Russian counterattack) "retired" from the front as "too old." I am serving as a mechanic, out of harm's way, which I guess is better than being shot at!

I trust the December date is still acceptable. I will have plenty of leave time built up by then to take you on a proper honeymoon somewhere away from the war. Think about where it is in Finland that you might like to go.

Will Alexis be able to make it back from Hiiumaa Island to be your maid of honor? I will have Rintala accompany me to serve as my best man. He too, unless some lucky Russian puts a bullet in his skull, will have plenty of leave time.

Well, it is dark and my candle is almost gone. You know what I feel. I don't need to write it down, do I?

Matti

The letter sat on the nightstand in her bedroom. She had read and reread Matti Peltomaa's words every night as she slid towards sleep.

Thank God he is no longer in danger, she thought, over and over. *Thank God.*

Elin dressed for work. It was late afternoon. She was taking a last sip of lukewarm tea when there was a knock on the door. She stood up from the kitchen table, adjusted the hairpins confining her shoulder length hair in a tight bun, and moved with grace.

"Yes?" she said as she turned the handle and opened the door.

The bright white light of summer entered through a bank of windows in the common hallway. Two tall men in black summer weight overcoats stood in the entry.

"Mrs. Goldfarb? Mrs. Elin Goldfarb?"

She nodded. "Yes, that's me."

"Inspector Salminen and Inspector Nevonen. State Police. We'd like you to come with us."

The introduction startled Elin.

The Valpo? What does the Valpo want with me?

"There must be some misunderstanding. I am a night manager at a hotel. Why would the Valpo want to speak with me?"

Salminen, a stereotypical Finn with thick blond hair and blue eyes and a slender build, nodded towards the stairway.

"There's no mistake. Just a few questions about your status. Come along with us, ma'am."

Nevonen, who was darkly complected with thin black hair, spoke. "No need to cause a disturbance, ma'am. Just routine questions. Come along now."

"I need my purse."

Salminen nodded acquiescence.

Elin slipped back into the apartment, picked up a small brown leather satchel, and closed the wooden door to the flat as she stepped into the hallway.

"Follow me," Nevonen said quietly.

The woman complied. Salminen stepped in behind her as the three of them descended narrow pine stairs.

The room where she was interrogated was not reminiscent of the interview room where the NKVD had questioned her. The office in the State Police headquarters in downtown Pietarsaari, a single story brick building on a side street, was bright and airy. Windows overlooked the harbor and offered a view of the famous globe atop the Strenberg Tobacco building. The room, with its fine draperies, overstuffed chairs and couches, and impressive brick fireplace surrounded by finely grained birch wainscoting and mantle, seemed more akin to a business executive's office than a space reserved for interrogation.

"Ah, Mrs. Goldfarb," an unimpressively ordinary man said as he entered the office. "George Ollinen," the man said, offering his dainty hand.

Elin Goldfarb returned the gesture.

"Please, have a seat," Ollinen said quietly, his gray eyes obscured by the thick lenses of his eyeglasses as he pointed to a comfortable chair next to a desk devoid of papers save for a thin manila folder in the exact center of the desk's blond surface.

Elin complied.

"I think we'll be fine," the little man said to the two officers who had accompanied Elin.

Nevonen and Salminen left the room.

"Now then," the Valpo commander said, reaching across the desk for a fragile teapot, "would you care for some tea? I gave up coffee some years back. Doctor's orders. There's nothing like tea to ease the nerves, don't you think?"

Elin shook her head.

"Well, I'll have a cup in any event," he said.

The officer poured tea. The windows were open. A breeze moved through the room.

"You must be curious as to why you are here."

Elin cleared her throat. "My supervisor at the hotel will wonder what has become of me."

Ollinen smiled. The gesture displayed sharp teeth.

Like those of a weasel.

The policeman opened the file. "Ah yes, night manager at the *Hotellet Jacobstad.* Impressive," the little man said quietly as he paged through documents. "Started as a chambermaid and moved into management. No easy task for an immigrant with no Swedish language skills to do in this city."

Elin squirmed.

"Inspector Nevonen is calling the hotel to advise them that you'll be late for work. He'll be discrete. You won't suffer any reprisals from your employer. Trust me on this, Mrs. Goldfarb. I know the hotel owner. We're old friends."

The disclosure did little to mollify the woman's concern.

"You must know, Mrs. Goldfarb, that, though you have, shall we say, a most 'intriguing' background, I am more interested in certain of your neighbors than you at this juncture."

What neighbors is he talking about?

The puzzled look on the woman's face caused the man to smile a crooked little smile. It was the first inkling that Elin had that their interview was not going to be confined to idle pleasantries.

"Who, you ask? Who is it that I am interested in? I can see that question in the furrow of your brow, by the increase of the pulse in your neck."

Elin swallowed.

"And a lovely neck it is at that," the man observed, stroking the skin of his own scrawny throat in a way that caused Elin's stomach to turn.

"No need to worry, Mrs. Goldfarb. Like I said, I am interested in a neighbor of yours. Actually, two neighbors of yours. The Cohens."

"Rosi and Walter?"

Ollinen nodded.

"But why?"

The officer sipped his tea and considered the woman. A subtle but complete change in the pleasant demeanor that Ollinen had exhibited at the beginning of the interview overcame the policeman.

"Dr. Cohen, for that is what he calls himself though he has no credentials to practice medicine here, represents a problem. I don't wish to share all of the details of why that is so, except to say that the good doctor has repeatedly been assigned to Kemijärvi and has repeatedly left that camp without permission. Did you know this?"

Elin nodded.

"How? How did you come to know this?"

I don't want to betray Rosi's trust. But she told me about her husband's disgust, about how he felt demeaned, a trained physician, being sent to a camp where he was expected to work in the fields.

"I know why you hesitate, Mrs. Goldfarb. You are considering your loyalty to Mrs. Cohen. Understand: She has, so far as the Valpo is concerned, done nothing wrong. She has stayed in Pietarsaari as her papers require. She has not done anything untoward. And yet her husband flaunts freedom, freedom he has not yet earned, freedom that is not yet his, by gallivanting all over the countryside and by practicing medicine when he has no business doing so."

Elin drew her purse into her bosom.

"You've learned these things from Mrs. Cohen?"

Though her throat was parched, Elin was able to answer in a weak voice: "Yes."

"Good. Honesty will do much to curry the favor of the Finnish government. It will do you well to cooperate so that, when your own situation is reviewed, there will be something positive on your side of the argument."

What does he mean, "When my own situation is reviewed"?

The flash of concern in Elin's eyes caused the officer to digress.

"Another day, another time, Mrs. Goldfarb. Today, I am only interested in where Dr. Cohen is. He has once again left the work camp without authorization. I am growing very tired of finding him, plucking him from wherever he's staying, and sending him back to Kemijärvi. He is, to state it plainly, wearing out his welcome."

The woman stared at her hands.

"You know where he is, don't you?"

She raised her eyes and looked directly at the policeman. Her aspect was one of timidity, not defiance.

"Then tell me. He will never know who gave me the information. His wife will not know. Only I will know who told me the whereabouts of Dr. Walter Cohen."

Elin swallowed hard.

I am to be married before Christmas. I am a guest in this country. If I don't cooperate, they may send me back to Russia. If that happens, I will likely die. I will not have my insulin and I will be sent to some far-flung place to die of a diabetic coma. I have no choice in the matter.

"Turku," she whispered.

"Where in Turku?"

"I don't know the address. But I believe he is staying with the brother of the rabbi there."

Ollinen smiled again. "Thank you, Mrs. Goldfarb," the little man said as he stood up and extended his soft, pink hand to the woman. "I'll have Inspector Nevonen drive you to work."

Elin shook the policeman's hand without sincerity. "I think I'd rather find my own way."

"Suit yourself, Mrs. Goldfarb, suit yourself."

The woman walked towards the door. Before she left the palatial office, Ollinen spoke again.

"Don't be surprised, Mrs. Goldfarb, if you and I sit down to discuss *your* situation in the very near future," the officer said cryptically, as he reclaimed his chair.

The heel of Elin's left pump caught the edge of a throw rug just outside the door. Elin Goldfarb stumbled, but did not fall, as she sought to escape the man's presence.

CHAPTER 20
Raasiku, Estonia
December 1942
(Nigul's Story)

***September** 5. Dust settles over the train station in Raasiku, twenty miles to the southeast of Tallinn. Flags on the front of a steam locomotive display black swastikas against a white and red background. The pennants ripple as the train rolls to a stop. Thick smoke roils from the stack of the coal-fired boiler powering the drive wheels of the massive engine. A coal tender and a string of cattle cars packed with human cargo pull in behind the locomotive.*

This train, and another that will arrive in a week, bring Jews from other countries to Estonia. In all, over 2,000 men, women, and children will arrive at the depot in the little village. The trains will arrive without fanfare. The unfortunate beings in the cattle cars will be unloaded on the platform of the station under the watchful eyes of Estonian police and German soldiers, but it will not be the Germans who decide the fate of the people on the trains.

Estonian Police Commander Ain-Ervin Mere and his Estonian adjutant, Lieutenant Aleksander Laak, the officer in charge of the Jägala Labor Camp, will decide which men and women are spared immediate execution in the pits of Kalevi-Liiva and are sent, however briefly, to work at Jägala. All the children and all the old men and women from the trains will be directed to trucks idling nearby. These unfortunates will climb into the trucks and vanish. Of the Jews sent to Ain-Ervin Mere by the SS from Thereisenstadt, only 300-400 souls will escape the execution pits upon arrival. Their fate will be decided later—after the German advance into Russia is stopped and the Red Army begins its counter-offensive.

In the end, Estonians collaborating with the SS and the Gestapo will be complicit in the murder of thousands of European Jews transported to Estonia by the Nazis. But these are not the only innocents murdered as part of the Final Solution in Estonia. Virtually all of the Estonian Jews who remained behind when the Russians evacuated Estonia will die. Most of the Estonian Roma population will be executed. And tens of thousands of Soviet prisoners of war forced to labor in the oil shale fields of northeastern Estonia will perish, either by being worked to death or at the end of a gun.

There will be many who claim to be unaware of what transpired. There will be some—a minority to be sure—who, like Aleksander Laak, cast their lot with the Nazis. One of these men was a man I knew. His name was Ernest Raun.

I did not know that Ellisabet Raun was living in Tallinn until months after she returned from Germany. I had not seen her since she was a young girl wrestling with me in the warm straw of a barn in Tartu. I, of course, knew nothing of Ernest Raun's involvement with Aleksander Laak and Jägala Camp before reconnecting with Ellisabet. Hell, at the time, I was not cognizant of what was happening to the Jews in Estonia. I had some knowledge, from scuttlebutt and rumor, of what Hitler was up to with respect to the Jews in the rest of Europe. Not the exact details, not the grim reality of six million people destined for fake showers, gas, fire, smoke, and ash. That was not something I appreciated in detail. But most of us knew that Jews were being herded up and confined to labor camps, ghettos, and places of that sort. We just didn't comprehend the utter evil of the plan behind the rumors. And I had issues of a personal nature occupying my attention at the time, issues that caused me to ignore the broader perspective of what would come to be called the Holocaust.

Karl had moved to Hiiumaa Island and was working as a teacher in the same school where Alexis Gustafson taught. From what I heard through the grapevine, Karl was living with Alexis in the very apartment where she gave me the final brush-off after displaying the love poems and gushing letters of adoration my brother had sent her. Of course, I didn't read the poems or the letters so I can only guess as to their content. But Alexis made it pretty clear to me that day in Kärdla what my little brother had been up to. I didn't have to read the goddamned poems to know Karl's intentions. However, I did know that the bastard was now sleeping with my girlfriend! OK. That's not true. She wasn't my girlfriend. But I wanted her to be. And Karl knew this before he slunk into her arms like some serpent from a Biblical story and captured Alexis's heart in a way I could never hope to.

So what did I do? What did a lovesick bachelor electrician do when betrayed by his brother? I went back to the only person I knew would have me. I returned to the flabby arms of Liisu Koidula.

The Russians were long gone. Liisu had tried and failed to curry the favor of a German officer, a captain I believe, whom, while briefly interested, had no intention of making a permanent commitment to the Estonian fleshpot.

Late one night, after a long shift working on a messy wiring problem in a German oil tanker, Big Peeter and I were in need of a cold beer. The Water's Edge was the closest tavern to the shipyards. I'd avoided visiting the bar after my unfortunate row with the skinny Russian sailor and his pals. I had little interest in rekindling whatever Liisu and I once had. But Big Peeter was parched and insistent. And so, I agreed to one beer.

"Nigul!" the fat woman said excitedly, as if we had never left off. "How nice to see you again!"

Big Peeter and I sidled up to the bar and sat on battered wooden stools. Three or four dockworkers and shipyard grunts sat on stools snugged up to the bar. There were no customers sitting at tables or in booths. Dim light fell upon the varnished surface of the bar and was reflected by the polished wood as I nodded to Liisu but said nothing in reply.

"He's a bit miffed," Big Peeter.

Liisu waddled over. "How so?"

The big man grinned, exposing foul breath and worse teeth. "He was in love."

Liisu laughed. "Nigul Kristian is always thinking he's in love. Every girl that wiggles her cute little behind as she walks down the sidewalk after smiling at him is the next girl he's in love with," Liisu said through a wide grin. "Isn't that right, sweetie?"

Her plump fingers came to rest on the back of my wrist. I wanted to pull away. Her gesture was too intimate, too friendly for my state of mind. And yet, her touch rekindled something, some vague expectation.

It wasn't that Liisu Koidula was disgusting: far from it. Though Liisu was fat and ungainly on her feet, there was allure in her dimpled cheeks and darting eyes. I wouldn't call it beauty. Liisu was not beautiful. But like those robust women in old Dutch paintings, there was a definite appeal to the woman that, even pissed off at my erstwhile brother, even while lamenting the loss of a truly handsome woman, I could appreciate.

I nodded. I *had* to nod. She was right. I *was* the type of man whose heart, at least in my youth, was easily captured by the woman closest at hand.

"Who was she?"

I knew what Liisu meant: *Who was the woman I was lamenting, the woman I had lost to my brother.* I wasn't about to get into it with the fat woman. Not in a bar. Not in front of Big Peeter. Though, in those days, I often wore my heart on my sleeve, I wasn't about to expose my wounds in public. Unfortunately, my companion knew my story and was not inclined—after quickly downing the mug of tap beer Liisu poured for him and starting on a second—to keep his big mouth shut.

"Stunning woman. A teacher in Hiiumaa with an interesting history. Came to Karelia from America with her mother and stepfather. Stepfather vanished in one of Stalin's purges. Her mother disappeared but is apparently living in Finland. Pietarsaari, isn't that right, Nigul?"

I gulped my first mug of beer and didn't respond.

If he wasn't so goddamned big, I'd knock him off that stool. But I know Peeter. You could hit him with a sledgehammer and he'd ask, "Was that a mosquito?"

"Seems like he doesn't want to talk about it," Liisu observed, compassion clear in her words. She didn't remove her hand. Curiously, I didn't remove it either. "Maybe you should just let it be, Peeter."

My friend was quickly getting drunk and listening only to himself. "So Nigul falls in love. But he makes a mistake. He introduces the girl to his brother. His smarter, better looking..." Big Peeter slapped my back as he said this, "...and more refined younger brother. The *Professor* writes goddamned love poems to her. And by the time poor Nigul shows up on her doorstep with flowers and candy and hope of something permanent, she's fallen for Karl. Sad, sad story, eh friend?"

The big man embraced me in a bear hug. I sat mute, staring at the empty mug in front of me, wondering why I'd ever agreed to drink beer in Liisu's tavern.

After five beers and two shots of cheap vodka, it didn't take Liisu Koidula much effort to lure me into her bed. I don't remember how the sex was. I don't even remember what we did. All I remember is lying on top of Liisu and crying into the fat woman's cigarette-afflicted hair as she stroked my neck and whispered words of comfort and condolence. That night, I renewed a perverse relationship with a woman I would never love. It was a connection I needed at the time and one welcomed by Liisu without conditions. We were lovers for two months. Despite the immorality inherent in such a relationship, I don't regret my time with Liisu. In the end, we did not part (as we did during our first break-up) because of a fight or an argument or something sinister. My relationship with Liisu Koidula ended the day I saw Ellisabet Raun standing on a sidewalk in downtown Tallinn waiting for a bus.

CHAPTER 21
SS Hohenhörn
Gulf of Finland
November 6, 1942

Elin Goldfarb was afraid.

Why is this happening? I am not a Jew. I was married to one, that is true, but he never sat Seder so far as I know. Seder: I know enough about Jewish ritual to understand the irony involved in thinking about the Passover as this German ship chugs through black water. The plague of Nazi discrimination did not "pass over" me. I am on this ship, the 28th name on a list of people bound for God knows where. Some Jews, some not, but all rounded up by the Valpo for real or perceived infractions against the government. In my case, I made a mistake. I said "no" to Commander Ollinen when, in return for his ignoring my communist activism and writings, I would become his mistress. I had no interest in satisfying that man's lust. I was finally, fully in love with Matti Peltomaa and would not, for any reason, betray that sweet man's devotion to me.

I was whisked away from the hotel by Valpo agents twice: once for my first meeting with Ollinen, during which I disclosed the whereabouts of Walter Cohen, and then for a second sit-down with Ollinen when he had me brought to an expensive restaurant where he explained his untoward proposal. The Valpo officer smugly revealed that I was "making a big mistake" by rejecting his advances, that he wasn't expecting exclusive rights to my "charms," and that I should reconsider, for the safety of my beloved, who, though an old man with an impressive combat record, could be sent back to the front. But I wasn't listening to Ollinen; I was thinking about how I could contact Matti and summon him back to Pietarsaari so he could explain to the policeman how we were going to be married, as if, in the face of the Valpo's power, one Finnish soldier could save me.

Ollinen didn't immediately act against me. It was a month before his men returned for a third visit. During that interval, I was unaware of what was taking place in Finland concerning certain foreign Jews. I only know that, when I told Commander Ollinen that I would take my chances regarding my long-stalled petition for residency, the Valpo commander simply smiled that crooked smile of his and said, "Alright."

The case of Dr. Walter Cohen, his wife, and their son caused the Finnish authorities consternation. Though there was no agreement between the Finns and the Germans to turn over Finnish Jews to the Germans, certain foreigners, including foreign Jews, had been identified by the Valpo as worthy of deportation.

The Deputy Chief of the Valpo sent a list of eleven names to the head of the Gestapo—the German Secret Police. Only one of the individuals cited for removal was a Jew but that first list set the stage for further intrigue. Though Dr. Cohen's name was not on that initial inventory, he continued to be a person of interest. Suursaari Island became another Finnish labor camp after General Pajari's men liberated it. Walter Cohen was sent there from Kemijärvi but he promptly left. Cohen was again arrested and held in Helsinki Prison until powerful Finnish friends intervened. The Jewish doctor was released and ordered to return to his apartment in Pietarsaari, but again, Cohen did not comply. Instead, he resumed his walkabout through Finland, which, to the Valpo, looked suspiciously like the meanderings of a spy. When Dr. Cohen returned to his wife and child in Pietarsaari, he was arrested and sent back to Helsinki Prison. From there, he was returned to Suursaari Island.

Valpo Chief Anthoni was so aggravated by the misbehaving doctor that he wrote to the Gestapo.

Throughout his stay in Helsinki, Cohen has intrigued against the State Police, has gained for himself undeserved advantage, thru influential acquaintances, has practiced medicine without a license, and attempted to delay his duties as a work conscript.

The point of Anthoni's letter was to add Dr. Walter Cohen, his wife, and their son to the second roster of persons being deported from Finland. The Gestapo acknowledged Anthoni's letter.

I confirm the transfer of the Jews mentioned…About this matter, the commander of the security police in Tallinn has been informed so that negotiations might be undertaken.

While this intrigue was taking place, Elin Goldfarb, a Jew in surname only, remained ignorant of the fate awaiting her. Upon her dismissal of Ollinen's proposition, Elin's life in Pietarsaari and her work at the hotel continued on as before. Her application for Finnish residency was neither refused nor granted. The powers that be simply ignored her request while the local Valpo commander determined her fate. She was aware Dr. Cohen had been arrested, released, and then arrested again. But the reasons behind the arrests, the existence of lists being sent by the Valpo to the Gestapo—these things were unknown to Elin Goldfarb until she read an editorial deploring the Valpo's conduct in the *Helsingin Sanomat*.

By the time Elin read the newspaper piece, public discussions about what to do with immigrants deemed troublemakers had grown loud and angry. The one man possessing the prestige and power to stop the Valpo from expelling *foreigners* (it was clear that the Finns had no intention of deporting Finnish *citizens* of any religion or ethnicity) chose to do nothing. Publicly, Mannerheim remained silent on the issue. Privately, he deplored the Valpo's intentions towards certain foreign refugees. But when asked about the situation "on the record," the Commander-in-Chief claimed the issue was a "civil" matter and not within the military's jurisdiction.

Despite the public outcry, the Germans in Estonia received a "final" list of foreigners being deported from Finland. Dr. Walter Cohen and his family were added to the list. But just before the Cohen family was snatched up, George Ollinen received word from his superiors that the Jewish doctor and his family were not to be touched. Instead of being handed over to the Gestapo, the Cohen family was inexplicably allowed to remain in Finland. Immediately after receiving word to release the Cohen family, Ollinen contacted Chief Anthoni with a special request. He asked that he be allowed to add one name—a communist sympathizer, journalist, and Jewess—to those being expelled. Anthoni was never advised that the woman in question was an American citizen, a detail that, if provided, would have caused the Valpo Chief to decline the entreaty. But Ollinen was an intelligent man, well versed in diplomacy, and he did not inform Arno Anthoni of Elin Goldfarb's nationality.

The day after Elin read the editorial deploring the impending expulsion of foreigners, she found herself being escorted away from the *Hotellet Jacobstad* by the Valpo. Two days and nights went by. She was, during that time, treated kindly by the matron assigned to guard female prisoners in Helsinki prison. And she was allowed, as the other prisoners were, to write a single letter.

November 5, 1942
Helsinki

Dear Matti:

Tomorrow I will be sent away. There is not much time to explain so I will only say this: The Valpo is convinced that I am a communist, a Jew, and a danger to Finland. I have been labeled "undesirable" and will be handed over to the Germans once I arrive in Tallinn. Of course, these things aren't true. I am no longer a communist and I am certainly no threat. A Valpo officer fabricated these allegations when I refused an untoward offer I won't detail here.

I hope you can find me and have me released. I have heard rumors of what will happen in Estonia. You know that Hitler is killing Jews. All across Europe, he is taking away their rights, their property, confining them, and, ultimately, killing them. That I am a Jew in name only is of no consequence. Find me. Save me. I implore you.

Elin

She had wanted to say more, to express her love for the man who had saved her life. But the electric light in the drafty cell she shared with Janka Kollman and Kollman's twenty-month-old son, Frans Olaf, had blinked twice, signaling "lights out." Elin hurried to finish her plea. She folded the single piece of inexpensive writing paper, placed it in an envelope, addressed it to Matti Peltomaa's reserve unit in Viipuri, and handed the documents and the pencil stub to the matron before the prison cell had plunged into darkness.

They stood on the deck of the ship. It was to be a short voyage, only three hours across the icy waters of the Gulf of Finland. The *SS Hohenhörn* wallowed in swells. Elin felt the pitch and roll of the freighter as she stood alongside Janka Kollman, Frans Olaf asleep in his mother's arms; the women and children separated from the men. Georg Kollman had not spoken to his wife or held his child since his family was rushed from their apartment under the cover of darkness. All the deportees were dressed in the clothes they had been taken in. Elin was one of the lucky ones: She had grabbed her overcoat and scarf when the Valpo came for her. But she did not have her insulin and, other than one bowl of meager gruel and a crust of stale bread provided in prison, she had not eaten in two days. As Elin spread her shoes for balance, she sought to conceal her dizziness, throbbing headache, and fatigue—symptoms of her uncontrolled diabetes. Elin Goldfarb knew she was in danger of being deemed unfit for hard labor and she had a good idea of what such a designation would mean once the ship docked.

"You Jews and other agitators," a rotund Gestapo agent said loudly in poor Finnish, "stop complaining!" Dressed in a thick winter coat and wearing earmuffs, winter boots, and black leather gloves, the German scrutinized the prisoners, a Lugar held loosely in his gloved right hand, as he continued: "It won't go well for you if you don't stop wagging your tongues."

"Ja," a tall, thin soldier in a SS uniform holding a submachine gun added, "there's no reason to complain. It's not that cold. Besides," the soldier continued, "if you die aboard ship, you'll save on the gas needed to dispose of you."

The guard's candor stunned Elin.

So the stories are true! Men, women, and little children sent to their deaths by gassing! I didn't believe the rumors. It seems impossible that an entire nation could allow one man, one bastard of a man, to lead them down such a path. But there it is: proof that I will likely never see Matti, or Finland, or America, again.

"We have done nothing to deserve this!" Georg Kollman shouted. "We are innocent of any wrongdoing!"

The Gestapo agent approached Kollman and placed the muzzle of the pistol against the man's temple. Janka Kollman shrieked.

"You," the fat policeman said precisely, gouging Kollman's skin with the cold steel of the Lugar, "shut your ugly Jew mouth. And you," the agent said in the same menacing tone as he turned towards the woman and child, "keep quiet or I will take that runt from your arms and toss it into the sea."

Janka whimpered. Elin moved to her side and embraced her. Wind sang through the ship's rigging. It was near midnight and the warmth of the sun was long forgotten.

"Ja," the skinny SS soldier added, "that would save even more gas. Toss the little Jew bastard into the ocean."

The Gestapo man retreated to a nearby ladder, leaned against the rungs, holstered his pistol, retrieved a silver case from the pocket of his overcoat, removed a cigarette from the case with gloved fingers, and lit the cigarette with a butane lighter. White smoke billowed from the glowing fag as the Gestapo agent judiciously considered the unfortunates shivering in front of him.

"Jews," the agent muttered. "Why the hell were they ever born?"

CHAPTER 22
Jägala, Estonia
February 1943

The woman shuffled through ankle deep snow towards the main office of Jägala labor camp in east central Estonia. It had snowed incessantly since she arrived in mid-November. Her survival was nothing short of miraculous and had endued her with renewed faith in either luck or God. She was unable to determine which of those two forces had saved her, but Elin Goldfarb recognized that she was a fortunate woman, whatever the cause of her salvation.

When the *SS Hohenhörn* pulled into the docks of Tallinn, she had fully expected to meet her end. The comments by the young soldier about the fate of the undesirables aboard the German-flagged vessel—that they were destined for destruction in some unnamed extermination camp in some undisclosed location—had been unnerving. The Valpo agents accompanying the human cargo said nothing. They made no protests on behalf of the captives. They did not intervene in the slightest way. It was clear that the Germans were, from the moment the twenty-eight unfortunates were herded onto the exposed deck of the freighter, in charge. It was a reality, a truth that, in Elin Goldfarb's mind, did not bode well for her.

Elin had followed Janka Kollman, who carried little Franz Olaf in her arms, as the prisoners were led from the ship onto the concrete pier. Her disease was rapidly taking control of her body. She had all she could do to put one foot ahead of the other without stumbling. Elin Goldfarb knew that, as a woman, she had a small chance of being saved from immediate death. She also knew that if she did not appear healthy, even that slim window of survival would disappear. It took great effort for her to keep up appearances in the face of her rising blood sugar and she had no idea if her deception would prove successful.

Stern-faced men stood above the dock and leaned against an iron railing as the deportees were herded along a cement walkway and ordered to stand at attention. German soldiers and Estonian police officers stood guard with rifles and machine guns poised to shoot anyone foolish enough to try to make a run for it.

Where would I go? Elin had thought to herself as she watched the sun edge above the towers of Old Tallinn. *I know nothing of this country, this land. To run, for me, for any of us, would be folly—even if there were no angry men with guns.*

She later learned that the men making the selections that day included SS Colonel Martin Sandberger, Gestapo officer Rolf Linden, Jägala camp commander Lieutenant Aleksander Laak, and Laak's assistant, Ernest Raun.

"Move the women and children away from the dock," Sandberger had said evenly, the steady tone of his voice concealing the ugly task he was charged with. "Hold them at Tallinn Prison until the next train arrives. We'll let the camp commander at Birkenau decide what to do with them," Sandberger added, pursing his lips as he spoke, knowing full well what awaited the women, the children, and the infirm in Poland.

Lieutenant Laak had a particular interest in young women of a certain age. The Estonian selected young Jewish females sent to Estonia and used their bodies in unimaginable ways at the labor camp he operated.

"That one would have been a good choice," Laak said through gritted teeth, pointing at Janka Kollman, "but she spoiled it by having a brat. Now, she's likely too loose. There's no point in wearing a stocking that no longer fits."

"See anyone else you'd like for the camp, lieutenant?" Ernest Raun had asked, his small eyes distorted by the thick lenses of his eyeglasses.

"No. There's no one here I can see myself spending time with," Laak replied.

"What about that one, the one with the long hair?"

Raun had pointed to Elin Goldfarb with the index finger of his gloved right hand as he spoke.

"I don't fuck old women," Laak responded.

"She's pretty, though, despite her age. Striking, actually," Sandberger said agreeably.

"Looks fairly intelligent too," Raun added.

"You want her? She's yours, Ernest. My gift to you. An early Christmas present," Aleksander Laak had said.

Ernest Raun nodded to the guard nearest Elin. "Bring that one over."

"You—move along," the Estonian policeman said gruffly.

Due to her rapidly failing mental acuity, Elin hadn't appreciated the command even though she had a basic understanding of German. The guard prodded her with his Mauser and urged her forward until she stood precariously, her balance nearly failing, her perception of events clouded by advancing decline, at the base of the platform holding the officials.

"What is your name?" Ernest Raun had asked in Finnish as he looked down on the woman.

"Elin. Elin Goldfarb."

"Ah," the lawyer said with satisfaction, "So you *are* a Jewess. At least you're not a communist. Am I right about that? You're not a communist, are you, Miss?"

"It's Mrs. Goldfarb. And no, I am not a communist. In fact," she had replied in a voice barely audible to those standing above her. "I think a mistake has been made."

Rolf Linden had frowned.

"The Gestapo doesn't make mistakes."

She shook her head.

I must be firm, but deferential, if I am to avoid being sent off with the others.

"I am an American. I am not a Jew. I was married to one but he is dead."

It took concentration for Elin to form words in Finnish, a language she knew by rote. Her answer came out slowly and the words were slurred.

Laak adjusted the brim of his officer's cap to get a clear view of the woman.

"She's insolent. And she appears ill. She will likely cause nothing but trouble, Raun. Send her off with the others."

Ernest Raun brought his gloved right hand to his chin and considered the woman. "You sound like an educated person Mrs. Goldfarb. Are you, educated, I mean?'

"I was a teacher. I completed college in the States." Elin had determined, in the instant before responding, that she would not reveal she had also been a newspaper reporter.

The little man clapped his gloved hands together like a child finding a lost toy. "Do you understand German?" Raun asked in that language.

Elin Goldfarb wasn't fluent in German but knew enough of the language to carry on a basic conversation. Even in her depleted condition, Elin understood that her answer meant the difference between life and death.

If I can learn Karelian, learn Russian, learn Swedish, I can improve my German.

"Jawohl."

There had been a slight pause in the discussion. The wind came up. Snow began to drift down upon the near frozen harbor.

"Lieutenant, she's just what I need!" Raun blurted out joyfully in German, "an administrative assistant, to deal with paperwork and correspondence. I say we bring her back to Jägala with us."

Laak shook his head. "She is trouble, Ernest. Her color isn't good. The last thing we need is to bring typhus or some other disease into camp," Laak had whispered. "Are you ill, Jew?" Laak asked loudly. "Are you sick?"

Elin struggled to find the words to reply in German. "I am diabetic. My insulin was left behind in Pietarsaari."

"Shit," Laak said with disdain. "Old, Jewish, and sick. What the hell good is she to us, Ernest? Answer me that. What the hell good is she to us?"

Raun had stared hard at the woman. "What if she is, as she claims, an American? I don't think we want to be in the business of sending Americans, even Jewish ones, to Birkenau. What do you think, Colonel?" Raun asked.

Sandberger focused on the woman. "If you want her, Mr. Raun, that's your business, not mine. I can justify it to my superiors. Say that there were questions about her origins, that she *may* be an American. That will satisfy the 'powers that be,' if you will. You decide."

"Lieutenant, I want her. Insulin is readily available. It will be no trouble to keep her well. That's not an issue. I'm convinced she will be of use to me," Raun said after a considerable pause.

"Rautinen," Laak shouted to the guard standing next to Elin, "show Mrs. Goldfarb to the truck. She's coming with us."

Rolf Linden looked out over the remaining men, women, and children shivering in the cold.

This is the best Finland can do? We supply Mannerheim with arms and tanks and planes and men; and a few dozen Jews and communists are the only cows the Finns are willing to cull from the herd? What the hell was Hitler thinking when he agreed to work with the Finns?

"Deliver the remaining Jews to Tallinn Prison," Linden had finally said. "There'll be a train coming soon enough to haul them away," the Gestapo officer added matter-of-factly, as if he was a farmer disposing of unwanted kittens. "The others can be sent to work the shale oil."

Georg Kollman, his wife, their son, and five other Jewish deportees were held in Tallinn Prison for two weeks before being sent to Germany. After arriving in Berlin, the unfortunates were herded onto cattle cars. Georg Kollman never saw his wife or infant son again. The family was separated in Tallinn and upon their arrival in Birkenau, Janka and Franz Olaf went directly to the showers. Georg and the other men were put to work in a labor camp where nearly all of them were worked to death or gassed. Of the foreign Jews given over to the Germans by the Valpo, only two survived. One of them was Georg Kollman.

CHAPTER 23
Puhja, Estonia
April 1943
(Nigul's Story)

I was very uncomfortable. I did not know that Karl and his new girlfriend would be visiting Mother and Father the same week I went on holiday. Despite Big Peeter's words of wisdom, and despite the fact that I had reconnected with Ellisabet Raun, literally bumping into her on the streets of Tallinn, it still rankled that my brother would stoop so low as to steal my girl from me. I know, I know. Big Peeter was right: Alexis Gustafson was never *my* girl. We had a few laughs and shared a kiss or two—hardly enough to constitute a valid claim on her affections. And yet, that is exactly how I felt. I believed Alexis was destined to be mine and I hers, and when Karl imposed on *our* equation, well, it was a tremendous blow. So, having my brother flaunt his victory in our parents' home didn't sit well with me. Not a bit.

I should have been a bigger man than to let jealousy interfere with my relationship with Karl. I mean, after all, I had found Ellisabet Raun again and she had grown into a handsome young woman with striking raven hair, rare emerald eyes, and a mature figure.

The girl has become a woman.

When we met in downtown Tallinn that day, it was as if no time had passed between us. Ellisabet was willing to take up right where we had left off. Whatever she'd been doing in Germany, apart from her studies, she was an accomplished lover. There was nothing she wouldn't do for me or *to* me, or allow me to do *to* her, when we were in bed. Ellisabet was completely free of shame and guilt about lovemaking. I should have been a happy, contented man. Even Ellisabet's National Socialist outlook didn't deter my ardor. There was nothing about my renewed connection with the daughter of the man who was assisting Aleksander Laak in running the Jägala labor camp that should have caused me to envy Karl. And yet, when I saw my brother and Alexis together, that is exactly what I felt.

"Hey," Karl said to me as I stepped into my parents' house from the stormy day swirling outside.

They were sitting on the sofa in the parlor. Karl sat disturbingly close to Alexis, the hem of her skirt hiked up, her legs provocatively displayed. The blouse she was wearing, red with printed yellow flowers, was too large for her. The collar was loose around her smooth, swan-like neck. The aperture was at least a size too large. A gold chain, simple and austere, rested on her breastbone. The chain held a small Orthodox crucifix depicting Jesus in torment. I wanted to ask her about the icon but held my tongue. Her mismatched eyes would not engage mine as I stood with a small valise in my hand and considered what to say.

"Nigul," Father said evenly, as he appeared in the doorway leading from the living room to the kitchen, "welcome home."

Father slapped me hard on the back and smiled that slight, difficult smile he was prone to rely upon when emotional.

Father is aging.

I took in the gray hairs sprouting from my father's nose and ears, the decline in his posture as he started to wither, to return to the earth from whence he came, and the small potbelly that was now lodged above the distressed leather of his one and only belt.

Far faster than I imagined.

I stood there with my mouth closed, nodding, and uncomfortable about what I saw both on the couch and in my father.

Mother's flighty entrance broke the sober, ungainly mood. "Nigul!" she twittered, as she scampered across the bare wood floor and hugged me. "So nice of you to visit. We were just talking with Karl and Alexis about their plans."

I kissed Mother's downy cheek. She moved aside and wrapped an arm loosely around Father's waist.

I set my valise down in a corner and nodded to Karl. "Hey yourself, Brother," I finally replied.

"You're looking well," Alexis said quietly.

"And you…" I stopped to think about how I would say what I wanted to say, "…Hiiumaa Island seems to agree with you, Miss Gustafson."

The words came out strained, but the sentiment was true: Her face was aglow as she sat next to my brother.

Karl stood up and motioned for me to follow him. "We need firewood," he said, moving towards the kitchen and the back door. "Lend a hand, will you?"

I hadn't taken off my wet boots. I bent to unlace them and carry them across the floor.

"No need, Son," Mother interrupted. "I'll just take a mop to it. Go on—help your brother. Alexis, would you mind lending a hand with dinner? I've got some turnips and potatoes and carrots and onions from the cellar that need peeling and slicing."

Alexis stood up, smoothed the fabric of her skirt until it hung properly below her knees, and followed Mother into the kitchen.

Karl and I slid around the women, opened the back door, went outside, and clambered down the slick wooden stairs off the home's rear stoop.

The rain had diminished to drizzle. As I followed Karl towards the three-sided shed protecting Father's hand-sawn and ax-split firewood from weather, I didn't say a word. I wanted my brother to be the first to speak, to offer an explanation. But I was sorely disappointed. Alexis was not the topic that Karl brought up as I held out my forearms and Karl loaded them with birch.

"You know that the puppets in Tallinn have instituted the draft," Karl said matter-of-factly. "Men between the ages of nineteen and twenty-three are being called up. I'll be dragged back into it. But working in the shipyards, you are likely exempt," Karl said, as he filled his own arms with wood and turned to follow me back to the house.

The dank day was waning. The dull sky was melting into the spectral landscape. Oak trees stood in clusters, their forms black and linear like vertical dividers against the pewter sky, adding no color to the world because their new leaves had not yet unfurled. My boots shuffled through pools of water, mud, and remnant winter debris covering the exposed brown grass as I followed a path worn into the ground by my father's boots.

"What are you going to do?" I asked Karl, as I kicked the bottom of the door leading to the kitchen.

Mother appeared with a pleasant smile still affixed to her plump face and let us in. We tromped past Alexis, who was sitting on a kitchen chair, a wastebasket between her legs, her legs open but her thighs covered by her skirt, as she peeled potato skins into the trash. The scene embittered me, reminded me of Karl's betrayal. But again, I held my tongue.

Karl and I unloaded the wood into the cast iron rack in the living room, taking care to neatly stack the pieces. Father would not countenance a mess in his wood rack and we had no desire to be chastised.

"Karl?" I repeated, as I untied my boots and placed them near the woodstove to dry.

Instead of addressing the issue he'd brought up, Karl changed the subject. "I didn't mean for it to happen."

Not now you dumb bastard.

"I'm not interested in having this discussion," I said, gritting my teeth, clenching my fists as I stood next to the woodstove warming my backside.

Karl dropped his boots next to mine. "If not now, then when, Nigul? We have to talk."

I shook my head. "No, we really don't. At least, not now, not while the wound is fresh."

Karl bit his lip and grasped my shoulders with his hands so that I was forced to look at him. "I am truly sorry it happened this way."

There was much sincerity in Karl's expression. Maybe that's why my right hand felt the need to crash into the side of his jaw. I was tired of Karl's sanctimony and I wanted to beat it out of him.

The punch stunned my brother and knocked his glasses off his face but did not, as I had hoped, drop him to the floor. Instead, he shook his head and managed a dazed smile.

"Not a good idea," Karl said, just before I lunged at him, hoping to wrap him up in a bear hug and throw him on his back where I could pummel the piss out of his boyish good looks.

My move was telegraphed and Karl avoided my crude attack. He sidestepped me and as I sailed past him, he gave my ass a kick with his big foot, sending me crashing face first onto the floor. Then he was on my back, trying to pull my right arm behind me, trying to gain a submission hold before the fight had even started.

He's stronger now, I noted, as his arm worked against mine, *but I've still got him by a good fourteen kilos.*

I twisted and managed to free my left hand from beneath my body. I wasn't too proud to grab Karl's long blond hair and yank his head back: There are no rules in brotherly warfare except "thou shalt not kill."

"Goddamn it, you're pulling my hair like a girl!" Karl yelped.

The women scurried into the front room.

"Nigul, Karl, stop this right now!" Mother screamed as her hands gripped her cheeks.

"What's gotten into you two?" Alexis added. "Stop this childishness before you break something!"

My unorthodox move was successful. I regained the advantage and broke free. I rolled across the floor to a place where I could stand and face my brother.

Father had left for the store to buy the newspaper and wasn't a witness to the row. Had he been there, no doubt he would have grabbed the nearest implement—a broom, a fire iron, an ash shovel—and used it to end the fracas. But he was gone so we were free to fight.

"Goddamn you, Nigul, I think you tore out a piece of my hair!" Karl screamed as we circled each other with balled fists.

"Good. That long hair makes you look like a woman anyway," I sneered.

The insult enraged my brother. He launched a wild left hook. The attempt grazed my right cheek.

I hit him hard with a right to the mouth and a left to his midsection. His stomach did not give: My fist met solid muscle.

No longer the kid I used to have my way with. Better get to it before he lands another punch.

While I was busy admiring Karl's physique, he was busy finding a weakness in my defense. His right hand struck my cheek with force. The punch staggered me.

"Good one, little brother," I said as I spit blood. "Nearly knocked out a tooth."

Karl smiled wickedly and threw a follow-up left but missed by a mile. I ducked and brought every ounce of my strength into his belly with an uppercut. I could feel breath leave my brother. I knew Karl was ready to go down. I landed another right to his thick Estonian skull and dropped him to the floor.

"Nigul, stop it this instant!" Mother screamed as she rushed to Karl's side.

I stood over Karl, blood dripping from the corner of my mouth onto my brother's face. He shook his head and sat up.

"That was a hell of a punch," Karl whispered, massaging his jaw, and reaching for his eyeglasses. "Didn't know you could hit like that," he added as he placed the spectacles back on the bridge of his nose.

Alexis stood off in the corner, her eyes wide, unwilling to intervene.

"Are you all right, Son?" Mother asked, touching the bright red bruise on Karl's face with tenderness.

"Nothing a little ice won't fix," Father said, as he stood in the doorway, newspaper in hand, staring at the disheveled room. None of us had noticed his arrival. "What the hell went on here? I'm gone for five minutes and you two decide to have a wrestling match?"

"More like a boxing contest," Alexis observed.

"And I lost," Karl said, as he stood up and extended his hand to me. "No hard feelings?"

I eyed Karl with suspicion. That last punch had felt good, damn good, but it hadn't erased my antipathy. Still, my brother was offering his hand in peace. So I took it.

While the women did the dishes and Father slumped in his chair fast asleep after dinner, his cigarette smoldering in an ashtray on a nearby end table, Karl and I went for a walk through Puhja. We did not head for the tavern: We simply went for a walk.

"What will you do now?" I asked. I posed the question in the manner of a father asking a man dating his daughter, *what are your intentions?*

Karl understood this. "We will marry. When, I'm not sure. But she's an Estonian citizen. Has dual citizenship, actually: Estonian and American. We both plan to continue teaching." Karl said quietly. "We may stay on the island or find work here on the mainland."

I bit the inside of my cheek.

"And you?" my brother asked in turn.

While it was true that I was seeing Ellisabet Raun and that there might be something substantial, something permanent in our connection, I was not ready to forgive my brother's behavior. So I said nothing about Ellisabet. Instead, I turned the conversation to another topic. "How will you respond to the draft?" I asked.

We came to the end of Puhja's main street, where pavement ended and gravel began. We looked up at the clearing skies, our hands in the pockets of our jackets, our hair moist from the mist that had lifted. A full moon rose. Shadows fell across the town's buildings.

Karl looked at me, thought for a moment, and then replied. "I'm going to Finland. To fight the Russians."

My brother's answer, in the face of the revelation of his love for Alexis, shocked me.

"What the hell…?" I asked.

We started towards home.

"Many of us going," Karl added in a confident voice. "And the Finns, unlike the Germans, will let us serve under our own officers. The Finns will face a counterattack before too long. I think it's the right thing to do, don't you, to go to the aid of the Finns?"

I blew cool air over my teeth. "What about Estonia?" I asked. "What happens when the Russians come back? You know they will, Karl. You know they won't let the Germans stay here forever."

We walked slowly as we talked.

"The Germans have St. Petersburg surrounded," Karl said. "They're racing towards Stalingrad. Moscow's threatened. I doubt the Russians will be back on Estonian soil any time soon."

I stopped beneath a streetlight and weighed my brother's optimism. "You're wrong," I said. "The Russians will push the Germans back to Germany. They are too many and the Americans and British are supplying them with tanks, airplanes, guns, ships, and food. And the Germans are overextended. They are tied up from Tripoli to Murmansk. They will tire, and when they do, the Russians will come streaming across the Narva like bees seeking blossoms. Mark my words, little brother, it will happen."

Karl shook his big head. His blond hair whipped like wet rope in the moist air. "Maybe. Maybe not," he replied, as we stood in front of our parents' house. "But I am going to Finland. Alexis knows, and while she disagrees with my decision, she will, in the end, accede to my choice."

I nodded. And then, I did something I hadn't intended. For, as I have said, Karl was the soldier and I... well, I was something less than a soldier. Maybe I said what I said because I still had something to prove. Or maybe, as the older brother, I still felt the need to protect Karl. Whatever the reason, I said what I said: "I'm going with you."

CHAPTER 24
Viipuri, Finland
February 1943

Weather blew in from the Arctic. Matti Peltomaa shuffled his ragged leather boots across frozen ground. His toes were frostbitten. Despondency and resignation were apparent in the old man's posture as he exited the barn his unit utilized as a repair facility. He had received Elin Goldfarb's letter and the impact of the message on the old man was devastating.

Had he been on the line with Juha Rintala and the Raiders, the letter would not have lost its sting but Matti would have had close friends with which to share his upset. In Viipuri, he had no such mates—only acquaintances. As Peltomaa trod from the barn to the log barracks, his fingers curled and uncurled inside the wool liners of his leather choppers.

I need to do something, he thought. *She is afraid, alone, and likely on the verge of being sent to some camp from which she will never return. The Gestapo will not provide insulin: They will show no such kindness. And what if the rumors about the camps are true? It is hard to believe, I'll grant you. But what if all of it is true? What hope does she have of making it out alive?*

As Peltomaa walked, the weight of disrupted love heavy on his shoulders, he encountered men moving in the opposite direction.

"You're going the wrong way," Erik Larsson, a Swede-Finn from Ostrobothnia said as he approached with two other men. All three Finns were younger than Matti Peltomaa by decades. "The food, as bad as it is, is this way," Larsson said, pointing towards the kitchen with a gloved finger.

Peltomaa nodded but said nothing.

"Cranky old bastard," a tall, lean man walking with Larsson remarked.

"He received a letter, a 'Dear John,' I think," Erik Larsson said quietly. "He's not a bad sort—just preoccupied with bad news."

Voices faded. Daylight waned. Peltomaa reached the bunkhouse as dusk engaged and the last rays of the sun were swallowed by night. He stood in front of the rough-sawn door to the building and looked up at the blue-black sky. Stars were emerging. The old man hesitated. There was nothing inside the bunkhouse but stale air: air tainted by sweat and cigarette smoke and other odors left behind by the fifty men who called the low-ceilinged building "home."

What the hell can I do? I have no idea where she is. The Valpo: They did this to her. Because of her connection to that Jew doctor. He paused and rethought his invective. *That's not right. This isn't Cohen's doing. Self-important as he is, and I only met the man once, he's right. He should be able to doctor his people without restrictions. He's not a spy. He's not a danger. But the damn Valpo won't let him alone, won't let those who associate with him alone. Elin got caught up in being a good person, in trying to help the Jew woman with her child. See what her kindness brought her? To some goddamned camp in Estonia! But where? Where in the hell in Estonia, if that's where she remains, is she? I can't do a goddamned thing about it until I know where she is.*

Matti opened the door and walked into the long, narrow common room of the bunkhouse. It was pitch black inside. He found a kerosene lantern by touch, pulled a match from his jacket pocket, struck it on a nail head, and lit the lamp. Smoky yellow light revealed crude bunks lining the log walls. Had the bunkhouse been meant to be permanent, the logs would have been peeled and the corners dovetailed. But the building's construction had been a rush job and the niceties of craftsmanship had been lost to expedience.

The old man removed his choppers, tucked them in a pocket of his coat, picked up the lamp, and shambled down the aisle. His sleeping platform—a straw tick placed on boards supported by a log frame—was the bottom bed in a tier of two bunks. The man who slept above Peltomaa, a cook named Aaro Kyyhkynen, was so large that the two-centimeter thick pine boards supporting the man's heft groaned every time the cook turned in bed. Peltomaa feared that he would eventually be crushed when the boards gave way and Kyyhkynen came crashing down. Matti's fears were never realized but the constant creaking of the abused wood above him made the old man leery.

Matti Peltomaa placed the lamp on a footstool and retrieved his packsack from beneath his bunk. Opening the pack's canvas flap, he withdrew a box of cigarettes: a prize rescued from a Russian supply truck a Finnish patrol had ambushed.

Peltomaa had traded a bottle of good Swedish vodka, liberated from a demolished truck that he and Erik Larsson had encountered when they were sent on an errand, for the cigarettes. A Russian plane had strafed the truck, killing its driver and delivery boy, a youth of no more than twelve, moments before Peltomaa and Larsson chanced upon the scene. Though the driver and his helper were both dead, the vodka was unscathed. Peltomaa and Larsson quickly transferred the precious cargo into the wagon they were using to travel to town, cautiously aware that the Russian plane could, at any moment, roar back over the open road and fire on them. After the vodka was tucked safely into the cargo bed of the buckboard, shallow graves were dug but no words were said over the departed because Peltomaa and Larsson did not know the victims.

Praying over souls who might not appreciate religion was something the two soldiers were unwilling to do. The horses strained in their leather harnesses and the truck was dragged off the road. Peltomaa and Larsson stashed the booze in the shed of an abandoned farm before returning to their unit. The vodka was as good as Finnish currency and Peltomaa had retrieved a bottle of the purloined booze and bartered it for a carton of purloined cigarettes.

The old man lit the cigarette as he sat on the edge of his bunk. The wool blanket of his bed was pulled taut. A goose down pillow, its white linen case smudged and dirty, was wedged against the cold wall. An unframed photograph of Elin Goldfarb holding little William Cohen was tacked to the bottom of Kyyhkynen's bunk so that Matti could study Elin's beautiful smile, night after night after night. Peltomaa unbuttoned his coat, clenched the cigarette between his lips, bent over, and untied his boots to thaw his toes. His wool stockings were full of holes despite his efforts to darn them. There was so little fabric left, describing them as "threadbare" would be optimistic. He rolled onto the bunk, propped the pillow behind his head, and stared hard at the black and white photograph. Smoke curled from the end of the cigarette as he puffed in silence and studied Erin Goldfarb's face.

"Shit," Peltomaa muttered.

His stomach growled.

"Shit."

Wind discovered cracks in the mud chinking of the log walls and teased the man's face. Matti finished the cigarette, sat up in his bunk, and considered whether or not he should go to supper. His stomach growled again.

I need to eat.

Letting go, giving up, would not bring Elin back, would not ensure her safety. He needed to be strong, to be alert, to find some way to right the wrong that had been done to her by the Valpo.

But what can one man do?

He mussed his hair. A tear formed in his eye.

Stop it, damn it. Stop it. Sentiment won't save Elin.

Peltomaa exhaled and stood up. He dropped the cigarette on the unvarnished planks of the floor, bent over, slid his boots over his stockings, did up the laces, and stood up again. He crushed the smoldering butt with the toe of his boot, picked up the cigarette, and put it in his shirt pocket. Matti buttoned the front of his great coat, lifted the lantern, and moved towards the door. In the building's entryway, he tamped the lantern's wick, placed the lamp back were he'd found it, removed his choppers from his coat pocket, and slid them over his fingers before opening the heavy door and exiting the building.

Stars were on display. Millions upon millions of pinpricks of light had manifested in the inky sky. There was no moon. Peltomaa's boots crunched hard snow as the rattle of silverware, the clank of glasses and plates, and the din of conversation enticed the old man to dinner.

CHAPTER 25
Hiiumaa Island, Estonia
June 1943

***15** March 1943*
Dear Miss Gustafson:

It is with sadness that I must tell you that the Valpo took your mother. She was expelled from Finland due to a misunderstanding. You will recall that she befriended a Jewish woman, Rosi Cohen. Mrs. Cohen is the wife of a German doctor, Walter Cohen. The doctor disregarded many orders of the Valpo. For this, Cohen, his wife, and infant son were to be deported. The Cohens were spared at the last minute but your mother was sent to Estonia in their stead. I have tried, through military channels here in Viipuri, to find out exactly where your mother was taken. I have been advised that others deported with your mother were sent to Germany. The good news is that no one can verify that your mother accompanied them.

I am trying to find her. However, I am not free to leave my unit. I would ask that you inquire through whatever sources you have available as to your mother's current situation. I am certain the Valpo will not provide you with information since the newspapers have condemned the police for their conduct in this affair. The fact that some of the individuals handed over to the Gestapo were Jews has left the Finnish government with egg on its face. Finland has prided itself on maintaining an anti-Nazi political outlook while fighting alongside the Germans. The fact that a handful of foreign Jews were expelled is a troubling episode and one the government wants to forget.

Please do what you can to find out information about your mother. You may write me in care of: Corporal Matti Peltomaa, 3rd Division, 14th Mechanical Brigade, Viipuri, Finland.

Sincerely,
Matti Peltomaa

The letter arrived just as Alexis Gustafson finished teaching for the year. Summer vacation was at hand when she sat down at the kitchen table in her flat in Kärdla to read Matti's plea for action. The apartment, the same one that Alexis had occupied since she first came to the island, had been shared with her fiancé. But Karl Kristian was gone. Karl, Nigul, and 3,000 other Estonian men had ignored the conscription call of March 1, 1943 and had left their native land to serve in the Finnish Army, in the *Soomepoisid*, the Estonian 200th Regiment.

"Why are you doing this to us?" Alexis had asked tearfully, when Karl revealed that he had enlisted in the Finnish Army.

They had been walking on a beach. The early summer sun was high and hot, making the sand painful on the soles of their bare feet. Alexis wore a sundress, the straps tight against her sunburned shoulders, the breeze billowing fabric away from her tan legs. She wore her aviator sunglasses and a wide brimmed straw hat, the style of hat old women who are afraid of the sun wear to the beach, though Alexis did not fear the sun. She simply did not want her hair to bleach.

Karl wore slacks and a loose fitting polo shirt, the tail of which flapped in the breeze. He too was reddened by the sun and his cheeks and neck burned further as they walked. There were other sunbathers and swimmers—couples and families on Törvanina Beach that day—but Alexis didn't notice them. She was only interested in the man walking beside her.

"Don't act so surprised. I told you I was thinking about going," Karl had said curtly. "I don't want to fight under German officers. Estonians who fight for the Germans generally end up dead."

Alexis shook her head. "You have no right to do this…to us. I thought we were to be married, in the fall, in your village church."

Karl had stopped walking and grasped her by the wrists. He turned the diminutive woman to face him as he spoke. "I swear that I will come back to you, to marry you, in Puhja, just like we planned. But I am vulnerable right now. The conscription will take me and I have no desire to fight, as I have said, under the Germans. No desire at all. You understand?"

Alexis looked away, to the north, across the sea, as tears clouded her eyes. "Why the hell is Nigul going with you? He's an electrician in the shipyards. Surely, he is exempt from the draft."

Karl had nodded, released his grip, and they had resumed their walk. "He is."

A puzzled look had crowded Alexis's face. "Then why is he going?"

Karl smiled, revealing big, white teeth, teeth untainted by coffee or tobacco. Unlike his older brother, Karl Kristian had never smoked and limited himself to one cup of coffee a day. "He thinks he needs to watch over me," Karl said, concealing the incongruity behind that statement.

Try as she might, Alexis had been unable, though she argued long and hard, to dissuade Karl. The day Karl took the ferry from Kärdla across the water to Haapsalu on the Estonian mainland, Alexis did not leave her bed. She made no attempt to walk to the pier to say goodbye. She had burrowed beneath the soft down comforter, despite the burgeoning heat of the summer day, unable and unwilling to acquiesce to Karl's decision.

By the time the letter from Matti Peltomaa arrived in Kärdla, Karl and Nigul Kristian had been in Finland for two weeks. Alexis received no word from Karl—no indication of whether he was training, or in combat, or simply biding his time until Mannerheim figured out what to do with the Estonians.

There are likely delicate politics involved, she thought, as held Matti Peltomaa's letter in her hands. *How does Mannerheim smooth over the upset of his ally? The Germans cannot be pleased that Estonian men are now wearing Finnish uniforms to avoid conscription.*

Alexis's mind wandered as she studied the old man's sweeping penmanship.

Mother's no Jew. Don't they know that? Doesn't the Valpo understand that she is an American who endured the death of her husband at the hands of the NKVD, suffered the loss of her honor at the hands of Tartar soldiers, and killed to attain her freedom?

The young teacher re-read Peltomaa's letter.

I can go to Tallinn. I can ask subtle questions of people I know there. Of people Karl and Nigul know there. What is that German woman's name, the one whose father is a Nazi? Raun. Something Raun. She might be able to find out what happened to Mother. After all, she is seeing Nigul and should, at least, be willing to talk to me. Karl says she's anti-Semitic like her father. But maybe if I explain Mother's history and how there has been a terrible mistake made in her case, this Raun woman will be moved to help. But what is her first name?

There was no time for Alexis to write Karl and obtain the woman's full name and address but that did not dissuade Alexis.

Tallinn isn't that big. It's not like I am going to stumble around Moscow or New York. Peeter Saul will help. He didn't leave Estonia to fight in Finland. His obligation to his wife and children prevented him from going. I know where Peeter lives. He's Nigul's closest friend. He'll know how to find the Raun woman. Big Peeter has always liked me, even after I did what I did to Nigul. Wait. That's not right. I didn't do anything to *Nigul. I simply made a different choice than he wanted me to make. Had to: I saw no future with Nigul. But with Karl? I have a future. We have a future.*

The bells of Kärdla's town hall clock announced noon. Alexis folded the letter, slid it into its envelope, and placed the papers in her purse. The woman stood up from the kitchen table and walked into her bedroom with resolve. She tossed clothing, toiletries, and her Bible into a small valise. Tears threatened, but Alexis drew upon her *sisu* as she shut and locked the door to her apartment. She was able to best her emotions, to think clearly and logically, as she walked towards the pier.

CHAPTER 26
Jägala, Estonia
August 1943

Ernest Raun made no demands on Elin Goldfarb's honor. Unlike the love stories that developed in some of the Estonian labor camps—the best known being the case of SS Officer Heinz Drosihn and Jewess Inge Sylten who fell in love and attempted to escape the Ereda Labor Camp, only to be captured and shot by the Gestapo—Ernest Raun made it clear from the beginning that he was not interested romantically in the American woman. In fact, over time, Raun came to acknowledge his sexual preference: that he was attracted to men, not women, despite the love he still held for his departed wife, the mother of his only child.

Jägala was small by concentration camp standards. When Elin Goldfarb arrived at Jägala, there were fifty-three men and one hundred and fifty women working the fields and forests surrounding the camp. Most of the women, the old men, and all of the children sent from Tallinn to Jägala never saw the camp. They were driven to Kalevi-Liiva, shot, and buried in a common grave. The number of Jews, Roma, and other "undesirables"—executed by Estonians working for the Security Police in this fashion—was in the thousands.

The barracks housing Jägala's residents were crude: hastily erected frame bunkhouses with inadequate heat, leaking roofs, and uninsulated plank walls. The food, as Elin quickly discovered, was the same thin beet or potato soup for dinner every night. Breakfast was weak rye tea and a slice of stale black bread. There was no lunch provided, despite the backbreaking labor that the men and women of the camp were assigned. Elin was lucky. After lapsing into unconsciousness one evening while working with Ernest Raun (a lack of carbohydrates was responsible for her demise), her sugar levels were quickly restored through prompt intervention by the camp doctor at Raun's insistence. After this unfortunate episode, Ernest Raun ensured his administrative assistant was adequately supplied with insulin and needles and that she received hard rolls and hearty soup for lunch. Raun's motives in keeping Elin healthy were not altruistic; he was a lonely man given to fits of depression who simply relished the company of another intelligent human being.

Throughout the winter and spring of 1942-43, Elin assisted Raun in a small office in the same building that housed Laak's office and living quarters. There were many days, as Raun attempted to dictate a letter or a memorandum to the American woman, that the sounds of Laak's trysts interrupted their work.

"That is disgusting," Raun would whisper, as noises leaked through the thin walls. "Why can't he wait until evening to bed his Jewish whores?"

Elin's face would flush at the invective, but she would not reply. She would simply still her fountain pen on the paper resting in her lap and wait for the consummation of desire in the next room so that her boss could begin his recitation anew.

Elin came to understand what was in store for the young women who spent time with the camp commander. It was always the same. Once Laak tired of a girl's hair, her eyes, her charms, she would vanish. Girls did not simply leave Laak's harem and return to the general prison population. No, Laak's vanity, his pride, his sense of ownership over his conquests, would not allow them to remain alive once they had satisfied his lust. Though Elin did not know for certain, she believed the camp gossip, which asserted that Laak's spurned concubines found final rest in the wet earth of Kalevi-Liiva.

If I am not careful, if I do not keep my thoughts to myself, I may be next.

More than once, as they passed each other in the hallway or within the barbwire perimeter of the camp, Elin felt Aleksander Laak staring at her. She knew the fact that she had been saved from the execution pit was a sore, a burr under the ass of the camp commander. But it was Ernest Raun, not Laak, who kept the camp running smoothly, while Laak occupied himself with his girls. As a consequence, whatever Raun wanted, Raun got. It was as simple as that. And so, despite the obvious disgust Laak held for her, Elin Goldfarb was left alone.

"How did you come to Finland?" Ernest Raun had asked Elin Goldfarb not too long after she arrived in camp.

She told him, in the slenderest of words, how she and Hiram had come to Karelia, how she and Matti Peltomaa escaped from Russia, and how there had been a mistake made with respect to her deportation. She did not include certain details of the story because there was no need to provide personal information to the man who held her life at his whimsy. But she had attempted, from her first private conversation with the lawyer, to appear friendly. Elin Goldfarb knew that her survival depended upon creating an emotional bond with Ernest Raun.

They had shared other conversations that touched upon Elin's education, her family in America, her work as a reporter, and her daughter. It was the topic of Alexis that, when first broached between the lawyer and his assistant, convinced Elin that, so long as Ernest Raun was at the camp, she would not be harmed.

"How intriguing," Raun had observed, as they worked in his office, Elin typing away on a distressed typewriter, a relic from Raun's law practice. "We both have girls as our only children. How intriguing that we have daughters as a common denominator."

Elin had not revealed to the lawyer that Alexis was actually her half-sister and not her daughter.

There is no need to say too much, Elin thought, as she described Alexis. *Besides, she is, as she has always been, my daughter in every way except biology.*

When Raun discovered Elin was a fan of Whitman and that her copy of *Leaves of Grass* had been left behind in Finland, he had shown another facet of his humanity: He purchased a used copy of the poetry collection in English from a Tallinn bookstore and surprised Elin with the gift.

As their relationship progressed and as Elin Goldfarb studied the man, she came to trust him. She did not like him. She could not like him or admire him because of the job he had chosen to do. And yet, she felt something, some sort of perverse attachment to her captor that she could not explain. Raun had a way of ingratiating himself to her, despite the cruel reality of what was taking place in the camp: the forced labor; the disappearance of Laak's women and the sick and the injured, the poor food, and the inhumane conditions. She survived the winter of 1942-43 because she owned a thick wool coat and a heavy wool scarf, was given her insulin, was provided more food than the other inmates, and because she worked indoors in a heated office while the other female prisoners toiled outside in the bleak snow, wind, and cold. Elin Goldfarb knew she was privileged and every night when she returned to the common barracks she shared with twenty other women she was careful not to arouse their envy by comparing her situation to theirs. She became introspective. Beyond the occasional greeting or casual discussion about the weather, she refrained from personal interaction with other prisoners.

I cannot be their friend and also work for Mr. Raun. I do not share their work, their toil, their punishment and I will not pretend that I do.

By the beginning of summer, as flies and mosquitoes replaced snow and cold as afflictions of the season, she learned that the camp was nearing its end.

"By September, Jägala will be no more," Ernest Raun disclosed one day in early June.

Elin was working on a food inventory when her boss made the statement. The comment caused her immediate upset, though, because of her precarious situation, she displayed no emotion.

What does he mean? Where will we all go?

"I did not mean to alarm you, Mrs. Goldfarb," the little man added quietly, looking up from correspondence on his desk.

Elin ceased typing and realized that her cessation of work had tipped Raun off to her upset.

"Uncertainty is never a good thing," she said quietly, her fingers poised over the keys.

Raun nodded and removed his bifocals as he sat across the room and considered her. "Nothing untoward will happen to you. You will go with me to Tallinn Prison, along with some of the others. At the prison, you will continue to assist me just as you do here."

"Along with some of the others..." What will happen to those who are not moved to Tallinn?

She knew better than to ask Raun what he meant by the cryptic phrase. She resumed working in an effort to calm her nerves.

The lawyer smiled.

"Nothing untoward will happen to those who do not accompany us," Raun said after a long pause. "Those who do not follow us will be sent to Vaivara, to work the shale. The bigwigs in Tallinn have decided it is more productive to have prisoners release oil from the ground than to work in the woods or in the fields. You should not," Raun said, in a lowered voice, "concern yourself with things over which you have no control."

Elin nodded but didn't respond. She knew better than to ask questions. Ernest Raun was her lifeline, her only chance of hanging on until Matti Peltomaa could find her. As much as she despised what the lawyer stood for, she knew better than to voice her opinion at such a critical juncture. And so, she resumed typing.

By the time the truck came to transport Elin and the remaining inmates and guards to Tallinn, Jägala Camp was nearly empty. Prisoners had been moved in small batches during the months of June, July, and August. By September of 1943, when Elin left Jägala in the back of a German troop truck—the heavy canvas top removed, a light rain falling on her bare head, the volume of Whitman tucked inside her sweater, her heavy wool coat hanging loosely over her left arm as she sat on a wooden bench in the cargo area of the bounding truck—there were only six Estonian guards, Ernest Raun, and ten prisoners, including Elin, left in camp.

Aleksander Laak was already gone, accompanied by one of his Jewish lovers, his driver, and his bodyguard. Elin happened to be out in the prison yard when Laak's car left the camp through the main gate, a gate that was no longer guarded by sentries. She watched the distinctive black sedan roar down the gravel road leading from the camp. When the car did not turn towards Tallinn but swung onto the road leading to Kalevi-Liiva, she understood: The young Jewess riding in the motorcar would not live to see the inside of Tallinn Prison.

"Do not think too much about it," Ernest Raun said quietly, as he stood next to Elin on the dead grass of Jägala's parade ground. "It does no good to lament circumstances that cannot be changed."

Elin Goldfarb had nodded but when Raun turned to leave, she did not follow him. Instead, she stood alone, in the middle of the deserted camp, watching the black car become smaller and smaller against the horizon.

Elin Goldfarb fully expected the truck *she* was riding in would also turn towards Kalevi-Liiva.

There is nothing to be done about it.

Resignation overwhelmed Elin as the driver worked the clutch and urged the truck's transmission through its gears. As the transport carrying the last of the camp's prisoners and guards approached the intersection outside Jägala's main gate, the driver downshifted. The truck slowed. But instead of heading towards Kalevi-Liiva, the truck carrying Elin Goldfarb turned towards Tallinn.

CHAPTER 27
Viipuri, Finland
March 1944
(Nigul's Story)

We trained under the command of Estonian line officers. Karl—the exemplary soldier that he was—found the drills redundant. I, on the other hand, relished the organization, the day-to-day certainty of camp life. Because of my skiing prowess, I was detached from our regiment and sent with twelve other Finnish-speaking Estonians to the Karelian front as a scout. Karl was not one of the twelve. His skiing wasn't up to par. You should know that I did not seek this assignment. I did not relish the chance to once again display cowardice under fire. But there was nothing I could do to protest the transfer.

As my unit skied single file over thawing snow in thick woods outside Valkeasaari, the last undisturbed, undiminished bit of forest left from the vicious "to and fro" fighting of the Continuation War, I thought about Alexis Gustafson's letter to Karl and considered how small the world had become.

February 1, 1944
Dear Karl:

How are things going for you? I hope and pray that you keep your wits about you and your head down so that when the war is over, you come back safely to Hiiumaa Island. This is my selfish wish: That you do not suffer a wound or are killed fighting a war that cannot be won. This is the truth. The Russians are on the move. Narva is threatened and, <u>when</u> it falls—not <u>if</u>, for it will surely fall—the entire country will be open to attack. The Germans have lost the desire to fight and Estonia has too few men to make a difference. Our soldiers are but small drops of water amidst the sea that is the Red Army.

Mother is alive! That is the biggest news that I have to share with you. Tell Nigul that, through Peeter Saul, I was able to find and meet Nigul's friend, Miss Raun. She was helpful in discovering where Mother is being kept. Turns out, and this is no small coincidence, that Mother is working for Miss Raun's father in Tallinn Prison! Please tell Nigul that, while I am not necessarily impressed with Miss Raun's politics, I am impressed with Nigul's choice. She is educated and lovely. I'd say that Nigul has excellent taste in women but, given our history, that might seem self-serving.

I have spent time with Mother through Miss Raun's intervention. Mother, while technically an inmate in Tallinn Prison, has some freedom of movement. She and a number of the other women are released each morning to work in the shipyards as warehouse workers. They are needed in this role because, after the most recent conscription, there are so few men available for such work.

Mother's job at the shipyard is how Peeter Saul found out about Mother's connection to Miss Raun. Peeter met Mother as he was walking to his night shift and Mother was returning to Tallinn Prison. He had the chance to speak with her ever so briefly and learned of her situation so that when I approached him about making contact with Miss Raun, he already had information regarding Mother's predicament. Tell Nigul he has a good friend in that man.

Mother related to me what took place with the Valpo and what happened at Jägala. The conditions were terrible and the Jews, of which Mother is wrongfully accused of being, were treated the worst. The things that Lt. Laak, the man in charge, did with and to the young women he selected to be his "companions," well, I cannot write the words but you can use your imagination. Most of Laak's women disappeared. There are rumors about their fate that I tried to ask Mother about. She would not go into detail. She is nervous that she too might suddenly, upon revealing too much, "disappear." Then there are the circumstances of my visits with her. Contact with Mother takes place inside Tallinn Prison with Miss Raun facilitating the visits. Miss Raun has some authority, as she works for Laak as the assistant warden over the female prisoners. My time with Mother occurs only in Miss Raun's presence. Though Miss Raun has been discrete when supervising these visits, I remain wary of her loyalties. Why she is showing such kindness to me can only be attributed to the fact that I am engaged to the brother of the man she loves. I have not, of course, confided in Miss Raun that I once had a connection to Nigul. I see no point in raising a possible source of discord between us.

Mother's hair has grayed. It is quite long and she is very thin. But as Mr. Raun has been supplying her with insulin and sufficient food, she is in fair health. Her mental state is less clear. She longs for freedom and, with no promise of it being granted anytime soon, there is always the chance that Lt. Laak will order the remaining inmates removed to some other camp in some other country. That is not as far-fetched as it sounds. Though the press here has kept what is being called "The Jewish Situation" out of the newspapers, anyone with ears to hear and eyes to see now understands what is happening. Something similar could happen to Mother and I pray that I can determine some way of ensuring that it does not.

Mother is in turmoil regarding her fiancé, Mr. Peltomaa. The last information I have is that he was in a reserve unit somewhere near where you and Nigul are deployed. Perhaps you can find him and tell him that Mother is alive and between you, Nigul, and Mr. Peltomaa, you can advise me of some course of action to take. Though Mother is an American citizen, short of traveling to Sweden, where the U.S. still has an embassy, I can think of nothing I can do to enforce her status. And there is no guarantee that such a trip would yield results. The same thing can be said with respect to a plea to Finnish authorities. The American Legation in Helsinki has closed. Thus, I see no way of involving the Americans in Mother's case at this point. I believe the only recourse is direct action. But what action that might be remains unclear to me.

This is a long letter, which, if it falls into the hands of the censors, will likely not make it to you. But if you do receive this message, find some way of contacting me and giving me your advice as to how I should proceed. Mother is the only family I have left. I cannot afford to lose her.

Love,

'Lexis

By the time Karl got around to sharing Alexis's letter with me, I was one day away from being transferred to the front as a scout. I did not have sufficient time to digest the import of what Alexis was saying before I left my unit. But as I skied along behind Sergeant Reinhold Kreutzwald, a distant descendent of the author of the *Kalevipoeg*, my legs weary from traversing mushy spring snow, I thought long and hard about Mrs. Goldfarb's situation. It seemed, at the time, an impossible quandary. She was likely destined for further trauma now that the Germans were convinced she was a Jew. I could see no clear way of honoring Alexis's plea that Karl and I come up with a plan to save her mother. But I also knew that the bond between my brother and Alexis was strong and that, in the end, Karl would do anything he could to save Mrs. Goldfarb. I also knew that I would do anything I could to ensure Karl was successful in his quest.

It had been quiet when I arrived at the front. The Red Army was concentrating its efforts elsewhere. The Russians had broken out of St. Petersburg and were applying pressure along the Estonian border. The Karelian Isthmus was, when I arrived, a secondary frontier: something that the Russians knew they would eventually have to deal with.

In contrast, the situation in Estonia was urgent. President Ulots called for the conscription of all male Estonians up to the age of 40 to stand and fight beside the Germans. Nearly 100,000 Estonian men came under arms. Most of them were assigned to defend Narva where the Red Army had thrown its considerable weight.

As if to send a warning to the Finns, Helsinki was bombed by the Soviet Air Force in late February. Due to improved Finnish air defenses, these bombardments had little effect on Finnish resolve. But I should have known, upon hearing the news from Helsinki, that these bombing attacks on the Finnish capital were only a precursor of things to come.

When I returned to Viipuri from my stint on the Karelian front, I learned the awful news: Soviet bombers had leveled Narva. Civilian losses were slight because most of the population had been evacuated. But the buildings, the infrastructure, the monuments and parks of the city had been hammered to dust. The bombing of Narva was followed by an all-out attack against the city. Karl and I sat in our barracks in Finland, anxiously awaiting news from home but there was nothing we could do. We could not leave Finland. We would be stopped as we boarded a ship bound for Estonia and would be summarily tried and punished as deserters.

The dire situation at home caused Karl apprehension. After all, Alexis was an American who had only recently achieved Estonian citizenship.

What fate awaits her? was a question I know my brother asked himself as we waited for the Russians to attack Karelia.

"Finally," Karl said reverently, his eyes locked on the front page of the *Viipurin Sanomat* as we sat on wooden benches around a roaring campfire.

It was warm for early May. Hordes of black flies attacked any exposed flesh but did not venture inside the fire's heat. I made the mistake of leaving my comrades to relieve myself in a nearby thicket. The flies made doing my business miserable.

"What is it?" I asked Karl when I returned.

"We've stopped the Russians. Vent stopped them at Silvertsi. The fighting at Narva is over."

"For the moment," I corrected, savoring a cup of real coffee from a pot set on a flat stone near the edge of the campfire. "The Russians will not stop just because one Estonian officer did something brave."

The others in our squad, including Sergeant Kreutzwald, murmured in agreement. Our collective mood was pensive. We had seen no action. We had contributed nothing to the Finnish war effort, while back home the Soviets were on the doorstep of conquering Estonia.

"Maybe. Or maybe if Vent and the others can stall long enough, the British and the Americans will see the light and send in troops."

I guffawed. It wasn't the polite thing to do, particularly when the person I was deriding was my brother. But the notion that the Americans or the British—after investing billions of U.S. dollars and English pounds in the Soviet war effort—gave a good goddamn about Estonia, well, that was too rich for me to contain myself.

"Little Brother," I said, as my tittering subsided, "sometimes you are so foolish. Roosevelt and Churchill aren't about to start showing concern for Estonia. Or Latvia. Or Lithuania. They will do nothing to upset Stalin. He's their pal. There will be no miraculous beachhead landing of American or British forces in Estonia. There will be no attempt by the Allies to rescue our country. We will either defeat the Russians by fighting alongside the Germans, which seems very unlikely, or suffer the consequences."

Karl was illumined by firelight. I noticed that his cheeks were red—not from heat but from upset. It was clear that my brother didn't appreciate my candor.

"How do you know this? How can you divine what is in the mind of Roosevelt or Churchill?"

The questions were spat towards me like snake venom.

"I can't," I admitted. "But I know this: No one *outside* Estonia cares what happens *to* Estonia. That's been true ever since the Great War. We are a little country. We have nothing to offer the world in terms of resources. Militarily, we are weak. And we will always, no matter what happens in this war, be subject to the whimsy of great powers."

"Nigul's right," Kreutzwald said, taking a nip from a tin flask. "But even so, we're no good to Estonia here. We should be back at home, standing up to the Russians, dying like men."

A twinge of fear shivered my body. I looked around the circle of soldiers. No one seemed cognizant of my upset. I took a deep breath.

"Well," Karl said quietly, his anger dissipated, "we're here now. Until we are released by the Finns to go home and do as you urge sergeant, we are bound to them."

Our comrades nodded. I looked at Karl. I wanted to ask him what we were going to do about Elin Goldfarb: How we were going to respond to Alexis's plea. But there was nothing in my brother's expression that revealed he had a plan to save the old woman.

CHAPTER 28
Viipuri, Finland
June 5th, 1944

Matti Peltomaa sipped beer with deliberation. The tavern where he drank, its quaint ambience, the atmosphere created by the photographic gallery of skiers, hockey players, long distance runners, and other sportsmen covering the walls, dusty trophies awarded to celebrate their exploits displayed on crude wooden shelves, enveloped the old man like a warm blanket on a cold Lapland night. The beer was cold and went down easily.

Tomorrow I'm back in it, Peltomaa thought as he drained his mug of Olvi and motioned to the bartender, a dark skinned Finn with impressively long hair braided into an ebony ponytail, for another beer.

The bartender, short of stature but broad in the chest, wore a wooden peg strapped to his right hip by a leather harness. The man teetered up to Peltomaa, the peg thump, thump, thumping against the wooden floor of the tavern, swept up the mug, and shambled back to the tap at the far end of the bar.

"You look down in the dumps, friend," the barkeep offered, one eye on his work, the other on Peltomaa as he filled the glass with honey colored beer.

The American didn't reply. Instead, he looked out a dirty window and watched stern faced Finnish soldiers march towards a mobilization point east of Viipuri.

They look tired.

The news in Estonia, where Elin Goldfarb was kept prisoner, wasn't good. The Russians were attacking Narva with renewed vigor and when the city fell, all of Estonia would be open to the enemy like a compliant virgin. Tallinn would be in jeopardy once Narva was taken and the Russian juggernaut moved on. The possibility loomed, as Peltomaa considered what he knew about Elin's predicament, that his betrothed's situation had changed.

How can I be sure Elin is still in Tallinn and not on some cattle train bound for Poland? Christ, I feel so damned useless sitting here. But how can I do anything about it? Tomorrow, I will be back with Rintala. The Reds are coming. That's for certain. They've broken out of Leningrad. They will push through the Mannerheim Line. And what will we do? We will fight but we will not be able to stop them.

Rintala's Raiders was now assigned to the 3rd Division. The 3rd was given an essential role in the defense of the Vammelsuu-Taipale, the so-called VT Line. The VT Line was located on the Isthmus closer to Leningrad than Viipuri. The majority of the Finnish forces, including the 3rd Division, were directly in the path of the anticipated Russian attack. No one, including Carl Mannerheim, expected the Finns—as short of armor, artillery, anti-tank weapons, and air support as they were—to stop the enemy. Instead, and this was something Matti Peltomaa gleaned from the Finnish press, the Field Marshal was hoping he could hold out long enough to negotiate a favorable peace. But the handwriting, in Peltomaa's mind, was on the wall: All the gains made since the beginning of the Continuation War were about to be lost. Karelia would once again become part of the Soviet Union and, in all likelihood, so too would the port city of Viipuri.

The bartender waddled up to Peltomaa and placed a full mug of cold beer in front of the old soldier without spilling a drop.

"Damn peg leg," the thick chested man said as he stood in front of the saloon's only customer.

"How'd it happen?" Peltomaa asked, slurping froth as he eyed the bartender.

"Land mine. One of our own. Can you beat that? I stepped on a Finnish mine! The minefield had been laid by my regiment but wasn't marked on the map."

"Shitty luck."

"Not true. *I* was lucky. By the time my stupid ass captain realized where we were, what the danger was, half the company was inside the minefield. Ten men, ten good Finnish soldiers were blown to bits. Five more, including me, ended up being maimed. The only good thing? Our dim-witted captain ended up being one of the dead!"

Peltomaa grunted and took a swig of Olvi.

"Arno Paavola," the bartender said, extending a thick hand in greeting.

"Matti Peltomaa," the old man replied, shaking hands across the bar.

"American?"

Despite his despondency, Peltomaa couldn't help but grin. "How did you know?"

Paavola winked. "The accent. Gives you fellows away every time…"

The tavern's double doors swung open to the late afternoon air and interrupted the barkeep in mid-sentence. Sunlight infiltrated the dim space. Two lanky young men dressed in ill-fitting Finnish Army uniforms stepped over the threshold. The soldiers were in their late teens or early twenties, too young, in Peltomaa's eyes, to be fighting a war. But both men carried themselves with defiance, with a jaunty confidence, as they sauntered towards the bar.

"You Peltomaa?" the taller of the two men asked in passable Finnish.

Matti Peltomaa squinted and took in the faces of the new arrivals.

Arno Paavola spoke before the American could respond. "Who's asking?"

The second man, his shoulders held straight, his eyes clear and steadfastly brown behind wire rimmed eyeglasses, took up the conversation. "The Kristian brothers."

Matti squinted harder.

Kristian? I know that name from somewhere...

"I don't want any trouble in here," Paavola said evenly, his left hand snatching a wooden baton from a shelf behind the bar. The bartender's sudden movement had been concealed but he chose to brandish the cudgel for affect. "No fighting in my place."

The taller man grinned. "You don't know us, Peltomaa, but you know *of* us. Through a young woman, my brother Karl's fiancé, Alexis Gustafson..."

Peltomaa nearly gagged on his beer. "The Estonians," he whispered.

The two young men nodded in unison. One extended his right hand. "Nigul Kristian," the tall, young soldier said, as he shook hands with Peltomaa. "And this, if you hadn't already guessed, is my baby brother Karl."

Karl Kristian didn't offer his hand but smiled widely and spoke in a firm, concise tone. "You're a hard man to find," he offered. "Chased you all the way from the 3rd Division Headquarters to this—"

"Careful, Estonian," the bartender said quietly, returning the wooden stick to its hiding place, "don't you dare insult my bar."

The Estonians laughed.

Peltomaa eyed the young men and took another gulp of Olvi. "Beers for my friends," he said, after draining his mug. "And another for me."

After their beers arrived the men retired to a round table in a far corner of the bar.

"How is Alexis?" Matti Peltomaa asked as they sat down.

"Beautiful," Karl replied.

Nigul grimaced but did not protest even though the wound of his brother's betrayal had not completely closed.

"And Elin? What news is there of Elin?"

The brothers sipped beer.

"Well, out with it, damn you. What's the news concerning Mrs. Goldfarb?"

Karl shook his head. "Not good. Nigul's lady friend, a supervisor at the prison and the daughter of one of the higher-ups, a man who works directly under Aleksander Laak, the bastard in charge, says that the prisoners will be moved soon."

Peltomaa placed the palms of his weathered hands on the flat pine surface of the table. "Where?"

The Estonians did not reply.

"Goddamn it! Where are they taking Elin?"

"To Poland. A place called Birkenau," Nigul advised.

Peltomaa looked up at the tavern's tin ceiling and considered the Estonian's revelation. There was no need to verbalize what they all knew: Birkenau was adjacent to Auschwitz, a place rumored to be the site of mass killings of Jews and others by the Nazis.

Matti massaged his bearded chin with his right hand, closed his eyes, and thought hard. Moments passed. Other patrons entered the bar. The place became noisy. Still, the old man said nothing.

After minutes of silence, Peltomaa finally spoke. "There is a way we can save her," he began. "It won't be easy. It will take money, at least three or four men, some help from your lady friend..." Peltomaa said, looking directly at Nigul Kristian, "...at the prison. And a boat." The old man paused again and thought. "No, we'll need two boats. One large enough to get across the Gulf and one small enough to slip through German naval patrols close to shore."

Nigul Kristian nodded. "I think Ellisabet would do it. She likes your woman. Though she's loyal to her father's cause, she has a heart. She would do it if I asked. There's an opportunity to snatch Mrs. Goldfarb on her return to the prison after working in the shipyard. We'd need to know the route the women use. Ellisabet can give us that."

"Good," Matti Peltomaa said quietly, considering the thin pool of beer at the bottom of his mug. "But I still need men to go with me. I'll have to work through Captain Laurila. He'll not give me any trouble. But getting the higher-ups to go along with a furlough, with the Russians breaking out, will be dicey."

Karl Kristian stared at his beer through the lenses of his eyeglasses. "I'd guess boats aren't so easy to come by. What captain wants to risk losing his investment to the Germans?"

Nigul nodded.

"I know a man...with a boat. He helped me once. He'd likely be up to doing it again," Matti Peltomaa whispered. "For a price, of course," the old man added. "He's here, in Viipuri, ferrying troops and supplies between Finland and Estonia."

Karl Kristian drained his glass and licked foam from his lips. His brother did the same.

"I have a question for the two of you," Peltomaa said quietly, as he dug into a pocket, removed a leather coin purse, retrieved money, and placed a Finnish bank note on the table.

"Yes, we'll go," Nigul Kristian said, with vigor, as the men stood up from their chairs and walked towards the door. "Karl and I will go with you."

"Thanks," the old man said wryly, as they opened the double doors and encountered afternoon heat, "but that wasn't what I was going to ask."

The men walked three abreast towards the waterfront.

"Then what?" Nigul prodded.

Peltomaa stopped, rubbed his forehead, pulled a cigarette from his shirt pocket, placed the butt between his lips, flicked a match against the matchbook cover, and drew heavily on the unfiltered tobacco. "Where in the hell did you learn to speak Finnish?"

Nigul Kristian smiled. "From our mother, Mr. Peltomaa. From our mother."

CHAPTER 29
Tallinn, Estonia
June 20th, 1944

A ferry chugged through swells. Storm clouds paraded above the cresting sea. Heavy rain struck the woman as she stood on the deck of the old boat. She was a passenger on a vessel that had plied the Gulf of Riga between Rohuküla and Heltermaa, running the twenty-eight kilometer gap at a plodding pace, for over fifteen years. The vessel, the *Hiiu*, named after the county encompassing Hiiumaa Island, struggled to make headway against the tempest and belched black coal smoke from its single stack against the griseous sky. Despite it being summer, Alexis was bundled against weather in a coat, a thick woolen hat pulled down over her short blond hair, and woolen mittens.

The news is not good.

The Russians were on the verge of breaking through at Viipuri. Reports on the radio and in the newspapers painted a more optimistic view but the distance between Estonia and Finland was not so great as to hide the truth. The situation in Finland was one of impending disaster.

Karl and Nigul are in danger.

Alexis had no way of knowing that the Kristian boys had met up with Matti Peltomaa. She had no way of knowing exactly where the 200th Estonian Regiment was, or whether her fiancé was in the thick of the fight or safe in reserve. She also had no way of knowing for certain how her mother was faring in the custody of Aleksander Laak.

That bastard uses young Jewish women in inexplicable ways.

She knew the rumors of Laak's lecherous conduct to be true after talking with her mother and Miss Raun on prior occasions.

Miss Raun has assured me that her father will protect Mother, watch over her, and keep her from being defiled. But how much power does Mr. Raun really have?

Alexis had encountered Aleksander Laak once inside Tallinn Prison as Ellisabet Raun led Alexis to Ernest Raun's office. Alexis's eyes briefly met Laak's and, despite the fact she had dressed in as dowdy a fashion as she was capable of, Alexis felt Laak's lust. Laak's was a palpable, dirty presence, like that of an old man leering at young girls in a schoolyard. She knew, in that moment, how sick, how diseased the man's soul had become.

Blessed are the pure in heart: for they shall see God…I doubt if that Beatitude applies to Aleksander Laak. I can pray for him but I don't believe it will do much good.

Still, she did pray for Laak every night before bed. She prayed that he would not turn his eyes towards Elin Goldfarb, that he would content himself with unfortunate strangers. It was a selfish, horrific—in Alexis's mind—prayer because it meant that young girls whom she had never met would likely die. But her mother would live and that was all that mattered to Alexis.

The locomotive pulled into Tallinn under clear blue skies and a hot June sun. Alexis's underarms were damp from sweat as she descended from the train with a small suitcase in her right hand, her coat hanging limply over her left arm, and began walking towards Big Peeter Saul's apartment.

She had been in contact with Karl and Nigul through the post. The Kristian brothers had urged her, now that school was over, to take her leave of Hiiumaa Island and seek out Peeter Saul. The closer Alexis was to Tallinn Prison, the better, the Kristian Brothers believed, could a plan be hatched to free Elin Goldfarb. There had been no details forthcoming from the brothers as to how this miracle would be accomplished. Alexis was simply urged to pack up and go to Tallinn. And so she did.

In Finland, the 200th Estonian Regiment was in the thick of it. By the time Alexis arrived in Tallinn, the regiment was in place along the VT Line. Karl and Nigul were assigned to the 2nd Battalion and unbeknownst to Alexis, the brothers were engaged in the largest land battle ever fought in Scandinavia. Alexis knew nothing of the Kristian boys' situation, or of the whereabouts of Matti Peltomaa, who had been called back to active duty and rejoined his comrades on the VT Line. These things were beyond Alexis's knowledge. The men who had urged her to come to Tallinn had no way of writing to her now that the Russians were close to breaking through to Helsinki.

"Miss Gustafson," Ingrid Saul said with surprise, as she opened the door to the Saul apartment after Alexis's timid knock. "Peeter is expecting you but he's still at work."

The two women considered each other. They had never been introduced and there was a natural distance to their meeting.

Peeter is right, Ingrid Saul thought. *She is a striking young woman, what with her short blond hair, her unusual eyes, and that figure! Oh, to have my figure back, like that, again. But five babies made sure my figure is* kaput, *as the Germans would say. Still, despite the chaos and the turmoil, despite my being driven to the bottle and near insanity by the little ones, I wouldn't trade places with her for a second!*

"I don't want to inconvenience you Mrs. Saul. I can wait in the park across the street until he comes home," the young teacher said.

Strange. With five children in the house, you'd expect to hear the din of play.

"Oh, no. You must come in. The children are out. We'll have the place to ourselves. I have a little tea left and a nice piece of yellow cake. It's not much but it is sweet, made with real sugar. And the chocolate frosting! Peeter was able to find Swiss cocoa for me. Where he found it and what he had to pay for it, well, the less we know about that, the better!" Ingrid said, through a cheerful smile. "Please, do come in."

Alexis accepted the invitation.

She is clearly sober. Good for her, Alexis thought, as she sat on a clean, white sheet covering the front room's davenport. *Good for her.*

The women talked as two strangers around the reasons for Alexis's visit to the city. They never directly discussed Elin Goldfarb's predicament. After an hour of verbal fencing, the women understood each other as only women can. Despite the lack of words of substance between them, they had formed mutual respect for one another. By the time the Saul children tumbled back into the flat, their clothes filthy from play on the teeter-totters and swings in the park's playground, Alexis Gustafson was standing side by side with Ingrid Saul in the small kitchen of the apartment, chopping pork for a casserole that would serve to feed a family of seven and one guest.

"Hello."

The booming voice of the shaggy headed Estonian giant echoed through the apartment as Big Peeter Saul slammed the door and stomped into the living room. All five children mobbed the poor man, his body bent and tired from his shift at the shipyard. The youngest Saul children, a two-year-old boy and his three-year-old sister, climbed the electrician as if he was a tree and claimed perches on his broad shoulders. The other children simply wrapped their thin arms around the big man's thighs and waist and held on for dear life.

"Children," Ingrid said, wiping her moist hands on a towel hanging over the steel sink basin, "leave your father be."

The children responded immediately. Their reaction was a change in their behavior that Alexis could not appreciate as a newcomer. Before their mother's sobriety, the Saul children were wild, wooly animals, due mostly to the fact that Ingrid drank herself to oblivion on a daily basis and simply did not care to guide or discipline her offspring. But in her newfound sobriety, Ingrid Saul broached no dissension, no nonsense from her brood. The children knew that if they failed to obey their mother, a willow switch, kept on a high shelf in the kitchen, would be brought to bear upon their bare bottoms. This is not to say that Ingrid

Saul was a cruel or abusive. She was simply instilling the discipline and decorum in her home that had been lacking during her years of drinking.

"Don't be so hard on them," Peeter said, as he approached his wife, pulled her into his big chest, and kissed her cheek. "They just miss their papa."

Big Peeter forgot that Alexis was standing ten feet away. His hand involuntarily reached for his wife's behind and gave a playful squeeze.

"Stop that!"

Peeter shrugged his shoulders and pinched his wife's ass again.

"You are incorrigible," Ingrid mumbled.

The big man smiled and released his wife's buttock. "But loveable, no?"

"No," Ingrid said, straightening her skirt. "No, you are not loveable when you make a spectacle of yourself."

"Hello, Miss Gustafson," Peeter said cheerily, as he walked over to the icebox and removed a pitcher of cold water. "How was the trip?"

The Estonian poured a glass of water for himself and studied the young teacher.

"Rocky. The sea was in turmoil. But the train ride was uneventful."

"Ah."

Once they had eaten and the children had been put down after listening to a bedtime story told by their father—not read from a book but invented from the man's wild imagination—the three adults sat in the front room of the small apartment and talked.

"The boys," Big Peeter said, "how are the Kristian boys?"

"I have no idea," Alexis said, while waiting for her weak tea to cool, her feet and legs curled beneath her skirt as she sat in an upholstered armchair across from the Sauls, who sat on the davenport. "I haven't heard from Karl since the Russians broke out of St. Petersburg."

"I've been saying my prayers," Ingrid Saul said quietly, "for them and for our soldiers defending Narva."

Big Peeter scowled. "I doubt prayer will defeat the goddamned communists."

"Peeter! Watch your language. We have a guest and the children might still be awake."

The big man chuckled. "The children are sound asleep. But I do apologize, Miss Gustafson, for the curse. It's just, well, that I doubt God cares one way or the other about whether Hitler or Stalin wins this contest."

Alexis nodded. "Perhaps you're right Mr. Saul. But I think God does care what happens to those of us who haven't chosen war as a way of settling grievances. God may even care about the Finns despite the fact they've chosen to stand with Hitler. Not a good choice, of course. But what other choice could the Finns have made?"

Big Peeter shook his head. "The Finns made a terrible choice. They married themselves to a bully: an abusive husband. They could have married themselves to the Swedes: a husband with virtue. Or the Norwegians: a husband with morals. But no, they chose the Germans. What a debacle."

Ingrid Saul's eyes opened wide. "*Debacle*? Where in the world did you ever come up with *that* word?"

Big Peeter smiled sheepishly. "I read the dictionary during down time at work. Over lunch and when we are stuck, waiting for other sections to catch up. Why? Is it a bad thing to want to know more, to be well-read?"

Ingrid laughed lightly. "No dear. You just surprised me is all. For someone who quit school at age twelve, it seems a bit late in the game to try to become a scholar, don't you think, Miss Gustafson?"

Alexis shook her head. "As a teacher, I say: 'It's never too late to learn'."

Peeter Saul stroked his chin, thin stubble visible in the dim light of the apartment. "Miss Gustafson, what are we going to do about your mother?"

Big Peeter's question was at odds with the lightness of their discussion and caught Alexis unaware. There was a period of silence as she thought.

"Well, I was hoping to see her tomorrow. Miss Raun has been most accommodating. She apparently likes Mother."

Peeter nodded. "But what will happen to your mother once the Reds take Tallinn?"

"Peeter, don't say such a thing!"

The big man slid his arm around his wife's plump waist. "Ingrid, my dear. It does no good to deceive oneself. The Russians are coming sooner than you might think. The Germans are losing men as fast as leaves falling from an autumn birch. It is only a matter of time. The Russians will be here just as they were before. And this time they won't leave."

Ingrid Saul shook her head. Her unkempt blond hair tossed back and forth across her brow, covering the deep frown that interrupted her face. "Don't say that. Don't tell me that those bastards…Oh, I am so sorry, Miss Gustafson…but you understand my upset, don't you? I do not want my children, my babies, raised beneath the red sickle. No, I do not."

Alexis pursed her lips and thought for a moment before responding. "About Mother…" Alexis began, changing the subject, "I *am* worried about what Lieutenant Laak will do. That," she added in a firm, serious voice, "is far more important to me than what Stalin has in store for us somewhere down the road."

Big Peeter removed his arm from around Ingrid's waist and rubbed his stubbly chin again. "I understand. She is your mother. If it were me, I would feel the same way. But what is to be done about it?"

Alexis shrugged her shoulders and sipped her tea.

CHAPTER 30
Karelian Isthmus
June 11th-June 20th, 1944

450,000 men. 11,500 field artillery pieces. Countless tanks, armored cars, trucks, tracked personnel carriers, and command cars. Innumerable fighter planes and bombers.

150,000 men. 1,100 artillery pieces. 800 tanks—mostly captured from the Soviet Union or on loan from the Germans. Several hundred fighter planes and bombers.

The first calculation is the army that Joseph Stalin sent against the Finns on the Karelian Isthmus in June of 1944. The second computation is an accounting of the forces defending that line. Worse than this disparity of men and equipment was the complete lack of preparation by the Finnish High Command for what every soldier defending the Isthmus knew was inevitable. There had been, as the Finns waited in their defensive positions, no real appreciation by the Finnish commanders for what was about to happen. This inaction was not because the Finnish High Command was clueless as to Stalin's intent. Countless reports from scouts on the ground and reconnaissance in the air confirmed that enemy troop movements were taking place. But no one in authority, not even Mannerheim, took the reports seriously.

3,000 guns and mortars on the Soviet side of the line launched the largest artillery barrage of the Continuation War. Within four days, the Red Army routed the Finns. The Russians moved forward at a pace rivaling a German Blitzkrieg. The Finns fell back to the VT Line, only to have *that* defensive position penetrated as well. Finnish counter offensives achieved little. The weight of the invasion was too great for the haggard and ill-equipped Finnish Army to reverse. A decision was made to abandon the VT Line and retreat to new positions behind the Mannerheim Line. The Mannerheim Line had not, despite requests from Finnish field commanders, been reinforced or rebuilt after the Winter War. Again, Filed Marshall Mannerheim accepted the inevitable, and by June 15th, he determined that the Finns, whose primary goal was to retain Viipuri at all costs, had to abandon the trench system named in his honor.

The defenders retired to positions that included Viipuri in the west, Kupasaari in the center, and Taipale—the VKT Line. This fallback position incorporated the rugged geography east of Viipuri along the Vuoksi River, though a gap in the natural barriers of the Karelian countryside existed between Viipuri and Kuparsaari where the terrain was compliant and the Finnish defenders were vulnerable to the Red Army's superior armor.

"Shit."

Matti Peltomaa looked out from beneath his summer fatigue cap, the brim dirty and bent, his face filthy from days spent living in a shallow trench cut through the moist earth defining the center of the VKT Line. Peltomaa was tired. His bones told him so. His joints told him so. His mind told him so. There was no bravado, no false courage left in him, after years of fighting, killing, and watching friends die. He was more than weary. He was done in. He felt unable to resist what would come next.

And yet, as Peltomaa eyed the Russian tanks lining up across the flat expanse in front of him, the American knew he would fight. He would not run. He would not retreat unless ordered to do so. Instinct had been defeated. The urge for self-preservation, the common-sense notion that he should turn tail and escape the danger amassing across the sunlit plain, duck into the safety of the depleted forest, and run as fast as he could towards the sea, wasn't in his character. Oh, it would be easy for the old man to escape to the coast and make for Kotka where the *Lahti*, the tramp steamer owned and operated by Ismo Salo (formerly named the *Kiev* when it plied the waters of Lake Onega and spirited Peltomaa and Elin Goldfarb to safety) was making trips between Finland and Estonia. But that was not the old man's character.

I could desert and be aboard Salo's boat bound for Suursaari—where I could launch the small fishing boat that I bought to run between the island and Estonia—in a few days. No one would question me. No one would care. Salo is ready to go. I am trading the last of my share of the stolen vodka for safe passage across the Gulf and the return: Passage for me, the two Estonians, Elin, and Alexis. I need to find the Estonians to discuss the details of how we will do this, how we will find and steal Elin away from that bastard Laak. There's not much time. Not much time at all. The Estonian Regiment is hunkered down to our west. They fight well. They are proud of their Finnish uniforms. But they are too few to make a difference. We will all fall. Maybe not today. Maybe not tomorrow. But we will all fall.

"What are you so deep in thought about, *Sergeant* Peltomaa?" Juha Rintala, who despite his lack of polish and education was now commanding the platoon, crouched beside the old man and watched Russian tanks move into position across the flat land.

"Nothing."

Rintala grunted. "I don't believe you. But there's more serious business at hand than your daydreaming. How's your knowledge of the new rockets? Are you up to snuff on them?"

"The Panzerfaust is a good weapon," Peltomaa said, patting the tube of the recoilless rifle propped against the angled wall of the trench an arm's length away. "It beats the Lahti all to hell."

"Hit anything with it?"

"One T-26 back at the VT Line. Blew the shit out of it. I've fired and missed at T-34s but haven't hit one yet."

Rintala looked out at the gathering enemy. "Well, I hope to hell your aim is better today."

When the Russians attacked the Panzerfaust proved its worth. Peltomaa, with the assistance of a young soldier, a boy of only seventeen, Marko Tattinen, took out two of the exhaust-belching monsters as the Soviets commenced their offensive. But two destroyed tanks were but a drop in the proverbial bucket. Scores of the clanking iron beasts crawled forward. When it seemed like the enemy tanks, supported by wave upon wave of infantry, were about to break through, Stuka dive bombers destroyed or disabled many of the advancing T-34s. Soviet fighter planes were slow to react against the dowdy Stukas. The result of the German air assault was the stabilization of the Finnish center. Unfortunately, other portions of the VKT Line did not fare as well.

Feeling the brunt of the Russian assault, Finnish regulars of the 20th Brigade—who had just arrived by train from East Karelia—deserted en masse. Viipuri, the prize of the Continuation War, the one objective that Mannerheim vowed would remain in Finnish hands, was lost to the Russians without a fight.

"The bastards have taken Viipuri," Major Laurila said plainly to officers and noncommissioned officers meeting in his shelter, a hastily constructed lean-too of salvaged planks, boards, and timbers covered with a thick layer of sod and earth behind the main Finnish trench. "But despite the bad news, we're staying put."

In the no man's land between the combatant lines, smoke wafted from the burning hulks of the Russian tanks and half-tracks that Peltomaa and the other Panzerfaust handlers had left as testament to the weapon's efficiency.

So simple, Matti Peltomaa had thought, the first time he launched a rocket from the steel tube over his shoulder and watched it blow a hole in a Russian troop truck. *Why did we not have these until now? Greedy Germans, that's why. Keeping the best for themselves. With these rockets and a few more tanks and a few more planes, we could have threatened Leningrad and forced the Russians to parlay. Instead, here we are, fighting to keep a few meters of Karelia with the main goal of our defense, Viipuri, now lost. Laatokka-Karlelia will be next. Petroskoi will fall. And then, who knows? If the Russians push through to Imatra and take the rail line running from Joensuu to Helsinki, the shit will really hit the fan. There will be nothing Mannerheim can do. Nothing the Germans can do. The 250,000 German troops sitting on their hands as placeholders along the border near Salla are of no use. They can't be shifted to Karelia without opening up all of central Finland. The Germans in the Arctic are useless for the same reason. Their removal would open up the far north. There's no doubt Norway would side with the Reds. They've had enough of Quisling and his ilk, enough of Nazi rule. If the Germans hadn't been so selfish, had truly been our allies, had given us tools like the Panzerfaust at the beginning of the war instead of too late to be of consequence, who knows what we could have accomplished together?*

"The men are tired. We're nearly out of ammunition. The new weapons are effective but there aren't enough of them to stop the Reds," Juha Rintala said quietly as the group studied a map of Karelia tacked to the rough pine board wall of the dugout. "Though we have plenty of water, bread, and cold rations, the men haven't had a hot meal in two weeks."

Laurila nodded.

"These are hardships," the major agreed, his eyes staring at his men, his hands placed firmly on his hips, "which we, all of us, including the officers, must endure. The end is coming fast. Armistice will happen soon enough. But until then, we have to fight and fight hard. If we relent now the roads will be open to Helsinki. And you know what that means for our children, our women, our old folks. Do you want that? Do you want to live, and have your loved ones live, under Soviet dominion?"

Rintala placed a filthy hand on his chin and considered the admonishment. "No sir, I do not."

Peltomaa and the others muttered in tacit accord.

"Then it's settled. Get back to your men. Buck them up as best you can. There's not much else we can do at this point."

The 200th Estonian Regiment fought hard. Led by Finnish officers who were professional soldiers, the Estonian regiment managed to delay the Russian advance. The Estonians enjoyed the benefit of new anti-tank weapons from the Germans, including not only the Panzerfaust but also the Panzerschreck, the German equivalent of the American bazooka. Each was effective in its own right and each allowed the Estonians to destroy Soviet tanks. Despite their bravery, or perhaps because of it, Estonian defenders of the VKT line suffered casualties at a disproportionate rate. Hundreds of Estonian soldiers were wounded or killed in the days leading up to the fall of Viipuri. But these kindred troops did not, as the Russians expected, turn tail and run during fierce fighting. They remained in their trenches, firing their Mausers at will, their machine guns pouring lead on the advancing enemy, and held their ground.

"You OK?"

Karl Kristian, the wire bow of his spectacles held together with black friction tape, the right lens scratched and blurring his vision, fixed his eyes on his brother's drawn, tired face as he asked the question.

Nigul Kristian did not respond. Despite the intensity of the battle, the eldest son of Andres Kristian still hadn't killed a man, still hadn't fired a shot during combat.

"I know," Karl said softly, placing the butt of his rifle on the sun-hardened ground as sweat rolled down his downy cheeks from the heat of the day.

Nigul looked away from his brother and didn't respond.

The Russian advance had stalled. The enemy was dug in across a narrow strip of open ground a short distance from the Estonian line as Soviet officers considered their options. Finnish troops anchored each end of the Estonian position. Unlike their Estonian comrades, who had nothing but shallow trenches to shield them from the enemy, Finnish units to the east and west of the Estonians were protected by forest. From their more secure positions, the Finns had bucked up the Estonians when the enemy was close to breaking through. Captured Russian tanks newly adorned with blue swastikas had emerged from the trees, slammed into the enemy and, with the help of the ever-present Stukas, destroyed dozens of enemy tanks. Soviet soldiers had attained the lip of the Estonian trench but the Reds had been stopped in horrific hand-to-hand fighting. Karl had killed four Russians: two with his Mauser and two with a Walther .38, a pistol he'd taken off a dead Finnish officer, at close range. Nigul had watched in open-eyed terror as his brother methodically killed. But he, the older sibling, had been unable to pull the trigger on his rifle as he cowered against the wall of the trench. Nigul made an easy target and only Karl's vigilance had kept his older brother alive.

"Know what?" Nigul asked.

Karl's expression bore no recrimination, no measure of disdain. "That you cannot kill?" the younger Kristian whispered. "It has not changed for you since Tartu, has it?"

Nigul shook his head. Tears wet his grimy face. He looked away, out across the dead bodies, the smoldering tanks, and the wounded land.

Karl drew a deep breath. "There's no shame in it, you know. None."

Nigul shook his head and tears slid off his chin.

"Really, I don't think anything less of you, Brother."

Nigul knew this was a lie: his younger sibling was judging him. The shame of it was too great to bear and too real to deny. A shot rang out. A Soviet sniper had taken aim on a young Estonian soldier stupid enough to stand up to piss. The boy, no more than a teenager, gasped once, toppled backwards into the trench, and was silent. Karl picked up his Mauser, rested the rifle on the rim of the earthen trench, adjusted the Mauser's sights, and waited.

He's using that berm as cover.

Karl studied a mound of blackened earth one hundred and fifty meters away and momentarily forgot his brother's distress. A lieutenant walked carelessly along the trench. The officer's cap was visible above the sandbagged wall and presented an intriguing target for the sniper.

"Get your head down!" Karl yelled.

Crack.

Dirt showered the startled officer. The lieutenant ducked.

Crack.

The sniper's second shot missed as well. The barrel of the Russian's rifle reflected sunlight.

Crack.

The report of Karl's Mauser caused the sniper to look up. The bullet struck the enemy soldier in the head. The Russian dropped his weapon, jerked to his knees, and slapped at the hole in his forehead before toppling backwards.

"Nice shot," the officer said as he stood up, brushed dirt from his gray trousers with his bare hand, and replaced his cap.

Nigul looked at the lieutenant with pleading eyes.

"What's wrong with him?" the officer asked.

"He's tired," Karl said, "tired and ready to go home."

CHAPTER 31
August 5th, 1944
(Nigul's Story)

My shame was great. Though the paralyzing fear I felt during combat subsided and my nerves were no longer frayed, the residue of my cowardice lingered like the taste of raw onion in my mouth. Karl said nothing about my behavior beyond what passed between us in the trenches outside Viipuri. He did not chide or cajole me in any way. I doubt that I would have been so kind if our roles had been reversed. I am not made that way.

We retreated to Tali-Ihantala, in a desperate effort to stave off the invasion of Finland. Viipuri was already in Russian hands. There was great danger that the Soviet fleet would break out of St. Petersburg and threaten Finland and Estonia by sea. Once the cork was unstopped, Red wine, in the form of unlimited Russian ships and troops, would flow into the Baltic. But before Karl and I could think about returning home, we had work yet to do at Tali-Ihantala.

Mannerheim drew a line in the sand at Ihantala. Losing Viipuri had been a blow to Finnish pride. Allowing the Red Army to advance into Finland proper would likely destroy the Finns' will to fight.

I did not participate, other than being present and cowering in my section of dry, dirty trench, in any of the fighting at Tali-Inhantala. Karl, as he had done previously at Tartu and Narva and Viipuri, acquitted himself well. He killed or wounded half a dozen Soviet soldiers during his final battle. Had we stayed in Finland after the fighting subsided, Karl would likely have been a highly decorated soldier. But we did not linger once the fighting ceased. As soon as Matti Peltomaa received permission to leave the front, the three of us made haste for Kotka.

Peltomaa was, for an uneducated man, crafty. He possessed an innate resourcefulness of both mind and hands that, well, quite frankly, I had not witnessed in anyone other than my own father.

"Where in the hell did you get this truck?"

My question came as the three of us, crammed into the front seat of an old Ford pickup, rumbled down a road leading from the front to the Baltic coast. Peltomaa had shown up at our unit's headquarters after the fighting stopped and an uneasy truce was installed. The Russians had tried to smash the Finnish Army. The goal of their final assault had been to annihilate the largest Finnish fighting force ever assembled. But the line at Tali-Ihantala held and the Soviet offensive on the Karelian Isthmus stalled, leaving the area relatively quiet as politicians sorted out what was to come next.

"From the quartermaster. I made a trade. Five cases of vodka for the use of the truck."

Liquid treasure rattled in the cargo area of the pickup truck as we bounced towards Kotka. There were dozens of crates—hundreds of bottles of premium Absolut vodka imported by the Germans from Sweden—rattling in the back of the truck.

"Aren't you worried that you'll break bottles driving so fast on this shitty road?" Karl asked after a sudden jolt caused all three of us to leave our seats.

"No," Peltomaa replied, concentrating on the narrow swath of light the truck's headlamps cast on the dark, gravel road. "The bottles are secure. The load won't shift."

There was a moment of silence. The truck's six cylinders purred evenly as we gained speed.

"Besides," the old Finn added, "we have to make Kotka before first light or we'll end up like the poor bastard I took the booze from."

I nodded but did not reply.

Karl grasped my shoulder as the front wheels of the truck bounced over stones.

Once their attack on the Isthmus stalled the Russians turned their offensive towards the territory between Lake Ladoga and Lake Onega. The Finns abandoned Petroskoi on June 28th. Two days later—because of Finnish refusals to sever ties with Hitler—the United States ended all diplomatic relations with Finland. This snub was, to use a tired cliché, the beginning of the end for my homeland. There was no hope that the United States would intervene in Estonia once the U.S. withdrew its official recognition of Finland.

Karl and I were not in Estonia on July 26th when Narva fell. We were not present in our homeland to serve under Col. Vent when he fought to save Tartu. But we knew this bitter truth: Estonia could expect no military aid or intervention from the Finns. We recognized this truth because we understood that Finland was in political turmoil. President Ryti had resigned. Field Marshall Mannerheim succeeded Ryti. It was no secret why a man who had made his mark as a military tactician would become embroiled in the ugly world of politics. Mannerheim became Finland's president because he was given carte blanche authority to end the war. This turn of events would prove to be devastating for Estonia. Once peace between Finland and the U.S.S.R. was achieved another half-million Soviet troops would be free to swing south and chase the bedraggled German Army out of Estonia and back to Berlin.

"Just as promised," Ismo Salo said with admiration as he opened a crate of Absolut in the cool, early morning air. "I didn't think you were telling the truth."

Captain Salo was short, stocky, and powerful with blackened teeth and serious eyes. I liked him instantly. There was a palpable honesty to the man. He was near Peltomaa's age—that is to say, in his early sixties—and remarkably fit. His arms were well muscled and his stomach was as flat as a pan. And though both Karl and I towered above Salo, I knew neither of us would be much of a challenge for the old boat captain if we got in his way. He was bull, an ox of a man.

"Have I ever lied to you?" Peltomaa asked as the four of us stood in emerging morning light, not a cloud in the sky, black slowly burning to blue.

"Once. You lied to me once."

Peltomaa shook his head. "Not true. Failure to reveal information is not lying."

Salo snickered at the memory of Matti Peltomaa concealing the fact that Elin Goldfarb was to be the additional passenger leaving Lime Island on Ismo Salo's boat.

"You didn't come clean," the captain replied. "Still, the fact that you both made it through is remarkable."

"Enough chit-chat," Peltomaa finally said. "Let's get down to business."

"Agreed," Salo replied.

We followed Ismo Salo into his office. The room was sparsely furnished. A simple pine desk, an unadorned pine chair, a single steel file cabinet, and several stacks of documents organized on a corner of the desk were all the room contained.

"Sorry there's no place to sit," Salo muttered as he slid behind his desk. "Both boats are ready. The work you started on the little launch is finished. Your rebuild of the single cylinder gasoline engine is a masterpiece. The thing runs like a Swiss watch. My brother Pekka patched the ribs and planking. It's as good as new and it'll only cost you ten bottles for the job. Well worth it, I'd say."

Peltomaa nodded. Karl and I stood behind the old Finn, letting the men conduct business.

"So, you're really going to undertake this fool's errand?" Salo placed his hands on his broad lap and looked intently at Peltomaa as he asked the question.

"I am."

"She's a handsome woman," the captain observed. "But you understand that you have little chance of success. Sailing from Suursaari to Tallinn in a ten-meter motor launch, even under the best of conditions, isn't for the faint of heart. It takes an experienced sailor, and you, my friend, do not seem to fit the bill."

Peltomaa nodded.

"And still, you want to try, don't you?"

Peltomaa nodded again.

"Love," Salo muttered. "Many men have died trying to find it or keep it. And you," the captain said to my brother and me, his dark eyes flashing, "what the hell is wrong with you two? Bright, strapping young lads with their whole lives ahead of them. Why in God's name would the two of you sign on for such folly?"

I started to reply but Karl interrupted.

"His woman," Karl said, gesturing towards Peltomaa, "is my fiancé's mother. My fiancé is helping her mother escape from Estonia."

Salo shook his head. "Stupid. This whole idea is stupid. Yes, the Germans are distracted. But there are thousands of German troops in and around Tallinn. And then there are the Estonian police. I've run into them ferrying supplies and men across. They can't be trusted. You need a ready supply of German marks to placate their greed or you'll find yourself caught by the short hairs."

Matti Peltomaa nodded. "Ismo, I know these things. I know it's a risk, that there's little chance I'll be able to get Elin out of Estonia alive. But what other choice do I have? She's in prison, Ismo, a prison for Jews about to be sent off to a death camp. It's a wonder Laak hasn't sent her off before this. We haven't much time. I have to try. You have a wife. You love her. You understand even if you don't agree."

Salo shrugged his shoulders. "I'll get you to the island. I've got to deliver supplies to the Germans—they've taken over the island. I'd bring you right into Tallinn if I could. But that's not the job I've been assigned by the harbormaster. It would mean the confiscation of my boat to violate orders. I can't risk that. You understand, don't you? I'd do more if I could."

Peltomaa nodded again. "Let's take a look at the boats," he said, motioning for Karl and me to follow Salo and him out the door.

CHAPTER 32
August 7, 1944
The Gulf of Finland
(Nigul's Story)

I stared at the dwarf and marveled at what the hell I'd agreed to do for a woman I'd never met. No, that's not true. I had agreed to go on a fool's errand because I loved Karl. Despite my cowardice under fire, I had a deep and abiding desire to protect my younger sibling, to do what needed doing to keep him safe. If Karl was hell-bent on helping Matti Peltomaa find Elin Goldfarb then I was going to be there if trouble erupted.

The dwarf eyed me with reserved contempt as the small boat motored through the inky night over smooth water. I could feel the dwarf's beady eyes on me even though there was no light with which to see the tops of my boots resting on the finely varnished fir of the launch's deck.

How does the little man know? I asked myself, as the single cylinder of the old marine engine purred and sputtered, propelling the boat over the velvety sea. *How the hell does that little bastard know I am useless as teats on a bull when it comes to combat?*

Oh, I looked the part of a commando, all right, just like Peltomaa and my brother. What with Suomis strapped across our chests, grenades hanging from our utility belts, bandoliers of ammunition crisscrossing the thick fabric of our khaki utility shirts, and black watch caps covering our respective heads, the four of us, the dwarf included, looked like a covert team from the Finnish special forces. But the dwarf and Karl: They knew, or at least, in the dwarf's case, suspected, my cowardice—that despite my prowess with my fists and a knife, I was pretty well useless in a gunfight. How the hell that ugly little sonofabitch guessed my secret without being with me in combat, I have no idea. But I was convinced he knew and his knowledge of my secret was disconcerting as the little wooden boat chugged its way across the Gulf of Finland.

His name was Niilo Niskanen. He was Ismo Salo's brother-in-law and had helped Salo's brother Pekka refurbish the ten-meter unnamed open boat that would carry us from Suursaari Island to Estonia. Ismo Salo had insisted that Niskanen go with us on our fools' errand.

"None of you knows how to sail an open boat across a large body of water, am I right?" Salo had posed the question after we had inspected the *Lahti* and the small boat.

"It can't be that hard," Peltomaa replied. "I have a compass and charts. There's nothing between here and there except for a few German warships."

Salo had grinned. "I've always admired your bravery, Matti. But being brave doesn't mean you're wise. You'll need more than *sisu* to make the crossing, land the boat, do your business, and make it back in one piece. The tides, Matti—the tides can do a man in if he's not careful. And there's no end of rocks and reefs between here and there to snag a boat."

Peltomaa studied the motor launch snugged to the pier alongside the *Lahti*. "You're probably right. Want to come along?"

Ismo Salo had shaken his head. "Not me my friend. I have to supervise the offloading of the *Lahti*. If I'm not there the German harbormaster will grow suspicious and you'd likely end up in the sights of a German gunboat before you can make the mainland," the squat man replied. "But there's someone who can do it, who can guide you to Tallinn and back."

Peltomaa looked at Karl and me. "Who?"

"Niilo!"

It had taken a moment for the dwarf to crawl out from under a tarp on the deck of the *Lahti* and claim his full height, which, at best, was just shy of one hundred and forty centimeters.

"What the hell do you want?"

The little man had a squat head, short arms, a rotund belly, and inordinately stout legs. His ogre-like face was twice the size one would expect for someone so diminutive. He resembled a character out of the *Kalevipoeg*. His tone had been defiant and not at all in keeping with his stature.

"Your attention."

The dwarf walked over to the gunwale of the ship and stood looking up at us with squinty eyes and a furrowed brow. "Ya?"

"Peltomaa here needs someone to pilot him from Suursaari to Estonia and back. These two are going with. They want to bring a woman out of Estonia, a Jew who's about to be shipped off to a death camp. You know the way. Can you do it?"

The dwarf had squinted. "I don't like Jews," the little man spat, dislike palpable in his tone.

Peltomaa interjected. "She's not a Jew. She was married to one, is all. She's in Tallinn, but for how long, no one can say."

Niskanen had placed a thick, stunted hand on his chin. "Two hundred."

Salo looked puzzled. "How's that?"

"Two hundred Finnish marks to take these idiots across. I'll wait one day, no more. Then I'll leave whether they're back or not."

Peltomaa had nodded. "I can pay."

The dwarf grinned. "Half now and half when I land that piece of shit you call a boat in Estonia."

"Agreed."

Salo had concealed the four of us in his cabin on the *Lahti.* The passage to the southern tip of the island—where the crew of the Lahti launched the little open boat at night—had been uneventful. As I have said, the sea was calm and, with the dwarf at the wheel, we motored away from Suursaari without incident.

"What the hell are you staring at?" Niskanen's question interrupted my reflection.

"Nothing."

The dwarf spat. He stood as straight as a cedar fence post, the steering wheel clutched tightly in his thick hands, his short legs spread for balance, staring over the bow of the little craft. The passengers sat on wooden benches running along the gunwales in front of the dwarf. I was sitting next to my brother on the port side. Karl's chin rested on his chest. Deep snores echoed in the night. Peltomaa was on the bench across from us, also asleep.

"You say I am 'nothing.' Is that what you say, Estonian?"

I shook my head. "I didn't mean it that way."

Niskanen chortled. "Bullshit. You don't like me, do you? You don't like 'little people'. Got something against those who aren't perfect, like you and the 'professor'. Am I right?"

I shook my head again. "That's not true."

There was brief silence.

"I know you," the dwarf finally replied. "I have spent my whole life around people like you, people who can't get past my height and my looks to consider the man. Well," the dwarf said, pausing to study a compass under the red lens of a flashlight, "if you didn't have me to bring you across, you three would be dead before you set foot in Estonia."

Our plan was to motor south until we hit the Estonian mainland and then follow the coastline until we arrived at the beach running between Rohuneeme and Kelvingi. The dwarf had friends there, Estonian fishermen whom he could trust. The fishermen, who had been in contact with Niskanen over Salo's shortwave radio, were going to bring us to Tallinn. That part of the plan had been worked out. But our exit strategy? Presuming we were able to find Mrs. Goldfarb and Alexis, we had no real idea of what came next. And that, to my way of thinking, had the makings of a disaster. Also unsettled was what Karl and I would do once the women were retrieved. I was unsure if I would stay in Estonia or flee to Helsinki. And Karl was equally uncertain: Would he stay in Estonia with Alexis or bring her back to Finland?

To the dwarf's way of thinking the return trip to Finland was a simple matter. He made it clear that our only hope was to sail directly for Helsinki. There was not enough petrol to retrace the cautious route we were sailing *to* Estonia. We would escape Estonia by crossing open water in a tiny boat that could do no more than ten knots. German patrol boats could travel three times that speed, which meant that our path to freedom was based upon chance and the pluck of a dwarf.

Niilo Niskanen nestled the boat's bow into a cradle of sand stretching between a chorus of rocks and boulders. Two Estonian fishermen, one short, one tall, held the boat steady as we clambered over the launch's steeply sloped fir gunwales onto wet sand.

"*Tänan*," Niskanen said in Estonian. "Will she be safe until we return from doing our business?"

The dwarf's question to the fishermen caught me by surprise.

"I thought you were staying with the boat," I said, as our pilot brushed sand from his dungarees.

"Changed my mind. Thought you might need a hand," Niskanen said wryly. "Your brother's got an extra pistol, no?"

Karl overheard the remark, removed the Walther he carried in his campaign belt, and handed it to the dwarf.

"*Tänan*" Niskanen repeated, sticking the pistol in his own belt. "Is it loaded?"

Karl nodded.

"Ya," the tall fishermen answered. "We'll keep an eye on 'er until we come to pick you up. This stretch of beach isn't much visited, but one never knows."

"Let's get you boys into town," the short fisherman added. "My truck is just up the rise."

We climbed into the back of an antique Fiat and sat cross-legged on the wooden cargo bed. My fatigue trousers and underwear were immediately soaked to the skin. A strong breeze coughed steady mist. The short fisherman slid behind the steering wheel, turned the key, and tromped the floor starter. The engine wheezed and then caught, humming like a sewing machine as the driver engaged the clutch, shifted gears, and stepped on the gas pedal.

CHAPTER 33
August 7, 1944
Tallinn, Estonia

"They will be here today."

Ellisabet Raun, her form petite, agile, and prim in her brown guard's uniform, her ebony hair pulled tight against the back of her skull and secured by a hand-crocheted hairnet, stood near Tallinn Prison's gated exit and spoke softly to Elin Goldfarb. Early morning fog vanished as the sky lightened. The steeples and rooflines of Old Tallinn manifested as the sun sought height in the eastern sky. Elin knew what the Estonian woman meant.

Matti is coming. The Kristian brothers are coming.

"Keep your eyes open and your thoughts to yourself and this should work out just fine," Ellisabet Raun said in the same firm yet quiet tone.

Eight female prisoners including Elin, all that were left from the labor camp, the only survivors of Aleksander Laak's brutal reign—the others all having been used up and discarded in the ditches of Kalevi-Liiva or been shipped with tired men and boys to Birkenau and Auschwitz—stood in warming air in meager clothing as they waited for guards assigned to their detail to arrive. An involuntary grin emerged on Elin's face.

"Don't be so obvious," the Estonian woman said beneath her breath. "You must maintain decorum. No one can suspect that you have any reason to believe that today is not like yesterday or the day before yesterday."

Elin's grin disappeared. Two lanky Estonian guards, their brown uniforms sharply pressed, Lugers concealed in shiny leather holsters attached to matching black belts, Mausers held loosely in their right hands, the slings of the rifles dangling from the rifle stocks, tromped down a stone staircase and stood by the locked front gate at the head of the small column.

"How goes it today, Warden Raun?" the guard closest to the woman said, his eyes fixed upon the starched white fabric of Ellisabet's blouse and not the woman's eyes.

Ellisabet Raun noted the man's wandering gaze. She drew the two sides of her open uniform jacket tight and affixed the jacket's buttons to eliminate the distraction. "Excellent, Corporal Veimer," she said evenly, not revealing her pique. "Ready for another day in the service of my country. And you?"

The man smiled, revealing a broken front tooth. "Excellent as well, madam. Excellent as well."

The other guard nodded to a stocky turnkey wearing an unkempt uniform manning the prison's entrance gate. "It's time to leave," the second guard said loudly enough for everyone to hear. "Open up!"

The turnkey yanked a chain leading to the front pocket of his trousers, removed a skeleton key, placed it in a lock, turned the key, and opened the gate.

"Let's get a move on. We're already ten minutes behind schedule thanks to Private Köler's inordinate attention to his mustache," Veimer quipped.

Köler brushed the thick brown hairs of the moustache beneath his nose with his left hand, slid the leather sling of the rifle over his left shoulder, but said nothing as he moved to the rear of the little group.

Veimer slung his own Mauser over his shoulder, took his place at the front of the women, and began leading the column towards the gate.

"Stop!"

The contingent halted. All heads turned at the sound of the Aleksander Laak's voice. Laak's black leather boots clacked against cobblestones as he emerged from shadow.

"Not her," Laak said firmly, his right index finger pointing at Elin Goldfarb. "She stays."

A lump formed in Elin's throat.

God no.

"But commandant," Ellisabet Raun said with expression, "why?"

Laak straightened to his full height. "I have my reasons. Keep your impertinence to yourself, Miss Raun, or you might not like the consequences."

The commandant stared hard at Veimer. "You heard me, take the rest of these pieces of shit to the shipyard. But the old woman stays. Understand?"

Veimer nodded. With a steady hand meant not to injure but to ensure compliance, he urged Elin Goldfarb towards Laak.

"Let's move!" the guard said, gesturing for the remaining prisoners to follow him.

The women did not hesitate. They did not allow Aleksander Laak to change his mind and call for them as well. As the gate slammed behind Köler, Laak studied the woman standing in front of him.

What I could have done with you in your prime.

"Come with me," the warden said curtly after his brief examination of the American. "We have much to do."

And so, like the Tartars in the forest, he has finally come for me…

Elin Goldfarb sought to contain her dread as she followed the lieutenant up the narrow stone stairway to his office.

CHAPTER 34
Rohke Söökla

Alexis sensed something was wrong.

"I need a moment of your time," Ellisabet Raun whispered as Alexis stood at the cash register near the entrance to the diner. "Is there a place we can talk in private?'

Alexis eyed the woman.

How can I trust her? I know, I know. She's befriended Mother. At least that's how it appears. But she stands with the Germans. Her father is complicit with Laak. I best be careful dealing with her.

"We can use the office. Margit's out for the day."

Alexis wiped her hands on the apron tied around her waist and moved swiftly across the greasy floor of the noisy room. She had returned to work at the Plenty Diner during her time off from teaching. The money was good and she enjoyed bantering with customers, especially the workingmen who came in after a hard day's labor looking for a good meal. The warden followed the waitress through an open door into a windowless office. Alexis closed the door and waited for Ellisabet to speak.

"The men. Where are the men?" Ellisabet demanded.

Alexis knew *whom* Miss Raun meant by the question but the *way* the question was asked confused Alexis. The American studied the warden's face, looking for signs of duplicity. Alexis found none. There was nothing but stark honesty replicated in Ellisabet Raun's eyes as the two women squared off in the unlighted room.

"They landed last night. That's the information Big Peeter Saul conveyed this morning when he stopped in for coffee. The men are spending the day at his flat, lying low until the women are released from work and return to the prison."

It was a curious protocol that Laak had imposed. The women were led to their jobs in the morning by armed guards but Laak tempted escape by allowing the women to walk back to Tallinn Prison *unattended* at the end of the workday. Alexis had been told that the women remained compliant because Laak used threats against the prisoner's families as a way to keep them in line. Laak had convinced the women that their families had not been sent off to concentration camps but were alive and working in other territories occupied by the Germans. The handful of Jewish and Roma women who had tried to run while on Aleksander Laak's watch? They had been re-captured and sent to death camps.

"Why do you ask?" Alexis replied with a question of her own.

Miss Raun stared at her hands. Alexis followed the other woman's gaze and noted that Ellisabet's nails were perfectly trimmed and polished.

The hands of someone who has never done a hard day's labor.

"There's been a development, an unfortunate change in circumstances," Ellisabet whispered.

Alexis pressed her palms against her hips. "How so?"

"Your mother didn't go to work this morning. Laak has her in his office."

"Goddamn it," Alexis whispered, as she brought her hands to her face. "Goddamn it," she repeated, despite her religious nature.

The other woman nodded and touched Alexis's bare wrist. "He's shown no interest in her, in his usual way, up to now. I don't think that's what his intentions are…"

The revelation did little to calm Alexis. "Then what, goddamn it? Then what is he doing *with* her or *to* her in his goddamned office?"

Raun shook her head. "I have no idea."

Noise from the diner filtered in through the crack under the office door. Voices of patrons demanding service imposed on the silence between the women.

Ellisabet removed her hand from Alexis's wrist. "There must be some task—something he trusts her to do with paperwork—in the offing. Laak has a meeting with the SS this afternoon. I can get her to the gate when he leaves for that."

"But that would be in broad daylight! The men were going to come for her after her shift was done—when the sun was down and the evening provided cover. Taking Mother in broad daylight is risky."

Raun nodded. "I know. But under the circumstances, it's the best I can come up with."

A rescue in late afternoon is a suicide mission. Is Miss Raun springing a trap for the man she says she loves? I wonder.

The prison warden shook her head emphatically. "No."

"How's that?"

Raun looked intently at the other woman. "No, I am not leading Nigul into a trap. I love him. Always have. There's more between us than he or anyone else knows. I won't allow anything to happen to him."

Alexis stared at Ellisabet Raun. The steadiness of her gaze made the other woman nervous. Ellisabet touched the thin, small fingers of her right hand to her chin.

"What is there between you and Nigul that I do not know, that Nigul himself does not know?" Alexis asked.

The warden looked away.

"There can be no secrets between us, Ellisabet," the schoolteacher said, a hint of tenderness in her voice as she addressed the other woman with familiarity. "The men we love are about to risk their lives."

Ellisabet Raun exhaled. The hubbub in the diner grew louder. Customers became unruly as their orders remained unfilled. There was no one manning the till. Despite the din Alexis would not lessen the intensity of her gaze. After a period of silence Ellisabet Raun nodded and told Alexis Gustafson what Ellisabet Raun had vowed never to tell.

"There's a child. Back in Germany. Our son. He is called Nigul as well: Nigul Raun. He was conceived from our one night together when we were both very young. He lives with my aunt, a single woman in Dresden. Even the boy doesn't know. He thinks my aunt is his mother. He believes his father died in a traffic accident. He was told that they were to marry but that the man died before the wedding. And me? I am simply the boy's cousin."

Tears flowed down Ellisabet's face. Her shoulders sagged and her breath caught.

Alexis moved across the office and embraced Ellisabet Raun in a fierce, sisterly hug. "You must tell Nigul."

Raun shook her head. "I can't. I promised my aunt that no one, other than my aunt and my father, would ever know."

Alexis created distance. "It's not right. He's the child's father. He must be told."

Ellisabet grimaced. "Please. I beg you. Don't tell him. I am sworn to secrecy. I only told you because I am afraid for Nigul, afraid for them all."

Alexis closed her eyes and thought for a moment. "I won't say a word. But you, Miss Raun, you must, at some point, tell him."

They left the topic unresolved.

Ellisabet wiped tears from her eyes and cheeks with the sleeve of her uniform. "Four o'clock. Have the men at the gate at four. Your mother will be there."

The prison warden turned, walked to the narrow fir door, opened it to the bustle in the diner, and left Alexis alone to consider how she was going to tell Karl and the others that plans had changed.

CHAPTER 35
Tallinn Prison

"You are discrete for a Jewess, Mrs. Goldfarb," Aleksander Laak observed as he sat at his desk, watching the woman work her way through documents piled on the floor of the musty office. "You keep your mouth shut and your eyes to yourself. That's why I've allowed you to remain alive, working for Raun. That's why you are here, working for me today."

Elin knelt on the plank floor and fed documents into a raging fire in an open brick fireplace at the far end of the large room. There was so much material, so many pages of dispatches and lists and inventories and memoranda to be destroyed that she did not have time to read the content of the papers.

The allies would love to see these, she thought to herself as she fed the fire. *There is likely much truth in these documents, much revelation of the cruel nature of Aleksander Laak and his kind written down here. The Germans and their ilk are fastidious. Every "i" must be dotted and every "t" crossed even if they treat their victims no better than stray dogs. It is all here: the ditches and the dead. But there will be nothing left when I am done. Nothing but memory.*

Ernest Raun entered the room as the woman shuffled paper into the flames. "What's this, lieutenant?"

"Ah, Mr. Raun. Just the man I wanted to see. I need your files. Mrs. Goldfarb will ensure that they are destroyed along with our other records."

Laak sipped coffee at his desk and watched the woman work.

"Why are you doing this?" Raun asked.

Laak smiled a wicked little smile. "I'm meeting Colonel Brooten at three to discuss our withdrawal to Latvia. The Red Army has secured Narva. Two Soviet columns are racing towards Võru and Tartu. When those cities fall, my friend, Tallinn is doomed. And so, we must make a clean sweep of it. Leave nothing behind that might incriminate us. Leave no trace of our work here, as proud of it as we might be."

The lieutenant's smile faded, as if he didn't believe his own lie—that there was some greater good behind the murders and deaths of innocents he had personally engineered. Laak sipped slowly from the china cup and eyed Ernest Raun.

The lawyer nodded. "I understand."

The warden altered his expression as the prisoner tossed documents into the rising flame. "Careful. We don't want to test the mortar of that old chimney. Keep the fire small and patient. You have all day to finish your work."

"Yes sir," Elin replied quietly.

"I need a word with you, Mr. Raun," Laak said, turning his attention back to the lawyer, and placing the elegant teacup back in its matching saucer as he rose. "In private."

Raun waited for the taller man at the threshold and followed Laak through the open door. Elin noticed that Raun's face was leaking sweat as he glanced furtively in her direction.

"I know," Laak said, as the two men walked down the prison hallway.

Raun followed the warden but said nothing.

"Aren't you the least bit curious about what I'm talking about?"

Raun maintained his silence.

"Ah, cat's got your tongue?" Laak observed. "An interesting trait for a lawyer."

The men arrived at an interrogation room. Laak reached for the door handle and opened the door to a claustrophobic space.

A single light bulb provided light. Two uniformed Estonians, men Raun had never seen before, stood in shadow. Both men wore holstered Lugers on their belts.

"Have a seat."

Raun looked at Laak. "What is the meaning of this?" he asked insolently.

Laak smiled. "Please, Mr. Raun, have a seat. There's no reason to take that tone with me. I just need to ask you some questions."

Ernest Raun claimed a chair at a small metal table.

Laak followed suit and sat across from the lawyer. The men studied each other.

"Get him!" Laak barked.

One of the soldiers left the room and returned immediately with a young man—a boy no more than fifteen or sixteen years of age.

"Ah, nice of you to join us, Mr. Toew. Please stand next to Mr. Raun."

The lawyer's face turned as white as paste.

"I see you know this boy."

Raun remained silent.

Laak slammed his fist down on the steel surface of the table. "Damn it, Raun, no more lies! I know your secret, you hear me? I know that you and this, this faggot, have been meeting at his lodgings for more than a month, doing unnatural things, forbidden things. You want to deny this? Do you?"

Laak stood up and shoved his chin within inches of the doomed man's nose. "Do you?"

Raun blinked but did not speak.

Laak reclaimed his seat and addressed the boy. "Mr. Toew, do you deny that you have been in an unnatural relationship with Mr. Raun?"

The boy's brown eyes batted but did not tear. There was great fear evident on Toew's face but he did not cry. "No sir, I won't deny it."

"See there, Ernest? See how honest, how forthright this young man is? For his candor, I will be generous. Hiller," Laak said, turning to the soldier who had brought the boy into the room, "take him down to the street and release him."

"Yes, lieutenant. Come along boy. It looks like it's your lucky day."

The youth and the soldier left the room. The steel door swung shut with a thud.

"Now, Raun, what do you have to say for yourself?"

The lawyer buried his face in the palms of his hands and wept.

"Stop that you stupid old fool. Tears accomplish nothing."

Raun continued to sob.

Laak pushed him chair away from the table but did not stand. "I was always puzzled," the warden said softly, the tone of his voice at odds with the circumstances, "why I never sensed that you had become intimate with the Jewess. Yes, she is middle aged. But as you pointed out when you saved her from the camps, she is still attractive. And intelligent. And well mannered. I should have thought she would be a perfect companion for you. Having sired a daughter—a lovely young lady, I might add—there's evidence that you once fancied women. But your daughter's conception must have been an anomaly, a distortion of your natural preferences. Am I right?"

The lawyer placed his face on the cold tabletop and covered his head with his hands.

Aleksander Laak smirked. "Tomorrow, Mr. Raun, tomorrow there's a train leaving Tallinn—maybe the last one out. And you, unfortunately, will be on it. You and your Jewess and the other prisoners—all that remain of the work we once did together—will all be on that train. You will be taken to Birkenau. The rest? Well, you know the rest, I am afraid."

"Why are you doing this to me? I was loyal, did what was asked, followed the Party's line. It was something I couldn't control, something that harmed no one..." The words leaked out from lawyer as he raised his face and looked into the warden's dark eyes.

"There are rules, Mr. Raun—rules of nature that must be obeyed. You broke those rules. As a man trained in the law, a man taught to follow the rules, you, above all people, know that rule breakers must suffer consequences."

Laak stood up from the table with a look of disgust on his face.

"*Man was not meant to lie with man*, Mr. Raun. It's the most elementary, the most ancient of rules. You broke that rule and now, you must pay the penalty. Take him to the men's cellblock. He has a train to catch."

Elin Goldfarb carried paperwork from Ernest Raun's office and fed the documents into the fire. As she added armfuls of correspondence and memoranda to the flames, Elin was puzzled. The lawyer had vanished. She expected Raun would supervise the destruction of his files but he never came back from his meeting with the warden.

Aleksander Laak *did* return to his office. He sat behind his desk, refilled his cup with coffee, and resumed his scrutiny of the woman's work. The warden did not engage Elin as she went about her task and Elin Goldfarb did not inquire about Ernest Raun's whereabouts. There was an air of despair and hopelessness to the room as Elin stoked the flames and Aleksander Laak watched fire destroy the evidence of his work.

CHAPTER 36
Tallinn, Estonia
(Nigul's Story)

Our plans changed. Uncertainty weighed me down as I trudged past Fat Margaret's Tower. I was also *physically* weighed down by the duffle bag I was carrying. The canvas sack was filled with my Suomi, grenades, and ammunition. My brother, Peltomaa, and I looked like merchant seamen just off a ship and walking through the city in search of lodging with sea bags over our shoulders. The dwarf was not with us. As I said, our plans had changed and Niskanen's seafaring skills were more important to the success of our operation than was his ability to shoot straight. When it was clear that we would not be rescuing Elin on her way home from work, we sent Niilo Niskanen back to the boat. We did not want to risk our pilot, our only means of escape, in a firefight.

When Alexis encountered us at Big Peeter's place there was such kissing and fondling and groping between Alexis and Karl, well, I had been damned embarrassed by the show.

When their ardor was sated Alexis related the tale of what had happened to her mother.

"What the hell do we do now?" I had asked the question as we sat in Big Peeter's flat with the window shades drawn. The big man's children and wife were gone. Matti Peltomaa sipped tepid tap water from a glass.

"Miss Raun will have Mother at the front gate by four. No guards will be present," Alexis had related. "Laak will be out. And Ernest Raun won't be a problem. He's apparently vanished."

"Vanished?" I had asked.

Alexis nodded.

"Does Ellisabet know where he is?"

Alexis shook her head.

I had sighed. "He's been found out, hasn't he? That bastard Laak finally caught him with a boy," I whispered.

Rumors regarding Raun's propensities were not confined to the walls of Tallinn Prison. There had been much speculation as to why, in the face of Nazi persecution of homosexuals, Laak tolerated such hypocrisy under his nose.

"No one knows for sure," Alexis had continued. "But that would be a good guess. Ellisabet is beside herself with grief."

My brother loosened his embrace on the woman's waist as they sat on Big Peeter's couch. "Ernest Raun is a bastard. I hope the Germans ship him to Poland," Karl said.

I had frowned knowing how much, despite the lawyer's failings, Ellisabet loved her father. "Brother," I said quietly, "sending him off to a death camp solves nothing."

Karl shook his head. "It rids Estonia of one more cockroach," my brother sneered.

Alexis had touched Karl's mouth. "Shsssh, Karl. He is just a misguided man. He's not the devil. He's not like Laak."

Big Peeter stood at the far end of the living room and grunted. "I agree with Karl. If Raun is on a train to Poland, that's too good an end for the bastard. He betrayed his country, sided with the Germans in every possible way. He's a Nazi, Nigul. A fuckin' Jew killing Nazi. Surely you know what that means to someone like Alexis's mother."

Alexis frowned. "Mother is no Jew."

I had tilted my head. "There's no clear line of demarcation between who is and is not a Jew with men like Laak," I observed. "Your mother is as Jewish— because she was married to one—as if she had grown up going to synagogue."

"All the more reason to get her the hell out of Tallinn Prison," Karl said, changing the topic. "So what's the new plan?"

Alexis had smoothed her skirt before responding. "At four o'clock, you're to be at the front gate. Ellisabet will have Mother ready. Occupy yourselves with something trivial across the street. Miss Raun will open the gate and Mother will walk to you. And then, you must vanish."

I had smirked. "That's the plan? She's simply going to walk through the front gate in broad daylight?"

Alexis nodded. "If you wait until tomorrow, it will be too late," she added. "There's a train leaving for Poland tonight. The prisoners and Mr. Raun will be on that train: Mother will be on that train if you delay."

"Where in the hell will we stay until nightfall?" Karl asked. "Once Laak realizes your mother is gone, all hell will break loose. There will be soldiers and police scurrying around the city like potato bugs on a ripe crop looking for her."

"Not here," Big Peeter had said firmly. "My wife and children will be back. I'll not have you bringing the police or the Germans down upon them."

"Then where? We can't sail until after dark," Karl had added. "The dwarf will have the boat ready. His pals will have the truck here to take us to the beach but not until after ten o'clock. What will we do for six hours?"

I pondered my brother's question. "Liisu."

Big Peeter bit his lip.

"How's that?" Karl had asked.

"Liisu Koidula. We'll be safe in her flat above the bar until dark."

"You're expecting a bartender who sleeps with Nazis to hide you?" Alexis had asked skeptically.

I strained to remain civil. "Bar *owner*," I had emphasized, "it's her place."

"I stand corrected."

"You may not like her," I added, noting Alexis's objection to my former paramour, "or how she makes her living. But Liisu won't give us up. She has no love for Nazis. She'll keep us hidden until it's time to leave."

Big Peeter had nodded. "Nigul's right. Liisu can be trusted."

Alexis stood up from the couch, walked to a window overlooking the street, and lifted a corner of the shade. Her faded calico skirt shifted as she moved. Sunlight entered the room.

"I hope you know what you're doing," Alexis had murmured, her eyes fixed on the city displayed outside Big Peeter's apartment.

CHAPTER 37
Old Tallinn
(Nigul's Story)

Our route through the city brought us to Tallinn Prison's main gate. It was nearly four o'clock by the time we were in position. Oh, there were a few Estonian policemen who scrutinized our meander but none stopped or interrogated us, so convincing were we in our roles as sailors on leave.

Big Peeter Saul was given the task of talking to Liisu Koidula. I knew he would impress upon my former lover the need for discretion and secrecy. Our lives hung in the balance and depended upon my hunch, my belief, that Liisu could keep her mouth shut.

"I'd wager that's the main entrance," Matti Peltomaa said, resting his duffle on the cement sidewalk and pointing to a wrought iron gate interrupting an ominous stone wall, "but I don't see Elin or Miss Raun."

"It's five minutes to," Karl said, glancing at the watch on his left wrist. "We're early."

I fidgeted. My nerves were raw. I was not anxious to be caught standing on a main street of Old Tallinn with a satchel full of illegal weapons. I lowered my sea bag to the concrete sidewalk, pulled a cigarette from a crushed pack in my trouser pocket, struck a match against the wall behind me, sucked smoke, and pondered the situation.

"I hope to hell they're on time," Peltomaa said uneasily. "We can't stand here too long without drawing attention."

I nodded and took a drag from the cigarette. White smoke ascended against the blue sky as we pretended to talk about something other than the reason for our being outside Tallinn Prison. An alarm sounded. Bells clanged—alerting guards and prisoners alike that a fire had broken out somewhere in the bowels of the stone structure. I smiled.

"Ellisabet's smart. She's creating a diversion."

"Right at the stroke of the hour," Karl added, admiration clear in his voice. "Here they come."

We watched the female warden and an older woman, not dressed in a prison uniform but in the summer-weight blouse and skirt, emerge from shadows cast by prison buildings into a sunlit courtyard. Ellisabet carried a key ring in her hand. Her shoes clacked against cobblestones as she walked towards the prison's main gate with determination. Elin Goldfarb followed the younger woman through warm, sunlit air. The women stopped in front of the prison gate. The warden slid a key into the lock, turned the key, and pulled the gate inward.

"Quickly," Ellisabet said. "The guards and the prisoners not on work release will be searching for a fire. There's no time to waste."

"Thank you," Elin Goldfarb said.

Elin briefly embraced Ellisabet before passing through the prison gate, scurrying across the gravel road, and collapsing in the arms of Matti Peltomaa.

I deserted my companions and walked towards the prison gate.

"Nigul," Karl shouted, "we need to leave!"

I ignored my brother and arrived at the gate just as Ellisabet was turning the key in the lock. "Come with us," I begged. "Come with us to Finland."

My lover looked at me through iron bars with reluctant eyes. "I can't."

"Why?"

"My father—I need to find my father."

I shook my head. "Laak has him. There's no saving him now."

She nodded. "I know. But he is my father. He's all I have left."

I winced. "You have *me*."

She removed the key from the lock.

My hands gripped the weather-pitted iron bars as I looked into Ellisabet's eyes.

"No. We had something once, when we were children. That was long ago. Now there is only my father."

Sounds of boots approaching drew my attention.

"You need to leave," Ellisabet urged.

"Only if you promise you'll come to Liisu's after you search for your father. I won't budge unless you promise."

"Go!"

I shook my head. I gestured to Karl, Peltomaa, and the American woman. The men picked up their sea bags and began walking down the sidewalk with Elin Goldfarb concealed between them.

"I must try. I must try to save him."

"I know. But when you learn that it's impossible, I want you to come with me."

I stared hard into Ellisabet's green eyes but she did not blink. Her right hand reached through the scaly bars and touched my cheek.

"If father's situation is hopeless, I will meet you at the tavern."

I stepped back. "You swear?"

Ellisabet Raun nodded. A clatter arose as the first wave of guards and prisoners landed on the cobblestones of the courtyard.

"Say it. Say it aloud."

Her eyes darted towards the clamor and back to me. “I swear.”

I turned from Ellisabet, crossed the street, grabbed the sling of my duffle bag, hoisted the heavy sack onto my right shoulder, and broke into a jog.

CHAPTER 38

Rohuneeme, Estonia
August 9, 1944

No one in authority discovered them at Liisu's bar. By midnight, when the two Vaino brothers—Hillar, the taller of the two, and Jaan, the thicker, shorter of the pair—pulled up in the alley next to the service door of the rambling old frame building in the Fiat, though Estonian police were combing the streets of Old Tallinn and the surrounding neighborhoods for the escaped Jewess, their scrutiny had not yet infiltrated the shipyards or adjacent businesses.

Elin Goldfarb, her three rescuers, and her daughter exited the tavern and entered heavy mist and fog in the alley where the Vaino brothers waited with the truck. Ellisabet Raun was not with the group. She had sent a hastily penned note with Alexis in her stead.

Nigul:

There is not much time. I have been searching for Father but have been unable to find him. I am sorry I gave you a false impression. I said what I needed to say to make sure you were safe. I never intended to go with you. You talk of leaving Estonia for Canada or America to make a new beginning. I think that is wise. There is too much hardship, too much pain, too much death here. A new start for someone like you—who has skills—is a good plan. I have no skills. I have only worked in the prison under Laak's direction. The allies will likely find me out and give me over to the Russians so I might as well stay here and look for Father. What more can happen to me? Take care of yourself.

Ellisabet

"Shit." Nigul's reaction was unmitigated.

Alexis had spoken briefly to Ellisabet when the Estonian woman stopped by the diner earlier that evening. Alexis, upon joining the others at Liisu's, had handed Nigul Kristian an envelope smelling of Ellisabet's perfume. Ellisabet's words, memorialized as elegant cursive in India ink across fine linen paper, should not have been a surprise. Nigul should have known that Ellisabet's foremost loyalty was to her father. But the Estonian was blinded by love and failed to fully understand the woman he professed to care for.

"Christ!" Nigul's anguish was palpable as he stood at the threshold of the tavern's service door, reading and re-reading the short letter by dim light escaping from the speakeasy.

Karl placed a hand on his brother's shoulder. "We must go."

Alexis walked to the Fiat and joined her mother and Matti Peltomaa in the truck's wooden cargo bed.

"Christ!"

Karl picked up his duffle bag and tossed it onto the Fiat's bed before doing the same with his brother's sea bag.

Nigul shoved Ellisabet's note into a pocket of his trousers and climbed into the truck.

Karl closed the tailgate and joined the others. Peltomaa thumped the cab's rear window. Jaan Vaino gunned the engine and bald tires slipped on gravel as the truck lurched forward.

'Where is she?"

Alexsander Laak stood in front of Ellisabet Raun, a riding crop, his interrogation instrument of choice in his right hand, as he asked the question. Upon learning of Elin Goldfarb's escape Laak suspected who had conspired against him. Ellisabet had been arrested when she returned to the prison after delivering her farewell note to Alexis. The woman sat in a metal chair, her arms raised to shoulder height and tied by rope to iron rings secured to the wall in front of her. Her legs were tied to the chair with the same rope. Ellisabet arched her bare feet and strained against the ropes as she waited for the next blow to land.

This is where he learns secrets.

Her back bore marks from the crop. Her blouse and camisole had been removed to reveal a slender figure of alabaster skin. She sat facing the wall clad only in her skirt. She shivered. Her head turned to see her tormentor. Laak was leering at her nakedness.

Even now he remains a pig.

"Who, Commandant Laak?" She replied slowly, clearly, and without emotion despite her distress.

"The Jewess."

Ellisabet Raun shook her head. "I have no idea."

Smack.

Leather tassels cut skin. Blood trickled down the woman's back. Despite the welling of tears, Ellisabet Raun did not cry out.

"Where is the Jewess?"

There was no one else in the room. Laak's men were out looking for the prisoner. There was little need for them inside the walls of Tallinn Prison. Only seven women remained as inmates under Laak's charge and they, along with Ernest Raun and his daughter, were destined to be delivered to a train bound for Poland before sunrise.

Ellisabet shook her head again.

"I asked you a question!" the commandant screamed, upset pooling in his face, frustration overcoming his professional calm. Another blow landed. Thin leather inadvertently slapped Ellisabet's face. Skin opened. Blood poured from the woman's cheek and pooled on the floor beneath her chair. "Where is the Jewess?"

It was not courage but disgust that kept her from replying. Ellisabet Raun shook her head. Crimson flecks landed on Laak's freshly pressed shirt. The warden ignored the unintended insult and placed his riding crop on the table.

"This isn't going to go well for you, you know? I have the power to make your end painless, to save you from all this."

Tears flowed down the curves of the woman's face. Uncontrollable shivering overcame Ellisabet Raun's strong will. She lowered her eyes.

"Why? Why did you risk your life for someone you don't even know?" Laak's voice changed. Instead of a berating, accusatory tone, he was now asking her questions in the manner of a father seeking information from a child.

Ellisabet Raun did not reply.

Laak considered the woman's exposed breasts and nipples. The thought occurred to him that she was his for the taking.

But what's the use? I need to make an end of this place. The past must be the past and, once I find a way, I will leave Estonia behind. I will settle someplace I can blend in and start anew. I am wasting time with this one. She won't talk. Carnal satisfaction won't be given up by her and so, why am I thinking of her in that way? Fucking a woman who doesn't want it is like fucking the dead. There's no enjoyment, nothing fulfilling in that. To hell with her! She can accompany her precious father to Auschwitz. Let the SS have them both!

Aleksander Laak stared at the black leather handle of the riding crop. Silence passed as he decided whether or not to resume the interrogation. Ellisabet had closed her eyes. She was more resolved to her fate than Laak wanted. The warden relished a victim's fear, needed it to fuel his rage. But Ellisabet Raun was played out—she had only silent stubbornness left with which to rely upon against his anger.

"Understand, Miss Raun that I will find your precious Jewess. Somewhere in this city she is hiding and my men, or the Gestapo, or the Estonian Police, or the SS, will find her. And..." Laak leaned in close so he could smell the woman's nervous sweat before continuing, "...when she is taken, I won't send her with you and the others on the train. I will take her, as your father should have taken her, and then, once I have used her up, I will skin that fucking Jew bitch alive, bit by little bit, starting with her toes and feet and ending with the skin of her once pretty face. That is the end that she will endure because of you, Miss Raun. All because of you!"

It was dark and foggy on the beach where Niilo Niskanen waited. The heat of the late summer's day had dissipated. Visibility was nil. A breeze waxed and waned in cool gusts. The bow of the open launch rested on wet sand. Waves crashed against the little boat. Seawater spilled over the stern and pooled in the bottom of the boat. Niilo rested his overly large hand on the grip of the revolver tucked into the waistband of his dungarees as he waited for the others. A fisherman's shed atop the dunes cast a barely perceptible shadow. No lights illuminated the shoreline. The dwarf glanced at his watch. The numbers of the timepiece glowed in the dark.

"Midnight," Niskanen muttered. "They need to get here in the next hour or we'll be in for it when the sun comes up."

A glow appeared behind the dunes.

I hope to Christ that's them.

A Fiat 508 puttered across hard packed gravel and stopped behind the shed. Headlamps faded. The Vaino brothers exited the truck and removed a canvas tarp covering the human cargo in the pickup's bed. Niskanen started up the hill. His boots sunk into the sand with each step. The dwarf maintained silence, knowing that it was possible the Fiat had been followed, that danger was lurking just over the rise.

"Hey," Niskanen said in a whisper as he walked up to Matti Peltomaa and extended his hand in greeting.

"Hey yourself," Peltomaa replied, returning the gesture.

"Any problems?"

Peltomaa shook his head.

"Good."

Peltomaa and the two Kristian brothers opened their duffle bags and removed Suomis, grenades, and ammunition belts.

"You can keep the bags," Nigul Kristian said to the Vainos as he tossed his sea bag towards the truck. "We don't need them anymore."

Karl Kristian and Matti Peltomaa followed Nigul's lead and added their bags to the pile before locking and loading their machine guns.

"Just in case?" Niilo asked.

Karl nodded.

"We need to move quickly," the dwarf advised. "We must get past Aegena Saar before the sky lightens. The Germans and the Estonians will be out in force at daybreak. We'll be sitting ducks in *that*," the Niskanen added, pointing to the launch. "The old inboard can't outrun a German patrol boat. We need to rely upon the fog and this," the little man said softly, touching his head with a thick finger, "to make it back to Helsinki."

The women shivered in the dank night.

"I'm Niilo," the dwarf said, extending his hand to Elin and then Alexis in turn. "Doesn't look like you two dressed for weather."

"It's all Miss Raun had—the best she could do," Elin whispered.

"There's a couple of slickers in the boat," Niilo replied as the party moved towards the roaring surf. "They'll cut the wind and keep you dry."

Hissing erupted behind scrub brush and wind-affected trees. A star shell burst above the white fog and mist and roiling black sea.

"Shit!" Hillar Vaino shouted. "The bastards followed us."

Light from headlamps cut the fog.

"There's an army on our tail!" Karl Kristian cried out. "Make for the boat!" Karl shouted. "The Vainos and I will try to slow them down." Turning to Peltomaa and Nigul, Karl issued a command: "Give the Vainos your guns."

Nigul considered his brother's order.

"This is no time to debate," Karl insisted. "Get the women to the boat. You and Matti help the dwarf push the boat free of the sand. If they catch us in the open we're sitting ducks."

Nigul tossed his Suomi to Jaan Vaino. The fisherman cocked the machine gun and followed Karl into a line of trees extending from the boat shed along the ridge. Peltomaa handed his machine gun to Hillar Vaino. The tall fisherman joined his brother and Karl behind the trees.

"Push, goddamn it, push!"

Niskanen stood with his feet apart, his hands on the bow of the launch, struggling against the surf. Matti Peltomaa and Nigul Kristian joined the dwarf's effort and pushed the boat into deeper water.

Rat-a-tat-tat.

Gunfire erupted as the flare waned and the sky returned to black. Screams rose as bullets found their targets. The Estonian police had not expected resistance.

"Karl!" Alexis cried out.

Elin Goldfarb was already seated in the boat and wearing a slicker. Matti Peltomaa held the bow of the launch as the dwarf primed the motor and engaged the starter. The engine wheezed and, with some coaxing from the little man's thumb against the choke, caught fire. Peltomaa cocked his revolver, pointed the gun in the general direction of the conflict, and sent a round towards the enemy. It was a foolish gesture: Peltomaa could not discern his target and the distance was too great for accuracy.

"'Lexis, get in the damn boat!" Nigul shouted over the din. "You'll get us all killed."

"I can't leave Karl!"

Nigul Kristian snatched Alexis from the beach and handed her to Matti Peltomaa. The American dumped the woman unceremoniously into the boat and followed her over the gunwale.

"There's no time for argument. Keep your head down. And Niskanen, get this tub moving! Karl knows what he's doing," Nigul said. "He's my brother, and I love him but if we don't get away from this beach we're all going to die."

The dwarf shoved the transmission into reverse as Nigul watched the firefight on the beach with envy. Despite the fog and mist, he knew that the accurate fire of the defenders was taking a toll. Policemen fell. Transport trucks and police cars exploded as bullets hit gas tanks. Though the Fiat was also hit and went up in a column of fire and smoke, Karl Kristian and the Vaino brothers were getting the better of the fight.

"We can't leave him!" Alexis screamed as she struggled to escape Peltomaa's bear hug. "We can't leave him!"

Bullets slapped water. Nigul held his pistol aloft and waded alongside the boat. When the water reached his waist, Nigul Kristian placed the revolver on the launch's floor and dragged himself over the gunwale. With the lanky Estonian safely aboard, the dwarf slammed the boat's transmission into forward gear, turned into the wind, and opened the throttle. As the launch plowed waves, Nigul Kristian listened to sounds of urgent battle, pondered his brother's fate, and realized that, once again, he had not fired a single shot at the enemy.

CHAPTER 39
September 22, 1944
Klooga Labor Camp

Võru fell on August 13th and Tartu on August 27th. Tallinn, the crown jewel of Estonia, fell to the Red Army on September 22, 1944. Free of German occupiers, Tallinn was immediately declared the capital of the new Estonian Republic, Jüri Uluots was installed as president, and the blue, black, and white Estonian flag flew. But when the Soviet Army arrived two days later, the tri-color flag was ripped from its pole and replaced by the hammer and sickle. The flag of independent Estonia would not fly again in Tallinn for nearly fifty years.

Pärnu and Happsalu were taken on September 24th. President Uluots fled to Sweden—where he died less than four months later. The Germans, having been routed from the mainland, tried to reinforce their positions on Estonian islands in the Baltic. Vormsi was shelled on September 24th. Five days later, Soviet forces stormed Muhu Island. Retreating Germans blew up the causeway between Muhu and Saaremaa in an effort to slow the Red Army's advance and Hitler reinforced Saaremaa Island in a last ditch effort to maintain a presence in Estonia. Two months of intense fighting followed before Hitler gave the order to abandon the big island. The Germans evacuated Saaremaa on November 23, 1944, leaving Estonia entirely in Soviet hands.

Estonian trains no longer ran because Russian air power had destroyed the rails. Consequently, Ernest and Ellisabet Raun did not leave Tallinn Prison by train as Aleksander Laak had planned. Instead, the Estonian lawyer and his daughter found themselves bound for Klooga, one of the satellite labor camps operated by the Germans and their Estonian collaborators, in a transport truck. The Rauns arrived at a camp on the cusp of liquidation. As the Red Army advanced, as city after city fell, SS-Hauptstrumführer Hans Aumeier—the overall commandant of Klooga camp and a veteran of Dachau, Auschwitz, Buchenwald, and Vaivara—gave the order to ship the remaining prisoners to Stutthof concentration camp near Danzig, Poland. But by the time Aumeier gave the order to evacuate, Estonian trains no longer had tracks upon which to move.

Ernest Raun was afforded special dispensation and worked in the camp office as the commandant's assistant. But Ellisabet Raun did not fare so well. She was sent, along with the other women from Tallinn Prison, to toil in the fields adjacent to Klooga Camp.

"My daughter could be of use to you, Herr Aumeier," Ernest Raun had petitioned throughout August and September after the Rauns arrived in camp.

Aumeier had not been interested in Ellisabet Raun: not as an office worker and certainly not as a paramour. He did not share Aleksander Laak's propensity for coupling with female prisoners. He was efficient and business-like in his administration of the camp. He had no time, with the rail lines down and the enemy closing in, for such foolishness. But, rather than voice his position on the matter to the unfortunate lawyer, whose days, Aumeier knew, were numbered, the camp commandant simply grunted at the Estonian's repeated entreaties.

"Finish the inventory of the harvest," Aumeier said. "There's much to be done before the Russians arrive."

The commandant's words troubled the lawyer.

What are his intentions towards me? Towards Ellisabet? Surely, I deserve whatever fate awaits me. I've done things and allowed things to be done that condemn me in the eyes of man and God. But Ellisabet? She is so young, so impressionable. I convinced her to join the Party, though she, in the end—unlike me—did the right thing: She allowed the Jewess to escape. That may condemn her in the eyes of Laak and others. But not in the eyes of God. She does not deserve to share my fate.

"Yes, commandant. I'll get right on it, commandant."

Ernest Raun did not share his thoughts with the German. He knew the precarious niche he held in the disintegrating hierarchy of Klooga Camp. The Russians were on Tallinn's doorstep. Soviet fighters and bombers had repeatedly hit the camp. But each time the barbwire fences and guard towers fell, the Germans—despite the obvious futility of continuing the place—rebuilt Klooga. There was palpable finality in the air as the lawyer returned to computing the bales of hay taken in by the harvest, as he counted the eggs collected, the liters of milk churned into butter, the bushels of turnips and potatoes and carrots drawn into the camp's larder.

We receive none of this. We are fed the same gruel, the same disgusting mush day after day after day. An occasional lump of putrid bread is tossed onto our plates. Stale, warm water is poured into our tin cups. Thin, barely discernible coffee is our only treat, handed out sparingly and with much fanfare by the cooks. The fresh produce, the chickens that are slaughtered and roasted, the infrequent pig that is butchered, all of that bounty is for the men who run this place. None of it, none of it is given to us.

It was early morning and the lawyer knew that Ellisabet and a handful of female prisoners were already in the fields on their hands and knees amongst ripe turnips, pulling dusty plants free of the dry autumn soil, depositing the harvest in wicker baskets as they crawled between planted rows.

Ernest Raun had seen his daughter once since their arrival at Klooga Camp. Ellisabet had been standing in bright sunlight washing her face with cold water from a hand pump in the women's enclosure. He had not dared to close the distance, to speak with her, to find out how she was faring. He had been in Aumeier's company, following the commandant on his daily rounds, memorializing improvements to be made, repairs to be completed throughout the camp by pencil in a notebook—Raun's knowledge of German being another reason he'd been spared deportation to Stutthof. As Ernest Raun wrote down Aumeier's directives in clean script, the lawyer had glanced towards his daughter: once beautiful and radiant and proud in her warden's uniform, now haggard and worn in a dirty shift that the breeze threatened to raise indecently. He had wanted to call out to her, to tell her how sorry he was for leading her to this end. But there was no opportunity to do so. As a result, Ernest Raun had silently watched Ellisabet wash dirt from her delicate face and rinse dust from her closely shorn, ebony hair, unaware that he would never see his daughter again.

"Holets," the commander barked at the SS lieutenant entering the camp office, "the Russians are closing in."

Raun feigned disinterest and continued to work while eavesdropping.

"Yes, commandant," the younger officer replied. "They're but a few kilometers away. The army has abandoned us."

"Cowards," Aumeier fumed, running a thin, venous hand over his widow's peak. "Lousy cowards. I have nearly two thousand prisoners to deal with and the army simply folds its tents and runs away. What the hell am I supposed to do?"

Holets, a tall, stereotypical blond-haired, blue-eyed German in his middle twenties was, despite his age, one of the older men remaining under Aumeier's command: most of the other guards at the camp were teenagers. The veterans who'd once manned the camp had been snatched up by combat units to shore up the German defensive effort in Estonia.

The lieutenant removed his cap and looked intently at his superior. "Liquidate, sir. It's the only thing you can do. We need to put down the last of the prisoners and retreat," Holets said, his words taking on the same sort of matter-of-fact inflection one would use when suggesting the disposal of unwanted puppies.

Aumeier bit his lip and glanced at Raun. The Estonian remained at work, writing columns of numbers in pencil on a lined ledger. "He understands German," the commandant replied, his eyes fixed on the lawyer.

The lieutenant shrugged. "Won't do him much good, will it?"

Hans Aumeier stared hard at the dispatches sitting on his desk. The German frowned. "I guess not. Implement the order," the Hauptsturmführer said without conviction, "Execute the prisoners. Stack the corpses, dose them in petrol, and burn the bodies. Do it quickly—before the Russians arrive."

Holets saluted and began to leave the room but stopped before opening the door. "What about the women in the field?" the young officer asked curtly.

Aumier thought for a moment.

"We should secure them as well," Holets added before Aumier could reply.

The commandant nodded.

"Send some men to deal with them," Aumeier directed. "Estonian guards are watching the field workers so one squad of your men should suffice. Have the women dig a ditch and then line them up and shoot them," the older man said quietly. "Dispose of the Estonian guards in the same fashion. Bury them all together," Aumeier added without emotion. "Make sure no one survives. We want no witnesses to our work here."

"Understood." Holets replied before opening the door and leaving.

The pencil shook in Ernest Raun's right hand. Though an intelligent man, a learned man, the Estonian lawyer lacked courage and knew that, even if he was capable of great heroism, there was nothing he could do to save his daughter.

CHAPTER 40
Rovaniemi, Finland
October 9, 1944
(Nigul's Story)

Niilo Niskanen was as good a sailor as our little band could have asked for. The dwarf guided the open launch ferrying Matti Peltomaa, Elin Goldfarb, Alexis Gustafson, and me through fog and mist and rain and tumult from Rohuneeme to Helsinki. The Germans had more important things to worry about than an insignificant boat transporting a handful of escapees. Peace between Finland and the Soviet Union had been finalized. Hostilities between the two nations had ended. An armistice had been signed and, as part of the accord, President Mannerheim agreed to expel the German Army from Finland.

"Do you take this man, Matti Aatos Peltomaa, as your husband, to honor, obey, and cherish, until death do you part?"

Matti Peltomaa and Elin Goldfarb were married in Pietarsaari by a justice of the peace. The couple was given a weekend to complete their nuptials and their honeymoon. Alexis Gustafson, a few members of Rintala's Raiders (including Lieutenant Rintala), and I were in attendance for the uninspired civil ceremony. By the following Monday Peltomaa and me were trudging through heavy, wet snow with other soldiers to confront Germans who refused to leave Finland.

We missed the fight on Suursaari—Operation Tanne Ost as the Germans called it. Our unit, the 3rd Division, was on the mainland, moving north when the Finns defending Suursaari repulsed their former German allies. Matti Peltomaa and I also missed the excitement at Pudasjärvi, the first real battle between the Germans and the Finns on the mainland. However, the 3rd Division did not completely escape the Lapland War (as the new conflict between Finland and the unwelcome German occupiers of northern Finland came to be known).

A small Finnish force under the command of Lieutenant General Hjamar Siilasvuo sailed from Oulu to Tornio in northern Finland. The purpose of the operation was to appease the Soviet Union. Though Mannerheim had agreed to push the Germans out of Finland, nothing much had actually transpired with respect to Mannerheim's promise. The Russians were anxious to see their enemy gone from Finland. Siilasvuo's ambitious plan—to land Finnish troops behind German lines by boat and then, as the defenders pivoted to stave off the amphibious attack, bring a larger Finnish force to bear—was meant to allay Soviet concerns that Mannerheim wasn't honoring the terms of the armistice. Of course, Peltomaa, the other members of Rintala's Raiders, and I had no idea that we were about to participate in the largest battle of the Lapland War. As soldiers, we simply put on our boots, slung our rifles over our shoulders, and followed orders.

As we trudged through melting snow, standing water, and mud on the road between Kemi and Tornio, I mused that Matti Peltomaa had no idea of my legacy in battle. No idea that, despite being in countless engagements, I had never fired my rifle at the enemy. Shame would be too little, too small a label to affix to what I felt as I marched in my gray Finnish Army uniform and my mud and snow covered boots, a low Finnish cap tight to my scalp, a German-style helmet dangling from the back of my rucksack by its chinstrap, towards further humiliation under fire.

We had landed on the beach outside Kemi, a Finnish town a few kilometers east of Tornio. Kemi had once been the primary thrust of the operation but the plan was changed and our objective became Tornio. Other Finnish units would surround Kemi and prevent the enemy from breaking out. As an ordinary soldier on the line, I was not privy to such strategic details. I did not inquire into the overall strategy being implemented by the higher ups. I simply did what I was told.

"How are your feet?" Peltomaa asked, as we slipped and slid towards battle.

The American knew I was suffering. The new leather boots I'd been provided when I joined the Finnish Army had rubbed my feet raw in a matter of a few hours. I'd slapped tape and gauze over the gaping, weeping sores to no avail. The constant friction of stiff leather on flesh, my waterlogged stockings completely useless against the offense, continued. My only choice was to up my resolve, keep my mouth shut, and put on dry socks whenever I could.

"Terrible," I said quietly, my head turned to the rear of the snaking, winding column of gray as I watched dawn leak over the conifer studded horizon behind us. "Nothing seems to help."

"You'd best be careful, Kristian," another soldier said, upon overhearing our conversation. "Trench foot can be a bastard."

I nodded. The pain in my left heel was excruciating. The blisters were open and leaking blood. We stopped. Sounds of artillery and mortars and small arms interrupted the quiet. One hell of a fight was taking place over the rise. Every tree around us was mangled by war.

Shell holes—the snowy ground blackened around the insults—pockmarked a traumatized land.

"Gentlemen," Lieutenant Rintala said as he walked in front of us, "it's time to dump your packs. Leave them here but make sure you take plenty of ammunition and grenades. You'll need them if we're to break the backs of the Germans."

A rebuttal akin to the buzzing of angry wasps arose. Most of us were not anxious to fight. The collective thought was that, since the Germans had saved Finland from becoming another province of the Soviet Union, it was bad form to repay kindness with bullets.

Rintala knew this feeling, knew that many of us were reluctant to fight against our one-time ally. "I know, I know," he said quietly, his voice level, no anger present. "They were our brothers in arms. I know that this turn of events is unsettling. Well," he continued, "I can't have it."

The lieutenant's voice became forceful as he spoke, as he strolled in front of us. "You see," Rintala continued, "as awkward as this might be, it is your duty—it *is our* duty—to see this through. My friends, it is nearly at an end. War is almost behind us. After the Germans are gone, we can go back to fishing, taking saunas, drinking, working, and loving."

Tittering broke out from the ranks.

"Yes, loving, gentlemen. Is that not something worth fighting for? To hold a Finnish girl in your arms and make love to her? How better to forget this bullshit, this mud, this cold, this death, this war? That's what we're here for men: To make Finland safe for our women and our children. So unshoulder your rifles and your Suomis, chamber a round, and let's get to it!"

Cheers rose and fell in waves across the snowy plain as each platoon, each company, each regiment joined the 10,000-voice choir.

We were not among the first to fight. Our regiment was held in reserve for two days. But idle time before battle is not restful. I got no sleep. My eyes were red. My feet throbbed. We ate cold food. Though fires were permitted, they provided little comfort. We huddled inside our winter coats, balanced on our haunches, greedy for warmth, snow and rain and sleet coming down in waves as wind blew in weather from the Gulf of Bothnia to add to our misery. We had nothing to cook over the fire, nothing from which to create a hot, satisfying meal. There was no opportunity to pitch tents because we were only a few kilometers from the front. The report of the big guns was deafening. Sounds of bullets and mortar rounds and artillery shells were omnipresent. One could tell from the noise that hell was being unleashed beyond the next hill.

"When do we go in?" I asked, on the dawn of our second day of waiting.

"Soon," Peltomaa said, sipping hot water tainted ever so slightly with a speck of coffee. "Maybe today."

I nodded and shifted my weight. The slight movement inflamed my left heel. I winced but didn't say anything.

"Feet still bad?" Matti's voice contained concern.

He's a good man. A damn good man. And like Karl, one hell of a soldier…

The remainder of my thought remained incomplete for an instant before I completed it.

…unlike me.

"Once we're in it, you won't notice your feet."

I nodded again.

Damn right. I doubt I'll notice much, including where the trigger on my rifle is.

Peltomaa carried a Suomi. I was outfitted with a Mauser, a rifle taken off a dead German and handed out by our quartermaster.

Strange, I thought as I considered my rifle, *if I ever do fire the thing, I'll be shooting at the Germans with their own gun!*

The Mauser leaned against my belly and chest as we talked.

"You worried?" I asked, changing the subject.

My inquiry wasn't idle. In the months I'd known Peltomaa, he'd aged exponentially. The tufts of gray around his ears had turned as white as unblemished snow. His spritely gait had slowed. Where once the old man seemingly defied time, he'd been brought to earth, made human, by the travails of war.

Peltomaa shook his head and tossed the last bit of rust colored water onto the snow. He turned the empty tin cup upside down on a spruce stump.

I tried not to stare but it was impossible: There was fatigue and exhaustion in the old man's eyes. But that was not unusual. The Finns had been fighting against an overwhelming enemy since 1939 and nearly every Finn under arms was as tired as Matti Peltomaa. Men like Peltomaa had nothing more to give. The old man let my question pass without comment when Rintala suddenly appeared.

"Time to saddle up, cowboys," the lieutenant said, with a wry grin. "The general needs us!"

By the time our regiment made the front, our progress over the slushy ground inhibited by German artillery shells slamming us, thinning our already depleted ranks, the German commander, General Rendulic, had unleashed his reserves. Our regiment was given the daunting task of establishing a *motti*, an entrenchment around the German defenders while other units dealt with enemy reinforcements.

I was dog-tired, sweaty, my feet throbbing, and my hands frozen as I knelt in the narrow groove engineers had hastily dug next to the Kemi-Rovaniniemi Road. The old man and the rest of my platoon crouched behind the meager protection afforded by frozen earth, waiting—waiting for the order to attack. We would leave the protection of our trench, cross open ground, and push the stubborn enemy back to allow the completion of the *motti*. We would settle in for a siege. It would be our task, and the task of our artillery, to hassle and annoy the trapped Germans into capitulation.

"Check your weapons!" Rintala shouted, as he opened the slide of his Suomi and looked into the breach of the light machine gun. "It's time to make the devil dance!"

The sound of bolts sliding on rifles and switches clicking from semi-automatic to automatic echoed throughout the trench.

"There will be a five minute barrage," Rintala said quietly to Peltomaa, "and then, we go."

The American nodded and then looked at me with such awareness, I knew that Matti Peltomaa, like my brother Karl, understood what I was about to do under fire. How he knew my soul, my inner conflict, my cowardice, I cannot say. But it was clear that Matti Peltomaa knew.

"Nothing to worry about son," Peltomaa said as Rintala moved off at a duck-like waddle to speak with the next squad in our platoon. "Stay next to me and you'll come out of this just fine," the old man whispered, as he placed a gloved hand on my right shoulder.

I shook off the gesture. I knew Peltomaa was being thoughtful, trying to quell the bile rising in my throat. But I couldn't countenance it—couldn't allow such kindness to penetrate my façade.

"I don't know what the hell you're talking about," I said tersely. "I've seen this before," I added, pulling off my soft cap and affixing the strap of my steel pot snuggly beneath my jaw.

Matti Peltomaa didn't take offense. Instead, the old man tipped his helmet up so as to study the battlefield. The shelling came and went far too fast for my skittish soul. And then, the order to go over the top was given.

I followed Matti Peltomaa out of the trench, my rifle leveled at the Germans, my right index finger on the trigger, the safety off and ready to fire. The old man moved with uncanny speed and agility, relying upon habit and experience to buoy him in a way that mere youth failed me. A great roar erupted from the Finns as we raced over snowy ground. The winds out of the Gulf of Bothnia had, overnight, frozen everything solid. Wet sea-driven snowflakes floated against the gunmetal sky and whitened the blighted land. The ground was wet. There was much uncertainty to our footing. The distance between our lines and the Germans was only one hundred meters, and yet, the enemy did not open fire as we emerged from our trench.

They're combat tested and patient.

That thought increased my fear. These were not green recruits sent to Lapland, fresh out of German military school. These were seasoned soldiers who had fought the Russian Army, the greatest fighting force in the world, for three years, greatly outnumbered but never outclassed.

Fifty meters into the killing field, the Germans opened up.

Rat-a-tat.

Crack.

Boom.

Machine gun bursts and rifle fire and grenades and mortar percussions echoed inside the storm as we raced towards the enemy. A German soldier revealed himself. I raised my Mauser and trained my sights on the enemy but could not pull the trigger. I could not shoot the man as he, in turn, aimed at Matti Peltomaa, a man who had already suffered wounds in battle.

Smack.

The bullet struck the old man's thigh, the excitement of the fight having altered the German's aim to Peltomaa's benefit. Other shots rang out from soldiers inside the defensive perimeter. Another round struck Peltomaa in the left shoulder and dropped him. The American's Suomi clattered to the frozen turf. A bullet whizzed past my face. Another nicked my helmet. I fell to the ground, my rifle lost to snow, my gloved hands clutching the earflaps of my helmet.

"Fuck," the old man moaned. "Jesus fuck."

I was almost on top of Peltomaa as I watched comrades race past us, grit, if not bravery, clear on their Finnish faces. I don't know how long I stayed beside the stricken man. I do know that, as I watched our attack fail, as I saw Finn after Finn fall short of the Germans, something inside me broke—not in a bad way, not in a way that would make me afraid and fearful for the remainder of my long life whenever an automobile backfired or a firecracker went off—but in a way that was cleansing and freeing. I can't say that I became courageous or brave or heroic. Those are terms applied to soldiers by writers and poets and others who have never known combat. I will say that this change enraged me, emboldened me, and made me finally able to do what I had, for more than three years, been unable to do.

A heavy machine gun was raking our comrades with impunity. Matti Peltomaa moaned but did not thrash. Movement would have drawn attention—and German fire—to us both. I remained as still as a dead man, my face shoved into the snowy earth, my bare hands gripping my helmet while withering fire stunted the impact of the Finnish assault. There was an explosion. Someone had called in a mortar strike on the nearest German gun emplacement. Though the mortar round missed its mark, it created a whirlwind of snow and smoke and debris that gave me an opening. I threw my right hand away from my body, grabbed cold steel, and rose to my feet.

The concussion had stunned the enemy. Finns counter-attacked. The German gunner and his tender did not see me pull a grenade from my utility belt. German soldiers to the right and left of the machine gun crew did not appreciate my arrival inside their trench until it was too late, until I threw the grenade into their midst, until my right index finger pulled the trigger on Peltomaa's Suomi and did what it had been trained to do.

The offensive stalled. It became obvious that we would not be able to encircle the Germans and push them back inside the *motti*. Peltomaa's Suomi ran out of ammunition. I threw all of my grenades. Unarmed and mud smeared, I scampered back to where the old man had fallen. Retreating soldiers missed Peltomaa—missed the fact that he was alive. I knelt next to the old man and touched my left index finger to his throat and found a pulse. I located Matti's wounds and, ripping pieces of bandage from the roll I'd used to bind the wounds on my feet, I stopped the blood oozing from holes in the old man's shoulder and thigh. The flow was slight: the bullets had not struck a lethal blow. Matti Peltomaa was a slight man. I stood up and slung his unconscious body over my left shoulder. Other soldiers saw my predicament, stopped their panicked retreat, and provided covering fire as I carried the American back to our lines. Once safely behind Finnish lines, Peltomaa was transported by stretcher to a medical tent far from the turmoil of combat where surgeons could work on his wounds.

The attack petered out but the enemy was content to leave us alone. The German general was not inclined to counterattack. A waiting game ensued. Very shortly after Matti Peltomaa fell, the last German troops defending Kemi and Tornio vanished through the *motti* like ghosts. Though other Finnish units pursued the spectral enemy, my regiment held fast. We were not there at Rovaniemi when German soldiers leveled the town. We were not part of the fiasco that included the enemy taking civilian hostages in a misguided attempt to trade Finnish citizens for German POWs. And though elements of the 3rd Finnish Division—my division—chased the German Army all the way to Muonio, by the time the Finns organized their pursuit, it was too late: The enemy had avoided our trap and had withdrawn to Norway.

Shortly after I made our lines with Peltomaa on my back, someone noticed that I'd been shot. None of the three wounds to my back were serious. The bullets missed my spine and major organs. It was only after I'd placed the old man on the stretcher when someone noticed bloodstains on, and bullet holes in, my coat. I had not felt the impact of being hit. I was, and am to this day, unable to recall how and when I was shot. Field medics were able to dig out the bullets under the influence of morphine and stitch me up on the front line while fighting raged around us. Sixty plus years later, I still carry reminders of that day: three small scars blemish my very old back.

"I've put you in for the Mannerheim Cross in the Second Class," Lieutenant Rintala advised as we waited to board a transport ship in Kemi soon after the Lapland War had ended.

I was lounging on my rucksack along with thousands of other soldiers destined to board a cantankerous old merchant freighter, the *Pori,* on an early winter's day, snow melting from the warm sun, water flowing across the concrete pier, when Rintala approached.

"What you did at Tornio, how you took three bullets and never faltered, never stumbled as you carried the American to safety, well, that alone is remarkable," Rintala said. "But," the officer continued, kneeling down so that our faces were less than a meter apart, "the courage you displayed in taking out the German machine gun, killing eight of the enemy and saving at least that many of your squad," the lieutenant added as he placed a big hand on the shoulder of my coat, a new one to replace the one that had been shot to hell, "is the stuff of Estonian legends."

I stretched my legs. I knew that such an honor, such an award, which carried with it not only the prestige of heroism under fire but also a substantial monetary prize—50,000 Finnish marks, nearly $10,000 U.S. dollars at the time—was undeserved. I had, on one occasion under fire, after countless failures of will, experienced a surge of adrenaline sufficient to accomplish something extraordinary. Based upon my personal history, I could not accept Rintala's praise. Besides, I was Estonian: I didn't want to accept an honor named after the most famous of Finns, an honor that should be reserved for Finns.

"I don't deserve your praise," I replied, trying to be firm but deferential. "There's much about my service that stands against what you are saying, what you are trying to make of me."

Rintala stood up, frowned, and shook his shaggy blond head like some pissed-off Norse God. "I don't give a goddamn about what you did or didn't do under someone else's command in some other battle!" the Finn roared. The officer's voice escalated to where everyone within earshot stopped talking to listen. "And I sure as hell don't care what you did or didn't do in Estonia. You served under me, Private Kristian, me, Lieutenant Juha Rintala of the Finnish Army. You fought with bravery and distinction, saving the lives of your fellow soldiers in the battle of Kemi-Tornio. Matti Peltomaa? He's alive and back in Pietasaari living with his wife, loving his wife, because of what you did. I need to know nothing more about it, nothing more. You understand, soldier? This conversation is over. I have said what I have said and I have done what I have done and that's the end of it."

I gulped cold, salty air, exhaled, and looked up at the officer towering over me. I was ready to debate the man, to add layer upon layer of fact to our discussion: ample examples of cowardice and inaction supported my demur.

But the broad shouldered Finn pivoted on his heels and walked away, leaving me to ponder what the hell I'd done that was so different from what hundreds, if not thousands, of other men under arms had done during an horrific and unexplainable war.

BOOK FIVE:
THE SINGING REVOLUTION

CHAPTER 1
Otepää, Estonian SSR
1946-1949

The Forest Brothers continued to fight the Russians after the Germans abandoned Estonia. But contrary to Estonian mythology, these partisans constituted a small group: their number never exceeded ten thousand men under arms. Primarily single men in their early twenties and thirties who had stood and fought with Germany during the war, there were older men and married men in the mix as well. But though the guerillas occupy a place of romantic idealism in Estonian lore, in reality, the Forest Brothers had very little effect upon the Estonian Soviet Socialist Republic.

Karl Kristian survived the skirmish on the beach and followed the Vaino brothers inland. The trio skirted the Wehrmacht's panicked retreat as the Red Army pushed west. Against the chaos of impending defeat, no one in authority bothered three young Estonian men on the move. But as the men approached Puhja, they knew they could not linger. The Russians were breaking out of Tartu and pushing Germans and Estonian forces before them like storm water flushing leaves towards a gutter. Karl Kristian and the Vaino Brothers eventually found sanctuary near Otepää, the winter capital of Estonia and the place where Nigul Kristian had once competed in ski races.

For the five years he stayed with the Forest Brothers, clandestinely attacking Soviet military trucks and transports and destroying Soviet guard posts and Estonian police stations with improvised explosives, Karl Kristian lived off the land and the kindness of common folk. Men would come and men would go from the Forest Brothers and rarely did the Russian authorities or their lackeys ever find anyone out. The limited size of the guerilla force was due more to attrition than Soviet counter-insurgency tactics. After months, and in some cases, years, spent hiding beneath the earth in squalid dugouts carved from the muck and ooze of swampy hillocks or beneath canopies of conifers in dense forests, a Forest Brother would become depressed or despondent or stark raving mad due to the isolated nature of his existence. Infrequent forays into surrounding communities, sometimes involving appearances at village dances or at other festive occasions under cover of darkness in hopes of a quick tryst or, at the very least, a quick embrace and a memorable kiss, took a heavy, heavy toll. Most Forest Brothers left hiding after a few months. Those who stayed longer were either dedicated to putting their thumbs in Stalin's eye, simply stubborn, or daft.

Karl Kristian was the second of the three: He was intractably defiant in his pig-headedness. Once the Russians took Tartu and its university, smashing to bits Karl's dreams of becoming a literature professor, Karl Kristian simply had no reason to stop fighting.

It was during these years that Karl Kristian's poetry dried up. Serving in the Estonian and Finnish armies, Karl was always composing fragments of verse on remnants of soup can labels, scraps of stationary, and other bits of paper. After the firefight on the beach, where Karl had fired round after round into the foolhardy Estonian police, killing nearly a half dozen men in the engagement, he thought often of Alexis. He remembered her short blond hair, her differently hued eyes, her figure, her laugh, her smile, and the slight shrug she gave when asked a question she did not have the answer for. But more than all these things, Karl Kristian missed Alexis Gustafson's mind. They were alike in their precocious intellectuality. Alexis was as smart a woman as the young partisan had ever spent time with. This fact and this fact alone, coupled with the knowledge that he was unlikely to ever leave Estonia to find her, destroyed Karl's ability to construct verse. The result of Alexis's leaving was declarative, certain, and eternal and Karl Kristian vowed he would write no more poetry.

But Karl was no monk. The loss of the woman he loved did not end his needs—the elemental desire of an ordinary man. And so, when his fellow Forest Brothers left the dank, cold darkness of their sod dugout doused in cheap Russian cologne stolen under cover of night, their hair plastered to their scalps with hair tonic, their faces and hands scrubbed to shiny hygenity, their civilian clothes newly washed, dried, and pressed with an old flat iron heated on the hideout's woodstove, Karl Kristian did not stay behind to mope. He too ventured out, into the Estonian night, in search of love.

Russian soldiers were garrisoned only five kilometers from Pühajãrve, a village located on the northernmost shore of the lake bearing the same name and but a short distance from the marsh where the Vaino Brothers and Karl Kristian lived. The partisans' journey to the Midsummer's dance in Pühajãrve was not the trio's first foray into town. Hillar, the taller, better looking of the two Vaino brothers, had a paramour who lived with her mother, father, and two little brothers on Kesk Street in Pühajãrve. Hillar had made many visits to the toolshed behind the small bungalow where Keisa Urmi, the nineteen-year-old mousey-haired, big-boned girl Hillar spent time with, lived. Keisa had outfitted the shed's loft with a straw mattress borrowed from a friend's attic, sheets and a blanket her mother would never miss, and a kerosene lantern. Jaan Vaino—the shorter, thicker, and slower brother—was several steps behind Hillar in his search for love. Jaan remained a virgin at age twenty, a circumstance that provided significant fodder for teasing by his older brother.

To earn money for food, ammunition, and supplies Karl Kristian took a job as a field hand during the harvest. The appearance of squadrons of unfamiliar men on government-owned collectives throughout the countryside was something that the Estonian authorities, unless trouble occurred, chose to ignore. With the deportations at the beginning of the war, with the impressment of Estonian men into the Red Army—many of whom never returned home, with 80,000 Estonians having fled to Sweden and Finland as the Russians advanced in late 1944, with other Estonians having followed the retreating Wehrmacht through Latvia, Lithuania, and Poland back to Germany, and with another 20,000 men, women, and children deemed Nazi collaborators deported to Siberia after the Russians returned, farm managers weren't particular about who worked their fields.

• • •

Karl had offered his services to Kolt Sabbe as the two men chatted in Sihva, a small village to the south of Lake Pühajãrve. Sabbe knew who Karl Kristian was before the former teacher opened his mouth. Kolt's cousin, August Sabbe, a defiantly persistent member of the Forest Brothers, pointed out the strapping young partisan to the middle-aged farmer and vouched for Karl as "a boy born and raised on a Puhja farm." That was all it took for the older man to approach Karl at a harvest dance. Kolt Sabbe, though no communist, had been "selected" by the local Party to run what had once been his family farm. In return for this great privilege, the farmer was required to supply his own labor, supplies, seed, and gasoline (for what was once *his* tractor: it was now owned by the State) all purchased at State-run outlets from Sabbe's meager salary. With his only child ill-suited for farm work, with his wife dead and gone—shot in the head when she chanced into a crossfire between retreating Germans and advancing Russians, Kolt Sabbe was desperate. He needed manpower to bring in the barley crop on the 80 hectares of land he managed. The two men met and talked. Karl Kristian offered his services and those of Hillar and Jaan Vaino. A deal was struck and, as soon as Kolt Sabbe needed the men, all three made the journey to the farm.

"Hey," Lovelise Sabbe, Kolt Sabbe's daughter and only child, had said upon first encountering the tall stranger in the barn her family had once owned.

Karl wore a distressed brown felt fedora clamped over blond thick hair. His deep brown eyes were distorted by the lenses of his eyeglasses. Perspiration leaked from the sweatband of Karl's hat and trickled down his cheeks.

He's thin but exceedingly handsome.

This was the first impression that Karl made upon Lovlise as he hoisted squares of fresh hay in the barn.

Karl nodded but, other than this cursory gesture, did not reply.

He's either shy or uppity. Father told me that one of the new men attended university and was once a teacher. He looks, despite the muscles and the grunting and the sweat, to be the sort of fellow who could be a teacher.

The farmhand's quietude didn't dissuade the young woman.

"I'm Lovlise. Lovlise Sabbe. My father, Kolt, used to own this farm."

Kristian straightened the bale on the stack, plucked an errant piece of hay from his shirt, and nodded. The young woman appeared to be no older than fifteen. She smiled unabashedly, revealing overly large front teeth. The impression of her face was one of kind allure; the sort of girl you could fall in love with over time but one that did not strike immediately at your heartstrings or stir you in a catastrophic way. She was short, not much more than one and a half meters tall, with a slight bust and narrow, infantile hips. But there was something about her eyes, as blue and bright an indigo as Karl Kristian had ever seen, that struck a chord. Despite the attraction, the farmhand said nothing.

"All right then," the girl said without rancor. "I'll see you around."

He gradually fell for her. Not as he once had—head over heels, with sexual urgency and immediate angst—for Alexis Gustafson. No, Karl Kristian's attraction for the farmer's daughter took time to build, to grow, to ferment and yield admiration and respect. Though it was clear that *she* was immediately smitten with *him*, the same was not true of his attention towards Lovlise, who preferred, as they became further acquainted, to be called by her middle name, "Marju." Part of Karl's reluctance, his hesitation towards the girl's flirtations, was his perception of her age.

She can't be more than fifteen. She is too young to be making moon eyes at a grown man like me.

Such speculations were laid to rest when Karl found out from Marju's father—in a conversation that likely worried Kolt Sabbe to no end—that the girl was older than she looked.

"How far has Marju gone in her schooling?" Karl asked one day as the men tried to remove the left rear wheel of the farm's old Belarus tractor to replace the rim, which had cracked, and the tire, which was bald.

The farmer looked up, the lever of a pneumatic jack in his left hand, and bit his lip. Though the partisan's use of his daughter's middle name, her familiar name, was disconcerting, Kolt Sabbe tried to control his ire. "Why do you want to know this?"

Karl noted an edge to the older man's question and thought before answering. "She seems very learned, very educated."

Sabbe grunted and returned to lifting the tractor wheel with the jack. The tire rose in herky-jerky fashion until it was free of the ground.

"Have at 'er, boys," the farmer said to the Vainos who were waiting to remove the wheel and tire.

The farmer stood up and wiped sweat from his hatless brow.

Shit. I lose my wife to the war and now this slicker, this book-loving university man, shows an interest in my daughter. What the hell was I thinking bringing these boys onto the farm? Sabbe paused as he studied Karl's face and stroked his thin, gray beard with his left hand. *If he wasn't involved with that nonsense in the swamps, maybe, maybe I could give my blessing. But such foolishness! It never ends, this fighting, this goddamned war. I'm not happy that I lost my farm. I mourn the death of Lahja. But what good do these men, hiding in the woods, think they can do? The Russians are like goddamned fleas on a mongrel: There's no end to them. Shit. What the hell does he want, besides the obvious, with my daughter?*

"Lahja. My wife," Kolt finally said in a tone of absolute reverence, "she filled in what the schools did not teach. Marju finished her last year of local school, in Pühajãrve, at age fifteen: 1944—the year my Lahja left us. Marju was to go off to Tartu, to attend university, like you, that fall. But Lahja's death changed our lives, denied her that."

"I'm sorry," Karl said in as conciliatory a manner as was possible.

The only response from the farmer was another grunt.

Marju was a virgin on their wedding night. Make no mistake: Karl and Marju had groped and kissed before their nuptials, sometimes approaching the level of intimacy Karl desired, only to have Marju wiggle free, and with a teasing laugh dismiss his efforts with an "Oh, Karl, you are such a pig!" It was not that she was uninterested. Karl sensed that she desired him as much as he desired her. Her smallness, her delicate, fragile body, was ready for him. He knew this, or at least, as his fingers found skin beneath her blouse, he sensed this was true by the quickening of her breath, by the sounds that leaked from her diminutive mouth. But Marju's chest formed the boundary where Karl's explorations ended. There was no finality in what they did within the shadows of the barn or beneath the cool shade of the evergreens defining the far reaches of the field once owned by Kolt Sabbe. She was not Ellisabet Raun, his brother's first conquest, yielding herself on a bed of straw in a Tartu stable at age fourteen. Nor was she Alexis Gustafson, a young woman of considerable experience in such things before meeting Karl.

"When we are married, in Pühajãrve *kirik*, then, Mr. Kristian, and only then, we will be free to do what you are insistent about doing!"

Marju's declaration of *her* expectations had compelled much thought from the teacher.

Married? Have I given her false hopes? I had intended for that to be the outcome with Alexis. Indeed that was my plan, such as it was before the beach, before she left in that open boat with my brother and the others, unheard from until two months later, when a letter came telling me she was alive and living in Helsinki, working as a teacher in a refugee camp, trying to earn enough money to return to America. Was what we had a dream? Was it all a mirage? Or is Alexis that fickle, or, to be charitable, that "adaptable"? That's it, Karl finally realized. *Alexis is, given where she came from and what she endured in America, Karelia, Russia, and here, infinitely adaptable. She bears no malice towards me, or any regret for what we had. But she knows, as smart as she is, that "we" are an impossibility: That "we" are separated by an impenetrable Red wall. Estonia has been reduced to a buffer to relieve Stalin's paranoia. Those in the Forest Brothers who dream that our resistance will draw in the Allies to break down the Red wall are fools. It didn't happen in 1944 as the Germans collapsed and it hasn't happened since. I've spent years living in cold, darkness, mud, heat, and mosquitoes. I've given it my all and gained nothing. It's time to get back to living. I haven't seen Father or Mother since the Vainos and I passed through Puhja on our way to the swamp.*

Damn. For a smart man, an educated man, I have allowed my stubbornness to guide me rather than rely upon common sense. There it is again! Alexis is a woman of not only infinite adaptability: She is a woman of innate common sense. It's about time that I exercise some! But why am I replacing one Bible-quoting woman with another? What is it about them, these women who insist upon the Church being instrumental in their lives, that Christian teachings be part of their being, their relationships? Had we stayed together, there is no question Alexis would have made the same demands, invoked the same parameters. We would have said our vows in a church. Alexis may possess common sense and adaptability, but she is no worldlier, no cleverer, for all her education, than this common farm girl I have come to love.

After Marju revealed that *she* intended that they be married, and he came to understand that there was no escaping *his* feelings for the girl, Karl Kristian began the process of extricating himself from the Forest Brothers. Karl's unit had not been involved in an operation for months when he disclosed his intentions to leave, first, to the Vaino Brothers, and then, to his unit leader. There was little surprise expressed by anyone. Karl had been sneaking away from the dugout since his first day as a laborer at the Sabbe farm with regularity. It was his choice, his mates said—his choice to leave, his choice to stay. And so, on Midsummer's Eve, June 21, 1949, Karl Kristian left the Forest Brother's log and earthen dugout in the great swamp to the east of Lake Pühajãrve for good.

• • •

They were married on March 1, 1950 after what seemed to all concerned to be a suitable period after Karl's proposal to Marju and after he offered a stammering petition to Kolt Sabbe for the hand of Sabbe's only child. The farmer reluctantly gave his blessing with the caveat that Karl join the Lutheran congregation in Pühajãrve, where the bride had been baptized and confirmed, and where countless generations of Marju's ancestors had been baptized, confirmed, married, and eulogized.

Andres and Hele Kristian attended the ceremony. Other relatives and friends packed the Lutheran chapel. After a short, dignified service, the well-wishers retired to what had once been the Sabbe farm. In the little white house where Marju Kristian was born and raised, folks stood in small rooms or sat on sparse furniture, holding plates heaped with food and cups of coffee or glasses of libation in hand while chattering in intimate gaggles. It was, despite the omnipresent backstory of Soviet dominion, a slice of gaiety acted out beneath the hammer-fisted grit of the times.

Karl Kristian accepted a position in Pühajãrve and would remain a teacher at the local school for the entirety of his career. He often dreamed of returning to graduate studies at *Tartu Riiklik Ülikool* in literature. But though daily life in Pühajãrve was, by and large, unaffected by the Soviet occupation beyond infuriating lines at the stores, constant shortages of consumer goods, the one-sidedness of controlled news media, limited access to religion, and other restrictions on civil rights; Karl soon realized that the studies offered at the Stalinist-influenced institution did not mesh with his individualism. And so, Karl fed his need to challenge his mind by rediscovering verse.

The Kristian girls, Tiia and Jaanika—born, like their father and their unseen uncle, a year apart—would negotiate the treacherous waters of pre-Glasnost and Perestroika Estonia and stay out of trouble with their parents and the authorities. The girls would eventually move to the bright lights and bustle of Tallinn to find husbands. But to Karl and Marju's chagrin, neither daughter would ever bear children.

Andres Kristian would expire from a heart attack at the age of 62 while smoking his pipe and sanding the birch skin of a new *kannel* as he sat on a three-legged maple stool outside his workshop in the backyard of his home in Puhja. Karl attended the funeral at Puhja *kirik* but his older brother did not. Nigul's letter of condolence arrived at the Sabbe farm, where Karl and Marju lived, weeks after Andres Kristian was placed in the ground and after Hele Kristian came to live with her youngest son and his wife.

CHAPTER 2
Winnipeg, Manitoba
1953
(Nigel's Story)

Aleksander Laak "Anglicized" his name becoming Alexander, or "Alex" Laak, just as I became Nigel Christian when I left Helsinki for Toronto and followed Alexis Gustafson across the Atlantic.

I know. It was foolish of me to covet my brother's lover. But Karl was out of the picture. He was trapped in post-war Estonia and I was a free man. Oh, I wore a certain and heavy weight of guilt because of my younger brother's heroism on the beach. Added to this was the shame I felt at having left my parents, my friends, and my country behind. What would I have done had I returned across the Gulf of Finland to Estonia? One never will know because I chose not to take that road.

I lived, for a time, in a refugee camp outside of Helsinki at Sipoo. A wooden barrack of the Finnish National Ski Team was my home. I was only a building away from the woman I loved. But I did not forget Ellisabet Raun as my ardor for Alexis Gustafson reignited. I tried hard *not* to forget. I sought to recall the smells and the gestures and the face and the voice that made up the woman taken and lost in the fields of Klooga. There was nothing definitive. I have never seen an official document detailing the *exact* circumstance of Ellisabet's death. But I am fairly certain, from all I've gleaned over sixty years of searching, that Ellisabet died in a hail of bullets on the cusp of a shallow ditch. Her name appears on one list: the transport roster bringing prisoners to a work camp. There is no trace of her, no mention of her beyond that notation.

Her father Ernest Raun? His fate is easier to determine. His name appears on a ledger naming the undesirables who were transported to Klooga in August of 1944 *and* appears on another list: An inventory of corpses found and identified when the Russians liberated Klooga camp on September 22, 1944. The lawyer's body was one of a very few left in an identifiable state. Raun's nude and bloated corpse was discovered by itself, away from the smoldering pyres of dead prisoners, a single bullet hole in the back of the lawyer's head.

Alexis would have nothing to do with me in the refugee camp. I understood that she was mourning Karl. Still, I tried to engage her in gossip as there was much to talk about during the idle time we waited for the next act in our lives. The camp where we were interned in Sipoo, north of Helsinki, was full of news about the war, including the biggest question for the Finns: Would Stalin invade Finland now that the Germans were gone? Just because Mannerheim had made a promise to Stalin and Stalin had made a promise to Mannerheim, we all knew—as we waited the end of the war in the crowded camp—it didn't mean a goddamn thing.

Hell, Hitler promised he wouldn't invade Russia, that Germany and Russia would divide Europe like children sharing a cluster of grapes. See what became of that promise, would you!

But Stalin had no interest in losing more men on the northern front. He was pressing the Germans along a vast line from the Gulf of Finland to the Black Sea. The Red Army was on the move, intent upon reclaiming territory that had once been part of the Soviet Union. It was equally obvious that, unless the Allies objected, Stalin would extend his military and political influence throughout Eastern Europe. All of this was the stuff of talk and argument between the displaced Finns, Estonians, Karelians, and Ingarians living in the camp. But one thing that was not discussed was Finland's role as a co-belligerent of Germany.

As soon as the Germans left Finland, silence regarding this truth descended over the country like the final curtain on a bad play. "Now," folks chastised, "is not the time to deal with recent history, with whether or not the decision to stand with Hitler was the wisest choice or the best choice." Discussions of such things, did, of course, took place in living rooms, parlors, and kitchens of homes and log farmhouses and apartments from Helsinki to Oulu. But public discourse, an open rending apart at the seams of how and why such a thing was necessary or wise or required? Such introspection was not done in the open by self-respecting Finns.

This was because the peace agreement brokered by Mannerheim was a total and utter humiliation for Finland. Under the terms of the accord, the U.S.S.R. reclaimed all the territory the Red Army had conquered during the Winter War including Viipuri and most of Karelia. As the final border was drawn, hundreds of thousands of Finnish-speaking Karelians fled to Finland and were placed in refugee camps like the one in Sipoo. Finland was also required to pay significant reparations to the Russians. And finally, Porkkala (a seaport located within spitting distance of Helsinki) was leased to the Soviet Navy for fifty years. The message of Porkkala, more than any other aspect of the armistice, was that, at least in the eyes of Stalin, the Finns were untrustworthy neighbors who needed to be watched.

"*Hei*," I would say as I approached Alexis.

Her blond hair had grown out and was tied in a ponytail. Her feminine curves were concealed in hand-me-down clothing but I still found her striking.

"*Hei te itse*," was the only response I could elicit from the woman.

She must hate me.

I would claim an empty seat on a bench next to her at the long, wooden mess table she was sitting at, drinking her coffee, talking with other women. But try as I might, I could not get Alexis to engage, to open up about her plans or whether she held anything, anything at all, in her heart for me. I knew it was a long shot, as Americans like to say in sports parlance, a "Hail Mary." But I was in love. What else could I do? Our standoff continued for months until, as all of us at the camp made plans for our next adventure, I finally forced Alexis to talk plainly and openly about what had happened.

"You left him," she said. "You left him on the beach fighting for his life. And you left Ellisabet, someone you supposedly loved as much as Karl, to die. You are," she had said very softly, so the others sitting around the table could not hear the words, "no hero."

Delivered matter-of-factly and without rancor as it was, the accusation stung. And I knew, at least in part, that her observation that, despite the Mannerheim Cross, I was a coward, was true. But though there were facts to support Alexis's opinion of me, there was also falsity in her accusations. Karl, not I, had made the choice to stay and fight so *we* could leave. I did not "abandon" my brother. And Ellisabet? Alexis knew better on that score, for she was the one who delivered Miss Raun's letter to me before we left Tallinn. Ellisabet's determination to stay in Estonia was her decision, not mine. Certainly, I lamented the choices Karl and Ellisabet made and I could have objected to their decisions with more vigor but my protests would not have changed a thing.

But what Alexis Gustafson said about me on that afternoon, the day before she left Finland for Canada, contained a kernel of truth. I knew, in my heart, my own history more completely and more thoroughly than anyone except Karl. Karl had been by my side for every skirmish, every engagement, every battle save one: The one for which I was awarded the Mannerheim Cross of the Second Order.

The one time I did what I was trained to do and my damn brother is hundreds of kilometers away hiding in an Estonian swamp!

"You're right," I had finally conceded, as I drained my coffee cup and stood up from the roughhewn table under draped canvas. "I left Karl. I left Ellisabet. I'm a sonofabitch."

Though I'd walked away in a huff that afternoon, my upset did not cause me to abandon my quest. I followed Alexis to Halifax and then by rail to

Toronto, where we both changed trains and went on, with two dozen other Estonian expatriates, to Winnipeg. I tried to bump into Alexis at various cafés and pubs and public places in the Manitoban capital, even being so bold as to once show up (unannounced and very drunk) at her apartment on Dysart Road, which I am certain did not assist my cause. My persistence was to no avail. By the time my father died, Alexis had completed her biology degree at the University of Manitoba and had moved on to McGill University in Montreal where she enrolled in medical school. A letter I sent to Alexis at McGill was returned. The handwritten notation on the unopened envelope read: "Refused—Unwanted Mail." Alexis's message was undeniably clear: "Stay away from me. Get on with your life." So I did.

Soon after settling into a studio apartment near downtown Winnipeg, I was apprenticed as a lineman at Winnipeg Power. I was—my supervisor said—a quick study. Within a year, I was managing a crew, earning a good salary, and ready to move on.

News from home was, at first, nonexistent. A few years into Stalin's rule, contact with Estonia improved, though the post was still slow and censored. The few letters Karl and my mother sent told of a mundane life. There was little of substance to the brief notes I received. I was, of course, saddened to miss Karl's wedding and Father's funeral. But travel to the E.S.S.R. in those days was nearly impossible and, if possible, prohibitively expensive. In the mid-1950s, there was no easy way to get from Winnipeg to Tallinn. And so I missed important benchmarks in the history of my family.

Of significance to my time in Winnipeg was an incident that took place in 1949, my first full year in Canada. Maybe "incident" is too strong a word. "Encounter" is a more accurate term. My supervisor at work, Tunne Laar, a half-Estonian, half-Icelandic elf of a man with a shaved head, big feet, and a hearty laugh, had worked the forests of northern Ontario as a logger before accepting a job with Winnipeg Power. We became friends and, in an effort to broaden my social horizons, Tunne dragged me to a dinner-dance at the Estonian Heritage Society one chilly winter evening.

Here is what I remember about that occasion: Though Alex Laak seemed unremarkable in appearance when Tunne introduced Laak to me, I became interested in the man's story. The former Estonian officer was proclaimed by my boss to be a "war hero," a man who fought long and hard against the Russians for our beloved *Eesti*. What did I know? At the time, I made no connection between the war hero in front of me and *the* Aleksander Laak.

The evening was pleasant enough. The drinks: cold and refreshing. The food? I don't remember what was served. But, to the end of my days, I will remember my first encounter with Aleksander Laak.

CHAPTER 3
Biwabik, Minnesota
1960
(Nigel's Story)

I emigrated from Canada. Before moving to the States, I had visited Duluth, Minnesota—a modest city tucked into significant hills scolded by the angry waters of Lake Superior—on one occasion. In addition to the hills, the water, the conifers and birches, and the opaquely prescient gray skies, it was the intangible "mood" of Duluth that captured my heart and made me feel: *I am home.*

This is not, I learned, an uncommon reaction from folks who hail from northern Europe. The city struck me, gripped me, as I've related, like no other place I've visited. And there was work, during the heady expansion-oriented, post-war economic boom of the 1950s, for an electrician in Duluth. After a vacation visit to Duluth in the summer of 1953, I returned to Winnipeg with three job offers including the position I ultimately accepted: Head lineman for Minnesota Power. But a catch ensued. A Minnesota Power employee stationed in Chisholm (who wanted to move his homesick Duluth-born wife back to the city on the big lake) snatched the job I'd been offered.

"Sorry to tell you this," the Minnesota Power official I was dealing with said during a long distance telephone call, "but the job we had in mind for you has been filled."

I was stunned.

Is a deal not a deal in America?

"Mr. Christian?"

I remained silent.

"There is another option, Mr. Christian, one that we hope you'll accept."

I swallowed. "Yes?"

"There's an identical position opening up in Biwabik, up on the Iron Range."

I thought hard, playing the vision of Duluth's lakefront and the great blue field that extended from the city's downtown unimpeded to the north, a never-ending sheet of fresh water that made Lake Peipus, the largest lake I'd ever visited prior to being in Duluth, appear trivial, over in my mind.

But I want to live in Duluth!

"I know you're disappointed, Mr. Christian. Believe me, I'll understand if you don't want to leave your current situation in light of this change. But my boss has advised me that, given our needs in Biwabik and your talents and experience, I'm authorized to 'sweeten the pot,' so to speak."

"What does this mean, 'sweeten the pot?'"

"Ah. Well, it means quite simply that Minnesota Power will increase our salary offer by 25% and also agree to pay for your mileage, truck rental, and any other expenses you incur moving to Minnesota."

The hills and the lake are beautiful, but the money in Biwabik is better...

And so, I began my life in a mining town—a village really—on the eastern end of the Mesabe Iron Range. It was there that I learned to love again. I met my future wife, Grace Blatnik Sippola, the mother of my two daughters (Emily and Emma, born three years apart, 1957 and 1960) at a dance at the Biwabik VFW where, as a combat veteran and a nationalized American citizen, I was granted membership. No one at the Club knew about the Mannerheim. Even Grace, after we were married and settled into our house—the logs milled from red pine harvested from the forty-acre site I bought with money saved from my job in Manitoba—never saw the Mannerheim Cross. The medal was relegated to a maple box, along with several other service ribbons and pins from the Finnish and Estonian Armies, in a closet of our garage.

At first glance, Grace Sippola was not my type. She was loud and demonstrative and funny. And, most disconcerting to a fallen Lutheran like me, Grace was Catholic. These deficits were failings that I could overlook in a woman who was physically appealing. But in contrast to my preference for short, more fully figured women, Grace was tall and as thin as a rail: nearly six feet and a mere 130 pounds I'd gauge she was the night we first met. And Grace's dimensions never changed a whole hell of a lot over time. Oh, she'd gain twenty to twenty-five pounds during pregnancy. But she never showed it much. And she lost the weight, without residual flab or stretch marks, within a few months of delivering our children. But strictly from a physical standpoint, I have to admit: Grace wasn't my type.

All told, there were three. The two girls came first. Then we lost a son, Daniel, at birth. He was born full term but something went wrong in the delivery room of the Virginia hospital. Daniel died in 1962 and other than mourning our collective loss and having a seemingly futile Catholic funeral, there wasn't much more Grace or I could do about it.

Despite her religion, Grace sinned: she insisted I use condoms during any lovemaking we engaged after Danny's death until, when tubal ligations became prevalent, my wife chose surgery as a permanent solution to her fertility. She could not handle losing another child and wanted to put an end to the possibility of more grief, regardless of what the Church had to say about it.

Despite my resistance to finding Grace Blatnik Sippola attractive, that night at the VFW I fell in love with the tall, willowy Iron Ranger.

It was a great bargain I made, accepting someone different in stature and physical attributes from anyone I'd pursued. Grace was, like me, naturally conservative with money. She was raised by her mother after her father died in a car crash. Budd Sippola perished on a gravel road outside Ely, driving back to Virginia, where the family lived, from walleye fishing. He was traveling in the dead of night, having stopped at the Chainsaw Sister's Tavern for one too many bottles of Grain Belt. Due to the circumstances of Grace's upbringing, where every penny needed to be measured, she was as frugal a partner as I could have asked for. She was, however, if the circumstances were right, willing to take a risk, which is what we did in 1958.

I'd been with Minnesota Power for four years when we bought her father's electrical contracting business from Grace's Uncle Floyd (who had been named the administrator of Budd's estate). We paid Floyd over time: so much down and so much per month. The note was for ten years. We paid it off in five.

Before I sold the business (our girls expressed no interest in electrical contracting) there were over fifty men and women working for Sippola Electric. Grace and I also owned Christian, Inc.—a building construction firm—and E&E Ski Touring—a cross-country skiing bed-and-breakfast that Grace and the girls operated for a time. Along the way, Grace and I also bought up old buildings in Biwabik, Gilbert, Aurora, Ely, and Tower, all of which, save the business block in Biwabik that I still own, we renovated and sold at a profit.

As I became more prosperous, I became better known around the Iron Range and had the opportunity to interact with Grace's maternal relative, Congressman John Blatnik. It was through the Congressman that I was able to piece together the story of Ellisabet Raun's death.

One does not survive combat without wounds of some sort. My most significant wounds are not scars on the paper thin, draping skin of an old man's back nor are they flashbacks of Matti Peltomaa and other men I served with being struck down by enemy fire. No, when I reminisce, when my Biwabik apartment falls silent on a cold winter's day, the television off, a copy of the latest *Duluth News Tribune* resting in my lap, the Mannerheim Cross of the Second Order hidden in the same box, in the same closet where it has always been kept (in the garage adjacent to the log home Grace and I built overlooking Sabin Lake where our daughter Emily now lives rent-free as a divorced woman with her son Benjamin) my wound from that time stems from this reality: I did nothing to save Ellisabet Raun. Karl, despite the struggles he endured, has lived a decent life. I am not troubled by the memory of leaving my brother on that Estonian beach. But Ellisabet? What of her?

It could be said that, as a collaborator, she, in the end, got what she deserved. But did she? At personal risk, she saved Elin Goldfarb from the firing squad or, more horrifically—if one form of death is worse than another, you judge, I cannot—the gas chamber. Because of Ellisabet's bravery, Elin married Matti Peltomaa, resumed her work as a reporter, and lived a long and fruitful life in Pietarsaari.

Matti Peltomaa? Yes, I saved his life in one panicked misstep of heroic action. And he too lived. Not so long as his wife. But he lived long enough to enjoy peace in his adopted country. But these circumstances, in my humble view, are not equal because I did what soldiers are *expected* to do. Ellisabet Raun did the *unexpected*. She saved someone she was not obligated to save. And this is why a never-fading image of Ellisabet's face is the most debilitating scar I bear from the war.

"Thank you for seeing me, Congressman."

Nikita Khrushchev had opened things up a bit after Stalin's death. Though he was no great friend of the West, the Soviet Premier knew that, to continue on with the purges and horror and terror associated with Joseph Stalin would be counterproductive. Khrushchev's attempts—to loosen the strictures of daily life, to make things more tolerable and less onerous for ordinary Soviet citizens—allowed information concerning how the Soviet Union was dealing with the atrocities committed by the Germans and their allies to find an audience in the Western press.

My interest in Ellisabet's fate was fueled by articles in *TASS* and other news sources regarding the Holocaust trials that were set to begin in Estonia during the early 1960s. It was while reading one such article that the name "Aleksander Laak" came to my attention. Curious about what had transpired after I escaped Estonia, I read all I could find concerning the upcoming court proceedings. My study increased my interest in the man known to me as "Alex" Laak, the Estonian war hero I'd met in Winnipeg.

Is he the same man being discussed in the newspapers?

"You've been a generous contributor to my re-election efforts over the years, Mr. Christian. And being married to a relative of mine..." the tall, athletic looking ex-OSS man, a man who had parachuted into Yugoslavia during the war to confer with Tito, had said "...gives you a leg up on seeing me on short notice."

The formalities over, I sat down in a chair in front of the congressman's desk. Our meeting took place in Blatnik's office in the federal courthouse in Duluth, a copy of a Russian language newspaper in my lap. I took a deep breath. I sensed the congressman was busy, that he wanted me to get on with the reason behind my visit.

"You said this was about atrocities in Estonia, during the war, you say?"

I nodded, still uncertain of my suppositions.

"The Balkans, now there's a part of the world I know something about," the politician said through a smile, tilting his head, the lenses of his eyeglasses catching light. "But the Baltic? I'm afraid, beyond elementary school geography, I don't know a whole hell of a lot about the Baltic!"

I smiled. John Blatnik knew much more about world politics than he was willing to let on. I opened the newspaper to an article about the upcoming Holocaust trials.

"This article..." I began, "...I think I know one of the men named in it."

Blatnik leaned forward and looked at the photographs of the three men featured in the story. The captions included the names Jaan Viik, Ralf Gerrets, and Aleksander Laak.

"Which one?"

I pointed to Laak's picture with my right index finger.

"How do you know this man?"

I hesitated before answering. I wasn't certain that the man I knew as "Alex" Laak was one in the same as the war criminal sought by the Russians.

"I met a man named 'Alex Laak' when I lived in Winnipeg."

Blatnik frowned. "The same man as the one wanted for war crimes?"

"I think so."

"Are you certain? Absolutely certain? If you are, the people who need to know about this are the Israelis, not the Russians. The Israelis have been doing a fair job of finding these bastards."

I took a breath before making a concession. "I can't be absolutely certain. This photo is years old. Taken before Laak left Estonia. But it appears to be the same man. It's very likely him."

Blatnik folded the newspaper in half. "May I keep this?"

I nodded again.

"Do you know," the congressman whispered confidentially, "if he's still in Winnipeg?"

Another pause.

"So far as I know."

The congressman stood up. "I'll take care of it from here. Thank you for bringing this to me. You did the right thing, Mr. Christian, the right thing."

I did not move.

"There's more?"

I nodded. "I feel responsible."

"For what, may I ask? You're a decorated war hero, for God's sake. Mannerheim Cross—the equivalent to our Medal of Honor. Only one of those men here in Duluth. Fellow by the name of Colallilo. At the doorsteps of Germany when he did what he did, I believe. You're right up there with him, Mr. Christian. What do *you* have to feel responsible for?"

I hesitated before continuing. "There was a woman. An Estonian. A collaborator. Her father was a Nazi. She was in the Party as well. They both worked for Laak. I'm certain, from what I've been able to discover, that her father died at a place called Klooga: A labor camp where thousands were murdered just before the Russians liberated the place. Not Laak's doing. But just like something he *would* have done."

The congressman removed his glasses. "Bastards," he muttered. "Rotten stinkin' bastards.The woman, you knew her...?"

"We were..." I hesitated to use the word that fit best, "lovers" for fear of diminishing Ellisabet's reputation. I chose a less inflammatory noun. "...friends. She was very brave, saved the life of a Jewish woman I knew. An American actually. The woman and her Jewish husband went to Karelia as part of 'Karelian Fever,' in the 1930s."

"Communists, I'd wager."

I ignored Blatnik's observation. "The collaborator, Ellisabet Raun, saved the Jewish woman."

Blatnik claimed his full height and stroked his chin. "What happened to the collaborator?"

I gulped. "I think she was shot. Like her father."

The congressman frowned. "I'm sorry. I'll pass along what you've told me. I'll try to see if there's any information about the woman...what was her name again?"

"Raun, Ellisabet Raun."

CHAPTER 4
Winnipeg, Manitoba
September 6, 1960

The man felt isolated. He was not a person of wealth or power. He lived with his wife in a suburban tract house in a Canadian city that was large enough for the man to blend in, to remain inconspicuous, and remote enough from the prying eyes of the central government to ensure his anonymity. To be sure, he had come there—after the war—legally. His immigration and citizenship papers, his status as a refugee from Soviet terror, were all correctly documented. Every "i" had been dotted and every "t" had been crossed. But lately he'd been forced to ponder distressing events unfolding in his former homeland. The exaggerated accusations. The unfairness; his boss, Martin Sandberger, was given a death sentence and then, due to the efforts of German American politicians, granted clemency and released from prison. The inflated claims of sexual brutality; there were never any "orgies"—only occasional trysts between the man and his female prisoners. How could you trust accounts of ancient wrongdoing coming from Communist Russia? You couldn't, the man surmised. And yet, there it was.

There's no one to confide in.

His wife did not know what had gone on at Jägala, Kalevi-Liiva, and Tallinn Prison. At fifty-two years old and a retired soldier, he remained emotionally distant to the point of creating uncomfortable silence whenever anyone, including his wife, broached the topic of his status as a "war hero." And he found the Estonian Heritage Society outings insufferable: All those émigrés fawning and cooing over what they perceived he had done during the war.

If they only knew, he thought. *The work Sandberger, Viik, and I accomplished was demanding, exhausting, detailed—and underappreciated for its vital importance in stabilizing Europe. If Jews and other radicals had been allowed to roam free, to go about their political business, sowing seeds of dissatisfaction and discontent, well, there would have been no end to the riots and demonstrations and difficulties. Our work made the home front void of such unpleasantness. And the wealth confiscated from the usurious Jews was welcomed by the powers that be. That wealth kept tanks and planes and ships coming off German assembly lines. But the questions—I cannot bear the questions. The truth would be too complex, too difficult, for most people to understand.*

The TV was tuned to the CBC. He sat in his favorite overstuffed easy chair, a cold can of Labatt's on the table within reach, the can opener next to the beer, a bowl of saltines and a plate of pickled herring close at hand. His wife had gone to the cinema with a friend. He didn't like movies much and rarely went: He had little interest in fables. He had lived the biggest, most complex story of his age and could not fathom resorting to his imagination to supplement his real-life experiences.

As he sat watching the black and white screen flicker, a foreboding, a feeling of dread, entered the comfortable house like an errant draft.

The news is not good. Of course, it wasn't good in April of 1946 when the world learned what Jews, and angry Jews at that, are capable of. Nearly 2,000 sickened, hundreds dead, when the so-called Nokmin, *the Holocaust avengers, put cyanide in the bread of German prisoners at Nuremberg. 300-400 defenseless men died grotesque deaths at the hands of those vindictive scum! The plot was supposed to be the beginning of "an eye for an eye" series of revenge killings. The* Nokim *wanted to kill one German for every Jew who died in the camps. Of course, the number of claimed Jewish dead is a fabrication. Nowhere near six million perished. Of that, I am certain. Despite the lies, even the Canadian press is getting into the act. Papers here, and in Ottawa, and Toronto, and in Halifax, and in Vancouver are all hinting and guessing as to what I am, what I did. Fuck them! Fuck them all.*

The man picked up the Labatt's, his fifth since his wife went out, opened it, drained it, and placed the empty can on the imitation oak table. He closed his eyes, and soon, he was fast asleep, far away from his troubles.

The front door opened. Autumnal night air infiltrated the house. Three men stepped into the foyer. Their presence did not disturb the slumbering man. Even when the biggest, the burliest of the trio stood in front of the sleeping homeowner, the man in the easy chair did not stir.

"Wake up."

Alex Laak's eyes jetted open. "What the hell!"

"Keep your voice down," another of the intruders said firmly as he displayed a nasty looking silver plated semi-automatic pistol tucked in his belt. "We don't want to make this messy."

"Who the hell are you?"

Laak's eyes were blurry. As his pupils became accustomed to light, they focused on the man who had shaken him.

"There's nothing of value here," Laak said, his voice quaking. "No money. No jewelry."

The man standing in front of the Estonian was wearing a blue jacket, casual black slacks, and a powder blue button-down dress shirt. He wore no tie. The top button of the man's dress shirt was undone, revealing a clean, white undershirt.

"That's not why we're here," the tall man whispered.

"We know who you are," the third stranger, the shortest, burliest of the group, added.

"I am Alex Laak. What of it?"

There was a slight nod from the intruder standing over the victim.

"As in 'Lieutenant Aleksander Laak,' commandant of Jägala camp?"

Laak blinked.

"He doesn't disagree," the one with the pistol observed. "I'll take that as an admission."

Laak opened his mouth to object but found he had nothing to say.

"Better to simply listen, Mr. Laak," the tall man said. "And better to do this in your garage."

Laak stood up and walked towards the door leading to the home's attached garage. Despite his mounting fear, Laak kept up appearances. He held his head as if he was still an officer inspecting guards under his command. The men entered the cool garage. Petrol fumes hung in the air. The garage was empty: Laak's wife had taken the family car. Cold from the concrete floor leaked through Laak's socks and he began to shiver.

"Should have put on shoes, Mr. Laak," the tall one said. "It would be more dignified if you were wearing shoes."

Laak's face flashed concern.

"My wife is due home any moment."

The tall man glanced at his wristwatch and smiled.

"The motion picture won't be over for forty minutes. We have plenty of time."

A lump formed in Laak's throat. "What are your intentions?"

The tall man smiled. "I have a question before I suggest something to you."

Laak swallowed but didn't speak.

"Do you remember a woman at Tallinn Prison, an Estonian Nazi, a Miss Raun?"

The name did not spark recognition with Laak. He shook his head.

"She was the daughter of Ernest Raun, a collaborator you sent to Klooga. He died there. This, we have record of. The woman, she was sent there too. But as to her demise, there is no documentation. Do you remember what happened to her?"

Laak struggled to understand why he was being asked questions about someone so inconsequential. "I have no recollection of such a woman."

"Survivors said she was in the fields when the Russians liberated the camp. Does that ring a bell, Mr. Laak?'

An image of a dark haired, green-eyed young woman, a very prim and dignified and beautiful young woman, emerged from the mists of the past.

Ah. Ellisabet Raun! Yes, of course, I knew her. She died in the fields with the others. It's a pity that one so beautiful, and an Estonian girl no less, was sent to her death in such a fashion. I didn't order it. Klooga wasn't my camp. But I would have done the same thing. She helped that old Jew woman escape. An example had to be made of Miss Raun. Of course I remember her.

Laak did not reveal what he remembered.

"He doesn't know anything about her," the shorter man said. "Let's get on with it."

The tall man pulled a length of clothesline from a jacket pocket and nodded to the man holding the automatic. The man with the gun retrieved a stepladder leaning against a wall of the garage.

"What's that for?" Laak asked, gesturing towards the clothesline.

"We all make choices in life, Mr. Laak. For example, you could have decided—when the Germans came—to fight the Russians. That would have been admirable service to your country. But instead you chose to run a labor camp where innocent civilians, many of them Jews, died. That was the choice you made, Mr. Laak," the tall man said, carefully forming a noose with the rope as he spoke. "So here is another choice for you to make. You can slide this rope over your head and climb the ladder. I'll secure the other end of the rope to one of the rafters. And then, when you are ready, I will kick the ladder away. Or, if you have sufficient courage, you may step off the ladder yourself."

Laak began to tremble. "You have offered me only one choice: To hang myself in my own garage!"

"I am not finished. The second option, for you, lieutenant, is to allow us to take revenge upon you for all of our Jewish brothers and sisters slaughtered at Kalevi-Liiva. I am thinking that a suitable death for someone like you would be slow, and agonizing. Perhaps," the tall man said, pointing to a red petrol can sitting on the garage floor near the garage's far wall, "being burned alive. Yes, that would seem appropriate since many of the bodies you and your fellow murderers burned in Estonia were not yet dead when you put the match to them. Yes, being burned alive would be fair, I should think, for someone like you."

Laak's eyes widened. "Please..."

"There's no one here who wants to listen to you, Mr. Laak. One minute. I will give you one minute to make your choice."

Laak's hands trembled as he climbed the rickety ladder. Standing unsteadily on the last wooden step, Alex Laak looked down at the intruders.

"You aren't God, you know," the condemned man whispered, accepting the rope from the tall stranger, placing the noose over his head, and tossing the free end of the clothesline over the nearest rafter. "You aren't God..." he repeated as he tightened the rope around his neck.

"I never said I was," the tall man calmly replied as he tied the rope to a pine rafter. "In fact, after what I've seen, I'm not so sure I believe in God."

Alex Laak stood on the ladder's last step, the noose tight to his throat, the short drop ready to snap his neck. The condemned man inched his feet forward, took a deep breath, nodded, and closed his eyes.

CHAPTER 5
Pühajãrve, Estonia

Hele Kristian lived long enough to attend the 1985 Song Festival in Tallinn and sing the verses to *Mu isamaa, mu õnn ja rõõm* ("My Fatherland, My Happiness and Joy"), while other singers on stage and the entire audience—over 100,000 voices—joined her on the chorus. Hele's voice was no longer strong: It was but a faint whisper of what it had once been. But her optimism that day, standing as tall as her arthritic back would allow at the microphone, singing as loudly and as in pitch as possible, mirrored that of her country. When she died in her sleep on the Sabbe farm in Pühajãrve at the age of 88, Hele Kristian was a content woman; Estonia was on the cusp of freedom and she had lived "to see the worm turn," as she was prone to say.

It began with Khrushchev's efforts in the late 1950s; with his recognition that the leadership of the U.S.S.R. had to allow the Soviet citizenry access to consumer goods, decent food, and safe housing. By the 1960s, though there was still no freedom of speech, freedom of the press, or freedom of religion in the E.S.S.R., the lives of ordinary Estonians had become less onerous under Khrushchev's policies. There were bumps in the road, so to speak; the Hungarian and Czechoslovakian crises temporarily derailed progress. But that was in the past and as times and regimes changed, people throughout the Soviet empire began cautiously petitioning their leadership through quiet, non-public backwater channels for further improvements in their daily lives.

When Mikhail Gorbachev became the Soviet premier in 1985, he brought two new concepts to Soviet governance: *glasnost* (freedom of speech and criticism) and *perestroika* (individualized economic freedom under the umbrella of socialism). The new leader calculated that less authoritarian views would preserve the Soviet Union. But Gorbachev was wrong in his assessment: The liberalization he implemented created political movements that, short of armed intervention similar to the force utilized to quell unrest in Hungary and Czechoslovakia, could not be contained.

As Soviet dominion over Estonia weakened, Karl Kristian became active in the Estonian independence movement. Karl's involvement in radical politics did not happen overnight. He remained apolitical for the better part of three decades. But with the opening of Estonia's borders, Karl began to listen to Estonian scholars and scientists and businessmen and athletes returning from their travels. From these conversations Karl Kristian gained insight. He began writing poetry that, had it been published during Stalin's reign of terror, would have likely seen him "relocated" to Siberia or worse. Though never collected as a body of work until after independence, Karl's poems were privately circulated to friends, acquaintances, and Estonians at large, creating a hubbub of interest in his work. He became a featured speaker on the topic of intellectual freedom, free speech in Estonia under Gorbachev first coming to academia, and then spreading throughout the general public. His poem, "The Siege of Kurustamma," ostensibly a poem about an ancient Hittite warrior, but read by many as an omen of warning to the Soviet Union, became a favorite. Karl Kristian was called upon to recite the short, dramatic verses of the poem from memory at nearly every political gathering. In addition, the poem was featured in leaflets handed out on the streets of Tallinn and Tartu, urging the Russians to go home.

The Siege of Kurustamma
Chariots and horses
Followed by the feet of ten thousand men
Crashing at the gates
Of the City Kurustamma's walls.
Bolts and arrows fall
Striking the flesh of peaceful serfs
Cutting down the Hatti
At the City Kurustamma's walls.

Then the pestilence began
And the warriors ran
In fear
In their urgent quest
To seek a noble death
Without tears
Quiet in the meadow...

Laughter at daybreak
The siege of the city is over now
Labarnas lies asleep
Near his fallen army to keep warm.

Now the godly strife
Draws its bloody knife
To clean
In the city square

Children, wide-eyed stare
And dream
Quiet on the road...

Letters were exchanged between the Kristian brothers throughout their decades of separation. Twice a year, the teacher updated his older brother on news of the family, including reports regarding Hele's failing health. Twice a year, Nigel would respond in kind. But there were no telephone calls, no personal visits, no family reunions between the brothers until Hele's passing in1986.

"Brother," the telephone call began.

"Karl?"

"Yes."

"I can't believe it. I haven't heard your voice in what, forty-two years. You don't sound any different!"

They were speaking Estonian. Though Nigel was out of practice, having used his native tongue sparingly over the four decades away from his homeland, fluency returned as the brothers reconnected.

"Neither do you."

There was a pause.

"How is Marju?"

"Good. She runs the farm like a foreman in a Soviet tractor factory. Her father was wrong to question her abilities with dirt..." Karl said, injecting a bit of humor into an otherwise serious conversation.

"And the girls?"

"Still in Tallinn. They love the city. Tiia works as an aid in a hospital and Jaanika is a waitress in a restaurant. She's going to school to become an accountant."

A pause.

"And your family," Karl interposed. "How are they?"

"Very well, thank you. The girls are continuing on in school."

"And Grace?"

"As lovely as ever."

"Ah."

There was a lengthy break in the conversation as static interrupted.

"Shitty connection," Karl said apologetically. "Damned Russian phone lines."

"I take it there's a reason you called," Nigel said, getting to the point.

"Yes. There's no easy way to tell you this, Brother, so here it is: Mother passed away last night."

The news did not stun Nigel Christian. It was information that, given the semi-annual updates Karl had been providing in writing regarding their mother's failing health, was not unexpected.

"She did not suffer. She went in her sleep."

There was a long sigh from Nigel before he continued. "When is the service?"

"She wanted to be cremated. That was her wish and it's already been done. We can wait until you can get here to hold the wake and funeral."

Nigel calculated the business he needed to transact, the deals and contracts and agreements he needed to complete to keep the economic engine of his personal commerce running. But the elder Kristian brother arrested his selfishness before saying something he'd regret.

Christ, it's Mother, you idiot. Of course you'll drop whatever you've got going and find a way to get to the funeral.

"Is there a problem?"

"No. Just thinking how I can arrange a flight," Nigel lied. "It won't be easy, finding four last minute tickets from Minneapolis to Helsinki. But I'll get on it as soon as we're off the phone."

"Grace and the girls are coming?"

Nigel took a breath. "I think it's time that my daughters and my wife saw where I grew up, don't you? I assume the funeral will be at Puhja *kirik* so her ashes can rest alongside Father?"

"That's what I was thinking."

"That makes sense. Mother would like that."

Karl nodded, though of course, his brother could not see the gesture. "How long will it take you to make arrangements?"

Nigel thought a moment. "If you give me a week, I should be able to swing it. If need be, I can pull some strings through Congressman Oberstar's office. Grace and the girls have updated passports from our trip to Finland last year."

As the words flowed across the telephone wire and found his brother's distant ear, Nigel knew he had made a mistake.

There was a delay in Karl's reply. "You were in Finland? Why didn't you stop by for a visit?"

Silence. The emptiness elongated. Nigel Christian sighed. "After what happened on the beach, I guess I was afraid of what you might say to me, that you still blame me for losing Alexis."

Karl sniggered. "After over forty years? You're crazy, you know that? I've been married to a lovely woman, raised two daughters, and had a good life. Alexis Gustafson was a wonderful gal but that is so far in the past, I'm not sure I can even recall her face. The past is the past,

Nigel. I have nothing but love and deep affection," the phrase came out awkward, as if it embarrassed Karl to say it, "for you."

Tears formed in Nigel's eyes. "I'll call you as soon as I've booked a flight," Nigel finally managed to say. "Then you can work with the pastor to set the day and time for the service. We'll stay as long as it takes."

"And," Karl said as the call concluded, "you will stay in Pühajãrve, as guests at our farm."

"We couldn't impose," Nigel hastily replied. "We'll find a hotel."

"This time of year? With the snow so deep and skiers visiting in droves? There isn't a room available within 100 kilometers of Puhja," Karl asserted. "No, Nigel, you and your family will stay with Marju and I. That's settled."

After they said their goodbyes, Nigel Christian slumped in the chair behind his desk in the study of his log home, a birch fire crackling and popping in the woodstove across the room, natural light from the winter afternoon illuminating the warm space, and wondered how it would feel to stand on Estonian soil again.

CHAPTER 6
Tallinn, Estonia
January, 1986
(Nigel's Story)

Mother's funeral was sad—the end of an era. It also marked the loss of the last relation standing between mortality and me. Understand that I didn't then, at sixty-three, obsess on the topic. Even today, as I approach my tenth decade of life, death does not claim an inordinate amount of my attention. Oh, as the number ninety rears its ugly head, of course I contemplate the end: Whether, as my wife postulated, heaven will be the one place where everyone we loved during our earthly lives will be reunited with us or whether it is simply a long, restful slumber without end—a generous nap after a life of toil. Whichever version is true, or if death holds something more surprising, more unpredictable, I think I'm ready for it. I've lived as much as one man should live.

I reclaimed my passion for cross country-skiing after I came to Minnesota. At one point, I even contemplated seeking a place on the Olympic team—as an American, of course, since Estonia remained closed to me until the fall of the Soviet Union. I trained hard, hoping to rekindle the competitive spirit I'd felt on the ski track of Otepää as a boy. I came close to making the U.S. Olympic Training Team, a stepping-stone to the 1960 games in Squaw Valley, California. Hell, I was only thirty-three years old and in my prime. As with marathon runners, it is not youth but early middle age that is the best age for skiers. I was a few seconds off the qualifying time, excited to pit my speed, wits, and technique against Sixten Jernberg of Sweden and Veikko Hakulinen of Finland during the Games, when I tore the anterior cruciate ligament in my left knee and ended up a scratch. Despite a pretty decent surgeon from the Mayo Clinic rebuilding my knee, I lost confidence. The accident, a collision with a spruce at the bottom of a steep, icy grade, ended my racing days.

After Grace and I built our log home on Sabin Lake, I was asked to coach a local youth cross-country ski team. At first, my work, the complexities of starting a business and trying to prosper, to make good in my adoptive country, overpowered any desire I had to coach. But when our girls came along, I found myself wanting them to understand, at least in some small way, the life I had lived in Estonia. Skiing was something ingrained, imprinted in my Baltic DNA that I knew would create such a link, such a bond. And so, after numerous declinations, I relented.

The girls did well. Emily finished second in the state amateur finals her senior year, training on trails I helped cut from the second-growth forest at Giant's Ridge Ski Area, a stone's throw from our home. That was in 1975. Emma did her older sister one better. She won the state amateur championship three years running. So far as I could tell, Emily was not the least bit jealous of her younger sister's success. I was the one who had a problem with Emma. Not with her victories but with her decision to forego offers to ski collegiately. Emma turned down athletic scholarships from several schools in Maine and Vermont to join Emily at St. Scholastica, a Duluth-based Benedictine college in line with my wife's Catholic faith. Emily completed her post-high school education there, finishing after some fits and starts, switching from the RN program to physical therapy, graduating, and immediately finding work at Polinsky Rehabilitation in Duluth. After a promising marriage turned ugly, Emily and her son moved in with Grace and me and found a PT position at the nursing home in Hoyt Lakes. Emma transferred to another Catholic school, St. Catherine's, where she completed her RN degree. She works down there, in St. Paul—the mother of three sons—though unlike her older sister, Emma's marriage remains solid.

The snow had been quick as my niece Tiia led Emma and me through spruce, pine, and birch forest south of Otepää.

We had flown from New York to Helsinki and crossed the Gulf of Finland by ferry. Karl had been waiting for us in Tallinn in his 1962 Volga: a clanking, backfiring, rusted carcass of an automobile that, while roomy, had issues regarding reliability and style. I sat in the front passenger's seat while Karl narrated a travelogue. We took a detour so that my family could see what had once been the Kristian Farm and visit my parent's second home in Puhja. I won't deny that I shed tears, but it did me good to walk the snowy fields outside the abandoned farmhouse and stop alongside Kalevipoeg Creek—a frozen black fissure across the white landscape—and remember. Karl stood by my side as we considered the land, the fields, and forests of our youth and thought back to two young boys working the vegetable garden, fishing, hunting, playing pick-up soccer, and skiing. More tears flowed when I saw the snow-covered pile of boards that had once been our barn. But the strongest memory that struck me as I inspected the place where Karl and I hid from chores wasn't of *that* barn but of *another* barn, a barn in Tartu.

Shameful visions engulfed me as I stood on ground farmed by my forefathers. If Grace perceived my internal conflict, she didn't acknowledge it. Perhaps, after years of repressing such feelings, I was a good enough actor to keep my turmoil concealed.

Emily and Jaanika stayed at the farmhouse with Marju and Grace while Karl, who needed to correct papers at his school in Pühajãrve, drove us to the ski complex. It was a glorious January morning. Tiia was every bit as competitive as Emma. My niece had won her share of ribbons in local meets and proved to be more than an adequate foil for my youngest daughter. I tried to match the girls' enthusiasm. But visions of dying of a heart attack (like the one the one that claimed Minnesota conservation icon Sig Olson while snowshoeing) compelled me to slow down.

Still, Olson went out the right way, I silently admitted between deep breaths of clean winter air. *To die amongst such beauty,* I considered, *would not be a bad way to leave this world.*

After a quick tour of Old Tallinn, I had time to talk privately with Karl, to learn, from the perspective of someone living in the country, what was in store for Estonia as the mortar binding the Red wall began to crack. There was no jubilation in my brother's aspect: Only a steady, calm, reasoned confidence that freedom was just around the corner.

As we walked the cobbled streets of the historic merchant town behind our wives and daughters, I could've shared the details of my family's visit with Elin Peltomaa in Finland. But for some reason I did not relate the tale. Elin was ninety-one years old when the girls and Grace and I flew to Helsinki the year before Mother's death. The former reporter was blind from diabetes and her hearing was suspect when we sat and talked with her in a Pietasaari retirement home. But despite the ravages of time and physical infirmity, the old woman's mind had been sharp.

"How have things been, Elin?" I had asked as we talked in the community room of the old folks' home.

When I left the Finnish refugee camp, I kept in touch with Matti Peltomaa by mail, sending one or two letters a year and receiving short, declarative responses in like number, until the old soldier died quietly in his sleep. After Matti passed, I started writing his widow. We formed a warm, if subtle, friendship built upon decades of long-distance contact. At first, I wrote Elin sporadically. But as she aged and her vision began to fail Elin wrote more frequently and I replied in kind.

I learned—through Elin's precisely handwritten dispatches—of not only the ordinary circumstances of her everyday life, but also the details of her career as a reporter for *Pietarsaaren Sanomat.* She had accepted a position with the paper in the 1950s as Finland worked its way out of post-war debt, regained international dignity, and remade itself into a modern, industrialized, progressive nation. The old lady's letters were also filled with news of Alexis. Through Elin Peltomaa, I learned that after graduating from McGill, Alexis returned to Brooklyn, obtained her physician's license, and joined a clinic in Harlem providing free medical care to impoverished women of color. It was at the clinic that Alexis Gustafson met and fell in love with Elmore Tate, M.D.—a statuesque black man born and raised not two blocks from where they worked. Dr. Tate also happened to be Alexis's boss, but that didn't seem to matter. The couple was blessed, according to Elin, with two beautiful and bright children, one boy, one girl; both of who had finished college.

Elin also shared with me that Alexis had continued her serious embrace of Christianity that arose from her love of the Beatitudes, something that drew her and Dr. Tate even closer since he too was a fervent believer. The couple's retirement plans were to become missionary doctors flying across the world on behalf of the Evangelical Lutheran Church, supplying medical services to the poor and the less fortunate. I felt a twinge, a pang, of jealousy as the old woman related the couple's altruism.

What have I done for my fellow man? I lamented at the disclosure of Alexis's saintly intentions.

From the family photograph the old woman showed me, it was clear that Alexis had maintained her figure and was a poised and striking wife, mother, and grandmother. I was thankful that, given how well Alexis photographed, the image didn't dredge up old feelings.

Elin wrote for the newspaper for years after Matti's passing. But as her eyesight degenerated, she stopped working, sold the small house that she and Matti had built overlooking the Bay of Bothnia north of Pietarsaari, and moved to the old folks' home where we visited.

"Very fine. Alexis, Elmore, and the children came to see me not long ago," Elin finally had answered.

"How long were they here?"

"They were in Europe for a month but stayed only a week with me. Alexis wanted Josiah and Janine to see Finland, Estonia, and Karelia."

"Did your great-grandchildren visit as well?"

I knew from Elin's letters that Elin's grandchildren were now adults.

A look of longing came over Elin's still youthful face.

Her complexion, her skin. She doesn't show age as one would expect!

Grace and the girls sat quietly on the sofa as the old woman and I conversed in Finnish. Though Grace was of Finnish heritage, she never learned more than a word or two of the language. I translated what Elin said so Grace and the girls could follow the conversation. Though the girls seemed bored and distracted, Grace appeared genuinely interested in the old woman's stories.

A cardboard box had rested on the carpeted floor next to Elin's feet. I was curious as to the carton's contents but declined to pry.

"Sadly, they did not come with," Elin finally replied, with a slight tremor. "I've never met them. They are in school and their parents didn't think it was wise for them to miss an entire month of studies."

I smiled. "I seem to remember that Alexis was a teacher once..."

"Yes. In Kärdla. But that was a long time ago."

I nodded. "A *very* long time ago," I replied. "Those were very different times, weren't they, Mrs. Peltomaa?"

"Elin. Please call me Elin. After all these years and all the letters, we are on familiar terms."

"Alright."

My eyes focused on the box on the floor. Elin Peltomaa smiled at my curiosity. Her perception was uncanny given her lack of sight.

"You are interested to learn what's in the box?"

"I am."

"Before my eyes failed, before I was unable to use a typewriter, I decided to write down my story. No, that's not true: I began to write *our* story—yours, mine, Alexis's, Hiram's, and your brother's—what was his name again?"

"Karl."

"Ah. I knew that. Shouldn't have forgotten that, as close as he and Alexis once were. Anyway. I began writing what I could remember from that time. Why I waited so long, I have no idea. But wait I did..."

"You were working, as a reporter," my wife had said kindly after I'd translated Elin's words.

"True. But Matti had passed away. I had little other than work to fill my days. Still, I guess I needed the distance of time before I could write what, as Hemingway would say, was true."

"My brother loved Hemingway."

Elin nodded. "I remember that! He persuaded Alexis to read *For Whom the Bell Tolls*. She praised it to high heaven and sent me a copy in Finnish."

The sun sank below a line of trees surrounding the rest home. Shadows claimed what had once been an airy, sunlit room. Elin reached for the box with great deliberation. Age had been clear in her shoulders and hips as she lifted the carton in halting fashion, removed the lid, placed it on the arm of the recliner, and removed a carefully typewritten manuscript.

"You wrote all that?" Emily had asked.

"I did," Elin said in heavily accented English. "Very slowly."

Everyone laughed.

She handed me a piece of paper with carefully spaced typing.

"Yes," I said with reverence after reading the first page of Elin's memoir, "that is how it was."

The old woman smiled, accepted the page from me and returned it to the box. She fit the lid snuggly on the carton.

"I want you to have this," she had said, her ancient arms straining from the weight of her work as she held the box out to me. "It's a copy: I gave the original to Alexis so she can pass it on to her children and grandchildren. It's not polished. But it is true, at least so far as I can remember."

"I can't accept this," I objected. "It's personal, like a diary. I doubt you meant for anyone outside your family to read it."

Elin had removed her eyeglasses, the corrective lenses cosmetic given her sightlessness.

"No. I insist. It is your story *too*."

There had been something in Elin Peltomaa's voice—in the way the word "too" raised in a lilt—that caught my attention. I sensed, as my family waited uncomfortably in the rest home's community room, that Mrs. Peltomaa had something more to say, something delicate and private to reveal outside the presence of my family.

"Grace, would you take the girls out to the car?" I had asked my wife. "I won't be more than a few moments."

My wife acquiesced without objection. I moved my chair closer to the old woman, placed my hand on hers, and smiled.

"Is there something else?" I had asked, raising my voice so that she could hear me.

The old woman looked at me with absent, milky eyes.

"There *is* something else you need to know."

"Yes?"

"About that woman, the one who saved my life…"

I had surmised she was trying to recall Ellisabet's name. "Ellisabet? Ellisabet Raun?"

"That's it. I hate when I know something but I can't retrieve it!"

I smiled. "Me too."

"You?" The old woman had reared back in mock surprise. "You're still a young man. Wait until you're nearly a century old and then see what surprises, what tricks your mind plays on you!"

We laughed again.

"Ah," Elin finally said, "Ellisabet Raun."

Another delay ensued.

"There is something I was told about Miss Raun that concerns you. It was told to me a very long time ago. By Alexis."

I had frowned.

What sort of secret would be left to reveal years after Ellisabet's death? And why had Alexis been the one to reveal it? The old woman has apparently forgotten my connection to her daughter. There's no reason to dredge up that old memory!

The old woman had smiled tiredly. "Alexis told me this in the strictest of confidence. She said I was never to reveal it, not to anyone; but most assuredly, not to you."

What the hell game is this old woman playing with me?

I held my tongue and listened.

"The Raun woman was what, sixteen years old when you first met, when the two of you first…?"

Elin had smiled again, this time, with more strength—as if the image of my coupling with Ellisabet recalled moments of passion from her *own* life.

"Fourteen. She was fourteen. I was working for a man at her father's law office, putting in wiring," I replied, my face flushing despite the distance in time from the event.

The old woman nodded. "You were always an electrician, weren't you, Nigel?"

The question was rhetorical so I didn't answer.

"She went away not long after that?"

"To Germany. To go to school," I recalled.

There had been a deep sigh. "It's a story that was told often, back in those times, when a young woman found herself in trouble."

Trouble? What does she men, "trouble"? Wait. I understand.

"She was…pregnant?"

Elin Peltomaa had grasped my hand firmly and squeezed. "She gave you a son."

Emotion assaulted me in ways that I didn't realize were possible. I sat holding the old woman's hand tightly for a moment. "What is his name?"

She had smiled, exposing dentures. "Nigul. Nigul Raun."

I gulped air and tried to steady my nerves. "Do you know where he is?"

She shook her head. "Ellisabet told Alexis that the boy was raised in Dresden by an aunt. I'm sorry Nigel, but I have no other information. I debated about this for years. Once, long ago, I picked up a pen and was about to write to you in America. This was when Matti was still alive. But Alexis described the pain in Ellisabet's eyes, the turmoil on her face at having left her son to be raised as another woman's child. And so, in hopes of keeping my daughter's pledge, I didn't write. I *should* have. I am sorry. Maybe if I had, you would have been able to contact the boy."

Tears had streamed down my face.

What if he is alive? He would be a grown man—not a little boy. He has known nothing but East Germany since after the war and has likely no idea of me. Is it right to try to contact him? Whose purpose would that serve? And Grace. And the girls. How do I tell them? How?

My last vision of Elin Peltomaa was of her very old face looking up at me with sentimentality as I stood to leave.

"You need to find him, Nigel," she had said firmly. "For his sake he needs to know his father. That would be something anyone would want to know."

"Something wrong, Dad?" Emily asked as we waited in line to board the ferry to Helsinki.

Karl and his family stood behind a chain link fence near the dock, Marju and the girls waving goodbye, my brother standing stick straight and taciturn.

I didn't reply.

"Dad?"

Elin Peltomaa's disclosure occupied my mind as we moved towards the ferry.

"It's nothing, 'Em. Just a bit overwhelmed by it all, I guess."

My daughter gave me a hug.

"She was a wonderful woman," Emily said thoughtfully, as she handed her ticket to the agent at the gangway, her comment clearly a reference to Mother's passing.

But that's not how my mind interpreted the comment.

And she gave me a son.

CHAPTER 7
Tallinn, Estonia
August 1991

Estonian opposition to Soviet rule gathered steam. By 1987, environmental concerns over oil shale mining caused protests to erupt in the streets. A proposed mine was stopped: *Glasnost* provided a basis for Estonians to criticize the government's plans. This political success was followed by other protests throughout Estonia on the anniversary of the Molotov-Ribbentrop accord. The Soviet Union clung to the fiction that the secret pact was a legitimate treaty granting it the right to occupy and control Estonia. A public demonstration decrying the falsity of the Soviet position was planned. The event was expected to draw several hundred protestors to Hirve Park in Tallinn. Instead, tens of thousands of Estonians gathered to express their discord with the U.S.S.R.'s distorted view of history.

By 1988, the public outcry against the Soviet regime had gained a more united voice and, for the first time since 1944, tri-color Estonian flags began to appear at public gatherings, first in Tartu and then later that same year, on the Song Festival grounds in Tallinn. Before the opening of the All Estonian Song Festival in 1990, Estonian had been re-established as the official language of the country, historical tracts and literature critical of the Soviets Union were being distributed freely throughout the country, and all trappings of Soviet dominion had vanished from the Festival program. In the end, the crowd that gathered to sing *Mu isamaa, mu õnn ja room* was over 300,000 strong—nearly one-third the country's entire population. When a youthful leader of the protest movement shouted boldly from the Festival stage that "One day, no matter what, we will win!" the Estonian people had their slogan and the country had its momentum, momentum that was transformed into a 600 kilometer human chain of protesters holding hands along the main highway running between Estonia and Lithuania.

After issuing new passports for over 860,000 ethnic Estonians: one for every man, woman, and child in the country who didn't claim Russian ancestry; and after organizing the Congress of Estonia as a competing body to the Soviet-sponsored legislature, the freedom movement reached a breaking point. Either Moscow was going to allow Estonia its independence, or, as had happened in Hungary in 1956 and Czechoslovakia in 1968, Soviet tanks and soldiers would be deployed by Moscow to restore control.

Karl Kristian played an important role in this movement. The teacher attended nearly every rally, providing poetic support for the notion of liberty and quietly cultivating the countryside in search of men and women of like heart who were willing to drop what they were doing at a moment's notice to travel to Tallinn or Tartu or other Estonian cities to gather in protest. By August 19, 1991, when the Soviet Union's system of internal governance collapsed on the heels of Gorbachev's suggestion that the U.S.S.R. become a loosely-knit confederation, Karl Kristian was well-known throughout Estonia.

"What will the soldiers do?" a young man asked as Karl linked arms with the questioner on his left and an even younger protester on his right.

"Gorbachev's a prisoner in Crimea," Karl explained as Estonians forming a human wall blocked heavily armed Red Army soldiers hell-bent on capturing the Tallinn television tower. "This is not Gorbachev's doing: This is the work of others, those who wish to see empire continue. These Russians soldiers, boys too young to shave, will not hesitate to shoot. I've seen men with guns do such things. They won't hesitate to fire into a crowd."

The Tallinn television tower was Estonia's main portal to the outside world. After elite Soviet paratroops secured the Tallinn airport, Soviet tanks and armed personnel carriers and ground troops had swarmed across Estonia's eastern border and secured the major population centers as communists in the U.S.S.R. attempted to imprison their premier. Gorbachev's intention was to return from vacation and oversee the ratification of the new confederation he had proposed. But members of the Communist Party opposing Gorbachev's pragmatic approach seized power. This internal conflict threatened to turn deadly and plunge the Soviet Union into civil war.

"Will they, Mr. Kristian? Will they fire on unarmed men and women?"

Karl was a minor celebrity to the Estonians assembled at the television tower. He wasn't as well-known as some others in the Independence Party, the group he'd aligned himself with. He wasn't a household name like Heinz Valk, whose unintentional reference to the nonviolent protests as the "Singing Revolution" gave the Estonian independence movement its unofficial title. But Karl Kristian was a respected figure in the push towards Estonian freedom.

Karl nodded at the blond haired youth. "They will."

"Listen to him, lad," an older voice boomed from the second row of protesters, "he's a veteran, fought the Russians in Finland and here, in the army and as a Forest Brother. He knows what he's talking about."

Karl turned to see who was speaking. A man directly behind him, a man about Karl's age, nodded to the old teacher.

I have no idea who he is.

"Stand down," an officer at the head of the Soviet soldiers urged in Russian, pointing his machine pistol towards the civilians—male and female, all ages, sizes, and shapes—obstructing the road. "We have our orders. We will take the tower!"

Diesel smoke from idling personnel carriers, the heavy machine guns of the half-tracks manned by young Russians; the guns locked, loaded, and aimed at the Estonians, drifted through thick August air. Russian words and phrases leaked from the ranks of the hot, anxious, sweating soldiers, their dander up, their excitement palpable.

"*Nyet*," one of the young protesters said. "This is our country," he continued in Russian. "You will not stop us from telling our story to the world!"

The Red Army officer pointed his pistol at the civilian.

A sense of dread overcame Karl Kristian.

I've seen that look, the look of blood lust, before.

"Stand down!"

The young Estonian shook his head.

This won't end well…

But Karl Kristian was wrong. Russian President Boris Yeltsin—who was wanted by the leaders of the coup for disloyalty but who had the support of the Russian generals commanding the Red Army—raced to Moscow, climbed onto a tank, and addressed the crowd surrounding the Soviet White House. Yeltsin proclaimed that he stood with Gorbachev—that he opposed the coup. As the president of the largest ethnic group in the U.S.S.R., Yeltsin's position carried weight. Within hours, Red Army units began withdrawing from Moscow.

Yeltsin's actions rippled through the Baltics. After two days of non-violent siege, the Red Army withdrew from Estonia. When the two Estonian policemen guarding the Tallinn television tower against the invaders descended from their perch, the policemen were mobbed as heroes.

That evening, a special session of the Supreme Council of the Estonian S.S.R., the last vestige of Soviet rule in the country, affirmed independence by unanimous vote. On September 2nd, the United States recognized the Republic of Estonia. Back from the Crimea, with the Soviet Union rapidly heading towards disintegration, and without a shot having been fired, Mikhail Gorbachev, the last premier of the Soviet Union, declared the Republic of Estonia to be a free and independent nation.

CHAPTER 8

The old man dropped a smoldering cigarette and crushed the butt between the toe of his dress shoe and asphalt.

Grace and the girls nagged me for years to quit. Oh, I tried. The gum. The patches. Visits to a shrink. None of it took. None of the medicines or the hocus pocus could break my obsession. What the hell, the old man mused as he kicked the butt into a gutter. *I'm nearly ninety—too damned late for a leopard to change its spots!*

He removed a scrap of paper from a pocket of his coat and held the note in his right hand—the skin as yellow and thin as the flesh of an onion—and climbed stairs leading to the Gerald Heaney Building. It was an atypical December day for Duluth. The ground was free of snow and the temperature was forty-eight degrees Fahrenheit.

I hate these false winters.

The man's eyeglasses slid down his octogenarian nose as he labored. He stopped at the top of the granite staircase, removed a brown felt hat from his head, and resituated his glasses. He studied the blue-gray open water of Lake Superior unfolding below the city before continuing on. Inside the glass doors of the federal courthouse, the old man emptied his pockets. He placed his personal items in a plastic bowl and handed the bowl to a security guard—a man who appeared bored to the point of distraction—before walking through a metal detector with the scrap of paper still clutched in his right hand and the fedora in his left.

"Right on through, sir," a younger, seemingly more pleasant security guard encouraged.

The old man shoved the note into a pocket of his coat, held the hat loosely in both hands as he shuffled forward, and waited patiently at the end of a conveyor belt while his wallet and other items were x-rayed, retrieved, and handed to him.

"Have a good day, officer," the old man said politely, accepting his property from the bored security guard.

The man said nothing.

"You too," the younger guard replied cheerfully.

Riding the elevator, the old man pondered what he would say, where he would begin the tale he was being asked to tell.

So much happened, Nigel Christian thought. *So many who were part of what took place are gone. Matti. Elin. Ellisabet. Karl. Marju. Grace. Lovely, lovely Grace. And the boy—the son I never met. I tried. At least I can say that. I tried to find him after Elin Peltomaa told me he existed. I went there, to Dresden, in 1994 and looked up his name in the archives. I found, like so many things having to do with the*

Germans, that there was a list, an accounting. The British and the Americans claimed the attacks were justified, that the city was a military target. I don't know the truth of that. All I know is that on the page listing the "R's" I found this entry: "Nigul Raun, male, age five. Died in hospital of severe burns." I didn't cry upon discovering the truth. I never told Grace or the girls. There was no reason to. I tried to forget him, like I've tried to forget so much of what took place. It's been a long time, over six decades, since the last shot was fired, since the last German soldiers left Estonia and Finland. And yet, even as we, the old ones still alive, try to restrict our remembrances, the past rears its ugly head in ways that can't be anticipated.

How else do you explain the story that broke in September, 1978—twenty-five years after the last known Forest Brother accepted amnesty? There it was—an article proclaiming the death of August Sabbe—a Forest Brother who survived the swamps of Estonia for over thirty years. He was drowned in the Võhandu River near Paidra by the KGB for his fortitude.

How do you explain the world's interest in a water-decayed Brewster Buffalo lifted out of an icy Karelian lake in 1998, fifty years after Lieutenant Lauri Pekuri lost a dogfight and crash landed in the lake, losing the plane but living to fight another day?

Or the tales about ex-Nazis and their collaborators such as John Demjanjuk, an eighty-nine year old American citizen who it turns out was not a gentle, loving, grandfather but a sadistic, murdering guard at the Sobibor extermination camp who was deported to Germany to stand trial for crimes against humanity?

Or the 1987 deportation of Karl Linnas, an Estonian collaborator who commanded a concentration camp near Tartu? Linnas immigrated to the United States in 1951 and worked as a land surveyor until a United States District Court Judge stripped him of his citizenship because his actions during the war "offended the decency of civilized society." A federal appeals court upheld the ruling and the United States Supreme Court declined to consider the case. Linnas was sent to St. Petersburg to face a death sentence but died in a prison hospital awaiting execution.

Or the 1994 ceremony held at the site of the Klooga Labor Camp dedicating a memorial to the Jews killed there?

Or newspaper articles from May of 2005 noting that the Prime Minister of Estonia had finally condemned Estonian collaborators of the Holocaust?

Or the July, 2005 unveiling by the Estonian president and the Israeli Ambassador to Estonia of a memorial in honor of the victims of Klooga?

Or the renewed interest of an awakened Finnish people as demonstrated by articles in the Finnish press beginning in 2007, sixty years after the war, discussing the fact that over one-quarter of all Soviet soldiers captured and detained in Finnish prison camps died from untreated diseases and malnutrition?

There remain many other unanswered, and perhaps, unanswerable questions about what took place during that time. But why, fifty years after his death, are the FBI and the INS suddenly interested in Aleksander Laak?

An elevator bell announced Nigel Christian's arrival on the floor housing the local office of the FBI. The door swooshed open. The old man stepped onto highly polished marble, switched the hat to his left hand, removed the scrap of paper from his coat pocket, and studied it. Satisfied, he returned the writing to his pocket before moving with confidence down the brightly lighted hallway.

And what of Alexis? the old man asked rhetorically. *Last I knew, she was living in New York City, the place she lived before going to Karelia with her parents. She worked for many years in a Bowery clinic providing free medical services to poor women and their children. That's what Elin Peltomaa said when I visited the old woman in Pietarsaari. Elin also told me that Alexis married a doctor who was a good man, Elin emphasized, a very good man.*

Nigel Christian thought he understood, as he walked towards the interview, why he'd been selected to come in. Very shortly, the old man would be asked to relate what he knew about Aleksander Laak and provide a narrative about what had taken place in Estonia and Finland a very long time ago. As he shambled towards the FBI office, Nigel remembered he'd read somewhere that Canadian intelligence had uncovered links between Laak's death and a cell of Israeli operatives who functioned as avenging angels.

What the old man did not know was that, when the Canadian government re-opened its investigation into Laak's death, the names of United States Congressman John Blatnik and Estonian émigré Nigel Christian came to light. Blatnik was long dead. But Nigel Christian was, to the delight of Canadian authorities, very much available for questioning.

Despite being ignorant of the exact details as to *why* he was being summoned to Duluth, the old man had a fair idea of the motives behind the invitation. He also suspected that questions would be asked about the large sum of money Nigel Christian had donated to a certain charitable foundation in Tallinn whose executive director was Jaanika Kristian: an organization that funded the "Karl Kristian Center for the Study of the Holocaust" at the University of Tartu. Financial transactions regarding the charity *seemed* suspicious. Investigators had hinted skepticism about Nigel's involvement with the charity during the brief time they spent with the old man in his Biwabik apartment.

They wouldn't understand, Nigel mused as his aged hand clasped a shiny brass doorknob. *If I told them the money came from the Mannerheim, they would be incredulous. They would object that such a small stipend could create such a large endowment. But the $10,000 I invested for more than sixty years was worth more than a million when I sold my Minnesota Power shares and wired the funds to my niece. It's money that Karl should have had during his lifetime. He was the war hero, not me. The Mannerheim and its stipend should have been his, not mine. He's gone now, like the others. Giving money in Karl's name, allowing his daughter to* *administer it, is the best I can do to honor his memory. I can try explaining this to the men in suits but they will never understand.*

Nigel Christian opened the door and entered the FBI office. After exchanging pleasantries with a receptionist, a woman of short stature and curt speech, Nigel was ushered into a windowless conference room and shown a seat. He claimed the green vinyl cushion of a government-surplus chair and sat quietly with the brim of his fedora held loosely in both hands while he waited. He did not remove his coat. Very shortly, three men, men interested in the past, would enter the room and claim identical chairs across the table from the Estonian. Preliminary questions would be asked, questions which Nigel Christian would politely answer. And then the old soldier would be asked to tell a story.

THE END

Resources

Books

Bliss, Michael, *The Discovery of Insulin.* Chicago: University of Chicago Press (25th Anniversary edition), 2007.

Cotter, Arthur. *The Finns.* New York: Episcopal Diocese of New York, 1923.

Engle, Eloise, and Pannanen, Lauri, *The Winter War.* Mechanicsburg, PA: Stackpole Books, 1973.

Hammond's Superior Atlas of the World. New York: C.S. Hammond & Co., 1938.

Hietamies, Laila (translated by Borje Vahamaki), *Red Moon Over White Sea.* Beaverton, Ontario: Aspasia Books, 2000.

Hokkanen, Lawrence and Sylvia (with Middleton, Anita), *Karelia: A Finnish-American Couple in Stalin's Russia, 1934-1941.* St. Cloud, MN: North Star Press, 1991.

Komulainen, Ernest J, *A Grave in Karelia.* Ann Arbor: Braun-Brumfield, 1995.

Kraav, Fred, *The Partisans*. New York: Vantage Press, 1952.

Ktakja, Ville, *Finnish Dictionary and Phrasebook.* New York: Hippocrene Books, 2002.

Laar, Mart, *War in the Woods.* Washington, D.C.: The Compass Press, 1992.

Lunde, Henrik O., *Finland's War of Choice.* Philadelphia: Casemate Books, 2011.

Munger, Mark, *Suomalaiset: People of the Marsh.* Duluth, MN: Cloquet River Press, 2004.

O'Connor, Kevin, *The History of the Baltic States.* Wesport, CN: Greenwood Press, 2003.

Oskanin, Sofi, *Purge.* New York: Black Cat, 2008.

Raun, Toivo U., *Estonians and Estonia.* Stanford, CA: Hoover Institute Press, 2001.

Rautkallio, Hannu, *Finland and the Holocaust.* New York: Holocaust Library,1987.

Sevander, Mayme (with Hertzel, Laurie), *They Took My Father.* Minneapolis: University of Minnesota Press, 1992.

Tolstoy, Leo, *The Death of Ivan Ilych and Other Stories.* New York: BN Classics, 2004.

Trotter, William R., *Frozen Hell.* Chapel Hill: Algonquin Books, 1991.

Turri, Antti, *The Winter War.* Beaverton, Ontario: Aspasia Books, 2003.

Virrland, Arved, *Graves Without Crosses.* Clarke, Irwin &Co., 1972.

Whitman, Walt, *Leaves of Grass.* New York: The Modern Library, 1921.

Films

Ambush. Matila Röhr Productions, 1999.

The Cuckoo. Kinokompaniya CTB, 2002.

The Kruetzer Sonata. Mongrel Media, 2009.

The Singing Revolution. Mountain View Productions, 2006.

The Soviet Story. Labvakar, 2008.

Under the Red Star. Sheba Films, 2011.

The Winter War. National Filmi Oy, 1989.

Websites

"Accused Nazi Killer Demanjanjuk is Deported". *The Daily Mail* website. www.dailymail.com.uk/news/worldnews/article-1180707A (accessed 11/8/2010)

"Aleksander Laak." Wikipedia. www.en.wikipedia.org/wiki/Aleksander_Laak (accessed 7/12/2011)

"Ambush." www.imfdb.org/wiki/Ambush (accessed 4/20/2012)

"Arnold Rüütel." Wikipedia. www.en.wikipedia.org/Arnold_Rüütel (accessed 7/21/2011)

"August Rei." Wikipedia. www.en.wikipedia.org/wiki/August_Rei (accessed 7/21/2011)

"August Sabbe." Wikipedia. www.en.wikipedia.org/wiki/August_Sabbe (accessed 7/14/2011)

"Background Note: Estonia." United States Department of State website. www.state.gov/r/pa/ei/bgn/5377 (accessed 7/8/2010)

"Baltic Sea." www.history.com/topics/baltic-sea (accessed 3/8/2011)

"Baltic States: The Forest Brothers." www.fccorn.people.wm.edu/russiasperiphery/ef6072e29bcff51937 (accessed 8/8/2010)

"Battle for Narva Bridgehead." Wikipedia. www.en.wikipedia.org/wiki/Battle_for_the_Narva_Bridgehead (accessed 7/14/2011)

"Battle of the Ice." Wikipedia. www.en.wikipedia.org/wiki/Battle_of_the_Ice (accessed 11/8/2010)

"Battle of Stalingrad." Wikipedia. www.en.wikipedia.org/wiki/Battle_of_Stalingrad (accessed 7/21/2011)

"The Battle of the Winter War: Anti-tank Weapons." www.winterwar.com/Weapons (accessed 4/22/2011)

"A Brief History of Sunset Park." www.sunset-park-com/history (accessed 11/25/2010)

"Carl Gustaf Emil Mannerheim." Wikipedia. www.en.wikipedia.org/wiki/Carl_Gustaf_Emil_Mannerheim (accessed 11/25/2010)

"Col. Pajari during the Winter War." www.ww2incolor.com/finnish_forces/Pajari (accessed 7/6/2011)

"Control." www.diabetesnet.com/diabetes_controli_tips (accessed 1/4/2011)

"Crimes Against Humanity in Estonia: 1941-1944". Axis History Forum website. www.forum.axishistory.com/viewtopic.php?t=52004&highlight (accessed 7/21/2011)

"Criminal Cases". www.kapo.ee/eng/areas-of-activity/international-crimes (accessed 6/29/2011)

"Disillusionment on the Grandest of Scales: Finnish-Americans in the Soviet Union, 1912-1939". Weldenhamer, Emily. www.sras.org/finnish-americans_in_the_soviet_union (accessed 4/20/2012)

"East Karelian Uprising and Soviet-Finnish Conflict, 1921-1922". Wikipedia. www.en.wikipedia.org/East_Karelian_Uprising (accessed 11/9/2010)

"Edvard Gylling." Wikipedia. www.en.wikipedia.org/Edvard_Gylling (accessed 12/4/2010)

"Einsatzkommando Finnland." Wikipedia. www.en.wikipedia.org/Einsatzkommando_Finnland (accessed 4/18/2011)

"Emajõgi." Wikipedia. www.en.wikipedia.org/Emajõgi (accessed 2/8/2011)

"Estonia." www.fao.org/a.AGPdoc/CounprofEstonia/estonia (accessed 3/8/2011)

"Estonia." www.history.com/topics/estonia (accessed 3/8/2011)

"Estonia Country Page". NCSJ website. www.ncj.org/Estonia (accessed 11/8/2010)

"Estonian Cuisine." Wikipedia. www.en.wikipedia.org/wiki/Estonian_cuisine (accessed 3/8/2011)

"Estonian Immigration." www.immigration-online.org/99-estonian-immigration (accessed 7/21/2011)

"Estonian Legion." Wikipedia. www.en.wikipedia.org/wiki/Estonian_Legion (accessed 7/21/2011)

"Estonians." www.everycutlure.com/wc/Costa-Rica-to-Georgia/Estonians (accessed 7/8/2010)

"Estonians." *Encyclopedia of Chicago* website. www.enceclopedia.chicagohistory.org/pages/435 (accessed 7/8/2010)

"Estonian Soviet Socialist Republic". Wikipedia. www.en.wikipedia.org/Estonian_Soviet_Socialist_Republic (accessed 1/5/12)

"Estonian Volunteers in Finland During WWII, 1939-1944." www.ww2f.com/eastern-europe/21967-estonian-volunteers-finland (accessed 7/21/2011)

"Estonian War of Independence." Wikipedia. www.en.wikipedia.org/wiki/Estonian_War_of_Independence (accessed 11/8/2010)

"Estonia's Return to Independence: 1987-1991". Estonian Embassy website. www.estemb.org/estonia/history/aid-2850 (accessed 1/14/2012)

"Estonia in WW II." Wikipedia. www.en.wikipedia.org/Estonia_in_World_War_II (accessed 7/14/2011)

"Finland and Germany in WWII: Brothers in Arms-and Partners in Crime?" *Helsingin Sonomat* website. www.hs.fi/english/article/Finland+and+Germany+in+WWII (accessed 4/18/2011)

"Finnish Air Force." Wikipedia.
www.en.wikipedia.org/wiki/Finnish_Air_Force (accessed 4/22/2011)

"Finnish Army 1941-1944."
www.ww2total.com/WW2/History/Orders-of-Battle/Finland (accessed 7/6/2011)

"The Finnish Civil War". Wikipedia.
www.en.wikipedia.org/wiki/Finnish_Civil_War (accessed 11/8/2010)

"Finnish Infantry Regiment 200." Wikipedia.
www.en.wikipedia.org/wiki/Finnish_Infantry_Regiment_200 (accessed 7/11/2011)

"Fokker D.XXI." Wikipedia.
www.en.wikipedia.org/wiki/Fokker_D.XXI (accessed 4/22/2011)

"Forest Brothers." www.enotes.com/topic/Forest_Brothers (accessed 6/24/2011)

"Forest Brothers." Wikipedia.
www.en.wikipedia.org/wiki/Forest_Brothers (unknown access date)

"'The Forgotten Transport' Films: Illuminating 'Places Left in Obscurity': A Story of Human Lives." *The News of the Czech Center* (pp.11-13, unknown date or date of access)

"Forgotten Transports: To Estonia". Mememsha Films website.
www.mememshafilms.com/forgotten-transports-to-estonia (accessed 7/21/2011)

"Forgotten Transports: To Estonia".
www.jbspins.blogspot.com/2009/01/nyjj-forgotten-transportstoestonia (accessed 12/31/2010)

"German Occupation of Estonia during WWII." Wikipedia.
www.en.wikipedia.org/German_occpuation_of_Estonia_during_World_War_II (accessed 11/8/2010)

"Greater Finland". Wikipedia.
www.en.wikipedia.org/wiki/Greater_Finland (accessed 11/08/2010)

"Hanko". Wikipedia. www.en.wikipedia.org/wiki/Hanko (accessed 6/23/2011)

"Harlem." Wikipedia. www.en.wikipedia.org/wiki/Harlem (accessed 11/26/2010)

"Heimosodat". Wikipedia. www.en.wikipedia.org/wiki/Heimosodat (accessed 11/8/2010)

"Heterochromia." Wikipedia. www.en.wikipedia.org/wiki/Heterochromia (accessed 11/9/2010)

"Hiiumaa." Wikipedia. www.en.wikipedia.org/wiki/Hiiumaa (accessed 4/17/2011)

"The History of Diabetes" and "History of Diabetes: From raw Quinces to Gruel to Insulin." Sattley, Melissa. Diabetes Health website. www.diabeteshealth.com/reade/2008/12/17/715/the-history-of-diabetes (accessed 17/7/2010)

"History of Estonia." Wikipedia. www.en.wikipedia.org/wiki/History_of_Estonia (accessed 6/4/2010)

"History of Rail Transport in Estonia." Wikipedia. www.en.wikipedia.org/wiki/History_of_rail_transport_in_Estonia (accessed 3/8/2011)

"Holocaust in Estonia". www.estonica.org/en/Holocaust_in_Estonia (accessed 01/02/2013)

"The Holocaust in Estonia". Wikipedia. www.en.wikipedia.org/The_Holocaust_in_Estonia (accessed 7/12/2011)

"Holocaust Trials in Soviet Estonia". Wikipedia. www.en.wikipedia.org/Holocaust_trials_in_Soviet_Estonia (accessed 7/12/2011)

"Home from the War: the Discovery in Russia." www.warbirdforum.com (accessed 6/22/2011)

"How to Create the 'Great Finland'". www.win.ru/en/school/4159.phtml (accessed 11/8/2010)

"Human Rights and Special Prosecutions." United States Department of Justice website. www.justice.gov/criminal/hrsp (accessed 11/8/2010)

"The Images of Neighbours: Estonians and their Neighbours." www.herkules.oulu.fi/isbn9514266331 (accessed 11/8/2010)

"Ingria". Wikipedia. www.en.wikipedia.org/wiki/Ingria (accessed 11/8/2010)

"Jäger Movement." Wikipedia. www.en.wikipedia.org/wiki/Jäger_Movement (accessed 8/3/2011)

"Jagala Concentration Camp". Wikipedia. www.en.wikipedia.org/Jagala (accessed 7/12/2011)

"Jatkosota: 1941-1944-Continuation War." www.rajajoki.com (accessed 9/23/2010)

"Jatkosota 1944: Finland at War." www.flamesofwar.com/Defaultaspx?tabid=112&art_id (accessed 6/26/2011)

"Jews in Finland During the Second World War". Vuonokari, Tuulikki. Finnish Institute website. www.uta.fi/FAST/FIN/HIST/tv-jews (accessed 6/16/2011)

"Joensuu Railway Station". Wikipedia. www.en.wikipedia.org/wiki/Joensuu_railway_station (accessed 4/23/2011)

"John Blatnik." Wikipedia. www.en.wikipedia.org/wiki/John_Blatnik (accessed 1/6/2012)

"Joseph Stalin." Wikipedia. www.en.wikipedia.org/wiki/Joseph_Stalin (accessed 1/8/2011)

"Jüri Uluots." Wikipedia. www.en.wikipedia.org/Jüri_Uluots (accessed 7/21/2011)

"*Kalevipoeg.*" Wikipedia. www.en.wikipedia.org/wiki/Kalevipoeg (accessed 2/10/2011)

"Kärdla." Wikipedia. www.en.wikipedia.org/wiki/Kärdla (accessed 5/1/2011)

"Kärdla Favorites."
www.virtualtourist.com/travel/Europe/Estonia/Hiiumaa/Kärdla (accessed 5/1/2011)

"Karelians". Wikipedia. www.en.wikipedia.org/wiki/Karelians (accessed 11/9/2010)

"Karelian Fever: Some of the Survivors". Kinnunen, Sylvia. *Marquette Monthly* website.
www.mmnow.com/mm_archive_folder/00/00/10/feature (accessed 11/10/2010)

"Karelian Fever Survivors" and "North American Finns in Karelia after 1938." www.d.umn.edu/~apogorel/karelia (accessed 11/9/2010)

"Karl Linnas". Wikipedia. www.en.wikipedia.org/wiki/Karl_Linnas (accessed 1/16/12)

"Katyn Massacre." Wikipedia.
www.en.wikipedia.org/wiki/Katyn_massacre (accessed 12/31/2010

"Klooga Concentration Camp". Wikipedia.
www.en.wikipedia.org/Klooga_concentration_camp (accessed 7/12/2011)

"Konstantin Päts." Wikipedia.
www.en.wikipedia.org/wiki/Konstantin_Päts (accessed 3/12/2011)

"Kulak." Wikipedia. www.en.wikipedia.org/wiki/Kulaks (accessed 12/14/2010)

"Ladogakarelia Winter War Dec. 1939." Wikipedia.
www.en.wikipedia.org/File:Lagodakarelia-winterwar (accessed 5/1/2011)

"Laestadianism." Wikipedia. www.en.wikipedia.org/wiki/Laestadianism (accessed 4/18/2011)

"Lahti L-39." Wikipedia. www.en.wikipedia.org/wiki/(accessed 7/6/2011)

"Lake Onega." Wikipedia. www.en.wikipedia.org./Lake_Onega (accessed 11/19/2010)

"Lake Peipus." Wikipedia. www.en.wikipedia.org/Lake_Peipis (accessed 11/8/2010)

"Martin Sandberger". Wikipedia. www.en.wikipedia.org/Martin_Sandberger (accessed 7/17/2011)

"Mayme Sevander Still Looking for Ten Young Men". Markkanen, Kristiina. *Helsingin Sanomat* website. www2.hs.fi/English/archive/news.asp?id=200010171E14 (accessed 11/1/2010)

"Memorial to Jews Imprisoned and Murdered at Ereda Camp". www.emorialmuseums.net/eng/stettens/view/889 (accessed 7/21/2011)

"Military Organization." Wikipedia. www.en.wikipedia.org/wiki/Military_organization (accessed 7/6/2011)

"Moonsund Landing Operation." Wikipedia. www.en.wikipedia.org/wiki/Moonsund_Landing_Operation (accessed 6/29/2011)

"Narva." Wikipedia. www.en.wikipedia.org/Narva (accessed 11/8/2010)

"Naval War in the Baltic Sea 1941-1945." www.thecensureofdemocracy.150m.com/naval_war (accessed 6/29/2011)

"Nazi Concentration Camps". Wikipedia. www.en.wikipedia.org/Nazi_concentration_camps (accessed 6/26/2011)

"New York City Neighborhoods." www.nyc.gov/html/hd/buyers/nychome-neighborhoods (accessed 11/25/2010)

"No Socialist Paradise for Finnish Defector Family". Mustranda, Emily. *Helsingin Sanomat* website. www.hs.fi/english/article/No+socialist+paradise+for+Finnish+Amer (accessed 11/8/2012)

"North American Finns Caught Karelian Fever". Ziegeid, Joy. *St. Petersburg Times* website.
www.sptimes.ru/index.php?action_id=2&story_id=8672 (accessed 11/09/2010)

"Northern Crusades." Wikipedia.
www.en.wikipedia.org/Northern_Crusades (accessed 11/8/2010)

"The October Revolution: Communism in Russia." www.white-history.com/hwr60 (accessed 11/25/2010)

"Paul Vent." Wikipedia. http://en.wikipedia.org/wiki/Paul_Vent (accessed 7/21/2011)

"Phase II: The German Occupation of Estonia In 1941-1944." http://www.historycommission.ee/ (accessed 01/02/2013)

"Places that Matter: Finnish Progressive Society Hall." www.placematters.net/node/1174 (accessed 11/25/2010)

"Rail Transport in Estonia." Wikipedia.
www.en.wikipedia.org/wiki/Rail_transport_in_Estonia (accessed 3/8/2011)

"Red Army." Wikipedia. www.en.wikipedia.org/wiki/Red_Army (accessed 5/1/2011)

"Resistance: Estonian Citizens in the German Armed Forces." www.okuatsioon.ee/en/occupation-period-overview/26 (accessed 6/29/2011)

"Responsibility for the Holocaust". Wikipedia.
www.en.wikipedia.org/Responsibility_for_the_Holocaust (accessed 11/8/2010)

"Revenge". Freeland, Jonathan. *Guardian* website.
www.guardian.co.uk/world/2008/jul/26/second.world.war (accessed 7/12/2011)

"Russian Baltic Shipyard No. 890, In Tallinn, Estonia SSR (SC RR 104)." www.faqs.org/cia/docs/104/0000496611/RUSSIAN-BALTIC (accessed 3/8/2011)

"Some Kind of Solution: Estonia, Finland and the Enlargement". *Helsingin Sanomat* website. www.hs.fi/english/print/1076152642289 (accessed 7/7/2010)

"The Strength of Native Ties: Social Networks of Finnish Immigrants to Estonia". The Free Library website. www.thefreelibrary.com/The+strength+of+native+ties:+social+networks+of+finnish+immigrants+to+estonia (accessed 11/26/2010)

"Saaremaa." Wikipedia. www.en.wikipedia.org/wiki/Saaremaa (accessed 4/17/2011)

"Saint Petersburg." www.russianinpetersburg.com/saint-petersburg (accessed 1/12/2011)

"Saint Petersburg State University." Wikipedia. www.en.wikipedia.org/Saint_Petersburg_State_University (accessed 12/6/2010)

"1936 Soviet Constitution." Wikipedia. www.en.wikipedia.org/wiki/1936_Soviet_Constitution (accessed 1/8/2011)

"SS Rank Table." www.oradour.info/appendix/ssrank01 (accessed 7/21/2011)

"State University, St. Petersburg." www.encspb.ru/en/article.php?kod=2804012305 (accessed 3/24/2011)

"Sunset Park also Rises." www.therealdeal.com/newyork/articles/sunset-park-also-rises (accessed 11/26/2010)

"Suomi KP/-31." Wikipedia. www.en.wikipedia.org/wiki/Suomi_KP/-31 (accessed 6/22/2011)

"Suursaari." www.jaegerplatoon.net/Suursaari (accessed 7/15/2011)

"T-26." Wikipedia. www.en.wikipedia.org/wiki/T-26 (accessed 4/22/2011)

"T-28." Wikipedia. www.en.wikipedia.org/wiki/T-28 (accessed 4/22/2011)

"Talk: The Holocaust in Estonia." Wikipedia. www.wn.wikipedia.org/wiki/Talk: The_Holocaust_in_Estonia (accessed 01/01/2013)

"Tallinn Prison." www.tripadvisor.com/Attaction_Review-g274958-d219 (accessed 11/28/2011)

"Tallinn Tram." www.hot.ee.tallinntramm/history110 (accessed 3/8/2011)

"Tanks in WW II." Wikipedia. www.en.wikipedia.org/wiki/Tanks_in_World_War_II (accessed 4/22/2011)

"Tartu in the 1941 Summer War." *Baltic Defense Review* (No.9, Vol. 1/2003) (accessed online, date unknown)

"Tartu Railway Station." Wikipedia. www.en.wikipedia.org/Tartu_railway_station (accessed 3/8/2011)

"Transportation in New York City." Wikipedia. www.enwikipedia.org/wiki/Transportation_in_New_York_City (accessed 11/25/2010)

"University of Tartu." Wikipedia. www.en.wikipedia.org/wiki/University_of_Tartu (accessed 2/8/2011)

"Valtiollinen Poliisi (The Valpo)". Wikipedia. www.en.wikipedia.org/Valtiollinen_poliisi (accessed 6/16/2011)

"Viipuri, Goodbye for Now". www.uralitca.com/antti.hrm (accessed 11/8/2010)

"Voices from the Second World War." www.sp.uconn.edu/~wwwcoh/TIMELINE (accessed 1/19/2011)

"Volga-Baltic Waterway." Wikipedia. www.en.wikipedia.org/wiki/Volga-Baltic_Waterway (accessed 12/3/2010)

"War Criminals Find It's Harder to Hide from Past." *USA Today* website. www.usatoday.com/news/washington/2010-10-01-warcriminals (accessed 11/08/2010)

"Why did the Estonians Fight Together with the Germans. www.hot.en.com (accessed 7/7/2010)

"The Winter War: Death in the Snow." Hickman, Kenneth. About.com website. www.militaryhistory.about.com/od/navalbattles1900today/p/w/winter war (accessed 4/22/2011)

Winter War Data." www.mailer.fsu.edu/~akirk/tanks/finland/finland (accessed 4/22/2011)

"Winter War." Wikipedia. www.en.wikipedia.org/wiki/Winter_War (accessed 3/16/2011)

"Women and Diabetes." www.diabetesnet.com/diabetes_information (accessed 1/4/2011)

Biographies

Historical fiction often involves the fictional treatment of real people used by the author as characters in the story. Here are brief biographies of some of the real people who appear in *Sukulaiset.*

Arno Anthoni
Anthoni became the chief of the Finnish State Police (the Valpo) in 1941. As head of the Valpo, Anthoni approved the deportation of 27 individuals to Estonia with the understanding that these non-citizens would be handed over the German equivalent of the Valpo, the Gestapo.

Eight of the individuals sent to Tallinn were Jews. All but one died at hard labor or in the gas chambers of Auschwitz. Anthoni was tried for his crimes against humanity by a Finnish tribunal after the Germans were expelled from Finland. He was convicted of the relatively minor offense of neglecting official duties but his conviction was overturned. Anthoni then sued and recovered substantial damages from the Finnish government for the three years he spent in custody.

Elin Goldfarb is a fictional character added to the list of 27 by the author as part of artistic license to create a story.

Hans Aumier

Holding the rank of *SS-Sturmbannführer* (Major), Aumier was one of three German officers in command of the Vaivara labor camp complex in Estonia after having served in Auschwitz. Klooga camp, as depicted in the story, was one of twenty subcamps under Aumier's control in the late summer, early fall of 1944. Whether it was Aumier or the day-to-day commandant of Klooga, Wilhem Werde, or another German officer who gave the order for the liquidation of Klooga as the Red Army advanced is unclear. For the sake of plot consistency, the scene involving Aumier and Holets (a wholly fictional encounter) is the author's version of what *may* have transpired.

After the fall of Klooga, Aumier continued serving in the SS, ultimately being arrested by the British, transferred to the Americans, and tried by the Polish government as a war criminal. He denied causing the deaths of any Jews at Auschwitz and denied having any knowledge of the gas chambers. He was hanged on January 28, 1948 in Kraków.

John Blatnik

Congressman John Blatnik was born in 1911 in Chisholm, Minnesota and was of Slovenian descent. A schoolteacher, he was elected to the Minnesota State Senate and served until 1942, when he volunteered for the Army Air Corps. He was assigned to the OSS (the predecessor of the CIA) and served as the American liaison to Tito in Yugoslavia, spending nearly a year with the partisan commander.

Blatnik returned to NE Minnesota after the war and was elected to Congress as a Democrat. He served in Congress until 1975 (when he was replaced by his long-time aide James Oberstar) and died in 1991 at the age of 80.

Oscar Corgan

The editor of a socialist newspaper, *Työmies* in Superior, Wisconsin, Corgan was a promoter of the Karelian Fever among American and Canadian Finns during the late 1920s and early 1930s. He moved his wife and children (including daughter Mayme Sevander, see below) to Petroskoi (Petrozavodsk), located in the Autonomous Region of Karelia within the U.S.S.R. Corgan was taken from his home by Soviet operatives in 1937 and was never seen again.

The details of Corgan's death, as depicted in this story, are fiction.

Edvard Gylling
Born in Finland, Gylling was elected to the Finnish Parliament as a Socialist Democrat. At the end of the Great War, he became active on the side of the Reds during the Finnish Civil War. When the communists lost the civil war, Gylling fled to Sweden. He later immigrated to Karelia and from 1920-1935 he was the primary political force behind promoting Finnish Karelian autonomy and welcomed Oscar Corgan and other Finnish speakers from North America. His nationalistic tendencies, however, did not comport with Stalin's views and he was arrested and executed in 1938.

Adolf Hitler
Synonymous with Germanic evil, Hitler was not German by birth, but Austrian. After briefly considering the Catholic priesthood as a vocation, Hitler attempted to live the life of a watercolor artist in Vienna. He was a failure as a painter and ended up living in a homeless shelter. A resident of Munich at the outbreak of WWI, Hitler volunteered, as an Austrian national, to serve in the Bavarian Army. He was wounded in battle and received the Iron Cross. After the war, he became involved in right wing extremist politics, ultimately being sent to prison where he wrote his noted work, *Mein Kampf.*

Upon his release from prison, Hitler's mercurial rise as a politician during an era when Germany suffered economic calamity saw him acquire absolute political and military power. His egomaniacal leadership of Germany into another world war, as well as his insistence of eliminating Jews, Roma, and mentally and physically handicapped individuals is well documented. He committed suicide on April 30, 1945 to avoid capture and punishment for his crimes against humanity.

M. Georg Kollmann
Mr. Kollmann, one of the eight (the author added the fictional character Elin Goldfarb to the list for the story) foreigners expelled by Finland and handed over to the Gestapo in Estonia in November of 1942, survived Auschwitz and lived out his life in Israel. His wife and child perished in the death camp as depicted in the story.

Aleksander Laak
Laak, who was born in Estonia in 1907, was a lieutenant in the Estonian armed forces during World War II and commandant of the Jagala Labor Camp. It is estimated that Laak had a hand in the deaths of 2-3,000 Jews and other detainees under his control, most of who perished by firing squad at Kalevi-Liiva. It is believed that Laak used female inmates as concubines. Following the German withdrawal from Estonia, Laak

immigrated to Winnipeg, Manitoba. After a decade of living a quiet life in Canada, Laak's name resurfaced as a person wanted by Soviet officials for questioning regarding war crimes committed in Estonia. Laak died on September 6, 1960 at his home in Winnipeg, either the victim of his own hand or murdered by the Israeli Mossad.

Carl Gustav Mannerheim

Born in Aiskainen, Finland in 1867 at a time when Finland was part of Czarist Russia, Mannerheim was a Swedish speaker who would later learn Finnish as well as four other languages. He became a cavalry officer in the Russian Army and served in combat during the Russo-Japanese War (1904-1905), the Great War (1914-1917), and the Finnish Civil War (1918). He was appointed Commander-in-Chief of the White forces, and upon the defeat of the Reds, resigned his commission to return to private life.

After refusing entreaties by the Lapua Movement (a Finnish Fascist group) to be its leader, Mannerheim accepted the position of Chair of the Defense Council with the rank of Field Marshall. Mannerheim was named Commander-in-Chief of the Finnish military shortly before the Soviet Union commenced The Winter War. He served in that capacity throughout the Winter War, Continuation War, and Lapland War.

With the resignation of Risto Ryti in August of 1944, Mannerheim accepted the Presidency of Finland and concluded negotiations with the Soviet Union to end the Continuation War. Upon the cessation of hostilities against the Germans, Mannerheim resigned the presidency and returned once again to private life. Plagued by ill health, he died on January 27, 1951, one of Finland's most beloved public figures. June 4th, his birthday, is celebrated annually as Flag Day by the Finnish Armed Forces.

Aaro Pajari

Pajari's rapid rise in the ranks of the Finnish Army was due to his uncanny bravery and intellect. Born in Asikkala, Finland in 1897, Pajari, who began his service during the Winter War as a Major, eventually rose to the rank of Major General by the end of the Lapland War. He was, as indicated in this book, the master of clandestine special projects involving small, quick-strike type units. He died in 1949 at the age of 52.

Konstanin Päts

Much of Päts's biography is incorporated into the story as background and does not need to be repeated here. He was born in Pärnu County, Estonia in 1874 during the period when Estonia was part of Czarist

Russia. After beginning his career as a journalist, Päts became active in Estonian politics during a period when Baltic Germans controlled municipal affairs. As Estonian speakers began to assert political control over the urban areas of Estonia, Päts became more active in electoral politics. Päts also served as an officer in the Imperial Russian Army during the Great War until the advance of the Germans threatened Tallinn. When the Russians retreated, the Germans arrested Päts. Once Germany surrendered to the Allies, Päts was released and accepted a governmental post with the newly founded Republic of Estonia.

Following a period of turmoil and authoritarian rule, Päts was elected the first president of Estonia in 1938. He served in that office until the E.S.S.R. was formed following the Soviet take-over in 1940. He was forced to resign as president, was arrested and imprisoned in a mental institution in the U.S.S.R. where he remained until his death in 1954.

Lauri Pekuri

Born in Helsinki in 1916, this courageous Finnish pilot and ace flew slow and cumbersome Brewster Buffalo fighters during the Winter War and Continuation War. He crashed a Buffalo in a Karelian lake on June 25, 1942 after a dogfight. Pekuri obtained another fighter (a German made Messerschmitt Bf 109G-2), but was shot down behind Soviet lines and taken prisoner. Upon his release from Soviet custody, Pekuri continued to fly, eventually becoming the first Finnish pilot to break the sound barrier. Pekuri retired in 1968 at the rank of Colonel. He died in 1999.

August Sabbe

In 1978, August Sabbe, the last of the Forest Brother partisans hiding in the swamps and forests of Soviet-era Estonia, was located and killed by the KGB. The Soviets allege he drowned while trying to escape but the evidence would suggest otherwise. He was 69 years old and had succeeded in eluding capture for nearly thirty-five years!

Martin Sandberger

Colonel Sandberger was born in Germany in 1911 and lived to the ripe old age of 98. He was an SS officer who assisted, and in some cases, directed, the Holocaust in the Baltic States. As described in *Sukulaiset*, Sandberger was in Tallinn, performing duties related to Hitler's "Final Solution" up through September 1943 and would have been present when Elin Goldfarb landed in Tallinn.

After the war, Sandberger was put on trial for executing Jews and other prisoners. He was convicted of war crimes and sentenced to death by hanging. Political pressure from United States Senator Langer of North Dakota, who had many German American constituents, ultimately prevailed on post-war German authorities. Sandberger avoided the noose and was released from prison after serving eleven years in custody. He lived out the remainder of his life in comfort in his native Germany.

Mayme Sevander

The eldest daughter of Oscar Corgan, Mayme was born in Brule, Wisconsin in 1923. As indicated, she accompanied her father, mother, sister, and brother to Karelia as part of Karelian Fever in 1934. Following Corgan's abduction, she continued to investigate, as best she could from inside the U.S.S.R., her father's disappearance.

After the disintegration of the Soviet Union, Mayme moved back to Superior, Wisconsin, where her father had been a newspaperman. She then returned to Russia to investigate KGB and other files that had been opened by the Russian government to public scrutiny, where she uncovered evidence that her father had been executed in 1938. She died in Sweden while visiting her daughter in 2003, at the age of 79.

Joseph Stalin

As the leader who replaced Lenin as the head of the Soviet Union, Stalin led the Russian experiment in communism from 1924 until his death in 1953. In the late 1930s, around the time of Gylling and Corgan's deaths, Stalin instituted the Great Purge, a campaign to rid the Soviet Communist Party of rivals. The purge allowed Stalin to consolidate his power while keeping a wary eye on events in Germany.

As indicated in *Sukulaiset*, Stalin entered into a non-aggression pact with Hitler in 1939 that allowed Germany and the U.S.S.R. to invade and divide Poland. It also gave Stalin the ability to attack Finland without fears that Germany might intercede. However, the Finns proved their mettle and while they did not defeat the Red Army, they inflicted enough damage to thwart Stalin's intentions. Within a year, Hitler, with the acquiescence of Finland, launched Operation Barbarossa, the German invasion of the U.S.S.R. However, despite his seemingly inexhaustible need to murder or confine the best scientific, literary, and military minds of his nation (killing more of his own citizens through purges than died at the hands of the German invaders) Stalin was able to galvanize the citizens of the U.S.S.R. into action. In bloody battles from the Black Sea to the Barents Sea, Russian forces stopped the Germans and their allies, turned the tide, and began moving with speed towards Germany. In the end, the size and determination of the Red Army, resupplied by the Americans and the British, pushed Hitler's forces back to Berlin.

Stalin died in 1953 and his immediate successor, Nikita Khrushchev, wasted no time in denouncing Stalin as a monster equal to Hitler with respect to the nature and extent of his cruelty to his fellow man.

Paul Vent

Vent, like Mannerheim in Finland, served in the Russian Army while Estonia was part of the Russian Empire. He became an officer during the Estonian War of Independence against the newly formed communist government of Russia. After Estonian independence, Vent remained in the Estonian Army, rising to the rank of major by the time of Estonian capitulation in 1940. The new communist government of Estonia disbanded the army and Vent escaped execution. He returned from hiding when Germany invaded Estonia and served in the Estonian Legion at Narva and Tartu, where it is believed he was killed in action in 1944.

About the Author

Mark Munger is a life-long resident of Northeastern Minnesota. Mark, his wife, René, and one of their four sons live on the banks of the wild and scenic Cloquet River north of Duluth. When not writing fiction, Mark enjoys hunting, fishing, skiing, and working as a District Court Judge.

Other Works by the Author

The Legacy (ISBN 0972005080 and eBook in all formats)

Set against the backdrop of WWII Yugoslavia and present-day Minnesota, this debut novel combines elements of military history, romance, thriller, and mystery. Rated 3 and 1/2 daggers out of 4 by *The Mystery Review Quarterly*.

Ordinary Lives (ISBN 9780979217517 and eBook in all formats)

Creative fiction from one of Northern Minnesota's newest writers, these stories touch upon all elements of the human condition and leave the reader asking for more.

Pigs, a Trial Lawyer's Story (ISBN 097200503x and eBook in all formats)

A story of a young trial attorney, a giant corporation, marital infidelity, moral conflict, and choices made, ***Pigs*** takes place against the backdrop of Western Minnesota's beautiful Smoky Hills. This tale is being compared by reviewers to Grisham's best.

Suomalaiset: People of the Marsh (ISBN 0972005064 and eBook in all formats)

A dockworker is found hanging from a rope in a city park. How is his death tied to the turbulence of the times? A masterful novel of compelling history and emotion, ***Suomalaiset*** has been hailed by reviewers as a "must read."

Esther's Race (ISBN 9780972005098 and eBook in all formats)

The story of an African American registered nurse who confronts race, religion, and tragedy in her quest for love, this novel is set against the stark and vivid beauty of Wisconsin's Apostle Islands, the pastoral landscape of Central Iowa, and the steel and glass of Minneapolis. A great read soon to be a favorite of book clubs across America.

Mr. Environment: The Willard Munger Story (ISBN 9780979217524: Trade paperback only)

A detailed and moving biography of Minnesota's leading environmental champion and longest serving member of the Minnesota House of Representatives, ***Mr. Environment*** is destined to become a book every Minnesotan has on his or her bookshelf.

Black Water: Stories from the Cloquet River
(ISBN 9780979217548 and eBook in all formats)

Essays about ordinary and extraordinary events in the life of an American family living in the wilds of northeastern Minnesota, these tales first appeared separately in two volumes, *River Stories* and *Doc the Bunny*. Re-edited and compiled into one volume, these are stories to read on the deer stand, at the campsite, or late at night for peace of mind.

Laman's River
(ISBN 9780979217531 and eBook in all formats)

A beautiful newspaper reporter is found bound, gagged, and dead. A Duluth judge conceals secrets that may end her career. A reclusive community of religious zealots seeks to protect its view of the hereafter by unleashing an avenging angel upon the world. Mormons. Murder. Minnesota. Montana. Reprising two of your favorite characters from *The Legacy*, Deb Slater and Herb Whitefeather. Buy it now in print or on all major eBook platforms!

10% of all gross sales of CRP books are donated by CRP to SmileTrain in hopes of helping children born with cleft lips and palates across the world. Learn more about SmileTrain at http://www.smiletrain.org/.

A special thanks to Finlandia Foundation for the grant that allowed this book to become reality!

Find out more about this wonderful organization at www.finlandiafoundation.org.

Paul Vesterstein

This is a work of fiction. No character, other than the historical figures portrayed, is meant to depict a "real" person. However, the preceding story was inspired by actual events including the emigration of the author's friend Paul Vesterstein from Estonia to Duluth in 1949. The photograph above is of Paul (at age 19) boarding a steamer for his new life in America after spending four years in a displaced persons camp in Augsburg, Germany.

Born in Otepää, Estonia in 1928, Paul grew up—much as the fictional Nigul Kristian did—skiing the forests of Estonia. The youngest of five children, Paul fought alongside the Germans as a fifteen-year old volunteer soldier during the battle of Narva in 1944. When the Red Army overwhelmed the defenders, Paul fled Estonia and eventually arrived in Germany. There he and nearly 3,000 other Estonians awaited the outcome of the war. When hostilities ceased, a young Estonian woman made arrangements for Paul to immigrate to Duluth where he became a successful collegiate skier, businessman, husband, and father of five children. He was awarded the White Star of the 4th Order by President Rüütel of Estonia in 2003 for his continued involvement in Estonian cultural and business affairs. (Sources: Paul Vesterstein archives, http://www.d.umn.edu/unirel/homepage/11/estonia.html, and http://vp2001-2006.president.ee/en/duties/?gid=34104.)